ruf

CW00321607

Tom Clancy's
POWER PLAYS

ruthless.com

CREATED BY
TOM CLANCY
AND
MARTIN GREENBERG

PENGUIN BOOKS

PENGUIN BOOKS

Published by the Penguin Group
Penguin Books Ltd, 27 Wrights Lane, London W8 5TZ, England
Penguin Putnam Inc., 375 Hudson Street, New York, New York 10014, USA
Penguin Books Australia Ltd, Ringwood, Victoria, Australia
Penguin Books Canada Ltd, 10 Alcorn Avenue, Toronto, Ontario, Canada M4V 3B2
Penguin Books (NZ) Ltd, Private Bag 102902, NSMC, Auckland, New Zealand

Penguin Books Ltd, Registered Offices: Harmondsworth, Middlesex, England

First published in the United States of America by Berkley Books
by arrangement with RSE Holdings, Inc. 1998
First published in Great Britain in Penguin Books 1998
1 3 5 7 9 10 8 6 4 2

Copyright © RSE Holdings, Inc., 1998

Printed in England by Clays Ltd, St Ives plc

Acknowledgments

I would like to thank Jerome Preisler for his creative ideas and his invaluable contributions to the preparation of the manuscript. I would also like to acknowledge the assistance of Marc Cerasini, Larry Segriff, Denise Little, John Helfers, Robert Youdelman, Esq., Tom Mallon, Esq., the wonderful people at The Putnam Berkley Group, including Phyllis Grann, David Shanks, and Tom Colgan, and Doug Littlejohns, Kevin Perry, the rest of the *ruthless.com* team, and the other fine folks at Red Storm Entertainment, as well as Hank Beard for his help sabotaging a Cessna. As always, I would like to thank Robert Gottlieb of the William Morris Agency, my agent and friend. But most important, it is for you, my readers, to determine how successful our collective endeavor has been.

ONE

THE FREIGHTER HAD BEEN CHRISTENED THE *KUAN YIN,*
after the Chinese goddess of mercy, but what doubt can
there be that its crew felt abandoned by their guardian
spirit at the end?

They had set out from the city of Kuching in Eastern
Malaysia at eight P.M., the cargo deck of their fifty-foot-
long, half-century-old steamship loaded with palm oil and
spices tagged for distribution in the wholesale markets of
Singapore. Despite intermittent rain, gusting winds, and
reduced visibility, the chop was moderate and the pilot
had maintained a steady speed of fifteen knots almost
from the time he got under way. He expected an un-
eventful run followed by a night of drinking in a dockside
bar; even now in the wet season, the main sea lane was
short and direct, taking just less than four hours to cross
the strait and then swing up the coast to Sembawang
Wharf, on the north side of the island.

With little to do until they reached port, the four members of the loading crew were playing cards in the vessel's
boxy hold by nine o'clock, leaving the upper deck to the
pilot and boatswain. The former, of course, had no choice
but to remain at the helm, although any sympathy his
shipmates might have felt for him was blunted by their

resentment of his superior attitude, higher salary, and relatively spacious bridge, with its soft leather chair and posters of nude women tacked up among the charts.

On the other hand, the boatswain was extremely well regarded by his fellows, and had been invited to join in the gambling. A man named Chien Lo, he ordinarily would have accepted with enthusiasm, but tonight had chosen instead to remain on deck with the freight. Given the bad weather conditions and his conscientious nature, he was understandably concerned that the lashings might come loose in the strong ocean winds.

Around ten o'clock the tropical downpour eased off a little. It was in all likelihood only a brief lull, and Chien resisted the urge to go below with the others. Trouble waited with the greatest of patience, his wife was fond of saying. Still, he decided it would be a good time to break for a smoke.

As his dear, loving spouse had also told him—she was quite *full* of advice—it was best to enjoy life's small pleasures while one could.

Even as Chien Lo put his match to the tip of his cigarette, two Zodiac inflatable watercraft had glided from the rushes and mangrove roots rimming a tiny islet some forty degrees east of the freighter's bow. Fitted with stabilizing fin rails and powered by sound-baffled ninety-horsepower outboards, they planed across the water at close to fifty knots, fast enough to eat up the *Kuan Yin*'s lead in minutes, cutting parallel wakes that roiled out behind them like the contrails of jet fighters. Soon the blot of land from which they had launched was swallowed up in darkness and distance.

There were twelve men in the pirate gang, its leader an

Iban tribesman of huge proportions, the rest natives of the southern islands, their number divided evenly between the fast-moving inflatables. The designated thrower in each group wore leather gloves and had a coiled nylon rope ladder snaplinked to his belt like a mountain climber. All had concealed their features, some with plain canvas sacks that had holes cut out for the eyes, nose, and mouth, others with old rags and T-shirts they had simply tied over the lower halves of their faces. They had identical kris knife tattoos on the backs of their hands as symbols of their criminal brotherhood. They wore swim vests over their dingy, tattered clothes. They were equipped with assault rifles and carried daggers in scabbards at their waists. And they were ready to put their weapons to lethal use without compunction, as the expressions of cold malignity under their face masks might have shown.

While the seizure of a freighter was an act they had committed scores of times, their present job was unusual in that it would not involve theft of the ship's cargo, nor robbing the crew of personal valuables that could be fenced on the black market—except perhaps as fringe benefits. Yes, the bars, whorehouses, and cockfight parlors of Sibu would have to do without their patronage for a while. Tonight they would be taking the ship into Singapore, and once there would have other things to keep them busy.

As the silent-running Zodiacs approached the stern of the *Kuan Yin,* they veered off in separate directions, the headman's craft swinging toward its port side, the other angling to starboard, both of them slowing to match the larger vessel's speed.

For perhaps two minutes after pulling abreast of it, the pirate boss stared measuringly at his objective, sweeping his gaze over its rust-scabbed metal hull. He wore a denim jacket, a scarf around his forehead to keep his long, rain-drenched black hair from whipping into his eyes, and a bandanna over his mouth and chin. Reaching into his breast pocket for a small flask of *tuak,* he tugged the bandanna down below his lips and swigged back some of the potent alcoholic drink. He took a second deep pull and swished it around his mouth, his face tilted skyward, drizzle sprinkling his exposed, windburned cheeks. Then he swallowed again, slipped his mask back in place, jerked his head toward the short, wiry man with the rope ladder on his belt. "Amir," he said, and sliced his hand through the air, signaling him to proceed with the raid.

The thrower nodded, reached down between his knees, and snapped open the lid of a stowage compartment between the bottom of his seat and the Zodiac's aluminum floorboard. From this compartment he extracted a second rope, this one a twenty-foot single rope with a "bear-claw" grappling hook at its end. He let out a measure of slack, and then began laying up half the coils in his left hand, taking the half attached to the metal hook into his right. Finally he stood and moved to the side of the craft that had edged up to the freighter, his feet planted wide against the undulant rocking and swaying of the current.

Stepping down on the rope's bitter end, Amir turned toward the cargo ship and heaved the grappling hook up at it, letting the weight of the hook carry the line on, the rest of the line paying out of his left hand.

The iron hook clamped onto its gunwale with a solid thump.

An instant later the thrower heard a similar noise from the opposite side of the freighter, and exchanged an anticipatory look with his four companions. All of them knew that sound meant the other raiding party had also been successful in mooring their Zodiac to the *Kuan Yin*.

Chien was standing with his elbows on the starboard rail and the cigarette dangling from his lips when he heard a thumping sound off the quarter. Then, moments later, a second thump from the same general area.

He frowned, thinking the peace and quiet had been too perfect to last. The *Kuan Yin* was now twenty nautical miles southeast of its destination, chugging along amid the scattered outcroppings of rock, soil, and lush tropical vegetation that were some of the Raiu chain's smallest islands. Spread in clusters across a vast expanse of the South China sea, they were mostly nameless and undeveloped, and Chien always found the passage between them to be a welcome interlude before reaching the congested harbor of Singapore.

He stared out at the water and considered ignoring the noise until he'd finished his cigarette, but could not stop fretting. What if there were drums of unfastened cargo rolling and crashing about the deck?

Chien shrugged and flicked his still-burning cigarette stub into the water.

Responsibility had its burdens, he thought, and then turned to walk aft and check things out, unaware of the murderous presence about to slip aboard the vessel.

A moment after hooking on to the gunwale, Amir secured his end of the rope to a mounting ring on the Zodiac's floor. Smoothing his gloves over his fingers, he turned to face the cargo vessel. Then he straddled the line, grasped it firmly in both hands, and jumped off toward the freighter, his legs spread, the line pressed against his body for maximum tension.

His cleated boots braced against the freighter's hull, he climbed with a kind of rhythmic shimmy, and was on deck in less than a minute. Once aboard, he unfastened the rope ladder from his belt, tightly fixed the upper part of it to the handrail, and pitched the remainder of its length over the side of the ship to the inflatable craft below.

The man who caught it quickly began his ascent, placing his foot on the nylon sling ropes that served as spreaders between the vertical mainlines. He knew the others would follow one at a time to avoid putting too much strain on the ladder.

Scrambling to the top of the ladder, he reached up toward the first man's waiting hand so he could be helped over the gunwale.

His upper body and elbows were already on the freighter's deck when Chien Lo, coming aft to investigate the mysterious thumps he had heard moments earlier, discovered to his horror that his ship was under siege.

Crouched on deck, the first pirate heard the boatswain's footsteps a split second before he actually pivoted on his haunches to see him approaching. By then he'd decided what to do. He didn't know how many other crewmen would be on deck, but would not wait for them to be alerted. The man had to be taken out right away.

Chien Lo had halted several yards toward the fore of the deck, staring at the invaders in shock and dismay, his legs turned to brittle shafts of ice. He had perceived the intention of the man already on board even without being able to see his face. The dark, narrow eyes peering through slits in his hood told him everything he needed to know. There was murder in them, pure and simple.

Chien Lo broke suddenly from his paralysis, spun around, and ran for the vessel's bow, where he knew the pilot would be manning the bridge. But the smallish pirate's swiftness and agility were good for more than just climbing. He sprang to his feet and streaked after Chien, whipping his knife from its scabbard, moving almost silently despite the thick-soled boots he had worn to provide traction while boarding the freighter.

He overtook the boatswain in a flash, lunging at him, grabbing him from behind, locking his arms around his chest, the force of his tackle throwing him belly-down onto the deck.

Chien produced a little bleat of pain and fear as a hand twisted itself into his hair and yanked his head up and back. Then the hard, cold edge of the pirate's knife met the soft, warm flesh of his throat and sliced it open from ear to ear.

Chien felt no real pain, only something that shook through his nerves like raw voltage. Then the pirate released him and his face hit the deck again and he died with a long, spasmodic shudder, his nose, mouth, and eyes in a pool of his own blood.

The pirate rose to his feet, dragged Chien's body to the edge of the deck, and kicked it overboard. In the vastness of the open sea it seemed there was hardly a splash as it hit the water and was swallowed up.

When the pirate returned to where he'd tied the ladder to the handrail, he found that the second pirate had managed to haul himself aboard. The rest of their team and five of the men in the other raiding party were also on deck, waiting for the last pirate to complete his climb.

A moment later he was up and they were all racing toward the forward part of the ship.

The pilot sank beneath the wheel in a lifeless heap, his blood pattering from his maps and *Playboy* pin-ups like falling rain. His killer had made fast work of him after entering the bridge, stealing up from behind, and slicing open his throat just as the first man aboard had done to Chien Lo. Caught completely by surprise, he hadn't even known what hit him, let alone gotten a chance to hail for assistance.

Now a second pirate came in, sidestepped the corpse, and took the wheel. His eyes roaming over the instrument panel in front of him, he nodded to the first man, who clapped him on the back, sheathed his dripping blade, and then rushed outside to give the others the good news.

They had taken full control of the vessel. Next they would deal with its remaining crew.

"Get on you knees, hands behind you heads!" the Iban shouted from the stairwell. Although every one of the ship's hands looked like Malays, he'd barked his orders through his bandanna in a serviceable if unpolished English. The national language had many variations in dialect, and he wanted to avoid confusion.

The crewmen gaped up at him from the card table, faces stunned, playing cards spilling from their fingers in a fluttery welter. Footsteps clattered behind the pirate leader as the rest of his band followed him down the metal risers from the deck.

"Do it now or I kill you all!" the Iban grunted, noting the crew's frozen hesitation and motioning them away from the table with the snout of his Beretta 70/90.

The four men complied, making no attempt at resistance, getting up in such a rush they clumsily knocked over several chairs.

They knelt in the middle of the cramped little hold and looked at the raiders in silence.

The Iban noticed that one of the captives had slipped off his wristwatch and was holding it out in his hand, offering up the timepiece as if to get done with the affair as quickly as possible. He knew what the man was thinking, and almost pitied him. None of the recent anti-piracy operations by Malaysia, Indonesia, the Phillippines, and China had done anything to decrease the high incidence of attacks in local waters. With thousands of jungled islands and vast stretches of ocean to patrol, the naval authorities could not hope to keep pace with their quarry, let alone ferret out their hidden land bases. Regional shipping companies were well aware of this, and simply figured losses to theft and hijacking into the overall cost of their operations.

The pirate chief's eyes moved over the faces of the sailors. While they looked tense and anxious in the cast of an overhead light fixture, none of those faces seemed especially fearful. And why should they be? The men were seasoned hands. They would have been through hijacks before, and expected to be robbed and sent off safely in dinghies and lifeboats. That was how it usually went.

The poor, stupid bastards hadn't any idea what had happened to their mates up above.

The Iban waved over one of the pirates who had come rushing down the stairs at his heels. The man stepped up to him and leaned in close for his orders.

"I don't want their papers messed up, Juara," the Iban

warned in a coarse whisper, this time speaking his native tongue, Behasa Malayu. "That happens, all this is for shit, you understand?"

Juara's affirmative grunt was muffled by the dirty white towel shrouding his mouth and chin. A blockish, thick-necked man with a shaved head and lot of surplus weight around the middle, he gestured briskly to a couple of the other hijackers, who moved toward the kneeling seamen and ordered them to toss everything in their pockets onto the floor.

The ship's hands again did as they were told without challenge. Juara covered them with his rifle while his two companions went and gathered up their surrendered possessions, depositing them in a small heap on the table. When the hands had finished emptying their pockets, the pirates frisked them down to make sure they hadn't withheld anything.

Satisfied they'd gotten what they wanted, they nodded to Juara.

Juara motioned the pair back to his side, then turned to look at the Iban headman.

"Get it over with," the Iban said.

He tried to keep his voice hushed, but it was deep enough to seem almost booming in the constricted silence of the hold. A terrible understanding dawned on the crewmen's features as their captors swung up their rifle barrels.

Now they finally know, the pirate thought. *And they fear.*

One of the ship's hands opened his mouth to scream and started to his feet, but then the raiders triggered their weapons and he fell backwards, his clothes riddled with bullet holes, most of his head blown away. Swept by the hail of gunfire, the rest of the *Kuan Yin*'s crew also went down in a cloud of blood, bone, and tissue, their arms and legs sprawling out wildly in their final throes.

The big Iban waited for the guns to stop their racket, then stepped over to the card table and randomly lifted a wallet from the pile of items that had been taken from the crewmen. He was eager to finish this last bit of business and return to the open deck; his ears rang from the shooting, and the air down here stank of burnt primer, blood, and the voided bowels of the dead.

He opened the wallet and found a driver's license in a transparent plastic sleeve. There was more identification in the other compartments. The slain crewman to whom the wallet had belonged was named Sang Ye.

The Iban made a low, pleased sound in his throat. He hoped the sailor had lived his life fully and spent his money well. At any rate, his wallet and identity now belonged to someone who would make good use of them.

There were big things in the works, very big, and the Iban was eager to reach Singapore and get cracking.

He thought of the sheet of paper folded in his breast pocket, thought of the instructions that were written on it, thought of everything they were worth to him. Surely more than he'd made in any dozen hijacks.

The American, Max Blackburn, didn't stand a chance. No more than the crew of the ship had stood one. . . . Not the slightest chance in the world.

TWO

WHEN ROGER GORDIAN WAS THIRTEEN YEARS OLD,
he built a tree house in a scrub lot where he'd often gone
to play with his friends. As originally conceived, it was
to have been a lookout against adults who came within
homing range, and a refuge from older children who were
potential troublemakers. He'd sketched out the blueprint
for it himself, and realized those plans with the help of
his two best pals: Steve Padaetz, his next-door neighbor,
and Johnny Cowans, a fidgety little kid who'd been nick-
named "Clip" for no reason anybody could remember.
At one point, Roger had considered fortifying their tree
house against marauders with a ring of elaborate booby
traps, but none of the dozen or so he devised ever got
beyond the planning stage. Truth be known, the boys
hadn't really expected a raid of any kind—that had just
been a fanciful notion, something to enhance their frolics
with a tingly edge of secrecy and adventure. There were
very few kids in the neighborhood whom they considered
enemies, and even fewer who were interested enough in
their whereabouts or activities to hassle them.

Or so the boys thought, anyway.

The ladder and tools they'd used to construct the tree
house had come from Roger's parents' garage. Steve had

gotten the actual building materials from the hardware store/lumberyard owned by his dad, although Roger never really got around to asking whether they were obtained with Mr. Padaetz's knowledge or consent. Somehow it didn't seem important at the time; the boys had needed little to complete their hideaway besides some two-by-fours, a few sheets of wood siding, and a box of nails, the unexplained absence of which would hardly have been enough to put Padaetz Home Improvements, the biggest family-owned business in Waterford, Wisconsin, on the financial skids.

The Sentry Box, as the tree house came to be called, had been at the center of the three boys' lives for an entire summer, beginning shortly after they got their final-quarter sixth-grade report cards, and ending a couple of weeks before the opening bells of junior high rang out. During the two hot, dreamy months that stretched between, they had idled away the daylight hours in and around it, swapping baseball cards and comic books and bad dirty jokes, poking around the woods, and conducting fruitless searches for the Indian arrowheads that, at least as schoolyard mythology had it, littered the undeveloped fields of Racine County.

Sometime in late August, the boys had started fashioning what was to have been an outdoor gymnasium in the patch of grass directly below the tree house, using some additional lumber they'd managed to scavenge together over the long season. There were still two weeks to go before classes resumed, and they figured they had over a month beyond that until the weather got too cold for them to mess around outdoors after completing their homework and chores. They had built horizontal and parallel bars, and begun work on an exercise horse . . . but their expansion was abruptly aborted when the raid they'd once half-worried about became a devastating reality.

The kids—teenagers, really—responsible for marring that idyllic period were Ed Kozinski, Kenny Whitman, and Anthony Platt, who was Kenny's third cousin and bore an attitude of perpetual, surly belligerence that marked him as someone to avoid at all costs. Perhaps two years older than Roger and his friends, this ghastly trio had never before taken the slightest notice of them, concentrating instead on acts of petty vandalism, finding ways to filch beer and cigarettes from local groceries, and making crude advances to girls who, by and large, pretended they didn't exist. Somehow Anthony had learned about the tree house, and had gotten the idea that those girls might be more accepting of him and his cohorts if they had a nice, private, tucked-away spot where they could all go to get drunk and make out.

The moment that thought reared itself from the bottom sludge of Anthony's mind, the Sentry Box was effectively lost to the younger boys; they had wandered out to the tree house one morning and found Kenny and company occupying it like counterparts from some science-fictional negative universe. Their outdoor gym-in-the-making had been ruined, the pieces of wood they'd used to build their apparatus scattered about the field. The words "Jive Palase" were spray-painted across two sides of the tree house in huge, bright red letters, the second half of its new name unintentionally misspelled in what would have been a comical twist had the circumstances surrounding it not been so painful. To Roger Gordian, it felt almost like a desecration.

Watching Roger and his companions from the entrance, Anthony sat with his legs swung out over the side of the

box, a Parliament in his hand and a contemptuous grin
on his face. The comics, trading cards, and everything
else Roger's group had hoarded inside it had been uncer-
emoniously dumped, and lay among the welter of beer
bottles, empty potato chip bags, candy wrappers, and
crumpled cigarette packs on the ground beneath it.

Roger and company barely had time to register what
had happened before they were pelted with a fusillade of
stones from their own lookout post. They had briefly considered taking a desperate stand against the invaders, but
then one of those whizzing rocks had struck Clip dead
center in his forehead and he'd dropped into the dirt,
howling at the top of his lungs, blood streaming into his
eyes from a wound that would later require four stitches
and a tetanus shot. Roger had known then that he'd been
beaten; worse, he had known it was no contest, and felt
crushingly ashamed of his defenselessness. The other
boys were bigger, meaner, and tougher than anybody in
his little group. And they had been ready and waiting for
a fight.

As Kenny's gang had begun climbing down the tree
after them, Roger and Johnny had helped Clip to his feet
and fled the scene.

It had been Gordian's first experience with a hostile
takeover, and four decades and change later, the memory
still stung.

That the sting seemed especially acute tonight was
quite understandable, given the distressing little bulletin
his visitor had just delivered from the Wall Street front.

"We went back there maybe two, three months later,"
he said now, finishing his story. "By then Kenny and his
parents had moved out of town, and his cousin was, I
don't know, just sort of neutralized without him. Anyway,

we returned and found the tree house destroyed, same way the gym had been. Boards sticking out of the snow, nothing intact. I don't know if it had been deliberately trashed, or if the numbskulls that moved in on us brought it down out of carelessness and stupidity. Doesn't matter, I suppose. What *does* matter, and what still bugs me whenever I remember this sorry little episode, is that I surrendered the tree house to those punks in the first place. Let them take something that was mine, something I'd built from scratch, without a fight.''

Charles Kirby looked at Gordian a while, and then drank some of his scotch and soda. It was nine o'clock at night and he was exhausted and jet-lagged after a long flight from New York. Still, he had joined Roger in the book-lined study of his Palo Alto home because he'd felt the news he was carrying was too important to wait until morning.

Gord not only paid the law firm of Fisk, Kirby, and Towland a handsome retainer for their advice and representation in corporate affairs, he was also a close personal friend. When Kirby had learned that the Spartus consortium, UpLink International's largest shareholder, intended to sell off its twenty-percent interest in the company, he'd immediately known what it augured, and had decided to fly out and tell Gordian about it face-to-face.

Studying Gordian's troubled features, he knew he'd made the right decision. A lean, graying man of forty-five with intelligent blue eyes, jutting cheekbones, and lips so thin that even his broadest smiles seemed wan, Kirby was wearing a dark-blue worsted suit over a white dress shirt that had lost its necktie, and been unbuttoned at the collar, somewhere around cruising altitude . . . a sartorial anomaly Gord had remarked upon the moment

Kirby arrived at his house. *Chuck, you're the most fastidious dresser I've ever met. The guy who sent me illustrated instructions on making a Windsor knot, and taught me that it was traditional for the bottom of a sport jacket to line up with the knuckle when your hands are straight down against your legs. The tieless look gives me an idea something's wrong. Big-time.*

Accurate enough, Kirby thought, sipping his scotch.

"Well, at least the creeps didn't get to enjoy the place for long," he said from the plump leather chair opposite Roger. "Bet you ten to one they never got any girls up there with them either."

"Nice try, Chuck. But let's not skirt the issue," Gordian said. "I'm a grown man, for godsakes. You'd think I could do better than to make the same mistakes that I did when I was still looking ahead to peach fuzz and my first kiss."

"Gord, listen to me—"

"I want to know how I could have been blindsided. How I could leave myself open to having somebody try and grab UpLink right out from under my nose."

Kirby drained his scotch, lowered the glass, and rattled the melting ice cubes inside it.

"You want me to sit here watching you bash away at yourself?" he said. "I wasn't aware that was part of our professional arrangement, though I can check with my partners to be absolutely certain."

"Could you really?"

Kirby frowned at his sarcasm.

"Look," Gordian said. "I've established my organization in dozens of countries, placed my employees at extreme risk in some of them, lost good people in others. If I can't learn my lessons, can't compete when the stakes are high, I shouldn't be fooling around in the big leagues.''

Kirby sighed. Granted, they were looking at a very serious problem, but Gordian ordinarily wasn't the sort of man to let self-pity and defeatism through the door no matter how hard they tried shoving their way in. What the hell was wrong with him? Could this be a kind of delayed reaction to the encryption-tech controversy . . . a case of the psychological bends after finally coming up from leagues underneath it?

Kirby thought about it a moment, and supposed that might be the case, considering how long it had dragged on and the flak Gordian had taken because of his public stance against the new government export policies. Maybe the operative factor here was exhaustion, and Gord was simply tapped out from waging too many battles on too many fronts at once. Maybe. And yet he couldn't help but feel that something else was eating away at him, as well.

''I won't deny you were vulnerable, but why blame it on recklessness?'' he said. ''You've had a lot of strains on your financial resources lately, ranging from some outlays that were merely unavoidable, to others that you couldn't have anticipated without a crystal ball.''

Gordian's peremptory look told Kirby he didn't need to be further reminded. In that way the two men were alike: They made their points with a minimum of words. And besides, both of them had done the arithmetic many times over. There had been the huge price tag of manufacturing, launching, and insuring the constellation of low-earth-orbit, Ka-band satellites needed for UpLink's orbital telecommunications network, the multimillion dollar cost of rebuilding the Russian ground station after it was nearly leveled by a terrorist attack the previous January, and the simultaneous expenses of getting the ground stations in Africa and Malaysia fully operational.

An ambitious program of corporate initiatives, to be sure. But Gordian's diversification from the defense technology that had earned him his fortune, while to some extent spurred by military downsizing, was not essentially profit-motivated—and that had always impressed the hell out of Kirby. Gord was not an ego-driven person. Nor was he an acquisitive one. Having made enough money to last him ten lifetimes, he could have done what a lot of fabulously rich men did and rested on his laurels, gone on long cruises to warm places, turned to breaking Guinness world records, whatever.

More than anything, though, Gordian had a heartfelt desire to help create a better world, and believed to his core that the problem of eliminating global tyranny and oppression required communication-based solutions. Having grown up in an era of Berlin Walls and Iron Curtains, he was convinced that nothing—neither military buildups, nor leadership summits, nor treaties—had done as much to bring those Cold War barriers down as information seeping through their cracks. Information, he believed, was the ultimate key to personal and political freedom. His goal, his *vision,* was to provide that key to the broadest number of people he could imagine . . . which, Kirby supposed, made him a pragmatic idealist. Or was that oxymoronic?

Now Gordian began to speak again, leaning forward, his elbows on his knees, his hands clasped together.

"Make no mistake, Chuck, I'm not second-guessing my business decisions with regard to the company's expansion," he said. "But I do fault myself for not preparing a defensive strategy against a shark attack. And it isn't as if I haven't had good counsel. You've advised me time and again to implement staggered terms of office on the board of directors. My friend Dan Parker, the congressman, tried to persuade me to lobby more forcefully for specific anti-takeover legislation in this state. I did neither.''

''Gord—''

Gordian raised a hand to silence him.

''Hear me out, please. As I said, this isn't just a *mea culpa*,'' he went on. ''A minute ago, you said something about my needing a crystal ball to predict what's happened. Well, in a way, I had one. I don't think Spartus putting its stake on the market comes as a total shock to either of us. Look at the articles in the *Wall Street Journal*. The endless commentaries on those CNN and CNBC financial programs. Every aspect of my company's operations has been subjected to criticism and ridicule, a great deal of it originating from a single source. Is it any wonder the value of our stock has gone into the sewer?''

''For the record, my comment related to your expenses, not the devaluation of UpLink shares,'' Kirby said. ''But I agree that the great and exalted financial prophet Reynold Armitage has done a trash-and-burn number on you in the media. If he's the source you're talking about, that is.''

''None other.'' Gordian folded his hands on his knees again. ''Spartus panicked, and though I figured I'd be able to settle their fears when I called them, they can't really be blamed for not buying my reassurances. Tell me the truth, Chuck. Have you ever seen anything like Armitage microanalyzing our 10-K information on the air? And then putting such an incredibly negative spin on it? Because I find it damned curious.''

Kirby didn't say anything, just shook his head. Yes, Armitage was an expert securities analyst, able to sniff the wind for market indicators better than almost any of his peers. What did it matter to the general financial community that he was also a pompous, mean-spirited son of a bitch? Some sons of bitches got listened to without being liked very much—and when Armitage spoke, investors large and small perked their ears.

Which was understandable, Kirby thought. Since becoming a constant presence on the money shows, Armitage had helped many, many stockholders to better understand the market and choose successful ventures. But he had also occasionally hurt struggling firms with imprudent calls, skewing figures to suit his predictions, baiting corporate leaders, seeming to relish making them look foolish. As Gordian had pointed out, you had to be ready to take your knocks when you were playing in the big leagues. And despite his sudden attack of self-doubt, he *was* a player . . . one of the best. However, what had raised Armitage's campaign against UpLink—and campaign seemed the only appropriate word for it—to an inexplicable level of viciousness was the timing of his disclosures.

The very day UpLink had released its yearly report to stockholders, Armitage had gone on *Moneyline* with the firm's 10-K and charged that there were critical discrepancies between the two statements. That had been untrue. Certainly, the reports presented their data in different lights, but annual reports were traditionally intended to emphasize a company's strengths and future goals, while the 10-K form was a dry listing of financial statistics prepared for the Securities and Exchange Commission as a matter of law. By presenting those stats out of context—failing to weigh temporary debts and liabilities against projected venture profits, for instance—one could easily give the impression that a business had gotten into much worse shape than was actually the case. And Armitage had gone a giant step beyond that, exaggerating the significance of every expense, minimizing every gain, and analyzing profit-loss ratios in the worst possible light to depict a company on the verge of ruin.

Damned curious indeed.

Still without speaking, Kirby rose, went over to the wet bar in the opposite corner of the room, and refilled his glass with scotch, leaving out the soda this time. As usual, Gordian's mind was hitting on all its well-oiled cylinders. Why the constant attacks from Armitage? As far as he knew, Gordian had never stepped on his toes, never even met the man. *Why,* then? The question had been buzzing around Kirby's own head for weeks like a nettlesome wasp, and the only answer that came to him amounted to nothing more than a suspicion. It was one he'd hesitated to share with Gordian, feeling it would be rash to do so without any substantiation.

"Hope you don't mind me helping myself to more of the expensive stuff," he said, turning to Gordian.

"Get it while it lasts," Gordian said with a grim smile, downing what was left of his own drink, then holding it out toward Kirby.

Kirby stepped over with Gordian's own favorite Beefeater—and splashed a healthy measure into Gordian's glass.

Their eyes met then, the look that passed between them lasting only a brief moment. Yet it was significant enough to give Kirby all the confirmation he needed that Gordian was thinking the exact same thing he was.

It was, he guessed, time they aired what was on their minds.

"Gord, do you believe this takeover bid was orchestrated?" he asked, the words leaping out of his mouth before caution could prevail. "That Armitage has been going at you with the intention of destroying shareholder confidence and—"

"And provoking a sell-off," Gordian said, nodding. "This whole thing reeks of behind-the-scenes manipulation."

Kirby inhaled, exhaled. He could feel the silence of the room pressing down on him with a weight that was almost tangible.

"If that's true," he said, "it would at least suggest that Armitage is in somebody's pocket."

"Yes." Gordian's tone was flat. "It would."

The two men faced each other soberly, their eyes holding.

"You have any idea who that somebody might be?" Kirby asked.

Gordian sat there quietly while the antique clock across the room ticked off a full minute.

"No," he replied at last, hoping his sincerity would be accepted without challenge.

He was, after all, lying through his teeth.

THREE

"TAKE MY WORD FOR IT, THIS HERE COUNTRY WOULD be the perfect retirement spot for Barney the Dinosaur," an American expatriate in Singapore once told a visitor from New York City. Or so he was quoted in the press, at any rate.

The comment—which was made in response to an inquiry about where some risque entertainment might be found, and would later become famous throughout the island—was overheard by a magazine writer amid the cacophonous chirping, tweeting, and trilling of innumerable performing birds. It was a Sunday morning, and Singaporean bird fanciers, mostly ethnic Chinese, had brought their thrushes, *mata putehs,* and *sharmas* out for the weekly avian singing competition at the intersection of Tiong Bahru and Seng Poh Roads, hanging their bamboo cages from specially built trellises above the public benches and outdoor cafe tables lining the street.

"You want cheap thrills, you got literally two options: dream X-rated tonight, or head on over to Fat B's, at the east end," the expat had continued to the utter mystification of his visiting friend . . . and the gleeful amusement of the eavesdropping writer, who, realizing she'd stumbled upon a perfect opener for her regular Lifestyles column, listened carefully while the birds peeped and cheeped their bright, vacant melodies into the sunshiny air.

Indeed, Fat B's, a decadent hole-in-the-wall tucked away behind a rotted shop-house facade in a narrow Geylang District *larong,* was unquestionably the seediest bar on the island republic. It was also a very busy place, drawing patrons night after night despite the stringent national morals laws, clinging to its grubby existence like some resistant bacilli on an otherwise scrubbed and sanitized operating room surface. Exactly *why* authorities tolerated it was anyone's guess, although there were rumors of ongoing bribes to police officials, and compromising photographs that had been waved over the head of a high-placed government minister as insurance against a shutdown.

With its crumbling walls and ceiling covered with purple foil, bathed in black light, and decorated with giant crepe-paper rafflesias, painted wooden folk masks, blowpipes, bead strings, dragon banners, and century-old human skulls that had once hung in the longhouses of Borneo headhunters, the interior of the bar was outdone in crassness only by its owner, Fat B . . . who, contrary to what his name suggested, was not fat at all, but physically slight, and had gained a reputation for being a bold exclamation point of a man through a mixture of conspicuously non-Singaporean aggressiveness and flamboyance, characteristics he was supposed to have inherited from his wealthy Straits Chinese ancestors. Those who had business dealings with him also knew of a certain hard, forbidding look that became evident in his eyes when his anger or suspicion was aroused, giving him, at such times, the appearance of a wary crocodile.

Tonight Fat B was wearing a collarless yellow silk shirt printed with colorful explosions of peonies, black shark-skin slacks, a diamond stud in his right earlobe, and jade-encrusted rings on eight of his fingers. His jet-black hair was slicked straight back over his head and had an almost buffed appearance. He sat at his usual table in the rear of the bar, his back to the wall, keeping a watchful eye on every coming and going at the door.

"Here's what you came for, Xiang," he said, sliding a brown manilla envelope to the big, long-haired man seated opposite him. "Odd how so much effort goes into providing such a slim package. But it's just that way when you're trading in information. It weighs nothing and everything at the same time, *lah*."

Xiang just looked at him, then silently reached out for the envelope and lifted it off the table. Fat B tried not to show that he'd noticed the kris tattoo on the back of his hand, thinking his interest wouldn't be at all appreciated . . . not by this retrograde brute. Still, he continued to regard him with hooded fascination. In the old days, his people had run around the Malaysian jungles stark naked—or just about—their skin covered with dragons, scorpions, and the like, flaunting those tattoos as symbols of courage and manhood.

His eyelids half lowered, Fat B wondered if the muscular Iban's entire body was adorned with such markings, and considered what an impressive sight that would be. Impressive and, no doubt, very painfully achieved.

Seemingly oblivious to the barkeeper's scrutiny, Xiang unclasped the envelope, folded back its flap, and looked inside.

Fat B watched and waited. Pop music squalled from stereo speakers at the four corners of the room, Eastern lutes, harps, and cymbals looping discordantly over Western-style synthesizers and electric guitars. Strobes splashed the foil-draped walls with violet light. Bar girls in short skirts and tight, swoop-necked blouses, and with too much makeup on their faces, laughed showily with the men who were paying for their drinks. Most of the women carried small purses that opened only after they led their companions into the staircase behind the barroom, or up to the small, private rooms on the building's second floor. Then they would make their illicit transactions, willing flesh for cold cash, fifty percent of which went into Fat B's pocket.

For no particular reason, Fat B thought suddenly of an ancient Chinese expression: *Everything can be eaten.*

His lips puckered thoughtfully, he stared across the room at the pair of men who had arrived with Xiang. They hovered near the entrance in their shabby clothes, one dragging on a cigarette and looking directly back at him, the other gazing upward at the wall, apparently studying the painted folk masks. Both also would have the dagger tattoo on their hands, of course.

Glancing cautiously over each shoulder to make sure he wasn't being watched, Xiang unclipped the envelope and looked inside. It contained a stack of nine or ten photographs. Reaching in with one hand, he pulled them out just far enough to expose their upper borders, and then gave them a quick scan, riffling their edges with his thumb, ignoring the sheet of paper clipped to the last snapshot. Then he returned them to the envelope, closed the flap, and looked back up at Fat B.

"Who's the girl?" he said in English.

"It's all in the little fact sheet I enclosed. Her name is Kirsten Chu and she is employed by a company called

Monolith Technologies. Very attractive, don't you think?" Fat B offered the pirate a relaxed smile. "It's unfortunate her parents stuck her with a Western name, but I believe she was born and educated in Britain. So it goes."

Xiang stared at him, his eyes flat. "You know what I mean. I didn't expect there to be two of them."

Fat B tried to look as if there was nothing about the envelope's contents that should have required explanation.

"Listen," he said. "She's just a beautiful lure dangling at the end of a very short line, you understand? Her movements are easy to track. Stay on her and she'll lead you to the American."

"What's their connection?"

"I don't ask, our employers don't tell."

"She a national?"

Fat B waited a moment before he replied, listening to shrieky Chinese vocals pierce a loud disco rhythm thudding from the sound system. Ordinarily he enjoyed the ratcheted-up volume and uneasy merging of musical traditions, but now it was all starting to grate on him, the sweeps of electronic sound jangling his nerves, the female rap singer's falsetto highs tearing into his eardrums like steel spikes.

He'd been optimistic things would go more smoothly.

He took a deep breath, exhaled, then finally nodded, his smile tightening at the corners.

"Don't make more out of this than there is," he said. "It isn't that big a deal."

"Bullshit. You think I'm stupid? An American with no business being in this country disappears, it's one thing to clean it up afterward. But a citizen? A *woman*? You've got to be joking. Something goes wrong and we're caught, I can look forward to a lot worse than six strokes of the *rotan*."

Fab B chuckled. "In Singapore, a fellow with my habits and appetites is liable to receive that sort of punishment just for getting out of bed in the morning. It might be said that our system of justice stems directly from Christian notions of original sin."

Xiang looked at him with his dark, empty eyes but said nothing.

Apparently, Fat B thought, his little stab at humor had gone over the *ah beng*'s head. In fact, he himself was no longer smiling, his mood having taken a sharp and rather abrupt downturn in the past few seconds. It wasn't as if the money was coming out of his own pocket, but he didn't like being interposed between this thug and their mutual employers. Negotiation wasn't his favorite activity, and he'd hoped—perhaps foolishly—that the pirate would simply take the envelope and leave.

"Really, what's the problem?" he said. "If you can grab both of them alive, fine. But it's this Blackburn who's truly valuable to our employers. Your main concern with the woman should be making certain she isn't left behind as a witness."

"If this is so easy, why couldn't your people take care of it? They followed her. They took the pictures. They could have gone ahead with the next step."

"We each have different ways of making ourselves useful. This country is where I live, you understand? I'm here for the long term. You're in and out, *lah*." Fat B shrugged again. "Let's not waste any more breath discussing it. We're both already committed, after all."

Xiang was silent. Fat B stared past him at the door,

waiting for him to make up his mind, anxious for their transaction to be concluded. How had he wound up haggling with the brutish creature? The whole distasteful episode had given him a headache.

He waited some more, watching a couple of grimy men step in from the alley and then head over to the bar.

"All right," the pirate said at last. "But I better get the rest of my money soon as it's done. You better make *sure* of it."

Fat B looked at him with quiet malice.

"Of course," he said, nodding. "It will be my pleasure."

The two men regarded each other a moment without exchanging another word. Then Xiang stuffed the envelope containing the photos under his denim jacket, pushed his chair back from the table with his feet, got up, strode to the entrance, and departed, his two companions falling in at his rear.

A small hiss slipping through his front teeth, Fat B sat very still and watched the door swing shut behind them.

Blackburn had picked up the puppet at an open-air bazaar—this was a while back, during Dipvali, the Hindu Festival of Lights. Needing a break from his responsibilities at the ground station, he had taken a few days off and gone to the coast to enjoy the frenetic celebration, taking in the sidewalk dancers, musicians, and magicians, sampling the delicious curries and *satays,* browsing the crafts stalls, and just strolling at his leisure amid the exuberant banners, floral decorations, sprays of colored rice, and endless strings of candles, lamps, and lightbulbs brightening every door and window.

Wearing an elaborate turban with a peacock feather jutting straight up out of its bottom wind, a maroon shirt with glittery gold threads woven through its fabric in vertical stripes, and steel bangles on one skinny wrist, the vendor who'd sold Blackburn the puppet had looked like a street-corner sultan in his holiday finery. His open, spirited smile had revealed the black-stained teeth and reddened gums that were telltale signs of habitual *betel* chewing—an addictive concoction with mildly intoxicating properties, the betel probably made him look ten years older than his natural age.

Blackburn remembered the strong scent of exotic spice on his breath as he had stepped up close to make his pitch, a pair of two-dimensional leather puppets in each hand, waving them aloft on slender rods. He remembered their painted colors looking gaudy and brilliant in the midday sunshine, remembered the exquisite detail of their hand-tooled features, and most especially remembered admiring the workmanship of the one in the vendor's left hand. The one that had, in fact, first caught his eye, and was now hanging above him on the wall of his office—some sort of animistic figure, part elephant, part man.

"Fifty *ringgits,* twenty-five American dollars!" the man had been shouting as he manipulated the puppet over his head. Out of curiosity, Blackburn had stopped to ask the vendor which Hindu diety the puppet represented, speaking English because he had not yet become proficient in Bahasa, having been in Malaysia less than a month at the time.

Smiling his big, resin-stained smile, wagging his head up and down as if he'd understood Blackburn, the vendor had thrust the puppet into his face and enthusiastically hollered, "Yes, yes! Fifty *ringgits,* twenty-five American dollars!"

"It's Ganesha, son of Shiva. . . ."

The voice was female and carried a musical British accent. Blackburn had turned in its direction to see an Oriental woman of perhaps thirty or thirty-five, a strikingly *beautiful* woman with a sweep of angle-cut black hair, slanted brown eyes, and skin that had been tanned the color of almonds and cream in the perpetual August of the tropics. Wearing summer khakis, a loose cotton blouse, and sandals, she was carrying a Coach handbag over her shoulder, a bag he'd known must have cost more than the combined yearly income of everyone living in that village.

Blackburn remembered immediately noticing that she had a magnificent body. Even through her baggy clothes, he'd been able to tell. It was the way she carried herself, he supposed. But he'd always had an eye for that sort of thing.

One of your best assets in the field, he thought now, three months later, his face troubled, his inner voice edged with self-contempt. Sitting by the phone in his office, he couldn't remember whether the desire to go to bed with her, and the idea of convincing her to become a fly on Marcus Caine's wall, had been linked from the very beginning. Oh, he'd felt a superficial attraction right away, but when had he ever met a good-looking women he *hadn't* thought would be fun in the sack?

Actually wanting her was another story, though. Wanting her, and then deciding he could *use* her. . . .

He thought suddenly and unexpectedly about Megan Breen and how different it had been when they were together. Not better, but easier, without guilt. They had liked each other and felt lonely and isolated in the bleak Russian winter. Neither had held expectations of their affair going beyond what it was. There had been no secret agendas between them, nothing to hide. It had been up front and without manipulation, the lines and limits clearly defined.

Of course, he hadn't known who she worked for until at least five minutes into their conversation, which had begun with them chatting about the puppet.

"... a god representing man's animal nature," she had said.

He'd looked at her and smiled. "Thanks. Sounds like the perfect mascot for my office."

"You'll see his image on a lot of pendants and charms," she said, returning his smile. "They're worn as protection against evil and bad fortune."

"*Better* than perfect," he said. "Think I'll hang him right over my phone. For when the boss calls to check up on me."

Her amused grin broadened.

"I can tell you the asking price is very fair," she said. "A lot of time goes into making these *wayang kulit* puppets, at least the quality ones. This man's even have bison horn rods."

"Is that also supposed to be good luck?"

"Not if you're a bison, I suppose. But it shows quality workmanship. Most of the puppets they sell to tourists have wooden rods."

Blackburn looked into her dark brown eyes, and realized she was studying his own. "That phrase you used ... *wayang*...."

"*Kulit*," she said. "Roughly translated, it means 'shadow play.' An enactment of the Hindu epics using maybe a hundred puppets, and a full orchestra. It's an ancient form of entertainment in this part of the world, and a way of keeping certain traditions alive. These days, though, Nintendo beats it hands down for popularity.''

''Same old, same old, I guess,'' he said.

''Maybe so, but it's an awful shame. The puppet masters—they're called *dayangs*—spend years and years learning their craft. They make their puppets by hand, and provide the voices and movements of all the characters. During a show the puppets are manipulated behind a white cotton screen, with oil lamps throwing their shadows onto it—when the lighting's done right, the shadows are colored, you know. The audience is split into two groups, so that one group sees the shadow play in front of the screen, and the other sees the puppet show and musicians behind it.''

''Representing the separation between the material and the sublime, the self and the godhead,'' he said. ''Worldly illusion and ultimate truth—''

''Atman and Brahman,'' she said, giving him a look that was comprised of equal parts surprise and curiosity. ''I see you're familiar with Hindu philosophy.''

''The Beatles school, anyway,'' he said. ''I must have worn out five copies of George Harrison's *All Things Must Pass* when I was in college.''

They stood there silently a moment, facing each other, their eyes still in contact. The crowd jostling around them, the pungent smell of cooking smoke thick in the sultry air.

''Fifty *ringgits,* twenty-five American dollars!'' the vendor yelled at the top of his lungs, pushing up closer to them, obviously worried that he'd been forgotten.

Blackburn reached into his pocket for his wallet, got out two bills—a twenty and a five, U.S. currency—and payed for the puppet. The vendor gave him a little bow of thanks and briskly moved off into the crowd, leaving Blackburn holding his new acquisition with a faint look of bemusement on his face, like someone who has won a stuffed animal at a country fair shooting gallery and abruptly realizes he hasn't the slightest idea what he's going to do with it.

"Well," the woman said. "I'm sure the puppet will make an interesting conversation piece when you bring it to work with you. Don't see many like it in the States, I'll bet."

Blackburn gave her a quizzical glance, not quite sure what she meant. Only a moment later did it dawn on him that she was assuming his office was in America. A natural enough mistake, considering that he was obviously American, and that he'd payed for the puppet with American money.

"Actually, my pal Ganesha here won't be leaving the peninsula in the foreseeable future," he said. "Guess I should properly introduce myself. My name's Max Blackburn. I work security for a company called UpLink International, and right now I'm based at our regional headquarters in—"

"Johor, isn't it?" She suddenly burst out laughing as they shook hands, putting him at a loss as to what he could have said that was so funny. She recovered briefly, but then saw that the bemused expression he'd been wearing on and off over the last several minutes was very much back in evidence, and broke up again.

Still, he noticed she hadn't let go of his hand. Which was something on the plus side, anyway.

"I'm sorry, you must think I'm awfully rude," she said, getting control of herself at last. "I'm Kirsten Chu, and it happens that I work for Monolith Technologies, Singapore. The Corporate Communications Division. I'm here on holiday, visiting my sister and nieces.''

Understanding spread across Blackburn's features.

"Ah-ha," he said. "So *that* explains why you're in conniptions.''

"It does indeed," she said. "Our employers are very much archrivals, aren't they? For the past six months I've done nothing but huddle with our lobbyists and publicists about the encryption flap, brainstorming ways to counter Roger Gordian's opposition.''

Though Blackburn would not realize it until several months later, that was the moment he had decided to use Kirsten. The exact moment. It had been a calculating, unemotional decision, entirely separate from the genuine attraction he felt toward her. And all the time they had spent together since, all the nights their bodies had been locked in passion, using her had been very much a part of it.

"Well, judging by how badly things are going for us, you're doing a helluva job." He'd flashed an engaging smile, letting a hint of flirtatiousness slip into his voice. Calibrating both for maximum effect. "But does being on opposite sides of a professional dispute mean we can't make friendly overtures?''

"Overtures," she repeated.

"Right. A personal truce.''

Their eyes met.

"I suppose," she said, "it could be possible.''

"Then let's seal it over dinner tonight.''

"Well . . .''

"Please," he said, not giving her time to answer. "I guarantee a mutually agreeable resolution.''

She looked at him a moment longer. Smiled.

"Yes," she said. "I'd love to have dinner with you."

And that was that. The beginning of an affair that had turned out to be enormously satisfying for him. Great sex, great inside information.

What more could a man desire?

Now Blackburn sat in the silence of his office, his face troubled, looking out his window at the sprawl of low, prefabricated buildings that constituted the Johor ground station, hating to think of the danger he'd put her in, *refusing* to let himself think about it, instead turning his mind back to the part that was real for both of them, imagining her body moving against him, joined to him, their cries of pleasure mingling in the darkness of her bedroom, going on and on into the night.

Yes, that part of it was real.

Real.

He reached for his phone, dialed her office number, waited for her secretary to connect them.

"Max?" she said, picking up a moment later. "Did you get my messages?"

"Yeah," he said. "Sorry I couldn't get back to you till now. They're adding components to the alarm system, and I had to oversee the whole thing. Took me most of the morning to get the glitches smoothed out."

Her voice became hushed. "Guess I got a little anxious. Something's turned up, and I think it could be important. Perhaps the very thing you've been looking for."

"You'd better not say any more right now."

"Agreed. Even if I wasn't at the office, it would be much too sensitive to discuss over the phone."

"Got you. We'll talk about it in person, then."

"Will you be coming this weekend?"

"Yes," he said.

"Such enthusiasm," she said.

He told himself to put away the guilt.

"Just tired," he said. "Barring any unforseen developments, I'll be taking a lorry over the causeway tomorrow morning."

"Bringing along your overnight bag?"

"It's been packed since yesterday," he said.

"Not too full, I hope. Clothes won't be necessary for the weekend agenda I've planned."

"Toothbrush and deodorant?"

"Now *they're* absolute requirements." She laughed. "I have to run, Max. Love you."

Blackburn's eyes moved from the window to the spot where he'd hung the puppet on the wall.

Atman and Brahman, he thought. *Illusion and truth.*

"I love you, too," he heard himself say.

Wondering if the words sounded as empty and mechanical over the phone as they did to his own ears.

FOUR

"CONGRATULATIONS, ALEX. I'LL BET EVERY POLITI-
cal columnist in the country's writhing in the light of your
greater glory."

Alex Nordstrum smiled a little uncomfortably as he
walked into the conference room, hoping Gordian's comments, coupled with his late arrival, wouldn't give rise to
certain impressions about him. That they might be accurate impressions was beside the point. Why be blatant?
Conceit was a quality Nordstrum preferred to bear with
discretion; he had an old Harvard classmate who'd been
wearing his Phi Beta Kappa fraternity key on a gold fob
for the past twenty years, and it was never a pretty sight.

"So you've heard about my upcoming submarine
ride," he said, taking his place at the table. And how was
that for understatement? Or had he struck a false note
right there? Maybe it was a mistake trying to appear blasé
about being handpicked for the small group of reporters
who would accompany the President and several other
world leaders—all of whom were intent on milking a
treaty-signing event for every bit of public attention it was
worth—on a "ride" aboard a Seawolf nuclear sub.

Yes, maybe he ought to let the others in the room be
freely awed.

"May I ask who gave you the news?" he said, knowing Gordian could have gotten it from any number of political and business contacts, including at least a couple of the individuals present at the meeting. Although the list of invited reporters had been released only hours earlier, this was a plugged-in bunch if there'd ever been one.

"My source insisted on anonymity," Gordian said. "Anyway, Alex, you'd better pour yourself some coffee. We've got a lot to talk about this morning, and you just might feel like you're already underwater before we're finished."

A workable segue to more relevant matters of discussion, Alex thought.

He looked around the room, nodding his acknowledgment to the parties who'd arrived ahead of him. Most of the faces he saw were very familiar, belonging to Gordian's core group of friends and advisors. There were two UpLink employees at the table besides Nordstrum himself, who, as Foreign Affairs Consultant, was technically a freelancer: Vice President of Special Projects Megan Breen, seated to Gordian's immediate right, and Risk Assessment Manager Vince Scull at his left. Directly across from Nordstrum was Dan Parker, the congressman from California's Fourteenth District and Gordian's closest confidant since the days when they'd flown bombing sorties with the 355th Tactical Fighter Wing in Vietnam. In a chair alongside Parker sat another government official, Robert Lang, chief of the FBI's Washington, D.C., bureau.

The man poring over a document at the far end of the table was Richard Sobel, founder and CEO of Secure Solutions, a young Massachusetts-based encryption tech outfit. He both rounded out the small group and, by mere virtue of his presence, symbolized all the reasons it had come together this morning. Nordstrum couldn't have said whether it was more significant that a competitor in the field of cryptographic technology was here to offer Gordian his support and alliance, or that Sobel was the only one of fifty leaders in the software business to accept Gord's invitation.

"Okay, let's get rolling," Gordian said now, the intense gravity of his manner hardly lifted by a cordial smile. "First, I want to thank all of you for coming. Second, I want to be clear about how much I appreciate *why* you've come. It obviously would have been easy to remain silent and invisible. Our unified stance on the encryption issue has already caused most of us considerable problems, and it's a fair bet they're going to increase exponentially in the next couple of days." He paused and glanced over at Megan Breen. "The credit for putting together the statement I'll be reading at our press conference goes entirely to Ms. Breen. Assuming everyone received a copy by fax and has gotten a chance to review it, I believe you'll agree she's done a magnificent job of boiling our concerns down to media-friendly sound bites."

"Absolutely," Sobel said, looking up at her from the sheet of paper he'd been scanning. "Megan, if I thought I had any chance of poaching you from Roger, I'd make an offer right now and be off, never mind the order of the day."

Megan smiled at the compliment. A tall, slender woman of thirty-six, with huge sapphire eyes and shoulder-length auburn hair currently worn in a French braid, she looked crisp and able in a violet blouse and a gray designer blazer-and-slacks combination. Being that he was a heterosexual male with what he regarded as a good eye for attractive women, Nordstrum had long ago observed that she was a knockout. Being that she was a professional colleague, Nordstrum recognized it wasn't politically correct to give that observation any air time, and had wisely kept it to himself . . . although he reasonably suspected that many of her other male business associates, a couple of whom were in the room at that very moment, shared his atavistic view. Or hadn't there been a jag of envy in Scull's voice when he'd conveyed the rumors about Meg and Max Blackburn heating up the Russian winter last year?

"While Roger may have put it a bit too flatteringly, I *did* want to make our comments brief and straightforward," Megan was saying. "Still, I hope none of you will hesitate to let me know if there's anything that should be added, removed, or clarified. We have forty-eight hours before President Ballard signs the Morrison-Fiore Bill, which gives me ample opportunity to fine-tune any part of the statement that needs it. I think, though, that our message really is a simple one."

"Looks that way from where I sit, too," Vince Scull growled. His fringe of hair in a careless uproar around a shiny expanse of scalp, a frown creasing his bulldog face, Vince appeared to be on the verge of an angry eruption. This was nothing unusual to people who had been exposed to him for any length of time, since his total range of emotions ordinarily seemed as narrow as it was volatile, with splintery annoyance being the lowest gradient on the scale, blistering fury the highest, and radical fluctuations between these extremes occurring once every hour or so. "We put the crypto out overseas without restrictions, and presto, every bad guy with a computer link can buy himself electronic communications that law enforcement can't crack. If Ballard's got the high-wattage brain they say he does, he ought to be able to understand that without any problem. I mean, it's pretty damn obvious, isn't it, Bob?''

The FBI man shrugged. ''In all fairness, there are gray areas. A valid argument says the bad guys have *already* gotten their hands on the technology through Internet dissemination, not to mention American companies who've circumvented the law by selling crypto abroad through their international subsidiaries. Follow that line of reasoning, and you have to ask whether it pays to restrict our software manufacturers from competing on the foreign market.''

''Can't put the genie back in the bottle, so put him to work instead. That's the same crap I've been hearing for *years* from people who want to legalize dope. And let me tell you, it doesn't make any sense. Back when I was wearing a cop's badge, I saw—''

''Listen, you asked me something, I answered,'' Lang interrupted. ''If I needed to be persuaded, I wouldn't be here today, putting my career and reputation on the line. As Dan can attest, I've argued vehemently against deregulation before a dozen congressional committees.''

''I agree,'' Gordian said. ''There's no need to rehash the whole policy debate at this table. Our purpose should be to make sure we haven't overlooked any means of stopping Morrison-Fiore, or effectively presenting our case—and our solidarity—to the public, the government, and the rest of the industry.''

Nordstrum had been thinking precisely the same thing, and was relieved Gordian had gotten the static out of the air before sparks started flying.

"Regarding your last few points, I'd say reading our little declaration to the National Press Club on the day of the signing is perfect strategy," he offered. "It will stir up controversy, grab media attention, take a story that would otherwise appear on page nine of the dailies and put it right on page one, above the fold." Nordstrum paused thoughtfully, adjusting his wire glasses on the bridge of his nose. "As to throwing some last-minute hurdle in front of the bill . . . short of locking the President out of his office the day after tomorrow, or conspiring to break his writing hand, I honestly don't see how it would be possible."

"Any ideas, Dan?" Gordian asked.

"I opt for breaking his hand," Parker said, but Gordian could only manage a feeble approximation of a smile in response.

Parker studied his face, and for perhaps the fourth time that morning observed that he was not looking well at all. His cheeks were ashen, and there were deep lines under his eyes that gave him the appearance of someone who hadn't had a decent night's sleep in weeks. Gordian wasn't the sort of man who was quick to share his problems, but he generally got around to it with Parker long before they swamped him. He had opened up to him about his difficulties readjusting to freedom after five years in a Hanoi POW camp, confided in him when his marriage hit a rocky patch a while back.

Lately, though, he'd been sealed tight, leaving Parker to play guessing games with himself about what was wrong. His instincts told him it was something personal . . . but a hunch was a hunch, and with Gord keeping quiet, and the shit flying in every direction because of the crypto debate, he hadn't had a chance to pursue it very far.

Parker suddenly became aware of the silence around him, realized Gordian was still waiting for his answer.

"From a political standpoint, I think we ought to be looking ahead to the next session of Congress," he said, shoving his concerns about Gord to the back of his mind. "Take a hard line now to gain a public-relations edge, advocate a return to the previous Administration's policy of setting firm limits on the level of encryption software that's authorized for foreign sale . . ."

"And perhaps ease toward some compromise as things pick up again in the Hill," Gordian said, completing Dan's thought. "I like it."

"So do I," Lang said. "As it reads, I believe Morrison-Fiore will be calamitous to our national security. But certain changes could be incorporated that would mitigate its damage."

"Such as . . . ?"

"Off the top of my head, a clear-cut provision banning export of plug-in encryption cards, and critical components for multiplex encoding units, like the type used by our armed forces—the same type you and Mr. Sobel are refusing to market abroad."

"Another thing would be a tough set of international laws and standards managing the operation of key recovery centers," Parker said. "These places are essentially private banks where governments deposit the digital key-codes to their data-scrambling software. Right now, police and intelligence agencies can subpoena the banks to turn over the codes . . . although the civil libertarians are challenging that power in various courts."

He looked at Lang. "Correct me if I'm wrong, but my

understanding is that there are no effective international
treaties which would compel a key recovery center in one
country to turn its keys over to another, even if the nation
requesting them can prove they're needed to counter a
threat to its security.''

Lang nodded. "You're dead-on. A terrorist with sophisticated electronic equipment could theoretically crip-
ple our economy, even disable our military computers,
while the ambassadors are wrestling over what legitimately can and can't be done under existing cooperation
agreements.''

For a moment Gordian sat staring out the office's floor-
to-ceiling window at the San Jose skyline, and the vague
humps of the mountains off to the southeast. Then he
shifted his attention back to Dan.

"What about the Foreign Trade Commission?" he
said. "Setting our sights on the future, I'm wondering if
anybody there eventually could be nudged toward at least
some of our positions.''

"Never happen," Parker said. "Olivera, the head of
the organization, is a militant free-trader. More important,
he's a Ballard appointee who's been brown-nosing the
President since they were poli-sci majors at the University
of Wisconsin. Not for all the Chapstick in the world
would he tear his lips away from the President's backside.
Nor would he allow his underlings to stray.''

"Somebody in Congress, then. Preferably the NSC.''

Parker shook his head. "I know of several men on the
panel who are privately sympathetic, and one who actually views Morrison-Fiore as a poison seed in our national
defense system. But all come from states where the software industry has tremendous clout, and where people are
afraid of losing jobs because of an inability to enter for-

eign markets.'' He smiled ruefully. ''Do you have any
idea what my opposition to the bill has cost me in votes?
Being the representative from Silicon Valley? I'd probably have alienated fewer constituents if I got bagged for
armed robbery . . . with an Uzi and the stolen goods in
hand.''

Gordian looked outside again, past the broad stretch of
Rosita Avenue, to where the Diablos went marching up to
Mount Hamilton, its distant flank barely visible through a
thin veil of smog. Closer by, one could still see a few of the
aging food-processing plants and plastic factories that had
once formed the industrial base of the city . . . but they
were really nothing more than relics. Technological research and development had been San Jose's lifeblood for
over twenty years; its economic survival was dependent on
the hardware and software outfits that gave a huge chunk of
the population their employment. Dan Parker was deliberately understating the price he would have to pay for standing by his principles . . . and by his friend. In doing so, he
had quite possibly committed political suicide.

Gordian turned from the window and ran his eyes
around the table, letting them settle briefly on each face,
each member of the coalition that had gathered around
him. Parker was immediately—almost *physically*—struck
by the realization that some of the old steel had returned
to his gaze.

''We should discuss our travel arrangements for the trip
to Washington,'' Gordian said. ''I think we're ready for
the next round.''

FIVE

FROM THE *STRAITS TIMES*:

Investigation of "Phantom" Freighter Continues

Authorities Increasingly Look Toward Piracy As Explanation for Crew's Disappearance

Singapore—Nearly 48 hours after the freighter *Kuan Yin* was mysteriously abandoned by its crew in Sembawang Harbor, its undelivered cargo remains in the possession of local customs officials, who have revealed that they are consulting with their Malaysian counterparts and the Piracy Center in Kuala Lumpur regarding the possibility of a hijacking at sea.

According to Tai Al-Furan, a spokesman for the Customs Ministry, the vessel is licensed to Tamu Exports, a commercial shipper based in East Malaysia. Mr. Al-Furan confirmed that it left Kuching Harbor sometime on the

evening of Sept. 15 with a manifest of
general wholesale goods designated to
arrive in Singapore that same evening.
No other stops were scheduled in transit. It was also revealed that the ship
was fully laden when found at anchor-
age early on the morning of the 16th,
adding questions about the motive for
a pirate raid to deepening concerns
about the present whereabouts of its
crew, which is said have consisted of
almost a dozen seamen.

''The shipowner is being very cooperative and has provided our investigators with a complete list of those
who were legitimately aboard the
Kuan Yin when it set sail,'' Mr. Al-
Furan told reporters.

While Mr. Al-Furan acknowledged
fears that the crew members may have
been forced to evacuate at sea by a
hostile boarding party—giving rise to
speculation that the vessel was com-
mandeered as a means of gaining the
perpetrators false documents and illegal entry into Singapore—he expressed optimism that a more routine
explanation might be found for their
disappearance.

''We are keeping open minds about
what may have happened to them, and
see no reason to jump to any conclusions at this point,'' he stated.

Mr. Al-Furan would neither confirm
nor deny rumors that signs of armed
violence, including apparent bullet
holes, have been discovered by police
in the vessel's lower deck.

Despite joint efforts by the Associa-

tion of Southeast Asian Nations
(ASEAN) to combat maritime crime,
the frequency of pirate attacks in
China and throughout the region—
many of them sponsored by underworld syndicates—has increased by
more than 50% over the past decade,
with their level of violence also esca-
lating. Last year alone over 400 seamen were either assaulted or killed by
pirates, an alarming figure in light of
recent improvements in the equipment
and interdiction methods used by
counter-piracy patrols. . . .

They had been following the woman for two days. According to their information, the American would likely
appear tonight. And it would be tonight that they struck.
Otherwise, it might be another week before they had their
chance, a week during which the investigation of the
Kuan Yin hijacking would broaden and escalate into a
manhunt, and the assumed identities of the ship's crew
would become increasingly useless to Xiang and his men.
They wanted to be long gone from Singapore by then.

The guest house they had been staying in was a shuttered, run-down building crammed between two other di-
lapidated structures in a twisty *larong* not far from Fat
B's. They had booked three rooms at a cheap rate, and
though the accommodations in each were limited to a few
sagging cots, a shaky corner table ringed by some equally
lopsided chairs, and a washbasin with a dripping faucet,
the out-of-the-way location and sordid atmosphere dis-
couraged tourists and other meddling transients from
seeking the place out, which was Xiang's only real requirement.

In fact, comfort was the last thing on his mind this evening.

His tattooed chest bare, he sat with both arms on the table, having wedged a small piece of cardboard under one of its legs to steady its irritating wobble. On its surface before him was a photograph of Max Blackburn. To his right was a candle he had set to burning in a flat metal ashtray. Beside the candle was a long, thin needle with a round ceramic handle. Across the room from Xiang, two of his men, Sang and Kamal, had pushed their cots to one side and given themselves space for the supple, tiger-style martial arts exercises of *karena matjang*. The shades were drawn and the electric fixtures in the room were off, and the candlelight projected their weaving shadows onto the walls and ceiling.

Thrown loosely across one of the cots were the clothes they would be wearing when they took Blackburn and the woman later on that night. Nondescript khakis, denims, and long-sleeved cotton shirts. The clothes of soft, weak people who lived safe and easy lives.

I suggest you get something to wear that will let you blend in, the peacock at the bar had said. His advice had been well taken, though he'd thought Xiang too witless to detect the mockery behind his neutral expression. Perhaps assuming size and stupidity went hand in hand. It was a mistake people often made in dealing with the Iban. And it only played to his advantage.

Now Xiang reached out with his large right hand, lifted the needle off the table, and held its carefully sharpened end into the flame. Let the others practice their *kata*. He had his own special method of preparation, of steeling himself for what lay ahead of them.

He waited silently, holding the needle out by its handle,

watching it heat up. When it was red-hot he pulled it out of the flame, then raised his left hand in front of his face, his fingers straight up and close together. He stared at it for several moments, his eyes slitted with concentration, almost as if he were reading his own palm. The glowing needle was still in his opposite hand.

Now he brought the needle horizontally toward his left hand, aligning its tip with his little finger just below the upper joint. His lips pressed tightly together, he slid the needle into the finger, piercing the soft flesh behind its pad, pushing it through until the tip came out the other side with a little squirt of blood.

Perspiration filming the wide expanse of his brow, he drove the needle further into his hand. It penetrated the fourth finger below the knuckle, cauterizing his flesh as it lanced on through and then exited again, its point emerging to prick his middle finger.

Xiang continued pushing in the needle until it had skewered all of his fingers except his thumb, rotating it once or twice to avoid nicking bone. There was an almost trancelike absorption on his face.

Slowly, then, he curled the hand into a fist around the needle. A minute went by, two, three. His fist tightened. He felt the needle's heat and pressure blaze across the inner joints of his fingers. Blood greased his wrist and went splashing down onto the photograph of Max Blackburn. The more excruciating his pain became, the harder he squeezed down on the invasive metal, causing the skin of his fingers to stretch and bulge around its length. The dribble of blood quickened and intensified, slicking his forearm, covering the image on the photo. His fist tightened some more. The pain was a wave to be ridden and

crested by sheer force of will, and he did not want it to
stop.

He sat there with glazed and unblinking eyes, oblivious
to the other two men as they continued their ritual exer-
tions, their shadows slipping back and forth across the
room, integrating and drawing apart in the liquid patterns
of their millennium-old fighting techniques.

"It will be done," he hissed under his breath. "It will
be done."

His fist tightened, tightened, tightened.

A half hour later, Xiang pulled the dripping needle
from his flesh.

He was ready.

The second time they'd been together—the first was that
crazily exciting weekend in Selangor, when Max Blackburn swept into her life like a whirlwind, swept her into
bed before she had a chance to think about what she was
doing, or even ask herself whether anybody was at the
wheel in her swoony little head—the subject of Marcus
Caine's business ethics had come up in their conversation.
Actually, Max had *brought* it up. Over dinner at a Thai
restaurant on Scotts Road, she recalled.

They had finished their meal, and were on their second
bottle of claret, and a half hour later would be grappling
breathlessly in Max's suite at the Hyatt, the clothes they
had shed leaving a scattered trail to the door. In between,
though, they had drunk their wine and discussed her employer. Briefly, it was true. Very briefly, because they'd
both been looking forward to more delightful activities
than talking shop. But long enough to touch off a sequence of events that would eventually turn her world
inside out.

The workday over, alone except for the cleaning woman out in the corridor, Kirsten Chu sat in the quiet of her office knowing that she was about to blow her career, and perhaps her entire life, to smithereens. Maybe sometime in the future, just so it would make clear and easy sense, she would convince herself that it was done out of conscience, moral indignation, and her refusal to become a passive accessory to acts that went far beyond the boundaries of international law. *A woman of principle.* Yes, that assessment by way of fuzzy hindsight had a nice ring, and would make her feel good about her decision in the reflective moments of her dotage. But right now, running an internal truth check, she could find only one overarching motive for what she was doing.

Of all the damn reasons in the world, it was out of love and longing for a man she barely knew anything about.

How bloody romantic.

Kirsten glanced at her wristwatch and saw that it was five-thirty, almost time to be off; Max was meeting her outside the Hyatt in half an hour. She popped the disk that would be the instrument of her professional demise out of her computer's CD-R drive, and for several moments afterward just sat there shaking her head, staring at the lethal circle of plastic, remembering that conversation at the restaurant as clearly as if it had occurred only yesterday.

Ah, Max, Max, Max. The question he'd posed to her was fairly indelicate, and probably would have been off-putting if it had come from anyone else. But that was the essential Blackburn, wasn't it? He had a way of saying things to her that other people couldn't, not without instantly and appropriately causing her defenses to harden. Indeed, she had felt vulnerable to him from the beginning.

He somehow turned tactlessness into a disarming quality, perhaps because he knew it worked for him, and took such confident pleasure in his knowing.

What he had asked, seemingly out of the blue, was whether she had any strong feelings about her employer's "underhanded corporate tactics." As if it were an obvious *given* that there was something wrong with the manner in which Marcus Caine did business. The sky is blue, the sea is wide, Marcus Caine is an unscrupulous crook. Elementary, my dear Kirsten.

At first she hadn't known what to say, had just looked at him over the rim of her wine glass, wondering if he really expected her to say anything. And he had just waited, letting her know that he did.

"I think," she'd replied finally, still hoping to avoid the subject, "your question is in violation of our declared truce."

"Nope, I've checked the rules, and they're very clear that it's acceptable," he said, that self-assured, damnably engaging look in his eyes. "Feel free to answer without risk."

She had not understood why his question made her so uncomfortable. Not then, and not for a while afterward. She had not yet been willing to admit, either to Max or herself, that he'd touched upon an already raw nerve. That the financial irregularities she had been noticing at Monolith—*irregularities,* ah, yes, she'd always thought of them like that at the time, always trivialized the significance of anything suspicious that crossed her desk—could be routinely explained away.

"Well, I'm sure that's his reputation among sour-grapes competitors, and his adversaries in protracted political battles," Kirsten said, more sharply than she'd intended. Charming as he was, Max's cockiness had irritated her. "Otherwise . . ."

"Actually, I was thinking of the class-action lawsuit against him a couple of years back," Max said. "You remember it?"

As one among an army of publicists who'd worked to stem the tide of bad press arising from that affair, Kirsten had remembered it all too well. Because Caine's new operating system was second only to Microsoft Windows in popularity—and catching up fast—it was common practice for software manufacturers to provide Monolith with pre-release versions of their products for compatibility trials. This was a mutually beneficial, even crucial, arrangement, since an operating system was useless without programs that could run within its graphic environment, and a program was dead on the shelf unless supported by one of the three standard operating systems.

The problems occurred when Monolith began patenting and marketing software that the developers claimed was nearly identical to the beta programs they'd sent out for evaluation. Their charge was that Caine's techies had lifted their intellectual properties, made minor changes to their graphic interfaces and proprietary architecture, and then stamped a Monolith logo on the retail packaging. In essence, that Monolith had rapaciously stolen their products and sold them as its own.

Sitting across from Max in the restaurant, Kirsten had put down her glass and leaned forward, her arms folded on the table.

"You certainly must know the matter was resolved out of court," she said.

"With a huge cash settlement from Caine."

"That isn't the same thing as an admission of guilt.

When you're a public figure, it's sometimes worth a great deal to get an issue out of the spotlight. Especially when the alternative is to let it drag on and become an impossible distraction.''

Max had spread his hands. ''There are other bones to pick with Caine. His flagrant disregard of the OECD anti-bribery convention, for instance.''

''You just said it yourself, Max,'' she said. ''It's an international convention, not a formal treaty. Meaning that it has no teeth. It's hardly a crime or a sin for Marcus Caine to exploit the gutlessness of its signatories . . . especially the French and Germans, who until last year were giving *tax deductions* to companies that exchanged cash payoffs for foreign contracts.''

She paused, took a breath. ''For God's sake, I'm not going to sit here and defend everything my boss does professionally. Nor can I vouch for what he's like personally. But he's the first man to own a truly interactive cable television network with affiliates on four continents, which makes him an entrepreneurial genius from my standpoint. If his competitive methods are occasionally ruthless, than so be it. What counts to me is that they're legal—''

''Or at least have never been conclusively proven to be *illegal*.''

''—and that he pays his employees very, very well,'' she'd gone on, speaking right through his interruption.

''I'd point out that there's real merit to the old cliché about money not being everything, but that would be kind of a cliché in itself,'' Max said. He gave her a tight smile. ''Wouldn't it?''

She looked at him with an odd mixture of consternation and amusement.

"Tell me, Max," she said. "Do you extend your services to UpLink for free? Troubleshooting around the world like a knight errant in Roger Gordian's holy crusade to link all of humanity with cellular phones and wireless faxes?"

If not for Max's frank, earnest look, what he'd said next might have caught her altogether by surprise. As it was, it instantly made her regret her sarcasm.

"Roger Gordian is a great man, and I would lay down my life to protect him," he'd said simply.

Whammo.

Now, looking back at that night, she recalled nearly being blown off her seat by those words. Somehow, their incredible strength and conviction bulldozed through her remaining emotional barriers, and caused her feelings for him—feelings she'd believed, or wanted to believe, consisted overwhelmingly of physical desire—of *lust,* leaving aside the delicate frills and flowers—to soar toward honest-to-God romantic love at warp speed. That had been a new and startling emotion for her, and she hadn't quite known how to handle—

A voice from the doorway suddenly intruded on her thoughts. "*Wah!* Excuse me, Miss Chu. Thought everybody go home. Come back later or not?"

Kirsten had identified the cleaning woman by her Singlish even before she looked up to see her head poking through the door. When she'd first returned to Singapore after completing her education at Oxford, Kirsten's ears had been forced to undergo a crash readjustment to the local patois, an idiosyncratic hodgepodge of English, Hokiien Chinese, and Indian phrases that jangled unharmoniously in the air wherever she went, and seemed especially favored by working-class immigrants from neighboring islands and the Phillippines.

Perhaps, she thought wryly, this was because they enjoyed watching upscale *kiasu* suffer migraine attacks while deciphering the latest term that had been added to the mix.

"No, Lin, that's okay." She clicked her computer into its preset shutdown routine and turned it off. "I was just wrapping up here."

The door opened wider and Lin clattered in with her cart.

"Why you work so late, *lah*? Is Friday night, should go out, get away from office." She winked. "Where your handsome American?"

Kirsten smiled, reached for her briefcase, and put the CD-R into an interior pocket—right beside the digital audio recorder on which Max would find a little something extra that was bound to make him ecstatic.

"Actually, the handsome American and I are planning to meet at his hotel and then dance away the night at Harry's," she said. And, as far as she was concerned, drink it away too. After turning the information she'd uncovered over to Max, information that might bring down a company that had been more than generous to her with its professional advancements, and that the group-centered Eastern traditionalist in her insisted was deserving of her loyalty, come hell or high water, she would need a whole lot of something potent to wash away the bad taste in her mouth.

"You have nice time," Lin said, a grin breaking across her broad face. "Promise tell me about it Monday, *lah*?"

Kirsten snapped her briefcase shut.

"As much as I can without shaming myself," she said.

• • •

Blackburn hastened up Scotts Road toward the Hyatt, his shoes slapping the pavement, navigating his way through thick city traffic, hordes of department store shoppers, and countless tired and slightly buzzed office workers making their post-cocktail-hour migrations home. It was seven o'clock in the evening, but the sun was only beginning to lose some of its solid-feeling intensity. Perspiring heavily, his shirt already wet as a sponge, he felt in desperate need of a shower . . . ah, yes, great way to start the weekend. Worse, he had arranged to meet Kirsten at six, and while he had called her on his cell phone to let her know he'd be late, it bothered him that he was running even later than anticipated. That she would be alone with the hottest of hot potatoes in her possession, waiting for him to show and take it from her hands.

She deserved better from him.

Most frustrating for Blackburn was the fact that he had started out with ample time to spare, having caught a lift to the bus terminal in Johor Bahru with a member of his security team, and then hopped the JB–Singapore express heading across the causeway. In the past, he'd found this to be a fast and hassle-free means of transportation from the mainland—far better than driving one of the company Land Rovers—since the buses had their own designated lanes and normally bypassed the customs posts where trucks and automobiles would get bottlenecked for lengthy stretches of time. However, tonight everything on the bridge, including public and private buses, had been subjected to exhaustive checkpoint procedures, causing delays in both directions. And though no one conducting the inspections had bothered to explain the reason they were taking place, many of his fellow passengers were convinced they were tied to the *Kuan Yin* affair that had been monopolizing the news broadcasts all week. With nothing to do but wait out the extended stops, they had noisily formed a consensus that officials were searching for the cargo ship's hijackers, or for confederates who might try slipping across the border from Malaysia to assist in their getaway.

Max didn't know about that; he had been too preoccupied with a security analysis at the ground station to follow the story's every sensational development. Still, he had noticed men in the epauleted uniforms of the Singapore Police reinforcing the usual contingent of customs bureaucrats, and assumed something very much out of the ordinary was in the air.

Of course, he'd had other things pressing on his mind as the bus continued fitfully over the Johor Strait and then onto the Bukit Timah Expressway, skirting a lush, carefully managed flourishing of parkland as it bore south to Ban San terminal. If Kirsten had finally dug up the evidence he'd been hoping to obtain from Monolith's computer databases, then the shadow play he'd initiated the day they met was about to reach its conclusion. But at what cost to her? She would be finished at Monolith. And the hard, cold truth was that he would be nearly finished with Kirsten.

Yes, she deserved better, much better, than she was bound to get from him in the end.

Blackburn had discharged the matter from his thoughts for the remainder of the trip in. Upon reaching the station on Arab Street, he had switched to a city bus and ridden it into the center of town, where traffic had once again slowed to a crawl, this time due to typical rush-hour congestion. Convinced he could make better progress on foot, he'd gotten off on Orchard Road and strode hurriedly west past the sleek, glass-fronted shopping centers lining the street like modern crystal palaces, their facades reflecting hard-pointed sun-darts that stung his eyes in spite of his dark glasses.

Now he swung right onto Scotts, squinting into the glare toward yet another exclusive shopping strip and the high tower of the Regency beyond.

Kirsten was waiting at her usual spot beside the main entrance, her hair pouring loosely over the shoulders of an eggshell-colored dress, looking out into the busy one-way thoroughfare, probably expecting him to arrive with the steady stream of cabs and buses moving past the hotel. As he approached her, Max instantly felt the mingled guilt and desire that always swelled up in him when they met. She had given herself to him without inhibition, and in its own way his craving for her was equally fierce, but Max did not love her as she had come to love him, and he had told her that he did only because it forwarded his selfish objectives. And though his lies and manipulations had profaned even their moments of greatest intimacy, he knew that he would keep leading her down the garden path until he got what he wanted . . . and that it wouldn't even be that hard.

No, God help me, not hard at all, he thought, stepping quickly toward where she was standing.

Xiang sat behind the dashboard of a panel truck outside the Hyatt's service entrance on the uphill side of Scotts Road. Less than half an hour earlier, the truck's original driver had been delivering fresh linens to the hotel. Now his naked corpse was in back, wrapped in a red-stained tablecloth from the very pile of linens he had been unloading when the Iban stole up behind him. Blood trickled from the ear through which Xiang had inserted his six-inch *kanata* needle, rupturing the man's eardrum, driving the needle up into the soft meat of his brain via the auditory canal, killing him instantly and silently.

The white uniform blouse that had been stripped from his body had smears of blood on the collar and was almost impossibly snug on Xiang, but he felt confident no one would notice it while he remained in the truck. Still, he was growing anxious. Where was the American? He could not stay parked at the loading ramp indefinitely without arousing suspicions.

Wrestling down his impatience, Xiang dipped his head slightly to look as if he might be resting behind the wheel. And waited. With luck, the murdered driver would soon have company.

Back on the street, the rest of the strike team had assumed various positions around the hotel, two covering its doors, a pair in front of the Royal Holiday Inn complex across the street, another four dispersed between the north and south corners of Scotts Road.

The men were similar in general appearance. Black-haired and stony-eyed, with angular features, skin the color of sunbaked clay, and compact builds over which the muscles were strung like taut leather cords. Each had concealed a weapon of one kind or another in the loose-fitting, casual clothes that allowed them to troll unnoticed among the hurrying crowd.

The swarm of people posed no hindrance to them. Nor did the remaining daylight. It would have been riskier to strike in darkness, when the street was emptier and activity along its sidewalks would be less frenetic. At night their movements would draw the eye like sudden ripples in a still pond; now the noise and confusion of pedestrian traffic would camouflage them in plain sight.

The woman had been standing at the Hyatt entrance for some time, looking out at the street as if she expected someone to join her at any moment. And, of course, that was exactly the case. They had been stalking her for days like wolves on the hunt. Tonight she would draw their real quarry into their circle, and they would do the job they had been paid to do.

Now the woman chanced to look in the direction of Orchard Road and her eyes widened.

The watchers took note. She smiled, waved, her expression pleased and a little excited.

The watchers observed this as well.

They turned in the direction she was facing, their eyes keenly anticipant, tracking the path of her gaze. *Finally,* they thought as one. Though the man walking toward her wore aviator sunglasses, he was easily recognizable as the individual in their photographs. He raised his hand in an answering wave and stepped up his pace.

''Max!'' she called, descending the hotel steps.

The watchers moved in to take them.

SIX

"GET IT STRAIGHT, ALEX. IT ISN'T THE LOCKS, BUT the *keys* your friend Gordian should be training his sights on . . . ah, stuff it up this contraption's wire-clogged asshole, I'm falling behind the pacer!"

In his career heyday, Rear Admiral Craig Weston, Ret., had been among the biggest of the U.S. Navy's big fish in his position as chief officer of SUBGRU 2, the command organization for all attack submarines on the Atlantic coast, based, along with the primary student training facility of America's submarine force, in Groton, Connecticut. This included the three nuclear submarine squadrons docked along the deceptively tranquil New England shoreline, as well as two squadrons split between home bases in Charleston, South Carolina, and Norwalk, Virginia—a total of forty-eight SSNs, one research submarine, and numerous support vessels. Considering that the payload of conventional and nuclear munitions aboard a *single* SSN was sufficient to erase a major coastal city from the map, the magnitude of the destructive force that had been under Weston's control was, in a word, remarkable.

For Alex Nordstrum, the best part of observing Weston on the rowing machine at the Northwest Health and Fit-ness club was seeing how much of that force he seemed to have taken with him into retirement. A tall, lean man in his late sixties with a silver flattop crew cut, stormcloud-gray eyes, and a jaw like a lofty mountain ledge, Weston approached his morning workouts with utmost seriousness and concentration . . . and a biting ferocity that was often manifested as a rather prolonged salvo of expletives, characterized by creative anatomical references, and uttered at a volume just quiet enough to avoid violating the gym's rules of acceptable conduct.

"*Son of a bitch!* I'm on you now, you hungry fucking crotch louse!" he growled, accelerating the rhythm of his strokes. He was wearing gym shorts and an athletic shirt to showcase—quite intentionally, Nordstrum believed—a physique that would have been impressive on someone thirty years his junior, and been considered truly phenomenal on a man his age in the best of health. Having recently undergone a program of intensive chemotherapy to combat prostate cancer that had metastacized to his lymph nodes, Weston had almost achieved superhuman status in Alex's estimate. Lateral muscles bulged in his thighs as he began his drive. Abdominals and pectorals that looked two inches thick flexed under his tank top midway through his extension. Biceps swelled on his arms as he pulled the handles to complete his stroke, then leaned back in toward the flywheel for his recovery, his hips swinging slightly, the tension cord vibrating like a bowstring.

On the exercise bicycle beside him, Nordstrum glanced down at his own softening middle, felt a twinge of embarrassment, and fingered the touchpad to increase his level.

"I thought you'd be giving me background on the Seawolf today,'' he said, struggling not to sound winded. "So how come we're talking about Roger Gordian?"

"Don't be a wise guy," Weston said. "I'm not always this generous with my advice."

Alex frowned. "Okay, have it your way. But I really do need that information."

"And you'll get all you can handle in a minute."

Weston rowed, his sinews working, inhaling and exhaling softly through his nose. His eyes were centered on the rowing machine's video screen, where tiny red and blue boats were racing over green water past a strand of white beach in a computer-simulated regatta. Nordstrum waited for him to resume speaking, peripherally aware of the smooth-operating silence of the modern equipment filling the gym. There was the occasional pneumatic hum of inclines being raised on the treadmills, and now and then the metallic clank of weight adjustments on the presses, but what he mostly heard were the sounds of controlled human exertion in uncluttered acoustical space: measured expulsions of breath, the rhythmic pounding of feet on rubber.

"Let me ask you something," Weston said at length. "Which would be of more concern to you—a bunch of thieves moving next door with a home security system identical to yours, or those same crooks moving in without *any* security of their own, but having the tools and wherewithal to disable your system? To open your front door, switch off your alarms, and walk into your bedroom any time you're sleeping or gone?"

"Rhetorical as posed," Nordstrum said. "I'd prefer they have neither."

"So would anybody, but that wasn't one of my choices. Indulge me, will you?"

Nordstrum shrugged and pedaled, his upper body bent forward over the handlebars, the towel around his neck damp with perspiration.

"Suppose I wouldn't want them getting into my house," he said.

Weston looked at him briefly. "There it is. My whole point. Gordian wants to make his case about crypto tech to the public, it ought to be *his* point too."

"That as far as you're going to spell it out?"

"Yes," Weston said, and then turned toward the screen again. "What do you want me to tell you about the sub?"

Nordstrum wondered if he'd missed a segue. "Everything you can. I should probably know what sort of boat I'll be riding in."

"And writing about."

"As a conscientious member of the press, and someone who doesn't like looking foolish," Nordstrum said.

Weston eyed the screen, produced another stream of epithets, and pulled more forcefully at the cable.

"You ever see that old TV program *Voyage to the Bottom of the Sea*?" he said. "My boys used to watch it religiously when they were young. Sunday nights at seven. When I was on tour I'd have to call in and listen to their episode summaries."

Nordstrum shook his head. "We didn't receive American programming in Prague at the time. Blame my ignorance on the Commies."

"Sure, forgot where you grew up," Weston said. He drove, recovered. "On the show there was a futuristic sub called the *Nautilus,* named after the one in the Jules Verne story. The Seawolf's its real-life equivalent, loaded with capabilities that the designers of Los Angeles-class vessels could only imagine. Goddamn thing's a testbed for advanced naval warfare technologies. It's got a modular construction for limitless upgrades. New low-signature hydrodynamics, and integrated detection, telemetry, and communications systems. Carries the usual array of anti-ship Harpoons, Mark 48 torpedoes, mines, you name it, plus the new Block 5-series Tomahawk. A land-attack missile that can hang in the air for up to two hours and has more warhead options than I can rattle off, including Hard Target Smart Fuze munitions able to penetrate to twenty feet underground before detonation.''

He winked and lowered his voice confidentially. ''While the Navy doesn't *officially* have nuclear-armed Tomahawks aboard its subs, the capability naturally exists.''

''Naturally,'' Alex said.

''I should add that the Seawolf's able to operate in the littorals.''

''Near ports, cities, enemy strongpoints, other land-based targets.''

''Exactly.'' Weston examined his reflection in the floor-to-ceiling mirrors, swore disgustedly under his breath, and straightened his posture. ''Before I get into more detail, you ought to know why the Seawolf's deployment under SEAPAC isn't just one of the President's typical mental farts, but his worst stinking room-clearer yet.''

''Let me take a wild stab at it,'' Nordstrum said. ''You're troubled by the prospect of having Japanese, South Korean, and other regional crew components aboard, even in exclusively non-combat roles . . . medical, research, and the like.''

''You know me well, Alex. It's the treaty's dumbest provision.''

Nordstrum pedaled. Though Weston hadn't yet broken a sweat, *he* was already starting to feel bushed.

"I don't know, Craig," he said. "Maybe you used the wrong television show for your analogy. The better comparison might be thinking of the Seawolf as a kind of USS *Enterprise*. Representatives of the world's peace-loving peoples consolidating their resources to guard against the Klingons."

"Never understood how that sappy shit got so popular," Weston said.

Nordstrum smiled. "Be that as it may, you know our Asian Pacific allies have been moving toward greater participation in regional military operations for some time. The Japanese alone spend millions on joint ballistic missile defense research with us every year. And there *are* Klingons in their part of space. North Korea's got Nodong-2's capable of dropping chemical and biological weapons into the heart of Tokyo." He paused, feeling a little out of breath. "This isn't anything that was pulled out of a hat, but a logical evolution of existing strategic policies."

"So you've stated ad infinitum in the editorial pages," Weston said. "And here I thought you were only doing it for a free thrill-ride on a submarine."

Nordstrum gave him a look. "Should I be offended by that comment?"

"It was a joke," Weston said without a trace of humor in his expression. "Look, cooperation is one thing. But how did we go from that to letting foreign seamen live and work aboard a nuclear sub, a fucking leviathan of the deep? What were our defense and intelligence communities *thinking* when they allowed it? I've never been phobic about the Japanese, but they will do what's in their own best national interest. For the past few years that's included joint military exercises with China and Russia. They're reaching out in directions besides just *ours*."

"I've never suggested SEAPAC doesn't have its risks. Obviously there have to be tough security procedures—"

"You mentioned medical personnel. As you'll see for yourself in a couple of weeks, even the biggest sub feels like a claustrophobic tin can once you've been aboard a while. It's a short hop from the infirmary to the torpedo room. Or the control room. Ghosts have a way of floating between decks, Alex. Of going wherever the fuck they want without being noticed. Because they can make their damned selves invisible."

Weston rowed silently, seemingly with nothing more to add, and having shed very little light on the technical workings of the submarine. How had they gotten sidetracked onto policy matters?

Alex swung his leg off the bike and wiped his forehead with his towel.

"That's it for me," he said. "Feel like breakfast?"

"I owe this cocksucking torture machine another fifteen minutes of my life," Weston said. "Next time, though. We'll have some pancakes."

"Sure," Nordstrum said, starting toward the locker room.

"Alex—"

He paused and looked over his shoulder.

"It's the key, not the lock. Tell that to Roger Gordian. Before the press conference. Okay?"

Alex regarded Weston a moment, then nodded.

"Okay," he said.

SEVEN

THE SUBTLEST OF VISUAL CUES JACKED BLACKBURN to heightened alertness. He could not have expressed the feeling in words; it was instinctive, programmed into his neural circuits by long years of battle experience with the Special Air Service. And he trusted it no less than his eyes and ears.

The man who had triggered his reaction had been poring through a magazine as he waited at the bus stop—so why had his eyes flicked over the upper edge of the magazine as Blackburn walked by? And why the sharp look of recognition on his features, the abrupt stiffening of his posture?

Why, all at once, had Blackburn gotten the powerful sense of being *watched*?

Perhaps twenty yards ahead of him, Kirsten was starting down the stairs in front of the Hyatt's entrance. Max slowed his pace and pulled back his gaze. He ranged it from right to left across an area several feet away and parallel to him, then reversed direction, scanning a larger, farther sector until it once again encompassed Kirsten. His attention had divided itself, automatically and simultaneously keying into separate frames of reference: the particular and the general, the narrow and the wide, points and lines.

Blackburn marked the bodies of the people within eyeshot as stationary and moving objects, drawing correlations between their positions and the broader patterns of foot traffic. Scouting for any peculiarities in their interrelationships.

Several were readily apparent.

There was a man launching off the curb directly across the street to his left, beyond the pedestrian crossing, then weaving through traffic toward his side of the street—a rare sight in a country that punished jaywalking with steep fines. Another was advancing from a short distance up the sidewalk, shoving through the crowd. Two more were rapidly converging on the hotel from opposite sides of the entrance.

Blackburn snapped a glance behind him, felt the skin on the back of his neck prickle. The man he had passed at the bus stop was pushing toward him, the magazine he'd been holding no longer in evidence.

All four of the men were around the same age, Asian, and wearing the same basic style of clothing.

The entire surveillance took under eight seconds and left him with little to consider. He had learned to be aware of everything that happened around him and quickly digest what he observed. It was clear now that he had walked into a trap. A *closing* trap. He did not know for certain who his enemies were, how they were deployed, or even their total number . . . but he did know the positions of five of them.

He walked on, trying to control his nerves, making a tremendous effort to conceal the fact that he'd spotted his attackers. Kirsten was halfway down the steps now, the men nearest the hotel closing in on her. Which could only mean they—or whoever had sent them—knew something about the Monolith files. He had to to get her away from them. But *how*?

Scanning the area near the hotel, he came up with an idea.

Without wasting an instant, he reached into his sport jacket for his palm phone, flipped it open, thumbed the power button, keyed up one of the speed-dial numbers stored in its memory, and hit "Send." Hoping to God that *Kirsten's* cell phone was on, and that she would answer his call if it was.

Kirsten had almost reached the sidewalk when her cellular trilled in her purse. She paused, looked toward Max, and smiled. He had lifted his own phone to his ear. Was he going to mutter sweet nothings to her as he came up the street?

Moving against the handrail, she set her briefcase down on a step and got out the phone.

"Hi-ho," she said into the mouthpiece. "I see you're finally—"

"Don't talk. There isn't time."

Confused, she looked across the short distance between them and saw that his face was as serious as his tone.

"Max, what's wrong?"

"I said to be quiet and *listen*."

Her stomach clenched with tension. She swallowed, nodded, her hand squeezing the phone.

"There's a taxi stand up the block to your right. Walk over to it as fast as you can without running."

She nodded again, looking at him with wide, questioning eyes. The stand was in the opposite direction from Max. What was going on?

Suddenly the emotion gripping her middle was no longer anxiety but fear.

The disk. God, this had to be connected to the—

"I want you to jump into a cab and get the hell away from here. I'll contact you soon. Understand?"

She gave him a third nod.

"Go!" he said.

Her heart knocking, she replaced the phone in her bag, snatched up her briefcase, and hastened down the remaining stairs to the street.

The two members of the strike team nearest the woman saw her stop and pull out her cell phone, then looked down the street at Blackburn, saw him talking into *his* phone, and immediately knew they'd been discovered.

One of them raised a hand to signal this to the others.

Bare seconds later he saw her resume walking, reach the bottom of the steps, and swing away from Blackburn toward the cab stand.

He and his companion increased their pace, pushing through the crowd, confident they were close enough to intercept her before she reached it.

Blackburn was still a few steps away from Kirsten when he saw the man turn his head toward her, turn his head toward him, and then give what was clearly a signal to his companions.

Not good, Blackburn thought. If the man had seen both of them on their phones, he wouldn't have to be a genius to conclude they were talking to each other, and that his group's little ambush was no longer any kind of secret.

The gesture would have warned his friends to hurry up and make their move.

Kirsten had reached the pavement, turned away from him, and started hastily toward the taxi stand, where a line of robin's-egg-blue Comfort cabs were waiting to pick up fares. The pair of men who'd been covering the door had veered off after her, right on her tail, blocking her from Blackburn's sight.

His teeth clenched, Max bumped quickly past a group of women with shopping bags hung on their arms, shuffled past some dark-suited businessmen, and then moved up behind the pair at a fast walk, using every available ounce of self-restraint to keep from actually breaking into a run. If he did that, it was a safe bet his attackers would do the same, and he had no way of telling whether he'd made all of them, or whether there might be someone he *hadn't* identified even nearer to Kirsten than the two men in front of him—and in an easy position to outrace him.

He gained on the men, gained some more, and when he was almost on top of them suddenly swung around to their left, quickstepping off the curb, then stepping back onto it, passing them, putting himself between them and Kirsten. He was three feet behind her now, maybe less.

Almost close enough to touch her.

Almost. . . .

He heard hurried footsteps coming up behind him, and lunged ahead with a burst of speed, no longer checking himself, knowing there wasn't any room left for hesitation. Reaching her at last, he hooked his right arm around her shoulder and swept her along toward the idling cabs, bracing her so she wouldn't trip head over heels onto the asphalt, using his body to shield her from their pursuers.

Rigid with shock, Kirsten stumbled along uncomprehendingly for several feet, trying to resist—then all at once realized it was Max and loosened up, letting him steer her forward.

She glanced over at his face as they approached the cab stand, her eyes bright with distress, their cheeks almost touching. "Max, dear Heaven, *Max,* I thought you were one of them. I—"

"*Shhh!*"

Kirsten fell silent, her body trembling against him. She had no sooner registered that he was looking past her toward one of the standing cabs, than he reached out and tore open the taxi's door so violently she had the wild idea that its handle would come off in his grasp.

What followed would always be a blur in Kirsten's recollection. One instant they were together, she under his arm, Max practically carrying her along, and the next he'd shoved her into the backseat of the cab, and was standing on the street, standing there alone, leaning through the door from outside.

"*Selangor!*" he shouted at the driver.

The man behind the wheel jerked around to look at him through the safety partition, his shoulder rattling the clutch of religious trinkets dangling from his rearview mirror.

"Sorry, no long distance, *lah,*" he said, shaking his head.

Blackburn jammed a hand into his pants pocket, hurriedly yanked out his billfold, and tossed it into the front seat.

"There's more than two hundred American dollars in it," he said. "Take her and it's all yours."

Kirsten was gaping up at him with a kind of helpless desperation. The driver, meanwhile, had already lifted the billfold off the seat and was peering into it with astonishment.

"Max, I don't understand," she cried shrilly. "What's happening? Why aren't you *coming*?"

"Stay with your sister," he said. "If you don't hear from me in a few days, I want you to get in touch with a man named Pete Ni—"

Max felt a hand seize on his left elbow from behind. He tensed, trying to keep himself planted between the two attackers and the cab.

"Get moving!" he screamed into its interior, then pulled his head out of the door, slamming it shut with his right hand. He could see the reflections of the two attackers in the window—one still holding onto him, the other trying to scramble past him to the car.

For a seemingly endless moment the cab remained stationary, and Max was sure the driver wasn't going to bite at his offer. Then he saw him push down the lever of the meter to start it running, and expelled a sigh of relief.

Her face bewildered and terrified, Kirsten shifted around in her seat as the taxi angled from the curb, staring at him through the rear window.

Their eyes met briefly, his narrow and resolute, hers moist with tears . . . and then the taxi joined the heavy flow of northbound traffic, and was gone.

It was the last they ever saw of each other.

Max heard a short, frustrated breath escape the man that had taken hold of his right forearm.

"You come with me, *kambing*," he hissed, and tightened his grip. His lips were against Max's ear, his body pressing up behind him.

Max didn't budge. The man's partner had jogged after

the cab for several yards, then been forced to get out of the way of speeding traffic, scrambled back onto the sidewalk, and turned around—but he hadn't yet returned to where they were standing.

Which left Max with a small but workable opening.

Moving with reflexive swiftness, he brought his left arm around in front of him, reaching across his middle, shifting his weight onto his right leg to pull his captor sharply toward him. As the man staggered forward with one hand still clamped over Max's forearm, Max put his free hand over it, gripped three of its fingers, and bent them back hard.

The man released him with a gasp of pain and surprise, struggling to regain his balance.

Max moved away from him and wheeled in a full circle, glancing up and down the street. A few nearby pedestrians had paused to gawk at the scuffle, but most were hustling past as if they hadn't noticed anything unusual. Maybe they really had not, or maybe they were just mindful that, however prosperous, Singapore was still a dictatorship where it was best to mind one's own business.

Either way, he had more urgent concerns. The magazine reader was coming at him from the left, and now he had the jaywalker for company. A third member of the strike team was hustling toward him from the right. Counting the man he'd just shaken off, and the man who had been chasing the cab—both of whom were behind Max—the odds against him were at least five to one.

The only direction left open was straight ahead, toward the hotel.

He ran across the sidewalk and bounded up the stairs to its entrance.

•   •   •

Max cut a line through the lobby without a backward glance. He was acquainted with its layout from his regular stays in UpLink's long-term guest suites, and he knew what he was looking for. To the rear of the desk and main lounge area was a bank of elevators and, on their right, a short, straight corridor leading to a service entrance. Beyond that, a stairwell that would presumably take him down to the basement and loading doors. No hotel security guards on duty, or at least none in sight . . . and he'd been hoping their presence might turn aside his pursuers. Still, if he could reach the service entrance before his pursuers caught up to him—a big "if" since they'd been following right on his heels—he'd be able to shake them by ducking out the side of the hotel.

Max saw a clot of new arrivals making a commotion at the check-in desk, German tourists from the sound of them. Hoping for momentary cover, he plunged into the noisy, milling group, then moved on past the entrances to the hotel dance club and bar, past the elevators, and over toward the service entrance, still not looking back over his shoulder—no time for that, no time at all.

The gray metal door was slightly recessed from the wall and had a pane of wired glass set into it at eye level. No one was anywhere near it. Max turned the knob with his left hand, pushed the door open with the flat of his right, went through, and stepped from carpeting to bare concrete.

Blackburn took a hurried look around—narrow flights of stairs ran up and down from where he stood on a wide landing. He started toward the descending stairs, but got no further than the end of the landing before the door crashed open behind him, a hand clamped onto his shoulder, and he was pulled backward with tremendous wrenching force.

Max caught hold of the rail an instant before he would have gone stumbling off his feet. He whirled on whoever had grabbed him, found himself standing with a butterfly knife pressed against his throat.

"Come with me." It was Jaywalker. Facing him from inches away, his fist clenched around the weapon's double handle. "Now."

Blackburn met his gaze and saw no hint of human emotion in it, only a sort of cold, vortical emptiness. Then he heard muffled footsteps and broke eye contact, switching his attention to the door pane. Magazine Man and two others were approaching from the outer hall. They would burst through onto the landing within seconds. And there was still nobody else around.

Blackburn stood motionless. His hands at his sides. The blade against the right side of his throat, less than an inch below the ear, where it could easily slice into his carotid artery. Blood trickled down from where its razor edge had broken his skin.

His mind raced. He was carrying a Heckler & Koch MK23 in a concealment holster against his waist, but his assailant wasn't going to give him the chance to draw it. He was in the most vulnerable position he could imagine, and the close quarters left precious little room to maneuver.

So what, then?

He didn't have a split second to waste debating it with himself. Sweeping his left arm up from his side, he slammed the outer part of his forearm against the back of Jaywalker's knife hand, knocking the blade away from his throat, then grabbing his wrist to keep him from bringing it back up. Caught by surprise, Jaywalker tried to tear free, but Blackburn held fast to him, bringing his knee up into his groin. Jaywalker doubled over, gasping for air, his knife clattering to the floor. Max moved in closer and followed with a rapid combination of punches to the head—left cross, right jab, left hook. Gasping for breath, his nose and lips bleeding, Jaywalker staggered back against the rail. Max didn't relent for a heartbeat. His chin tucked low in a boxer's stance, he hit his opponent with another smashing blow to the side of his face, putting all his weight into it, wanting to take him out before he could recover . . . and before his friends came to his assistance.

But he only got half of what he wanted. As Jaywalker dropped to the floor in an unconscious heap, the fire door winged open and the others bolted through onto the landing. The one in the lead was small and wire-thin, wearing a baggy tan shirt, chinos, and Oakley sunglasses. Running up behind him, Magazine Man was perhaps a head taller and a good deal bulkier.

It was Oakley that proved to be trouble of a sort Max never could have seen coming.

He was reaching for his gun when Oakley dropped into a low squat, and, spinning on one leg, snapped the other leg out parallel to the floor, the side of his foot striking Max's ankle with shocking impact as the kick reached the end of its arc. Caught completely off guard by the move, firebolts jagging up to his knee, Max went staggering, fumbled for the rail, was unable to grab it this time, and tumbled down the stairs.

He rolled twice, somehow keeping his right hand fastened around the butt of his semi-auto, his other arm twisting underneath him as he threw it out to brace his fall. He hit the lower landing with an audible crash, winced, a huge flare of pain suffusing his entire left side.

There was little doubt he'd seriously injured his shoulder blade, perhaps even fractured it.

He still had his gun, though. Still had the blessed thing cocked and ready in his fist.

Rocking onto his back, he saw Oakley hurtling down toward the landing, toward *him,* coming on like a goddamned homing missile. The funneling, empty look hadn't left his eyes. Aware he'd be finished if his shot went awry, Max brought up the pistol, aimed dead center at his attacker's rib cage, and squeezed the trigger.

The report was oddly flat and unechoing in the concrete stairwell, but its effect was nonetheless dramatic. Blood and shreds of material blew from the front of Oakley's shirt as the heavy .45 ACP slug tore into him. His sunglasses whirled off his head and smacked against the wall. He sailed backward as if suddenly having been switched into reverse, his arms flailing, his eyes wide and unbelieving. Then he sprawled limply onto the stairs.

Max glanced past his body at the upper landing, saw that Magazine Man had slipped a hand under his baggy shirt, and fired again before he could pull whatever the hell he was reaching for.

There was another flat thud from his gun muzzle, another explosion of crimson, and Magazine Man went down clutching his chest.

Blackburn knew he'd only gained a brief reprieve, and struggled to a sitting position. The three men he'd overcome couldn't have been too far ahead of the rest of his attackers. If they'd stayed in contact with them—which was likely—the others would be coming through the door at any moment.

His situation was going to get worse, much worse, once they did.

He needed to move fast.

Max got to his feet, grasping the rail with one hand to support his weight. His ankle and shoulder wailed from their injuries. He looked up and down the basement corridor into which he'd fallen, saw large double doors perhaps ten or fifteen feet over to his right, and made a snap decision to see where they led.

He boosted himself off the rail with a small gasp of exertion, reached his goal with a few limping steps.

Suddenly there was a loud crash—the stairwell door flying open behind him.

Then footsteps.

Banging down the stairs.

Max felt a thrill of renewed urgency. It wasn't hard to visualize the newcomers' reactions when they saw what he'd done to their friends. They would not be pleased, to say the least.

He pushed the whole length of his body against the metal lock bar, and the doors opened out. Weak daylight flooded over him. Ahead was a loading ramp that rose to a short alley lined with Dumpsters. A delivery truck was parked at the curb at the mouth of the alley. The word "New Bridge Linens" painted across its flank in English, a delivery man on the driver's side of the cab.

Max paused. Saw that the delivery man's head was craned so he could peer out the passenger window. Saw the expression of menacing scrutiny on his features. And realized he'd been about to go running straight toward his opponents' getaway vehicle.

The delivery man turned toward his door, threw it

open, and emerged from the truck, hurrying around its front grille toward the alley. Max could tell at a glance that he was enormous, and did not feel like having to take him on. In the best of conditions it would be a tough fight, and he was far from at his best right now. His gun upraised in his right hand, he withdrew into the doorway, grabbed the lock bar with his left hand, and hauled back on it, praying he could find another way out before his pursuers overtook him—

Exquisite pain sliced through his right arm all at once. It jerked into the air as if snagged on a fishing line, jerked out of his control, the semi-auto flying from his fingers. A harsh breath escaped Max's lips as he glanced incredulously down at himself and saw that something *had* caught onto him below the elbow, tearing through his jacket sleeve, actually sinking into his flesh—a kind of metal grappling hook at the end of a thin chain, what he believed was a goddamned martial arts weapon the Chinese called a flying claw. The man grasping its handle ring, his stare devoid of mercy, could have been Oakley's twin.

The double doors flung wide open behind Max. With his peripheral vision he saw the bulking figure of the man move up on his left.

He desperately gripped the tautened chain with his good hand and struggled to tear it loose, but the claw wasn't coming out, the claw had gouged too deeply into his arm, the claw was buried inside him.

My God, who are *these guys?* he thought, his blood streaming thickly from his wound, dripping over the chain to the floor. The man at the other end of the weapon holding onto it like someone engaged in a deadly tug of war. *Who—?*

Before he could finish asking himself the question, the driver's massive hand swung out at his temple and the world exploded into blinding whiteness and then went black.

EIGHT

From *The Wall Street Journal*:

Industry Focus: Roger Gordian's Growing, Failing Monstrosity
BY REYNOLD ARMITAGE

There is drama in the numbers: by its own accounting estimates UpLink's earnings have fallen 18% in the past year, the largest slide in its third consecutive quarter of decline. Its stock prices continue to drop at an even more precipitous rate, having closed the week by falling $15.4656 to $45.7854 a share on Big Board composite volume of 100 million shares, a decline of 25%. As a result of these losses the corporation's market value has plunged by about $9 billion, considerably below even the gloomiest analysts' predictions and raising new questions about whether the high-tech giant can support its heavy investment in a global "personal communications satellite" network—one requiring the launch of about 50 LEOs and 40 gateway stations around the world, for a total investment of over $3 billion over the next five years.

There is drama in the numbers, but the entire story is more complicated than they reveal upon first examination. Certainly the defense and communications operations at the heart of Roger Gordian's past success desperately need to have the causes of their ill health diagnosed and remedied. But to completely understand the forces bringing down his parent company, one must look at the poor track records of its spawn. To offer but a few examples: the lackluster performance of UpLink's specialty automotive subsidiary, the chronic profit drain of its medical devices and power generation divisions, and the recent Dow losses suffered by its computer hardware and software offshoots due almost entirely to Gordian's imperious and unreasonable decree against the sale of cryptographic technology to emerging overseas markets. Indeed, the catalog of failures and borderline failures for what had been one of America's leading companies seems endless.

Unease runs deep among investors, who fear that Roger Gordian has created a patchwork monster, a multilimbed aberration whose lifeblood is being diverted away from its corporate center to sustain its unwieldy reach. To be blunt, as UpLink's once highly valued stock continues to lose ground, it becomes less critical to ask whether its problems are due to hubris, inattention, or simple bad judgment on the part of its executives, and fitting to state the obvious bottom line—its board has failed to uphold its basic fiduciary responsibility to shareholders, namely guaranteeing a premium return on their investments.

Let us pause here to consider an image of cojoined or "Siamese" twins—better yet, make them triplets—their bodies connected by an implacable tube of flesh, nerves, and intertwined blood vessels. In the cradle, they coo and embrace. As young adolescents they plan for a future that seems a bright, infinite frontier.

But adulthood brings change and discord. One of them grows to enjoy composing gentle romantic poetry. Another's great pleasures are drinking and arm-wrestling in rowdy taverns. The third simply likes to fish in the sun. Miscreated, mismatched, and miserable, they try to reach some lifestyle accommodation, equally dividing their time between preferred pursuits, but their basic incompatibility of nature causes all three to fail.

The poet cannot write because the long nights in hard bars make soft, lyrical thoughts impossible, and because he suffers hangovers from the alcohol flowing through their common bloodstream. The prodigal grows depressed and contrary while his versifying brother struggles to focus on the intricacies of rhyme and meter. Their constant arguing exhausts the fisherman,

> so that he merely sleeps away his mornings by the stream, and his rod frequently drops from his fingers to be dragged off into the water by a darting bass or trout, gone with a splash.
>
> Eventually the three brothers wane and perish. The cause stated on their death certificates? One does not know the medical term, but perhaps it might rightly be called overdiversification.
>
> What can be done to spare UpLink from a similar demise? For answers we might contrast the untenable generalism of its expansion to the cautious, focused growth of Monolith Technologies. . . .

Although it wasn't yet time for the reception to conclude, Marcus Caine was feeling bored and stuffy-headed in the packed United Nations chamber. From his place at the dais, he sat staring past exotic floral arrangements at a profusion of television cameras, cables, floodlights, and microphone booms, all manipulated by a crew of scurrying technicians. Behind him was a large collapsible backdrop showing the U.N. symbol, a globe viewed from the North Pole and surrounded by olive branches. Because this was a UNICEF event, there was the added touch of a woman holding a young child in the center of the globe. Caine's wife, Odielle, sat quietly at his right, her face thin and clamped. On either side of them were officers of the organization's Executive Board and high-ranking members of its parent body, the Economic and Social Council. Below him, rows of interpreters in headsets were translating their insipid, windy speeches into six languages.

As the current speaker droned away about Caine's philanthropic largesse, he absently glanced down the length of the table at Arcadia Foxcroft, *Lady* Arcadia, his connection to the Secretariat, and the woman who had arranged the ongoing event. Wanting to stop his mind from drifting off entirely, he stared at her, made her his fixed point of concentration. It wasn't hard. She had the sort of face one would expect to see on a fashion model's headshot—exciting, glamorous, provocative. Her peach-colored dress accented a spectacular figure. Lively blue eyes flashing, delicate lips parting over perfect white teeth, she was having a conversation with the fellow next to her, laughing at something he'd said. Though he couldn't hear the laughter from his seat, Caine was very familiar with the sound of it.

Somehow it always made him think of sharpened glass.

Caine watched her. A man-killer, Arcadia. And aware of it, as were all women of her type. She brushed back a wisp of auburn hair, revealing one of the diamond earrings that he'd bought for a small fortune at Harry Winston's and given her while they were in bed the previous night. He had dropped them between her thighs after they made love, and she had found that tremendously arousing. As she'd put them on, and then slid on top of him, groaning breathlessly, awakening him to delight again, he'd wondered how many other sexual dalliances she was having even while they conducted their affair, how many other partners were lavishing her with expensive gifts. Doubtless quite a few. Which was all right. Bad girl, Arcadia. He had his fair share of her, and thought it was only sporting to let the rest of the boys have theirs.

Besides, he liked to imagine her engaging in hidden, illicit acts out of his presence . . . just as he thrived on the tension of having his wife and mistress seated in the same room, rubbing elbows, making small talk, secrets running between them like unseen trip wires.

Caine was dimly aware that another speaker had taken the microphone. A famous Hollywood actress who had married a New York congressional leader, semi-retired from the big screen, moved out to East Hampton, damped her incandescent beauty behind scholarly wire glasses, and become a dedicated spokeswoman for children's causes. Caine wished he'd dated her when the chance had presented itself some years back. Now she was expressing her admiration of his professional standards, his accomplishments in wedding the mass media to computer technology, his inroads into new Asian cable television markets. She raised a chuckle from the crowd with a line that used the word "gizmo," shifted her tone to one of sober concern, and last but not least, praised his unflinching commitment to the Children, capital C. Thanks to Marcus Caine, she concluded wryly, it was truly becoming a small world after all.

Throughout the speech Caine kept his eyes on Arcadia, watching her flirtatious interaction with the dignitary beside her. He understood her quite well; indeed he and she were alike in a great many ways. Born in Argentina, the illegitimate daughter of a wealthy German expatriate and his one-time maid, she had been raised by her mother without paternal involvement or financial assistance, and was turning tricks in the streets of Buenos Aires before she was twelve. A decade and several wealthy clients later, having taught herself the manners and forms of sophistication, she slept her way into England's green and pleasant bowers, married a sputtering old lord who was ripe for the grave, secured his inheritance, and thus guaranteed her place in elegant High Society—make that capital H, capital S, please. She was a poseur, plain and simple. An urchin who had snuck into the ball and charmed her way into favor with the invited guests. No wonder her every gesture seemed an exaggeration. As if she constantly needed to prove herself *to* herself.

Yes, Caine understood her. As he sat among U.N. appointees chosen for their social status and connections, graduates of elite schools, men and women whose bloodlines and fortunes could be traced back centuries, pampered exquisites who were little more than walking family crests, how could he not? They were to the manor born. His father had been a sales executive who retired with a moderate pension after an undistinguished and psychologically anesthetizing career. His mother had taught third grade until she became pregnant with him and settled into being a housewife. Caine himself had been a good student throughout his youth, and attended Harvard for two years on a merit scholarship—but it had been withdrawn in his fourth semester when he'd gotten into some difficulties, and he'd never obtained his degree. Had he not fostered several important friendships before his expulsion he'd have been finished even before entering the race.

The fine ladies and gents in his company would have been astonished, completely astonished, if they knew what he thought of them, how *contemptuous* he was of them. . . .

A flurry of movement to Caine's immediate right, near the podium, suddenly intruded on his thoughts. He straightened in his chair, breaking his attention away from Lady Arcadia. The speaker presently delivering an encomium to his humanitarianism was Amnon Jafari, Executive Secretary ECOSOC, and he seemed about to wrap things up. A group of dark-suited men had appeared from behind the collapsible wall with a six-foot-long blow-up of Caine's endowment check to UNICEF—three million dollars, which he'd promised to double once it was matched by donations from other wealthy individuals. The mock check was backed with plywood, and there were two members of the group holding it at each end.

The Secretary's voice was a deep tenor, and its volume grew as he ended his speech, expressing his gratitude to Caine with a final burst of enthusiasm. Caine heard his name boom from Jafari's lips to the acoustical drop ceiling, and then carry across the chamber to the VIP floor and public galleries. Applause crashed through the room like thunder.

It was time for him to accept the accolades. He would enjoy standing before the cameras while trying to outdo the pompous verbosity of his hosts.

He rose, went to the podium, and clasped Jafari's right hand in both his own. Then the Secretary stepped aside and Caine turned to face the crowd, the oversized reproduction of his check making a splendid prop behind him. He began his comments by thanking the roster of U.N. officials responsible for the event, speaking without reference to notes or the Teleprompter—Caine's eidetic memory was one of his strongest assets.

"Yes, I am honored to be here," he said when he was through rattling off names. Flashbulbs popped, cameras dollied in for close-ups. "But more than anything, I am grateful for the opportunity to stand before you today with a challenge. As many of you know, I have long been committed to extending the global reach of interactive electronic media, and especially Internet technology—for it is my belief that they are the modern magic that can

unite the inhabitants and governments of Planet Earth and
truly make us one, the tools that will bring about our next
evolution as a species. Cyberspace allows us all, young
and old, rich and poor, the great and the humble, to meet
on a level field. A field with ever-expanding horizons and
limitless potential.''

He paused for some scattered handclaps, glanced over
his wife's head at Lady Arcadia. She met his gaze and
smiled at him, her lower lip tucked alluringly between her
front teeth.

"Yet as we take our first steps into the infant twenty-
first century, we must proceed boldly rather than tenta-
tively to assure that none are denied access to this
dynamic realm of information and knowledge. Those of
us who have been blessed with lives of material comfort
are obliged to share the rewards we have enjoyed. Listen
up and listen well: It is time to dedicate ourselves to guid-
ing and educating the children, so that they too may grow
without limitation, and attain new and fulfilling horizons.
Time for each of us extend a hand, and pledge a portion
of our wealth to bringing them technology that will im-
measurably improve their lives. It is a hard fact that advancement requires money. Schoolroom computers,
high-speed DSL modems, Internet connections—none of
these come free. From Bahrain to Barbados, from Af-
ghanistan to Antigua, from the industrial capitals of Europe to the emerging nations of West Africa, the youngest
and least fortunate of us must be guaranteed access. . . .''

Caine went on in that vein for perhaps ten more
minutes, and then decided to quit before he talked himself
hoarse. His standing ovation was punctuated with cheers
and bravos. He noticed that Odielle's clapping was rather
feeble and halfhearted, and that her pinched expression

seemed even tighter than it had been all morning—could it be she'd seen him exchange intimate glances with Arcadia, even knew something about his trysts with her? The thought made him tingle with a kind of giddy excitement.

But later for that. The show wasn't over yet, not until his Southeast Asian business associates—his *benefactors,* as they would have preferred to be considered—saw him run through his greatest hits. Doubtless, they would be watching and listening for them in front of their television screens.

Caine stood quietly until the crowd subsided, then announced that he would be taking a few questions from the press corps.

Predictably, the first one shouted at him had nothing whatsoever to do with his gift to UNICEF, or his challenge to the rich, or his crusade to put the deprived youngsters of the world on-line.

"Mr. Caine, as you know, the Morrison-Fiore bill will be signed into law the day after tomorrow." Caine recognized the reporter from the network newscasts; he had a scoop of dyed brown hair and an alliterative name. "Could you please give us your thoughts about that, and also about the fact that Roger Gordian is expected to simultaneously hold a press conference in Washington to declare his continuing opposition to the President's relaxed encryption policies."

Caine looked thoughtful. "I respect Mr. Gordian for his tremendous past accomplishments. But he has already expressed his views on the subject, and the people have voiced their grassroots opposition through their elected representatives. This is about our children and our grandchildren. About the *future*. Regrettably, Mr. Gordian has turned his eyes in the opposite direction.''

''If I may follow up, sir . . . as the bill's most vigorous proponent in the public sector, will you be going to Washington for the signing ceremony?''

''I haven't yet decided.'' Caine manufactured a smile. ''The President has been gracious enough to extend an invitation, but one day a week in the spotlight seems like plenty to me. Quite candidly, I've had enough of hotel rooms and am itching to get back to work.''

The reporter sat down and a second man sprang to his feet.

''Do you believe there's any link between Roger Gordian's stance on the encryption issue and UpLink's diminishing stock values?''

Beautiful, Caine thought.

''That's a question better asked of an investment banker than a software developer,'' he said. ''I'm really not here to speculate on my colleague's business difficulties. But if I may argue the obvious, the fortunes of *any* technology firm rise or fall on the willingness and ability of its leaders to look ahead rather than behind them.'' He paused. ''Now, if we may get back to the children's initiative I've proposed today. . . .''

But of course they didn't, which was exactly what Caine had wanted and anticipated. In the remaining minutes of the Q and A, Roger Gordian's name was mentioned half a dozen times, mentioned until he almost became an unseen presence at the press conference.

But not a participant to it, Caine thought. Today the floor was his, and his voice alone was being heard.

Engrossed in his own performance, he called on another reporter.

The future indeed.

That was very much what it was all about.

"Roger—"

Putting his hand over the phone, Gordian looked up at his wife as she appeared in the doorway of his study, wedged the receiver between his neck and shoulder, and held his pointer finger aloft.

"Just a minute, hon."

"You said that *twenty* minutes ago. Before you called Chuck Kirby."

"I know, sorry, we tend to get long-winded," he said distractedly. "Right now, though, I'm just buzzing the airport. I intend to fly the plane into Washington for the press conference, and want the mechanics to check it out...."

Ashley gave him a look that meant business. "Gord, what do you see in front of you?"

He cradled the receiver. "A wonderful but increasingly impatient spouse?"

She still wasn't smiling.

"Gorgeous, too," he said, knowing he was in for it.

"It's been three hours since I came home from the salon with shorter hair and blonder highlights than I've ever had in my life, and you've been holed up in here the entire time, too busy to notice," she said. "This is Saturday. I thought you were going to take the evening off."

He didn't say anything for a moment. Three hours since Ashley came home? Yes, he guessed it was. The afternoon seemed to have raced past before he'd managed to get a handle on it. As had the six months since his continual absorption with his work, his *calling* as she referred to it, had brought them to the brink of divorce. Always, he seemed to be trying to catch up. It was only after the murders of his dear friends Elaine and Arthur Steiner in Russia—a hail of terrorist gunfire having ended their lives and thirty-year marriage without reason or warning—that Gordian had awakened to what a gift he had in Ashley, and realized with terrible clarity how close he was to losing her. A half year of intensive counseling and earnest commitment had helped bridge many of the rifts between them ... but every now and then there were marital ground tremors that reminded him the bridges weren't all that steady. Not yet, anyway.

"You're right, that's what I promised." He stretched his neck to work out a kink of tension. "I apologize. Do you suppose we can start over from here?"

Ashley stood there in front of his desk, a trim, elegant woman whose youthful good looks had made no discernible concessions to early middle age, her sea-green eyes very still as they met his gaze.

"Gord, listen to me," she said. "I'm not a pilot. I don't even like to sit near the window in a passenger plane and be reminded there are clouds underneath me, rather than over my head where they *belong*. But you've always told me how being in the cockpit of a jet frees up your mind, gives you a feeling of perspective and ... what's that term you use? Ambient space?"

"Either that or altitude sickness," he said, smiling wanly. "You're a good listener, Ash."

"It's my best quality." She slowly crossed the room to his desk. "That space you talk about ... it's a kind of luxury that you afford yourself, and I'm glad you're able to do it. But sometimes I'm also a little jealous of it. Do you understand?"

He looked at her.

"Yes," he said. "Yes, I do."

She expelled a long sigh. "I'm not blind to what's going on. I read Reynold Armitage's latest bunk in the *Wall Street Journal*. I hear you and Chuck talking about stock sell-offs. I saw your face when the evening news carried Marcus Caine's remarks about you at the U.N. And I can imagine how it must sting."

Gordian started to answer, then hesitated, his brow furrowed, his lips pressed tightly together. Ashley waited. It was his nature to hold his thoughts in close, and she knew he often had difficulty raising the lid on them.

"I once met a snake-oil advertising man who would've called Caine's tactics a pseudo advocacy campaign," he said at length. "Or pseudo *adversary* campaign, it depends. He's been running both at once, you see. The basic idea is to use a public issue to gain attention for your firm, while promoting certain corporate agendas without being overt about it. You get the target audience to notice you by creating or stepping into a controversy, and then slip in the message you really want to convey between the lines. It's the marketing equivalent of a stage magician's top hat and cloak."

"And Marcus's so-called Children's Challenge obviously would be an example of the first type of campaign."

"A perfect example. Gives him an aura of take-charge philanthropism, a moral platform that's virtually attackproof. You know anybody who's against kids?"

She gave him a faint smile.

"I can think of a few times when our own bugaboos were young that *we* almost qualified, but you've made your point," she said. "The pseudo adversary campaign . . .

that would be his dispute with you over the crypto bill, wouldn't it?''

He nodded. "If you're going to play this sort of game, the potential rewards should always outweigh the risks, and Marcus is well aware that the issues surrounding encryption really don't excite much public reaction. The average person doesn't see how relaxing export controls is going to make any difference in his daily life. Nobody cares except special-interest groups within the high-tech industry on one side, and the law-enforcement and intelligence communities on the other.''

Ashley paused to digest it all.

"The strategy behind the UNICEF crusade isn't too down-deep," she said finally. "Let's give the kids computers and sell more Monolith software and have everybody feel good and pat themselves on the back. But what's he trying to achieve by taking you on over encryption? I don't see the . . . the *subtext*."

Gordian shrugged a little.

"You've asked the million-dollar question," he said in a vague tone. "And I'm not sure I can answer it."

Silence filled the room. Ashley realized he was sinking beneath it again, and leaned forward, lightly touching the fingertips of both hands to the edge of his desk.

"I understand how you feel, Gord," she said. "Do you accept that as a given?"

The question caught him by surprise.

"More than just accept," he said in a quiet voice. "Knowing that you understand . . . it's like a prize I've won without quite being sure how I did it, or whether it's even deserved. It makes me stronger than I'd be if I didn't know."

She smiled thoughtfully, looking straight at him. "I'd

never, never want to minimize your difficulties, or suggest there's anything in the world I wouldn't do to help you with them. But what I was starting to say before . . .''

He studied her face in the brief pause. ''Yes?''

''I was going to say that if you'd put those problems away for a few hours, if we could share some of the space you get up at thirty thousand feet right here on the ground, *together,* I'd trade UpLink, this house, our cars, every cent we have, everything we own. Or do you always have be to alone in the pilot's seat to let go?''

There was more silence. Ashley thought she could see the detached, inward-looking expression gradually lift from his features, but wasn't sure. Perhaps it was only wishful thinking.

She came close to exhaling with relief when he slowly reached out, covered her hand with his own, and let it rest where he'd put it.

''Let's go out to dinner, you name the restaurant,'' he said. ''Your enchanting new haircut deserves to be viewed by one and all.''

She smiled gently.

''You may have noticed,'' she said, ''that my membership at Adrian's spa and beauty salon wasn't among the things I indicated a willingness to surrender.''

He looked into the oceanic greenness of Ashley's eyes and smiled back at her.

''I very well may have,'' he said.

NINE

WHEN MAX BLACKBURN FIRST TOLD PETE NIMEC
that he'd gotten a line deep into the working guts of Monolith, and that he was using it to trace what he'd described
as "improper business practices and financial arrangements," Nimec had listened with close interest—and by
not ordering him to abandon his investigation posthaste,
had tacitly okayed its continuance. Still, as Chief of Security at UpLink, he had cautioned that UpLink would
under no circumstances be dragged into a situation that
might be perceived as corporate spying; the potential liabilities were far too great. Nimec had also pointed out
that it would be inadvisable for Max to provide any further details about the probe should he decide to move
ahead with it on his own string . . . unless or until he
turned up something of concrete significance.

Max had gotten the gist without anything more having
to be explained. Deniability had been established with a
nod and a wink—as it always was. If his activities came
to light, no one else at UpLink would be dragged into the
consequent chocolate mess. Nimec wanted clean hands
and fingernails from the level of clerk to upper management.

Officially, that had been the end of his involvement in

the fishing expedition. Unofficially, he had been eager to see what developed. And was becoming increasingly so as Marcus Caine's public attacks on Gordian intensified.

Their understanding kept very much in mind, Max had been exceedingly circumspect with his references to the matter in the three months since their initial phone conversation about it . . . when he mentioned it at all, that was. Nimec had gleaned that Blackburn's conduit into Monolith was a female employee with whom he'd originally formed a—quote, unquote—social relationship and only later enrolled as an informant. That she held a high-level position in the office of Corporate Communications, Singapore. Beyond these two pieces of information, he knew little else.

Of course there were other legitimate reasons for the men to stay in touch. Max had been sent to Malaysia for the purpose of emplacing security procedures at the Johor ground station, and many of his plans required Nimec's input and advance approval. Which was why he'd tried phoning Blackburn from his home office at four o'clock Sunday afternoon, making it the first thing Monday morning Johor time. After reviewing an expensive upgrade Max had proposed to the bionetric scanners last week, he'd decided to give him the green light to begin installation—only to learn that he hadn't yet arrived at the office.

"Mr. Blackburn was in Singapore for the weekend, and it's quite possible he's run into delays getting back across the causeway," his receptionist had said. "The causeway crossing has been awful lately . . . some sort of ship hijacking has Customs bollixed. Still, I'm certain he'll be in soon. Would you like me to try contacting him on his mobile?"

"No, it isn't anything urgent, just tell him I called when he gets in," Nimec said.

That had been eight hours ago, and Max still hadn't been in touch. Nor had *he* had a chance to give Max another ring; the child-custody arrangement Nimec had worked out with his ex-wife allowed him weekends with their son Jake, and he'd just returned from dropping the twelve-year-old off at home after taking him to a baseball game.

Still, Nimec wondered if his message had somehow gotten lost or slipped Max's mind, and wanted to try him one more time before turning in for the night. Blackburn's greatest weakness was a tendency to let curiosity lead him in too many directions at once, and he needed to be reminded that the ground station was his primary responsibility.

Nimec went over to his desk, picked up his phone, and keyed in Max's number.

"UpLink International, Max Blackburn's office."

"Joyce, it's Pete Nimec again."

"Oh, hello, sir," she said. Then hesitated a beat. "Mr. Blackburn hasn't shown up yet."

Nimec raised his eyebrows. "Not all *day*?"

"No, I'm sorry. Nor has he phoned in."

"Have you tried calling him?"

"Well, yes. On his cell phone. I think I suggested it to you earlier—"

"And?"

"There was no answer, sir."

Nimec was silent a moment. There had been something odd about Joyce's tone from the moment he'd identified himself, and now he suddenly realized what it was. She was covering. And had been right off the bat.

"Joyce," he said at last, "maybe its my imagination, but you're sounding very protective."

She cleared her throat. "Sir, Mr. Blackburn was rather vague about his plans before he left. But . . ."

"Yes?" he prompted

"Well, to be truthful . . . I think they were of a personal nature."

"You think he's cozied up somewhere with his girlfriend? Is that it?"

"Um, perhaps . . . I mean, not that he specifically told me—"

"Your loyalty to Max is admirable. But besides your suspicion that he's gone off on an amorous toot, are you sure you're not keeping anything from me?"

"No, sir. Absolutely nothing."

"Then let me know soon as he materializes," Nimec said, and hung up the phone.

Seconds later he rose from behind his desk, switched off the light, and headed for the shower. If Max was deliberately trying to stay incommunicado, he was either having much too good a time accommodating his Monolith executive, or—to be fair—becoming overly preoccupied with the more substantial aspects of his investigation. Both possibilities left Nimec feeling annoyed and a little uneasy.

When he finally got Blackburn on the horn, he intended to find out what he'd been doing, and if necessary remind him where he ought to be focusing his attention.

Independence was acceptable within limits, but no information was worth the problems Max could cause by taking things too far.

• • •

Its diesels purring quietly in the late-night fog and darkness, the twenty-six-foot pleasure boat was within fifteen kilometers of the northern Sumatran coastline when Xiang, gripping the foredeck rail, sighted the bright glow of a floodlight almost directly abeam.

He remained still and calm at the foredeck rail, checking his wristwatch.

The yacht was traveling with its cabin and running lights off, but there was a chance it had been picked up by the radar or thermal-imaging sweeps of a fast patrol boat. Only a very small and random chance, though. He was confident the vessel's theft would not yet have been detected; his men had taken it out of its slip after midnight, stealing aboard when the landing had been nearly deserted, disconnecting its uncomplicated security alarms with a few clips of a wire cutter.

Restrained and tranquilized, the American had been driven to the head of the landing in the panel truck his captors had used during his abduction, then been brought onto the ship while its motors were warming up.

No one had been there to challenge the pirates. Investigators searching for the *Kuan Yin*'s hijackers had established tight controls at the airports, causeway, and commercial shipping docks—the obvious corridors of departure—but there hadn't been any strengthening of surveillance and inspection efforts at the marinas where the wealthy berthed their yachts and sailboats.

Xiang had counted on the improvised cordons being spotty, and planned from the beginning to exploit their inevitable holes. Singaporean authorities were used to chasing common smugglers, and tracking down illegal workers from Thailand and Malaysia whom they would herd into detention camps, flog with a cane, and send back to their native countries with their heads shaved in disgrace. They had no experience dealing with a manhunt of any scope, and even with the computerized IBIS command-and-control system they'd purchased from the Brits making it easier for field units to coordinate their efforts, they were far out of their league. Unlike the boat people washing up on their shoreline as if they were beached fish after a storm, Xiang and his outlaws were neither desperate nor docile.

Now Xiang peered into the conical beam of light shining at a right angle to him and waited, his jacket flapping in the warm south breeze. He could hear the grunt of a small outboard above the slapping of wavelets against his keel. Good, he thought. The boats manned by naval task forces were sped along by turbocharged engines and water-jet drives. This was nothing so modern or formidable.

As Xiang stood leaning over the rail, the floodlight suddenly went out and the heavy-hanging sea mist knitted water and sky into a screen of undivided blackness. He dropped his eyes to his wristwatch again, waited exactly five seconds, then looked back out at the water.

The light blinked rapidly on, then off, then on.

He glanced over his shoulder. Through the cabin windshield, he could see several of his men in the cockpit. Behind the wheel, Juara looked out at the searchlight, then lowered his head to study a compass and chart in the faint glow of the binnacle. After a moment Juara straightened up and nodded to Xiang, confirming that they were at the proper coordinates for their rendezvous.

Pleased, Xiang unclipped the high-intensity flashlight from his belt, held it out in front of him, and returned the hailing signal with his response. On, off, on, off. Then on and off again after a fifteen-second interval.

He hung on the rail until he could see the outline of
the pickup launch, then went quickly into the cabin and
down the gangway to the lower deck, wanting to assure
himself that the prisoner was ready to be brought ashore.

TEN

"SERIOUSLY, JASON, THIS OUGHT TO BE CALLED 'Cholesterol Corner' or 'Arterial Sclerosis Way' or something,'' Charles Kirby said, looking down at his Rudy Guiliani hero sandwich, which contained a precarious mountain of corned beef, pastrami, Muenster cheese, and Swiss cheese, with a dripping mantle of Russian dressing and coleslaw at its lofty summit. Altough he had been tempted by the Barbra Streisand, with its multiple strata of turkey and roast beef, he'd found himself incapable of reading its name off the menu, thinking it had a rather unmanly ring.

"Why's that?" Jason Weinstein said, and stretched his mouth to encompass a pastrami, corned beef, and liver-heaped Joe DiMaggio, which he'd chosen over a Tom Cruise only because he'd never been a big fan of the latter's movies.

Kirby pushed his chin at the window. "Well, with that Lindy's Famous cheesecake place on the corner, and the Famous Ray's pizza joint across the street, somebody could build a famously successful practice opening a walk-in cardiac center on the block, don't you think?"

Jason shrugged indifferently, bit into his food, and reached across the table to grab a half-sour dill off the pickle dish, visibly chagrined over its nearer proximity to Kirby. Why Jason hadn't simply asked him to *pass* the pickles across the table rather than opting for the boardinghouse reach, as his grandmother would have called it, was something that Kirby couldn't for the life of him understand. He was a Wall Street lawyer, for God's sake. Where the hell were his dining manners?

He reached for his knife and fork, cut a wedge off his sandwich, and ate it in silence, having decided that any attempt to raise it to his mouth would result in an unstoppable landslide of sliced meat and cheese—Jason's ability to perform that gravity-defying task notwithstanding.

Suppose you need to have grown up in Brooklyn, he thought.

Jason chewed and swallowed with unfettered relish. "Better than sex, isn't it?"

"Maybe not for me," Kirby said. "But pretty good, I admit."

Jason gave him a look that said there was no accounting for taste.

"Okay, talk. Why'd you spring for lunch?"

Kirby sat for a moment.

"You represent the Spartus consortium. Or at least your firm does," he said. "I want to know who's buying its stake in UpLink."

"Whom *you* happen to represent."

"There isn't any conflict of interest," Kirby said. "The sale's a matter of public record—"

"Or will be once the i's are dotted and the t's are crossed," Jason said. "To be accurate."

Kirby shrugged. "All I'm asking is that you save me some legwork."

Jason lowered his Joe DiMaggio to his plate and regarded it with a kind of lusting admiration.

"You suppose they cure the meat themselves?" he said.

"Come on, Jase," Kirby said.

Jason looked him. "Sure, why not, but you never got it from me," he said. "The high bidder's a firm in Michigan called Midwest Gelatin. I don't guess I need to tell you its specialty."

Kirby scowled. "Some local jelly producer has the capital to buy up thousands of shares of UpLink? You're shitting me."

"I speak the truth," Jason said. "And that was *gelatin,* not jelly. It's used in everything from home insulation to sneaker insoles to ballistic testing. There's also a pharmaceutical variation which goes into the headache pills you gulp by the bottle. For your information, Midwest happens to be the largest chemical manufacturer of its type in the country."

"It public or private?"

"Number one," Jason said. "It's a subsidiary of a canning company which is wholly owned by a public corporation that manufactures plexiglass sheeting. Or chinaware, I frankly forget which."

Kirby considered that while Jason dove into his sandwich.

"Are you aware if there's anyone, um, of *note,* in Midwest Gelatin's upper management? Or that of its parent companies?"

Jason was looking at him again.

"You want to follow the paper trail, find out who's behind the move on UpLink, I suggest you talk to Ed Burke when we get to the park," he said.

"Our Ed?" Kirby pointed to the front of his uniform shirt, on which the word STEALERS was printed in gold capital letters. "The first baseman?"

"The canner's one of his biggest clients," Jason said, nodding. "Just *please* promise that my name won't enter the conversation."

"Thought I already had."

Jason shook his head. "No, no, you didn't."

Kirby made the scout's honor sign with his index and middle fingers.

"Promise," he said.

Satisfied, Jason turned to watch a thin, elderly-looking waiter scoot past the table with a tall stack of dishes expertly balanced on his arm.

"He's been working here since I was a kid," he said. "Three decades hustling on his feet, can't imagine how he does it."

"Could be he loves it here as much as you do," Kirby said.

Jason's gaze continued following the waiter's energetic trajectory down the aisle.

"Bet that's it," he said very seriously, and took another huge bite of his improbable sandwich.

Reynold Armitage's twenty-two-room duplex was in a palatial landmark building with balustrades and cornices and an ornate iron-and-glass marquee shading its Fifth Avenue entry opposite Central Park. The trappings of status and wealth were as evident—some would say *egregiously* evident—within his apartment as they were without; passing through the front door, one entered a long, wainscoted reception hall leading into an octagonal salon and then a living room with a parquet floor, massive fireplace, and haughty oil portraits under a vaulted ceiling. Continental silver gleamed on antique tables, Venetian glass goblets and decanters winked diamond points of light from breakfront cabinets, and dynastic Chinese vases perched like fragile blooms atop finely wrought marble gueridons.

Marcus Caine found it all very impressive, though not nearly so much as the scrupulous attention Armitage had payed to concealing the matrix of integrated electronic systems designed to compensate for his physical disabilities—most of which relied upon Monolith's leading-edge voice-recognition technology.

Ordinary men fit their homes with handicap access ramps, priviliged ones with lifts and elevators, he'd once told Caine. *I want you to give me something better than either.*

Caine sat sipping his vermouth as the parlor doors opened seemingly of their own volition, and the master of the house made his entrance ... the grandiosity of which was unaffected by his wheelchair-bound condition. In a certain way, rather, it lifted him from the merely pretentious and gave him an air of solitary dauntlessness. Don Quixote stalking windmills, Ahab versus the white whale, persistance against any odds. It was the warp and woof of highest drama.

''*Close,*'' Armitage said in a barely audible undertone, his power wheelchair carrying him forward with the faintest mechanical hum. Behind him the double doors swung quietly shut. ''No interruptions, take messages.''

He came up to his guest and halted the chair with a joystick on its left armrest. Once it had been on his right side, but over the past several years that hand had become too seriously atrophied to be of any use.

"Marcus," he said, raising his voice to a normal level. "Sorry to have kept you waiting, but I was on a call. Fortunately you look quite settled. Absorbed in meditation, even."

"Admiration," Caine corrected. He indicated his surroundings with a slight flick of his hand. "This is a fascinating room."

An intense man of fifty with a narrow face, dark, watchful eyes, and a widow's peak of straight black hair, Armitage appeared surprised.

"And here I've always seen you as all business," he said. "It seems you're *growing,* Marcus. In fact, my estimate of you soared to new heights after your appearance at the U.N. I really want to compliment you on that one."

Caine gave him a cool glance. "Do you, now?"

"Absolutely. You came across as very likeable, which is everything from a public relations standpoint. There are pollsters who measure that sort of thing, as you're surely aware. How else would we know which celebrities to hire for product endorsements and situation comedies?" A sardonic grin crept across his lips. "I'd give you a clap on the back if I could."

Caine tried not to look uncomfortable.

"Have you considered," he said, "that I may have learned a few tricks from watching *you* on television?"

Armitage shook his head. "I occupy a unique niche. My readers and viewers don't have to like me, just listen to me. And they will as long as my financial advice is solid . . . and I'm able to communicate it." He paused and swallowed, the muscles of his throat straining to perform the basic function. "Would you like Carl to refill your glass, or should we get right down to what you wanted to discuss?"

"I'll pass on the drink, thanks." Caine wondered if Armitage's brittle references to his disease were shading his own impressions of how quickly it was advancing, or whether his speech in fact seemed thicker than when they'd last sat face-to-face. It was entirely possible, he supposed. That had been well over a month ago, and the progression of ALS could be rapid even with experimental drug therapies. "Tell me how things went with the president of MetroBank."

Armitage looked at him. "Don't hold me to this, but I think I've convinced Halpern to accept your bid."

Caine felt a stir of excitement. "Are you serious?"

"What's important is that *he* seemed to be," Armitage said. "Of course, he's going to need his board of directors to rubber-stamp the sale, so it might be prudent to hold off celebrating until after he meets with them next week."

Caine ignored the caveat. His face was suddenly hot. "Their stock comes to, what, nine percent of UpLink?"

"Closer to ten, actually," Armitage said.

Caine made a fist and jabbed it stiffly in the air.

"Son of a bitch, this is fantastic," he said. "Fantastic."

They were quiet. Reynold's crippled right hand twitched a little as a dying nerve cell in his brain misfired, his padded wrist brace rapping the armrest of his chair. Caine looked away. Nine percent, he thought. Added to the stock purchase already in the works, it would give him a *hugely* dominant share of UpLink. He'd have what he wanted, and so would the goddamned Chink who had him by the balls.

Several minutes passed before Armitage broke the silence.

"I hesitate to do this," he said, "but there's something I'd like to ask you on another subject."

Caine shrugged absently. "Sure, go ahead."

"It concerns the problem in Singapore . . . that Blackburn fellow who was poking around over there."

"Forget it," Caine said. "It's finished."

Armitage cocked an eyebrow.

"How was it taken care of?" he asked.

Caine shook his head like a dog shaking water off its fur. The subject troubled him and he didn't like it impinging on his thoughts. What was it with Armitage's seeming compulsion to make him uneasy?

"I neither know nor have any interest in knowing," he said.

"Has anyone conclusively determined why the man was spying on you?" Armitage persisted.

"I told you, I stick to running my business. It isn't my direct concern."

"Not yet, anyway," Armitage said flatly.

Caine shot him a glance. "What the hell's that supposed to mean?"

"Don't be irritated," Armitage said. "I'm only pointing out that you'd do well to stay on top of even the more disagreeable aspects of your endeavors. If my health problems have taught me anything, it's that control can slip away in a blink."

Caine set his glass down on the table beside his chair.

"Well, thank you for the advice," he said, and rose to his feet. "I'll put it under my belt."

The thin, vaguely scornful grin had returned to Armitage's face.

"Leaving already?" he asked.

Caine nodded.

"I have a flight home to catch tonight," he said. "As

you suggest, I need to keep a close eye on things, which includes making sure the Left Coast hasn't fallen into the Pacific while I've been away.''

Armitage regarded him steadily,

"Marcus, my friend," he said. "You're finally learning.''

"This is all a bad dream," Ed Burke said. "Right?"

"I wish," Charles Kirby said.

It was the bottom of the eighth in the Stealers-Slammers contest with the Slammers leading 6–0, the Stealers at bat, one man languishing on second, and the third up, Dale Lanning of the law firm of Lanning, Thomas, and Farley, a strike away from going down to obliteration.

Huddled with his teammates in the dirt patch behind home plate, Kirby watched the Slammers' outfielders move in so close they could see the flop sweat glistening above Lanning's upper lip. While no one would have challenged his reputation for getting legal adversaries to back away from his clients, his display of batting skills had prompted a very different reaction on the diamond.

"Maybe he'll pull it out under pressure," Burke said.

"I'm not optimistic."

Kirby snatched at a cluster of dandelion pods floating past him in the diffuse early autumn light. There had been a time when you wouldn't have seen dandelions in the city any later than mid-August, he thought. But over the past decade New York summers had gotten longer and warmer, so that fall seemed more a calender event than a true seasonal shift. The previous year, in fact, the trees had remained in lush foliage until a January freeze finally snapped the deep-green leaves off the branches. They had hit the sidewalk and scattered like bits of glazed ceramic.

Deciding he'd postoned the inevitable long enough, Kirby turned to Burke and gave him a confidential little nod, motioning him aside from the rest of the team.

"Ed," he said, "I need to ask a favor."

"Let me guess," Burke said. "You want me to kill our batting ace before he causes us further humiliation."

Kirby opened his hand and released the dandelion seeds into the air.

"Actually, I'd like you to tell me who's behind the raid on UpLink," he said. "I'm talking about the person moving the chess pieces."

Burke looked at him. "What makes you think I've got that information?"

Kirby just shrugged. Burke pushed some dirt around with the toe of his sneaker. At the plate Lanning let a low pitch go by, and adjusted his grip on the bat.

"I give it to you, I'm putting in a great big whopping chit," Burke said.

Kirby nodded. And waited.

"There's a firm called Safetech in Danvers, Massachusetts, that designs and manufactures polymer glass replacement products," Burke said. "Security panels, hurricane-resistant windows, antiballistic laminates, and so on. Its clients range from real-estators to department-store chains to the State Department and DEA. Safetech is the corporate entity making the acquisition . . . through various offshoots."

"The person," Kirby said. "I want to know the *person*."

"I was just getting to that," Burke said. He looked down at his foot, still scuffing out tracks in the dirt. "Safetech's front men are a pair of MIT grads who were rich with technical know-how and nothing else. When they came up with their business concept, they took it to someone who offered them an interest-free startup loan in exchange for a silent partnership in the operation. A fifty-one percent share."

"Not an unusual deal if you need to raise finance capital," Kirby said. "Nor is it the worst."

Burke shrugged. "What counts is the two underfunded brainstormers found the lending terms acceptable."

"And the identity of the generous third party is . . . ?"

Burke looked at him again.

"Marcus 'Moneybags' Caine," he said. "Your boy Gordian's number-one detractor."

Kirby took a deep breath, released it, and gazed out at the plate in time to see Dale Lanning swing his bat a mile high of the ball.

Burke bent to pick their gloves up of the ground, and handed one to Kirby.

"That's *allll,* folks," he said, frowning. "Time for us to let the prosecutors score more points. I'm telling you, this has *got* to be a goddamn nightmare."

Kirby appeared to be looking out across the field at something Burke couldn't see.

"It is," he said, slipping on his glove. "It very definitely is."

ELEVEN

ALTHOUGH IT WAS ONLY A LITTLE PAST EIGHT IN THE morning, Zhiu Sheng had noticed a dramatic reduction of trade at the floating market as the motor canoe brought him to where the waterway narrowed and the wooden stilt houses of impoverished locals came crowding up on either bank. Most of the peddlers and buyers had appeared at daybreak, preferring to get their business out of the way before the heat and humidity became too oppressive—the former with their goods displayed on the decks of small boats or log rafts, the latter poling along in shallow dugouts, or arriving via *klotoks* like the one he had hired, forming long lines of slow-moving watercraft in the canals twisting through outer Banjarmasin like the tentacles of some languorous octopus.

Zhiu saw small boats loaded with bananas, star fruits, lichees, melons, and salaks; with green vegetables; with fish, eel, cray, and frog; with selections of precooked foods. Conspicuously, he did not see a single vender selling chicken meat, once the largest source of animal protein for Indonesia's citizens, now an imported delicacy served mainly to foreigners in Jakarta's expensive restaurants. Rising feed prices coupled with the devaluation of the *rupiah* had devastated the poultry industry when the so-called "Asian miracle" lost its glow, resulting in most of the native breeding stock being liquidated. The American chicken farmers had moved in to exploit the livestock shortage and essentially captured the market . . . their success ironically assured by the greed of Chinese and Malaysian feed producers, who had refused to lower their prices or extend credit to the Indonesians.

Zhiu understood supply and demand, but it vexed him nonetheless.

He rode in silence, looking with steady fascination at the other vessels winding along the canal. In addition to the market craft, there were postal boats, water buses, and tublike rice barges with sailcloth tops wobbling toward docks at the city center. It was a scene that brought back memories of his last visit to this district nearly three decades ago, when Sukarno's PKI was at its height of power and had sought to establish a united Communist front with the government in Beijing. He had come, then, as an official envoy of Zhou Enlai to help organize state construction projects . . . a straightforward assignment for a man whose revolutionary passion was still in full blush.

Like many things in life as one became older, the circumstances of his present trip were laced with greater complexity, Zhiu thought.

He accepted the differences and rarely looked back on his beginnings, but supposed returning to this place after so long a duration of years had made him reflective. How hard Sukarno had struggled to eradicate the stain of Western cultural influence, and how painfully he would have viewed its indelibility. Even here it could not be ignored. A few moments earlier, a group of white tourists had darted past in rented speedboats, reminding him of noisy macaques with their round eyes, sunburned red cheeks, and loud excited voices. But he'd clamped down on his annoyance, preferring, as always, to look on the bright side. At least the water spouted by their outboards dispelled the mosquitos, and added a relieving coolness to the semblance of a breeze coming off the Barito River.

"Pelan-pelan saya," Zhiu told his canoe guide in Mandarin-accented Bahasa. He pointed toward a woman selling rice cakes from a boat that had been cobbled out of warped old boards.

"Ya."

The canoe man cut his motor, paddled up to the rickety boat, and reached down beside him for a bamboo pole with a nail fastened to one end. Extending the pole across his bow, he speared a rice cake for Zhiu Sheng and held it out for him to sample.

Zhiu took a bite, swallowed, and tossed a bronze-colored coin onto the vender's deck.

"Terima kasi banyak," she said, smiling with gratitude.

Zhiu instructed the guide to restart the outboard, and settled back for his light breakfast.

A short while later, the canoe man turned a bend in the canal, swung toward a house and rice barn overhanging the near bank, and informed his passenger they had reached their destination. Zhiu did not bother saying that he'd already guessed it for himself. The further they had progressed beyond the market, the more he'd sensed eyes watching from behind shuttered windows, and noticed hard young men tracing his progress with quick, covert glances from the walkways connecting the ramshackle structures.

Khao Luan was like a feudal warlord to the people of this area, giving them just enough to keep them loyal, but not so much that they might become independent of him.

Now the canoe man again silenced his engine, and rowed up to a ladder running into the muddy water from the dwelling's front door. Three teenagers sat on separate rungs—two boys in faded denim shorts and T-shirts, and a girl wearing similar shorts and a halter of some sheer, revealing material that had been tied below her breasts to expose her midriff. There was a kind of affected sexuality about her that at once saddened and disgusted Zhiu Sheng. The boys also seemed to be playacting at roles they did not quite grasp, sitting with their shoulders hunched and smoking unfiltered cigarettes as they listened to an enormous radio blasting out American rock music.

They slouched under the hot sun, staring into the water as if they might find something other than aimless drifts of reeds and sediment beneath its torpid surface.

The Asian miracle, Zhiu Sheng thought dryly.

He saw them raise their eyes from the crawling water as his guide brought the canoe up beside the ladder. All of them had bad complexions. All looked dirty and undernourished. Their expressions were bored and impassive and uniformly sullen.

He waited until the canoe had been lashed into a berth composed of four vertical bamboo poles, then paid the guide, lifted his carryall onto his shoulder, and rose to step ashore.

The teenagers watched him a moment longer. Then the taller of the boys stood up to block his approach, crossing his arms over his puffed-out chest, doing what he thought was expected of him under some artificial standard of toughness.

It would probably kill him in a streetfight before he was twenty.

Zhiu Sheng finished his rice cake, then rubbed his fingertips together to wipe off its pasty residue.

"*Saya mahu laki bilik,*" he said from the prow of the boat. "I'm here to see the men inside."

The tall boy stared down at him, letting his cigarette dangle from his lips the way they did in American gangster movies. The smoke curling from its tip carried the pungently sweet odor of cloves.

"What is your name?" he asked.

Zhiu was in no mood. "Go on. Let the men know their friend from up north has arrived."

"I asked you—"

"*Berhenti!*" Zhiu checked him with a motion of his hand. "Stop wasting my time and do it."

The boy stared at him for a second, then turned and went up the ladder to the door, taking longer than he should have, wanting to save whatever face he could with his companions.

Let him have that, at least, Zhiu thought. *He may never have anything else.*

The boy knocked on the door—two slow raps, a pause, followed by three rapid ones—and waited a moment before pushing it open. Then he leaned his head through the entry and said something and waited some more. After a brief interval Zhiu heard a male voice answer from inside the house. Though the words were unclear to him, their tone was unmistakeably harsh and reprimanding.

The boy turned from the door and shooed away his friends, who climbed down to the landing and went hurrying off somewhere along the bank.

"*Ma'af saya,*" he said nervously, offering Zhiu Sheng a contrite bow. "I did not mean to offend—"

"Never mind."

His patience exhausted, Zhiu brushed past him and ascended the shaky ladder, half expecting it to buckle under his feet.

He was met at the entrance by a pair of lank, brown-skinned islanders with undulant kris tattoos on their hands. Was it not said that such a dagger could claim a victim merely by being driven into one's shadow? Perhaps so, Zhiu thought. But ancient myths aside, he believed the semi-automatic rifles slung over the men's shoulders would prove much more lethal.

"*Selamat datang,*" one of them said. He bowed his head deferentially. "Welcome."

Zhiu nodded and went inside.

The interior of the dwelling was a large rectangle, its floor and walls made up of bare plywood boards, the high peaked roof supported by tiers of slanting beams. Midway down the length of the right-hand wall was a closed door with a third islander standing guard in front of it. Towering and rigid, he had coarse features, long black hair, and was bare-chested under an open denim jacket with cut-off sleeves. The blockish muscles on his torso and upper arms were heavily covered with tattoos. In addition to his rifle, he carried a knife—a kris, no doubt—in an elaborately tooled leather sheath on his belt.

Zhiu ran his eyes over to the middle of the room, where the men he had come to meet—General Kersik Imman, Nga Canbera, and the drug trafficker, Khao Luan—were waiting at a long plank table.

Glancing up from a conversation with the others, Kersik was the first to acknowledge his presence.

"Zhiu Sheng, you look well," he said, dipping his head. "How was your trip?"

"Hot, tedious, and hopefully worthwhile," Zhiu said.

A smile touched Kersik's thin, lined face. While the eyes below his shaggy brows were as strong and sharp as ever, he had aged a great deal over the past several months and, in civilian clothes now, possessed an almost grandfatherly mien that hid his true severity of nature.

By contrast, Zhiu thought, Canbera looked scarcely older than the children outside, and like them seemed to be working at a role that was beyond him. Political subversive, champion of the poor. His soft features and vain demeanor put the lie to it, though. As did his social position. The eldest son of a diamond baron, Nga had been born into immeasurable wealth, and handed control of Banjarmasin's largest bank only to serve as a place marker on his family's sprawling financial game board. He understood nothing of human struggle, and less of material hardship. Nor did the spoiled upper-class activists with whom he secretly consorted . . . and whose national reform movement he was helping to fund.

He was a narcissistic dabbler, interested in gratifying his own conceits, and would leap for the safety net of privilege if the consequences of his actions overtook him.

"*Sawasdee.* My place isn't nearly as well appointed as Kersik's residence, but, as a humble exile and outsider, it's the best I can do."

This from Khao Luan himself. Seated at the head of the table, he raised his hands in the traditional Thai greeting, palms together as if in prayer, his fingertips just below his nose to indicate familiarity. On their previous meetings, Zhiu noted, he had steepled his hands lower and closer to his chest—the stranger's *wai*.

The significance of the gesture was not lost on Zhiu, and it admittedly distressed him . . . for was a man not measured in large part by his associations? Still, he returned it without hesitation. The time for misgivings was long past. And corrupt as his occupation might be, the Thai was without pretense and worthy of respect.

"Please," Luan said, indicating an empty chair on his right. "Make yourself comfortable."

Zhiu went over to the table and regarded him carefully. Round and balding, Luan had a smooth wide forehead, bow-shaped lips, and a light mustache and chin beard. His cheekbones were perfectly flat and covered with soft, shiny pads of flesh. He sat with his chair pushed back from the table, his short-sleeved batik shirt hanging out over his waist sash, straining at the seams around his big stomach, and unbuttoned at the collar to reveal a thick ring of Hmong silver. There were dark blotches of perspiration on his chest and under his arms.

"The American," Zhiu said, lowering himself into his chair. "Where is he?"

Luan nodded toward the door in the right wall.

"My friend Xiang and his sea wolves are keeping a close eye on him."

"Has he told you anything?"

Luan was silent a moment before replying.

"He's been, ah, unable to communicate this morning, but I expect he'll be coming around shortly," he said. "Maybe then we'll all learn what we want to know."

Zhiu darted a surprised glance across the table at General Kersik. "He was captured, what, four days ago?"

Kersik brought his head up and down, a slow nod.

"He's a tough one," he said.

"No need to be concerned, we'll get what we want out of him soon enough," Luan said. He smiled thinly. "The White Lady has her ways."

Zhiu raised his eyebrows. "Heroin?"

"They've scarcely been apart since we introduced him to her yesterday," Luan said. "She'll charm him into talking."

"It is barbaric."

"It is necessary," Kersik said. "And preferable to some alternatives."

"As our prisoner should conclude for himself before too long," Luan said.

They were quiet. Zhiu found himself staring at the enormous pirate. He seemed somehow to exist in his own space, immovable and dangerous, his calm unfeeling eyes those of a Mesozoic creature poised to strike.

"What I think ought to worry us is the woman," Nga said.

Zhiu shifted his attention to him. "Chu, is that her name?"

"Kirsten Chu. She's dropped out of sight. And there's no telling what she's discovered about our involvement with Monolith, or what sort of proof she's taken with her. A tremendous amount of information could have been routed through her division of the company."

"I assume we have people looking for her in Singapore?"

"And elsewhere," Luan said.

"Still," Nga said. "It could hurt us badly if the Americans learn of—"

"I've been trying to reassure Nga that he's jumping ahead of things," Kersik interrupted. "Let's stay with what we know. This could have been a case of industrial espionage, having nothing to do with us."

"She's repeatedly accessed Monolith's most sensitive financial databases from her office computer terminal. Made dozens of telephone calls to the UpLink groundstation in Johor . . . and probably many more that can't be traced because they went to a secure line,'' Nga said. ''Are you suggesting that we simply forget about her?''

''You really must try to become a more receptive listener,'' Kersik said. ''Without the American to guide her, it's likely she won't know where to turn, or what to do with any documentation she might have. Probably she'll surface on her own. If not, we'll eventually find her.'' He motioned toward Zhiu Sheng with a slow, gliding wave of his hand. ''Let us put speculation aside, and get to the point of why our comrade has traveled here.''

Zhiu nodded slightly. Despite his equable manner, Kersik was looking hard at him.

''I've brought positive news,'' he said. ''Those I represent are prepared to supply whatever munitions you require. The high-speed boats will be more difficult to obtain, but should also be forthcoming.''

''And the landing craft?''

''You'll have to settle for fewer than requested.''

''How many?''

''Three, perhaps four.''

Kersik pinched the bridge of his nose. ''The assault rifles, they've never been fired?''

Zhiu knew he was thinking about their integrated silencers, which quickly became ineffective with use.

''They are factory-new Type 85's.''

Kersik continued to look thoughtful. ''We must be guaranteed prompt delivery. As you know, our window of opportunity is quite small.''

''Any date we agree upon will be firm,'' Zhiu said. ''You have my word.''

Kersik drew a long breath.

''I'm concerned about how the reduced number of watercraft will effect our invasion capabilities,'' he said. "It means revising the entire operational plan.''

"Perhaps not as drastically as you might think. The attack boats are heavily armed. And the amphibious craft can be refitted to hold larger complements. Insofar as available manpower, there would likely be no difference at all. If you want me to go over the specific modifications—''

"Later,'' Kersik said. He hadn't taken his eyes off Zhiu's face. "Your government. What is its position toward our venture?''

"Officially, nothing is known of it.''

"And speaking practically?''

"I can tell you there will be no opposition at any level,'' Zhiu said, selecting his words with utmost care.

Kersik nodded with satisfaction.

"Yes,'' he said. "That much *is* good news.''

Zhiu let his eyes roam around the table.

"I hope, then,'' he said, "that none of you will object to the terms of payment.''

Luan pursed his lips, reacting with predictable wariness.

"Which are?'' he said.

"I'm obliged to require the full sum in advance.''

"What?'' Nga said, his eyes flashing incredulously. "You can't be serious.''

Zhiu remained very still.

"We are asking for a great deal on short notice,'' he said. "The suppliers have expenditures of their own. It is reasonable for them to expect hard currency in return for the risks they are taking.''

"And what of *our* risks?'' Nga said in a tight voice. "I've done much for you and the Zhongnanhai you represent. My bank's international position could be irreparably damaged if things go wrong."

"That is very much appreciated. But, regrettably, this isn't a situation in which my superiors can barter off a portion of the cost, or make any other concessions."

Nga bridled. "Forgive me, Zhiu, but it sounds to me as if you're offering up excuses for PLA profiteers. How can you expect us to—?"

"Enough," Kersik interjected. "I understand your frustration, Nga. But we are compelled by certain exigencies, and must acknowledge that our needs are rather special." He glanced at Luan. "What do you say?"

The Thai hesitated a moment, then shrugged his chunky shoulders.

"Attached as I am to my money, I nevertheless consider my portion of the expenses already spent, and suppose it makes little difference when I physically part company with it," he said. "Let's not bicker over what can't be changed, and instead move on to important matters of planning. We've been so focused on Sandakan and what comes after, that none of us are talking about the data-storage vaults in the United States. They are essential to our success and at least as highly guarded as—"

The door to the rice barn opened, surprising them. They fixed their attention upon Xiang as one of his pirates leaned through from the other side, addressed him in a low whisper, then withdrew into the barn, leaving the door ajar.

Xiang turned back around, looking straight at the Thai.

"The American's opened his eyes," he said.

The room went silent.

Luan smiled slightly and cast an eager glance around the table.

"Excuse me, brothers," he said, heaving his bulk off the chair. "I have to go to work."

He followed Xiang into the barn, pushing the door heavily shut behind him.

TWELVE

BLACKBURN CAME TO WITH A START, DISORIENTED, bathed in sweat, clusters of black motes floating across his vision. His eyes were battered and swollen, his body throbbing with pain in a dozen places. Where was he? Why couldn't he move his arms?

He realized he was in a chair . . . slumped forward in a hard, straight-backed chair . . . and jerked to an upright position. Too quickly. Dizziness washed over him and his stomach contracted. He fought to push back the nausea, the taste of vomit rising in his throat. For several seconds it was touch-and-go, but then the sickness began to recede.

He squeezed his pulsing eyes shut and sucked in breath after labored breath.

Okay. All right. Let's try it again. But slower.

He rolled his head to relax the aching tendons of his neck, lifted it an inch or two—slow, slow—and opened his eyes again.

Better.

Blinking, he looked himself over.

His shirt was bloody and torn. Had he been shot? No, no, he didn't think so. There had been a bad tumble in the hotel stairway. Then that iron claw, or whatever it was, sinking into his arm. He'd been trying to get it out, and then somebody or something had hit him. And afterward . . . ?

What had happened afterward?

Max gulped down another mouthful of air. *Come on, come on, what happened?* He got little besides brief, elusive flashes, and wondered if he'd sustained a concussion from the blow to his head, or maybe the fall down the stairs. There had been long periods of oblivion alternating with moments when he half awakened and took in confused snatches of reality.

At one point he'd been in a truck . . . the delivery truck outside the hotel. That was where he'd first been handcuffed, in the vehicle's rear compartment. There had been a body back there next to him. A dead man, probably the original driver. He had been stripped of his clothing, and a mixture of blood and some other, viscous fluid was oozing from his ear. Max remembered lying there beside the naked corpse on sheets wet with gore . . . and that was all. He didn't know how long he'd been kept in the truck or where he'd been taken afterward. Just had a vague sense of time slipping away. Then being lifted, carried a short distance, and dropped flat on his back.

More time passed. He'd been in a close space, registered monotonous rolling, pitching movements. It had been like that for a while. Then a strong, freshening wind gusted over him. There had been a salt breeze. An abrupt realization that he was on a boat, they were transporting him somewhere on a *boat* . . .

He'd slipped back into unconsciousness, awakened once somewhere else. Another truck? Another boat? It was no good, that part was almost entirely a blank. He could recall nothing about it except for having been moved yet again to what he supposed was his present location, a barn of some sort. It was wide and dim and stewingly hot with a thatch roof and steps rising to a loft. Both his wrists had been cuffed to the arms of the chair. The restraints were standard police-issue metal bracelets.

His watchdogs were anything *but* cops, though. He'd recognized a few from the bunch that had pursued him at the hotel, including the big one, the one he'd first seen waiting in the truck, and who had come at him through the service door. . . .

Blackburn felt his head clearing. With each interval of consciousness more of what had happened came back to him, his scattered bits and pieces of memory weaving into a coherent thread and drawing him toward a full recognition of his predicament.

Here in the barn he'd been asked questions, mostly by the one who seemed to be in charge—Luan, that was his name. Asked questions and beaten hard when he refused to answer. But that hadn't been the worst of it. Not by far. He had been through brutal ordeals before, and believed he could have withstood their interrogation for quite some time.

Oh, shit. These goddamned bastards came to the same conclusion, didn't they?

The hairs at the back of his neck prickling, he remembered the needle. How could he have forgotten it even for a *second*?

Maybe, though, that was why his mind had switched itself off for a while. To provide a cessation from what was otherwise unavoidable. To spare him from thinking about the needle.

The first time had been the roughest. They'd held him down, torn off his shirt sleeve, and jabbed the needle into the bend of his arm. Because he'd been struggling, the one with the syringe had botched several attempts at piercing a blood vessel. But eventually he'd succeeded, pressing the needle flat against his skin, inserting it down the length of the vein, drawing a little blood to make sure he'd gotten a good hit. And then depressing the plunger.

Blackburn had made a small sound, a kind of moan, and slid back in the chair, his head nodding, his eyes rolling back under their lids. Wildcat tingles had rushed up his arm in what seemed to be a direct line to his brain, then widened out into ripples of numbing warmth that spread through his flesh and bones and viscera until he went slack. And the horror, the really overpowering horror of it, was that a part of him had *welcomed* the nullity it brought. He'd trained his mind and body to endure the severest punishments, but to have his pain drawn out of him in a great merciful *whoosh* like heaven taking a deep breath. . . .

Baifen, Luan called it.

Chinese slang for heroin.

She was a seductive bitch, and that was what they were counting on.

His memories rushing back on him now, Max glanced at the inside of his left arm and saw the black and blue where he'd been injected . . . how many times? Five, maybe six. There were blisters under his elbow where the spike had slipped and some of the drug was inadvertently pumped between his skin and muscle. The first couple of times they'd shot him up, a ferocious rash had spread from his elbows to his shoulders and neck, but his system had adjusted, and the redness and terrible itch were slowly fading.

Blackburn was still taking stock when he heard movement to his right. He looked up and saw one of his guards—he'd counted four of them in the dimness—step over to a door on the opposite wall, open it, then lean out to speak with somebody on the other side . . . the big guy from the delivery truck, who was also apparently his superior. When he came striding into the barn a moment later, Luan was right behind him.

Here we go again, Max thought, steeling himself.

He watched in silence as Luan moved to a table about six feet away, where his captors kept the heroin and works, as well as a water pitcher and small gas burner for cooking the drug. He saw orange flame spurt from the burner, saw Luan drop a chunk of the heroin into a spoon, then saw him mix it with some water and then hold the spoon over the heat.

After perhaps a minute of boiling he dropped a cotton swab into the spoon, let it swell up with liquid, pushed the needle into it, and raised the plunger to filter the narcotic solution up through the cotton.

"My friend, you have kept your secrets against much persuasion, but sooner or later you must tell me what I need to know," Luan said, approaching with the hypo. He spoke English well enough, though his tongue kept bumping against the wrong syllables.

Max sat there without response.

"You will not compromise your honor by breaking your silence," Luan said. Coming closer. "Your employers would be pleased with you. A man cannot be expected to tolerate more than you already have on their behalf."

Max said nothing.

Luan shook his head. It had become something of a perverse, repetitive drill—the unanswered questions, the beating, and, once that failed, the junk. They were simply exploring their options, Max thought. Reasoning that sooner or later he'd either succumb to the pain or the desire for release. *Insidious cocksuckers*. Given intravenously, heroin rushed into the brain's pleasure centers within seconds. Addiction would take a while, but the craving for it . . .

That was the worst part, wasn't it? The part his mind had cringed away from acknowledging, and the reason it had shut itself down.

The craving had already wormed its fine but perceptible roots into him.

Luan came another step forward.

"I already know who you are, and who you work for, leaving only one thing unknown," he said. "What were you after, Max Blackburn?"

Silence.

"One last thing," Luan said. "Tell me."

It occurred to Max that he would have been interested in hearing Luan answer that very same question . . . and that his ignorance on that score was a good indication Kirsten had managed to stay outside his tracking range. You dealt with the uglies of the world long enough, you came to understand they could rationalize the vilest actions imaginable . . . his present circumstances unfortunately being a clear case in point. Had they gotten her in their talons, they would have used any means available to squeeze her for what they wanted.

No, they didn't have her. Or at least it helped a little to think so.

He kept staring at Luan in silence.

The Thai's face had grown sorrowful. "It shouldn't matter to me, but I want to give you fair warning. While you may not remember how to use your tongue at the moment, it is certain that you will before I leave here. You understand?''

Max swallowed dryly. No, maybe he didn't understand, not altogether. But he had an awful feeling that he soon would. He'd kept an eye on the big guard, watched him sidle over to the table, reach for a knife sheathed against his leg, then stand there near the burner with the weapon in his hand. It was a kris, its blade about six inches long and shaped like a sine wave. . . .

Something new and different, he thought

Luan was standing right in front of him now, regarding him with careful appraisal, his false sympathy only serving to counterpoint the menace in his gaze.

Finally he pursed his lips and discharged a sighing breath.

''No,'' he said resignedly. ''I don't think you're going to take my advice after all.''

He turned partially toward the big watchdog.

Nodded.

Max glanced over at the table and felt his stomach tighten.

The watchdog had raised his knife to the flame, was holding it over the flame, its blade rapidly heating up, becoming radiant in the dimness of the barn.

''Xiang,'' the Thai said.

The big man turned and advanced on Max, the knife flashing red-hot, almost seeming to pulse in his grip. Out of the corners of his eyes, Max saw two other guards suddenly appear from the shadows, one on either side of him. Each clasped a shoulder and pressed it hard to the chair, pinning him against the backrest. He strained against them, but their hands were as unyielding as the steel cuffs on his wrists.

He tensed throughout his body, his heart striking mallet blows in his chest.

In no hurry, Xiang hung over him a moment like a living, breathing mountain. Then he lowered the kris to his arm and sliced into his skin about an inch above the wrist, making a shallow, razor-thin incision that almost instantly withered around its edges from the heat of the blade. Max was seized with pain as Xiang carved into him, gliding the knife upward beneath his skin, stripping it away little by little, pushing the blade higher . . . higher . . . higher. . . .

Squeezing the chair's armrests, Max fought not to scream, clenched his teeth so he wouldn't scream, a raspy, wounded-animal sound tearing out of him instead. Veins bulged in his temples. His head whipped back and forth. He smelled the sickly-sweet odor of his own cauterized flesh and nerve tissue as it peeled away from the rising blade. He thrashed convulsively, heard the legs of the chair pounding the floor, banging on the floor, the loud thump of wood against wood matching the jerky violence of his spasms. He could see nothing beyond the insane, brilliant pain, think of nothing but the scream locked away in his throat, trying to tear free of his throat like a trapped thing with claws and teeth flinging itself against the sides of its cage.

Max only realized the cutting had stopped some thirty seconds after the Thai ordered it done. He thought it must have taken longer than that for Xiang to actually slide the knife out of his arm, flicking a long . . . *six inches* long, at least . . . shaving of skin to the floor.

Finally, the guards who had been holding him down backed off and he sagged into the chair, gulping down huge lungfuls of air, the muscles of his ravaged arm twitching and jumping.

He felt his consciousness draining and willed himself back to clarity.

Luan's face hovered in front of him.

"Your employer, Roger Gordian," he said. "Tell me what he wants."

Max sat there, motionless. Rivulets of sweat poured down his brow and stung his eyes. His arm felt coated with scalding oil.

Luan showed him the syringe.

"Tell me," he said. "I can make things better for you."

Blackburn met his gaze. Inhaled. Exhaled. And then gave him a slow nod.

Luan grinned and leaned in expectantly.

"My boss is . . . P. T. Barnum . . . and I'm looking for freaks for his tent show," Blackburn said in a weak voice. "Got them all here," he said. "A fat man"—he nodded toward the Thai—"a giant"—he nodded toward Xiang—"and more geeks . . . than you can count," he said, and rotated his head to indicate the guards standing to either side of him.

Luan's grin turned downward and mutated into something horrible and forbidding. He straightened, allowed the full weight of his gaze to press on Blackburn for a moment, then slowly shook his head.

"Stupid," he said, and then gave Xiang a command in Bahasa, pointing at Max.

Pointing at his face.

Blackburn saw the giant take a step toward him with the kris, the two watchdogs who'd restrained him once more appearing at the fringes of his vision.

He thought about how to prevent them from carving him up alive, decided there was probably nothing he could do, and figured he would try anyway.

Summoning what strength he had left, Max threw his weight forward as hard as he could, and managed to rock to his feet while still cuffed to the chair—his wrists chained to the armrests, the back of the chair a rigid plank against his spine, forcing him to bend at the waist so he was almost doubled over.

The two guards' surprise at his sudden move made them hesitate for only an instant, but that was all the time Blackburn needed to launch himself at the Thai, slamming him backwards into the table where he kept the works. As the heroin packets and still-flaming burner crashed to the floor in a welter, the fire hurling a wavery mesh of shadows about the room, he saw the watchdog on his left come charging straight at him, waited for him to get close enough, and wheeled in a semicircle, catching him across his middle with the upturned chair legs. The watchdog yelped in pain and dropped to his knees.

Max took a breath and steadied himself. Heard footsteps now, from his opposite side. The shadow pushing toward him might have been startling in its immensity had he not been braced for Xiang's attack. Still, his limitations of movement and balance made it impossible to avoid.

Gonna get hurt no matter what I do, he thought. *Might as well dish some hurt of my own.*

Whirling toward the giant, he lunged forward in a bullish rush, Xiang's torso looming up like a marble pillar as he drove in and butted him with his head.

Xiang snorted in anger and surprise, the kris dropping from his fingers. Max kept his head lowered and again slammed himself into his columnar chest. The gigantic islander staggered back but did not fall. His knife forgotten in his rage, he lurched forward like a wounded bear, his colossal arms spread wide, biceps expanding and rippling under his flesh. Snarling, he clamped his hands over Blackburn's shoulders and hefted upward.

Max felt a wrenching pain as his feet left the floor. Though he weighed a solid hundred-eighty pounds, Xiang lifted him seemingly without effort.

Blackburn saw an atavistic savagery in his features that instantly made him cold inside. The giant wasn't thinking about the information they were trying to get out of him. Wasn't thinking about what his boss wanted him to do. Wasn't thinking, period. His fury was a cyclone that had pulled him into its maw as it gained destructive energy and momentum. He was just along for the ride.

In a sense, they both were.

Xiang shook Max furiously, holding him suspended above the floor so they were almost eye-to-eye. He rattled out a groan, the strength he'd mustered through sheer willpower draining away, his body too hammered from abuse to comply with the demands he was making of it. Suddenly he knew what was coming, knew with such a sure sense of inevitability that he could almost hear a door shutting in his head. There would be no last-minute escape of the sort that might occur in a novel or film, no orchestral swells as the larger-than-life hero fought his way to safety. It stank, yes, but *real* life was like that sometimes, you never knew when the smell would come wafting up out of the kitty litter, and the best he figured he could do was express his feelings about it in a manner that would translate across any language barrier.

Filling his mouth with moisture, he spat in Xiang's face.

Xiang growled, actually *growled,* his cheek glistening with bloody saliva. He took a broad step forward, another, pushing Max up against the wall. Then, with a tremendous heave that bulged the muscles of his upper back and shoulders into a corded mass, he slammed Max backward with stunning force, pulled him in toward his chest again, slammed, pulled, slammed. Max tugged unavailingly at his cuffs, his upper body writhing, a mire of blood flooding his mouth, the chair splintering between his back and the wall, cracking into jagged pieces of wood that spilled to the floor underneath him as Xiang slammed and pulled and slammed. . . .

Lost in a roseate haze, Blackburn felt a snap somewhere in his neck, followed by a bright sparkle of pain. The haze darkened and solidified. From what seemed a great distance, he heard the Thai shout something in an agitated voice and a language he didn't understand. He had a sensation of disconnected free fall, as if he were a small stone plummeting into a bottomless chasm.

Then he ceased to feel anything at all.

"Stop!" The Thai clambered across the barn toward Xiang and grabbed his arm. "That's enough *lunacy!*"

The giant glanced over at him. An instant later, his face changed—the furious, wildly unreasoning look clearing from it. He turned toward the limp form he was pressing to the wall, stared at it a moment as if seeing it for the first time, and let it drop.

Luan knelt over Blackburn and hurried to check his

pulse. He didn't like the way his head was leaning, the rubbery tilt of his neck.

When his eyes jumped up to Xiang, they were glacial. "He's dead," he said.

THIRTEEN

EVERY WEEKDAY MORNING AT 5:30 ROGER GORDIAN
left his home outside San Jose, got into his raven-black
1984 Mercedes SE, then headed east along El Camino
Real to the San Carlos Street exit and through the down-
town area to UpLink's corporate headquarters on Bonita
Avenue. Like Gordian, the Benz was in generally fine
condition despite showing a few signs of age: a cranky
starter here, a clogged line and worn part there, nothing
that, in his estimate, couldn't be remedied with regular
maintenance and an occasional highway workout.

Still, those around him fretted. Concerned about its re-
liability, Ashley had been pressing him to drive one of
their newer vehicles to the office, but the Land Rover
seemed too damn big and the '01 BMW too damn small,
lacking substance and character, and resembling an electric shaver or a soap bar. Concerned about his personal
safety, Pete Nimec had tried convincing him to hire a
driver or bodyguard, but Gordian liked having the solitary
time for thought as overflowing rural greenery became
neatly fenced suburban yards and then a crowded me-
tropolis, the transition seeming to mirror the thrust of human advancement itself.

And he liked driving along with his hands on the wheel

as the big V-8 engine ran with a low satisfying sound that reminded him of a perfect, sustained note coming from deep in the belly of an operatic tenor.

And he liked how there were just enough motorists on the freeway to give him a sense of forward progress, of linkage to other people pursuing their daily objectives, each of them slightly ahead of the pack, moving toward their destinations in lanes that would jam tight only a few hours later.

On his way to work now, he was undeniably pleased that he'd resisted Pete and Ashley's urgings. There were a number of things on his mind, things he needed to sort through without interruption, and the driver's seat of his car was the ideal place to do precisely that.

It always comes down to will, timing, and maneuverability, he reflected. *You have to avoid getting stuck on any one battle, and make sure you're ready to exploit any possible chance to take the opposition by surprise.*

That was modern combat doctrine in a nutshell, although in this instance Gordian was thinking neither about armed conflict, nor even the martial art of highway driving, but business, which he had long ago learned was its own species of warfare—coldly opportunistic, full of hidden traps, and capable of heaping loss and carnage upon the unprepared, the indecisive, and the inflexible.

The night before, Gordian had gotten his call to war from Chuck Kirby, who had phoned to confirm what he'd already known in his gut, and what legal disclosure requirements would reveal to the public within days: The tender offer for the Spartus holdings had been made by Marcus Caine through a rather thinly disguised corporate surrogate . . . specifically, a Midwestern concern called Safetech.

Okay, next item, he thought. Having established *what* Caine wanted, the issue of *why* he wanted it still remained to be tackled. A takeover seemed the obvious objective, but things were not necessarily that clear. The Williams Act and a whole slew of California securities and anti-takeover statutes compelled Safetech to state the reasons for its stock acquisition in a Schedule 13D filing to the Securities and Exchange Commission, and in other documents it was required to exhibit to shareholders. Even playing strictly by the rules, however, Caine had plenty of wiggle room in which to obscure his intent.

His offer-by-proxy left no doubt that he at the very least wished to remain discreet—and one thing Gordian knew about Caine was that he never stayed in the background unless there were some very compelling reasons to do so. While Marcus was often unsubtle, he was not unsophisticated. If he was preparing to mount a raid, he would bide his time until he was in the best tactical position to execute it. Hands down, he would represent himself in the schedule as seeking *not* to wrest control of UpLink from Gordian and its board of directors, but rather to obtain a substantial minority interest that would give him a say in managing its assets, and allow him to protect his investment. Whether that position would bear up under scrutiny was immaterial, because all the courts were likely to do in the event of false or incomplete disclosures was order that they be revised.

Meanwhile, Caine would be getting exactly what he needed: time to woo other large shareholders to his side, time to sidestep the Williams Act's disclosure provisions by purchasing smaller blocks of UpLink stock on the open market, time to develop and refine any number of additional takeover strategies . . . assuming, of course, that a complete acquisition was his goal.

How, then, to anticipate it? Kirby and his trustbusters were already formulating a civil action on the grounds that there were several sectors of the communications and technology industries where Marcus Caine's various interests were in direct competition with UpLink. The lawsuit was a showstopper in that it would keep the lawyers and judges wading through a sea of complicated litigation, but unless the feds climbed aboard with a criminal antitrust suit of their own to bolster UpLink's challenge— something they were typically slow to do—it would result in a long battle of attrition with unpredictable results, and hunkering in had never been Gordian's style. As Sun Tzu once said, the possibility of victory lay in the attack. With all the resources at his disposal, there surely had to be a—

Gordian eased into the left lane to pass a lumbering trailer truck in front of him, a look of deep concentration on his features. Quite unexpectedly, his mind had turned back to the piece he'd read by Reynold Armitage in the *Wall Street Journal* the other day. What was it *he'd* had to say about Gordian's resources? The leadoff essentially had been a rant about his corporate diversification having led to wrongheaded management decisions, after which Armitage had drawn his grotesque Siamese twins metaphor, something about mismatched limbs and unsustainable growth. The article had prickled—but could it be Armitage had a *point*?

Gordian hesitantly had to admit that he might, and supposed part of his irritation over what he'd read stemmed from his having realized it from the beginning, if only on a semiconscious level. He could not afford to let his disdain for Armitage—or suspicions about his motives—

prevent him from intelligently evaluating his assertions. Emotionalism in a fight was blinding and corrosive. Regardless of its ultimate merit, his enemy had unwittingly given him a tip worth exploring.

And if it turns out he's right, what path does that take me down? Gordian thought, knowing full well that wasn't the question he needed to ask himself. The path was there before him, its direction clearly marked, and what he really had to learn was whether he'd have the strength and will to walk it . . . and accept the painful sacrifices to which it would inevitably lead.

Inhaling deeply, he glanced out the driver's window to see the sun perched fat and lazy above the mountains, as if it had found a comfortable nest where it might linger for all eternity, describing a constant, knowable horizon against which he could steer a warmly lighted path through the world.

Pity indeed life was never that simple.

It would have been a harried and difficult twenty-four hours for Pete Nimec under the best of circumstances. With only a couple of days to go until Roger Gordian and his closest advisors flew to D.C. for their press conference, a million and one security arrangements—everything from personnel selection to the job's involved Beltway logistics—needed to be finalized. In addition, there had been a series of unexplained lapses in the alarm net at the Nevada data-storage facility. And two of his Sword administrators at the Botswana satellite station had let a squabble over authority escalate into a bar fight that left one with cracked ribs, the other in a local jail, and Nimec with the problem of whether both deserved to be canned.

These were all matters requiring prompt attention, but it was Max Blackburn's unaccountable disappearance that had been occupying most of his thoughts . . . and the phone conversation he'd just had with Max's secretary had done a lot to exacerbate his worried mood.

On his previous call, which he'd placed from the UpLink building at six o'clock Tuesday night—eleven A.M. Wednesday, in Malaysia—Joyce had told him Max still hadn't returned to the ground station or contacted her with any explanation for his absence, making it almost four days since anyone had seen or heard from him. The protectiveness Nimec had detected in Joyce's voice when they'd had their initial talk had been replaced with a disconcerted, anxious tone.

"Joyce, I need you to be straight with me," he'd said. "Has he ever pulled a vanishing act before? Done anything like this at all?"

"No, sir," she answered without hesitation. "That's why I'm so confused. I honestly thought he'd be in touch at some point yesterday."

Nimec paused, thinking.

"The woman he's been dating in Singapore," he said after a moment. "Do you know how to contact her?"

"Well, yes, I'm pretty sure I have Kirsten's home and office numbers on file," Joyce said. "Max left both with me in case I—"

"I need you to do some checking," Nimec broke in. "Call this . . . Kirsten, is that what you said her name is?"

"Yes, Kirsten Chu—"

"Buzz her at work first, see if she can tell you what's happening. If you don't reach her, try her where she lives. And keep trying till you catch her. Let me know soon as you speak to her, okay? Doesn't matter how late it is here in the States, I'm a night owl anyway. You can take my home number.''

''Yes, certainly . . .''

In the six hours following that conversation, Nimec had attended to countless items of business, gone home, pushed himself through a strenuous *shukokai* karate workout in his dojo, showered, had a bite to eat, and then settled down in his den to read his E-mail—acutely conscious the entire while that hadn't heard from Joyce. She'd finally called back ten minutes ago, midnight PST, four in the afternoon Johor time.

''Any luck?'' he'd said, recognizing her voice the second he picked up.

''I'm sorry, no,'' Joyce replied. ''After we spoke I left several messages for her at Monolith . . . that's where she's employed, you know—''

Yeah, I know, all too goddamned well, he'd thought.

''—but she didn't return them. It was the same story when I tried her residence.''

Nimec waited. He could tell there was more, and didn't think it would be good.

''Sir, I noticed a long pause between Kirsten's outgoing announcement and the tone on her home machine,'' she'd said at last. ''It was the sort you'd get when there are already quite a few messages waiting. . . .''

''As if she hadn't been there to retrieve them for some time,'' he said, completing the sentence for her.

Another pause. He imagined Joyce nodding at her end of the line.

''Just before calling you, I took the liberty of phoning Kirsten's departmental receptionist,'' she went on. ''I said that I was a personal friend, and had been trying to get

163

in touch with her, and was wondering if it was possible that she wasn't checking her voice mail.''

''Yes? Go on.''

She breathed. ''Kirsten wasn't there. She's been gone since Friday and nothing's been heard from her. Everyone at her office is becoming very concerned. They say this is completely unlike her.''

Unlike her, unlike Max, unlike both of them. So where are they?

His head starting to ache, he'd thanked Joyce for her trouble, assuring her he'd be in touch, listening to *her* nervous assurances that she'd do the same the instant she had any news, and signing off.

Now, ten minutes later, Nimec's headache had exponentially worsened, becoming the type nothing but a good night's sleep would relieve. Except he was too wired to sleep, and therefore would have to suffer. Max was one of his most trusted and responsible men, and it was no use telling himself he was merely extending a weekend barn dance with his girlfriend. All signs were that he'd bitten off more than he could chew investigating Monolith . . . and God only knew what had gone wrong.

Nimec frowned as he stared at the wall opposite his desk, regretting his willingness to let Max go ahead with this thing in the first place. Yes, it had gone bad, he was becoming more convinced of it by the second. Exactly what to do about it would take a little thinking, but do something he would. . . .

And every one of his instincts told him it would have to be soon.

''I'm going to ask you a favor on a rather sticky affair,'' Nga was saying. ''Understand I would not trouble you if there were any other way.''

"It is ever my pleasure to be of help to you," Kinzo lied, though his true pleasure would have been to stay as far from Nga Canbera as possible. But face and money compelled one to do much that was disagreeable.

They were regarding each other across Nga's desk in his office at the Bank of Kalimantan, a sleek, bright space on the building's thirty-third floor that had a breathtaking ocean view, and was decorated in a modernist Oriental style: sparse furnishings, neutral woods, its walls unadorned except for a 17th-century Chinese screen depicting an idealized winter landscape.

"Perhaps you'll want to hold your decision until you hear what needs to be done," Nga said.

Kinzo waited in silence. Thin and small-eyed, with a face like a tight fist, he was vice president of Omitsu Industrial, an electronic components manufacturer in Banjarmasin that had originated as an equal Japanese-Indonesian partnership during the years of the tiger economy, and fallen under majority Japanese control after the tiger leaped too far for its own good and went crashing into a ditch.

This had been the typical story for Southeast Asian businesses in need of financial rescue at the end of the previous decade. While many Western analysts had been gleefully forecasting economic Ragnarok for the Japanese, they had done what they had excelled at doing throughout history—learning from their mistakes, adapting to changed circumstances, and ultimately turning misfortune into advantage. Their rebound strategy had been twofold. First, they had propped up joint ventures with companies in Thailand, Malaysia, Indonesia, and the Phillipines by offering infusions of operating capital in exchange for bigger pieces of the action: i.e., controlling shares. Second, they had reprioritized, shifting away from a dwindling Asian market and focusing on export to cash-rich American buyers.

Japan's shrewd exploitation of opportunity had not only yielded heaping economic dividends to legitimate businessmen, but also kept the sake flasks of *yakuza* criminal syndicates overflowing, bringing particular rewards to the influential Inagawa-kai, which was entrenched in the Asian banking community, which had itself capitalized a large percentage of the corporate buyouts. Indeed, a graphic analysis of these financial interrelationships might aptly portray a long line of smiling, satisfied men, each with his hand deep in the pocket of the fellow in front of him.

In the case of the Omitsu Industrial resuscitation, the Canbera family had both brokered the deal and provided lending capital to the Japanese investors under exceptionally generous terms of repayment. That the Canberas had myriad ties to the *yakuza* was something the borrowers knew and accepted from the outset. That they might be called upon to provide a host of illicit favors to their "black mist" creditors was likewise considered a distasteful but acceptable part of their payback agreement.

As the old saying went, Kinzo thought, it was necessary to cross many fjords in passing through the world.

"Let me tell you my predicament," Nga said, cursing Khao Luan and his barbarians for the onerous position in which they had placed him. "There was an accident yesterday involving a foreigner. A white man." He gave Kinzo a meaningful glance. "It was fatal, you see."

Kinzo sat there looking at him.

"I want to make it clear that I had nothing to do with what happened, and would personally choose to report his

death to the police,'' Nga said. ''But the circumstances—
and the parties involved—are such that I would have a
difficult time proving it was unintentional.''

Kinzo remailed silent.

Nga folded his hands on his desk, considering his next
words. This was the delicate part.

''There's a problem with the body,'' he said. And met
Kinzo's gaze with his own. ''With disposal of the body.''

Kinzo took a breath, released it, waited another moment. Then he slowly nodded, wondering what sort of
infernal madness Nga was flirting with . . . and dragging
him into as a reluctant participant.

''I have a shipload of cargo leaving Pontianak tomorrow afternoon,'' he said. ''It will be crossing the Straits
of Melaka en route to points west.''

Nga looked at him.

''Ah,'' he said. ''The open sea . . . is a lonely place.''

Kinzo nodded.

''Were a man to fall overboard on such a voyage,''
Nga said, ''I would imagine he might never be found.''

Kinzo moved his shoulders. ''Even should the currents
wash him ashore, the ravages of the sea and fish upon his
body would make it hard for anyone to identify him. Or
conclusively establish the cause of his death.''

Nga smiled a little.

''As always, my friend, you make perfect sense,'' he
said. ''Give me the ship's name and exact place of departure, and I can arrange for the luckless one we have
discussed to be brought aboard tonight.''

Kinzo saw the uneasiness at the edges of Nga's smile,
and decided to reinforce it with a cautionary word. He
disliked the banker and resented his outrageous imposi-
tion . . . and apart from that wanted to be sure Nga real-

ized this was no minor impropriety of the sort his father had been covering up his entire life.

"Since you seem to value my thoughts, I feel obliged to share some with you," he said. "If a man with no friends were to disappear without explanation, his loss would be a blank space that goes unnoticed and unfilled. But things rarely occur in a void, especially when it comes to human affairs." He paused, then leaned forward. "If there are people left behind to miss him, an investigation is a foregone certainty. Should it turn out to be persistent, even the total absence of physical remains might not be enough to keep the circumstances of his 'accident' from being unearthed. Attention must therefore be given to all possible eventualities. Do you understand?"

Nga stared at him. The smile had fled his lips.

"Don't worry," he said. "I'm taking care of everything."

Unconvinced, Kinzo didn't answer.

Kirsten stood looking at her sister in the kitchen of Anna's home in Petaling Jaya, neither woman speaking, their faces gravely serious. On the butcher block between them were neat piles of chiles, water spinach, bok choy, white radish, and other ingredients for the stir-fry they had been preparing for dinner. A bamboo steamer filled with bean sprouts sat on the stove top, the burner beneath it still unlit. Behind Kirsten, an electric rice cooker worked quietly.

Her face pale, Anna was trembling with distress, the knife she had been using to chop her vegetables forgotten in her hand.

"Maybe you ought to put that down before you cut

yourself,'' Kirsten said, nodding her chin slightly toward the knife. She gave Anna a strained smile. "Or me."

Anna stared at her as if she hadn't heard a word she'd said. The faint hiss of the rice cooker was all that broke the stillness in the room.

Kirsten opened her mouth to say something else, thinking even another tortured attempt at humor would be preferable to the silence . . . but then she decided to leave it alone. What had she expected anyway? Surely not sympathy. She had been staying with Anna and her family for several days now, having arrived with a concocted tale about needing to get away from things because of a romantic breakup, an emotional situation that had pushed her to the edge, all of it complete drivel.

It wasn't that she had meant to keep the truth from Anna and her husband, certainly not for this long, but whenever she'd started to share it with them, the words had refused to come. And so she had continued the deception until it had gotten out of hand—like everything else in her life recently.

At times, Kirsten had thought her guilty conscience and dreadful worries about Max really *would* drive her out of her skull, and by this morning had realized she couldn't bear her freight of secrets anymore. Her resolve firmed, she had planned to wait until her brother-in-law got home from work, sit him and Anna down in their living room, and tell them the truth, the whole truth, and nothing but the truth, so help her God.

But as a surgeon at a government hospital in KL, Lin was often detained with some emergency or other, and when he'd phoned to say that might be the case this evening—well, she had feared her determination might crumble before he arrived, and decided it might be best to make her confession to Anna alone rather than chance putting it off again.

Still, Kirsten hadn't been looking forward to it, and choosing the right moment had been difficult. Oddly enough, however, her mind had been on something else entirely as they'd started their dinner preparations a half hour ago, just before she came out with her story . . . or rather, before it had *leaped* from her mouth all on its own.

The incident she'd been remembering had occurred the previous day, when she was babysitting Anna's two kids, Miri and Brian. They'd been out in the condominium's small backyard playing, and Miri, who was five, had caught a grasshopper while poking around a flower bed, then started shouting for her older brother to find a jar to put it in. He'd run into the house in search of one, leaving her to stand there with her small hands cupped around the insect . . . but when he'd taken longer than Miri expected, her initial excitement over capturing it had turned into a sort of jittery dismay.

"It's getting away," she'd yelled, her eyes wide and frantic. "It's too *big*!"

In fact, it *had* been very big—that the local bugs were always of the king-sized variety was one of the harder things to which Kirsten had needed to get reaccustomed upon her return from England—even harder than the bloody Singlish—and what had presumably gotten her niece so upset was feeling the creature ricochet wildly around in her hands, beating its hard carapace against her palms as it strove to free itself, something that seemed much too large and alive to be contained for very long without inflicting a painful bite or sting.

Becoming aware of Miri's agitation, Kirsten had dashed over from where she'd been clipping a hedge across the yard, and had reached the poor kid just as she'd thrown her hands wide open to release the grasshopper, which had shot into the air like a rifle shell, escaping with a sort of ticking, clicking, fluttering sound that caused had Miri to jump with a shrill cry of startlement. It had taken Kirsten a while to get her settled down, and she'd only accomplished that after repeatedly assuring her the bug had gone away, *far* away, and would not be returning to exact some hideous insectile revenge upon her.

In a sense, Kirsten guessed that her own struggle to keep the truth locked up inside her had been akin to what happened to her niece—she had found herself scared and helpless, dealing with something that had proven much, much more of a handful than she'd bargained for.

And what in the world had she feared from Anna and Lin, anyway? How could any reaction be worse than letting them remain ignorant of the confusing, dangerous mess into which she'd gotten herself?

"Anna, please, listen to me," she said now, fumbling for words. "I'm so sorry . . ."

"*Sorry?*" Anna emitted a burst of harsh, pained laughter. "What am I supposed to say to that? What am I supposed to *do*?"

Kirsten was shaking her head.

"I don't know," she said. "All I can tell you is that I never intended to bring any of this into your home. And that coming here was a terrible mistake. I'll be out by tonight if it's what you—"

"Shit, will you stop making things worse?" Anna said sharply. "Bad enough you've been lying to us the entire time you've been here, letting us believe you're nursing a broken heart. Then I hear it's all about you being involved with spying on your employer, and this craziness about men *ambushing* you on one of the busiest streets in Singapore like something out of James Bond. And now, to make matters worse, you're saying *dzai-jyan,* good-bye, as if you think we'd be eager to see you walk out the door and get kidnapped, even killed, God only knows. I'm not sure whether to be angry, frightened, or insulted.''

Kirsten felt her throat getting thick with moisture, and swallowed.

"May I request," she said, "that 'forgiving' be added to your multiple choice?''

Anna held her gaze for a long, silent moment.

The silence grew.

"Yes," she said finally, nodding. "You may."

Kirsten expelled a ragged sigh. "I'm so mixed up, Anna," she said, her voice barely above a whisper. "Max . . . he knows my cell-phone number, and promised to be in touch within days. When I got into the cab, he was starting to give me someone's name, a person to call if I didn't hear from him, but I didn't catch it. . . .''

"Kirsten, if you want my opinion, the people you *ought* to be calling are the police," Anna said. "This Max is the one who got you into trouble in the first place. I understand that you have feelings for him, but how do you know for a fact that *he* isn't a criminal? That the men who were waiting outside the hotel weren't the authorities?''

Kirsten shook her head vehemently.

"No," she said. "It isn't possible."

"But you've only known the man a few months. Why are you so positive?''

"Because, while I may be five years younger than you, I'm not some little schoolgirl who's got her head screwed on backwards,'' Kirsten said, her throat filling again. ''Look, I won't deny I'm in love with Max. Nor will I deny having had doubts about whether he shares that feeling, or even wondering on occasion whether my position at Monolith made me . . . useful to him. But I know . . . I *know* . . . he cares for me.'' Kirsten wiped her hand across her eyes, and it came away wet. ''You can go on arguing about whether he respected me in the morning, but he's not some kind of manipulative crook, or con man, or whatever. He risked his life to lead those men away from me. I can't just turn my back on him now.''

Anna sighed. ''That isn't what I was suggesting, and if you'd stop being defensive for a second you'd realize it,'' she said. ''All I'm saying is that you—*we*—are in a very serious situation, and need to get help. What's so terribly wrong with the idea of calling the police? With at least considering it before some harm comes to you, me, Lin, or the children?''

Kirsten opened her mouth to speak, and realized she didn't have a clue what she wanted to say . . . but no, that wasn't right. That was being dishonest with herself, and she was supposed to be coming clean here. She had more than a clue. She knew, absolutely *knew* what needed to be said, and she could not allow pride and stubbornness to get in its way.

Suddenly she found herself overtaken by emotion, hitching out uncontrollable sobs.

Anna set her knife down on the counter, then came around to Kirsten's side and took one of her hands.

''Kirst, I didn't mean—''

''No, don't,'' Kirsten said, furiously swiping tears from her eyes with her free hand, *hating* the tears as they poured down her cheeks in an unbottled stream. ''You did mean it, every *word,* and you're absolutely right. You let me stay here unconditionally, and in return I've put your entire family at risk. And that can't continue.''

Anna stood beside her in silence, looking at her, still holding her hand.

Meeting her sister's gaze, Kirsten leaned forward and kissed her gently on the cheek.

''It's time for me to take some advice besides my own,'' she said. ''I'm calling the police.''

FOURTEEN

"YOU WANT TO *WHAT?*" CHARLES KIRBY SAID, GRIP-ping the telephone in his Broadway office. "I can't believe you're serious."

"Believe it," Gordian replied from clear across the United States. "I've given some hard thought to the idea."

Not easily jolted, Kirby felt like hanging onto his chair.

"We spoke less than two days ago, and you didn't mention—"

"That's because it hadn't occurred to me yet," Gordian said. "I said I thought hard about the whole thing. Not hard and *long*." He paused. "Sometimes it's a matter of recognizing when you've gotten a genuine inspiration."

Still trying to recover his equilibrium, Kirby held the phone away from his mouth, inhaled, then slowly counted to ten. He glanced out the window, where many stories below and across the street people were hoisting placards in protest of something or other near the steps of City Hall, a more or less daily occurrence for as long as he'd had his office here. What was it that had brought them out today? He squinted to read the signs, realized he couldn't make out a word they said, and promptly forgot about them as he exhaled.

"Our paperwork for the antitrust suit's already three inches thick," he said. "We're almost ready to file it."

"Then go ahead and do so," Gordian said. "We both know its real purpose is to buy time, and we can use all we can get."

Kirby frowned. "Gord, my job is to give you legal counsel and representation. I can't make decisions for you. But I hope you're aware of the risk you'd be taking by going ahead with this."

"I can accept it," Gordian said. "Talk to somebody with a cold and you might get sick. Stroll past a construction site and a brick might fall down on your head. You can't crawl into a burrow."

Kirby was silent. *Breathe. Count to ten. Let it out.*

"You know, it's always a little scary when you get philosophical," he said after a while. "Just tell me you won't lock yourself on this plan until after you're back from Washington."

"I'd rather get things in motion sooner," Gordian said. "As a matter of fact, I was going ask that you head out here to meet with me and Richard Sobel the morning before we fly."

"But that's Thursday. The day after *tomorrow,*" Kirby said, flipping through his appointment book.

"I'll obviously understand if you can't make it, Chuck. Just as long as *you* understand that if you have any compelling reasons to dissuade me, it'll be your last chance to offer them."

Reaching for his pen, Kirby crossed a Thursday lunch date with a very attractive female colleague out of the book, and substituted the words "To San Jose."

"So quick bright things come to confusion," he muttered.

"What was that?" Gordian said.

"I said I'll be at your meeting," Kirby replied.

Just as Alexander the Great severed the Gordian knot with a swift and decisive whack of his sword—thereby gaining the favorable auspices of Zeus—so had Megan Breen and Peter Nimec concluded early on in UpLink's worldwide expansion that it needed a similar rapid-response capability, a security team that could cope with crisis situations where both regional stability and the company's interests were threatened, sharing intelligence with host governments, using scenario-planning techniques to defuse most problems before they hatched, and prepared to counter violence with forceful action of its own should that option be unavoidable.

Since their employer had been cooperative enough to have a surname (and bold disposition) that invited comparison with the legendary Macedonian, they had dubbed this arm of their far-flung organization Sword. And because of Nimec's access to the generally *inaccessible* society of law-enforcement professionals—he'd started out a beat cop in South Philly, moved to Boston in mid-career to garner an illustrious and still-unmatched record of closed cases for the BPD's elite Major Crimes Unit, and after yet a second geographical move wound up Chief of Special Operations in Chicago, all in less than two decades—they were able to lure the cream of the crop away from police and intelligence agencies around the world, staffing their pet project with men and women who were equal to any job.

One of the impressive Young Turks with Sword's New York branch, Noriko Cousins, had been a handpicked member of Nimec's team during the Code Name: Politika investigation of about a year back, and was credited with being a major reason for its speedy progress and successful resolution. After her section chief, Tony Barnhardt, took early retirement due to injuries sustained during that probe, she had been a natural to fill his post, which, in keeping with Pete Nimec's loose-reigned executive approach, allowed her to run her show with very little topside interference. She rarely heard from Nimec unless it was important.

And so, when she got back from lunch this cool autumn afternoon to find three phone memos from him on her desk spindle, every one of them received during the hour she'd been out of the office, it struck her as safe to interpret the repeated calls as a sign that a matter of some urgency had cropped up.

Hustling over to the phone, she punched in his direct number without pausing to unzip her jacket.

He answered at once. "Nori, I've been anxious to hear from you."

No kidding, she thought.

"Is everything all right, sir?"

"I haven't decided yet," he said. "Look, I'm not going to twist your arm, but I'd like you to come out to San Jose, and would rather not explain why until you get here."

Surprised as Noriko was, she only needed a moment to decide. The personal and professional allegiance she felt toward her boss made it easy.

"When?" she said.

"Soon as possible. Tonight, tomorrow, if you haven't got anything else that's pressing."

"Nothing that my assistant can't handle," she said. "It's been quiet in these parts lately, knock wood."

"Good." He paused for several seconds, the prolonged silence somehow conveying the gravity of his mood even more than his tone of voice. "I know this is asking a lot, and apologize for being mysterious. But we really ought to talk in person."

"It's no problem," she assured him. "Let me get off the phone and start making arrangements. I'll get back to you soon as they're set."

"Later, then." Another pause. "And Nori?"

"Yes?"

"I suggest you pack plenty of lightweight clothes. We might be doing some traveling."

She rubbed the back of her neck, thinking that one over. *Curiouser and curiouser.*

"Will do, sir," she said.

It was what might have been called a perfect equatorial night at Pontianak Harbor, the air warm and clean, countless stars filling the sky, the water stretching off from the rim of the shore lustrous with their reflected light. At the docks, a flotilla of commercial vessels sat anchored amid a silent thicket of cranes and hoists, the off-loaded ships resting buoyantly beside others stacked from stem to sternpost with freight containers, their prows pushed deep into the water under the weight of their transport.

Most nights there was something of a dozing serenity in the quiet before daylight, when the roar and yell of dockworkers, and the constant, rhythmic swinging of booms, would forcibly overpower the soft lap of the current.

Most nights.

Tonight the loud rumble of a cargo truck had shaken the stillness, a muddy tarpaulin flapping over its rear as

Tom Clancy's Power Plays

it rolled up to the transit sheds at the north end of the dock, swung onto the ramp outside their loading doors, and came heavily to a stop.

Moments later a pair of waiting men emerged from one of the darkened sheds and turned toward the big hauler. Looking out from behind its steering wheel, Xiang saw them enter the wide yellow fan of the headlights, their short, slicked-back hair and cherry-blossom arm tattoos marking them as *yakuza,* barely out of adolescence, yet old enough to have been recruited from the *bosozoku* motorcycle gangs that were the equivalent of training schools for the Japanese underworld.

Xiang nodded to Juara, who was riding shotgun. Then, leaving the headlights on, he cut the engine, stepped out of the cab, and rounded the front grille to approach the pair of *yakuza.*

Punks, he thought, regarding them with stony eyes. The smuggling and drug-trafficking alliances Japanese crime families had formed with the Southeast Asian syndicates had not only yielded lucrative results, but had put strutting small-timers like these to good use. The cleanup job they were doing was the sort nobody else would touch.

"You're fucking late," one of the toughs said in Bahasa. "We expected you here an hour ago."

Xiang tipped his head backward slightly, saying nothing. The cargo truck's passenger door flew open and Juara sprang out, an FN P-90 assault weapon in his hands, the tiny lens of a laser aiming system under its silenced barrel. Expressionless, he stood beside the hauler and pointed it in the general direction of the *yakuza.*

"Never mind that," Xiang said. "I want you to tell me who sent you to meet us."

180

The *yakuza* seemed momentarily confused. "Why? We look like IMB to you?"

"You look like sewer rats who are too stupid to know they're about to get their heads blown out their asses," he said, and motioned to Juara.

Juara angled the small, molded-plastic gun sharply upward to center a red dot of laser light upon the *yakuza*'s forehead.

"Tell me who sent you." Xiang repeated. His eyes locked on the tough's. "*Now.*"

The *yakuza* blinked, shrugged.

"We're doing this for a man named Kinzo," he said.

"Doing what?"

"Taking a dead *gaijin* for a trip out to sea," he said. "You satisfied?"

Xiang continued to stare at him without moving for perhaps another half minute, then finally pushed his hand out at Juara. The second pirate lowered his gun.

"The body's in back of the truck, wrapped in a tarp," he said. "Get it out of there and onto whatever ship's taking it away. And don't ask any more questions, you little shitbag."

Trying to conceal his relief, the *yakuza* shrugged and said something to his partner in Japanese. Then both of them went around the back of the truck to do their work.

As he watched them lift the American's body from the covered flatbed and carry it off into the shed, Xiang suddenly remembered something that gave him a foolish but nevertheless powerful desire to hasten on his way. He turned back toward the truck, briefly pausing to gaze out over the black water licking at the quay—the water that would soon swallow Max Blackburn into its depths—and found himself unable to dismiss the unsetting thought that had occurred to him a moment ago.

Pontianak was named after the Malay word for vengeful spirits.

An involuntary shiver running through his frame, he ordered Juara to return to the truck, then climbed inside himself and drove off into the night.

As with any deadly combustion, the Jakarta massacre was inevitable once its explosive ingredients made contact under flashpoint conditions.

The protest organizers, mainly university students belonging to various political elements loosely gathered under the "pro-democracy" umbrella—and, in fact, representing everything from mendicant Communists to militant ultra-Nationalists—had been planning the demonstration at the Cultural Center for a great many weeks, distributing jargonistic leaflets, fliers, posters, and placards; slogan-emblazoned T-shirts and baseball caps; even compact discs filled with fiery speeches and protest anthems meant to be ratcheted from boom boxes during the rally. On and around Indonesia's largest campuses, movement leaders had sought out converts with the zeal of religious proselytizers, gaining thousands of student supporters and managing to stir up a large percentage of the usually apathetic working class, which had endured four years of grinding deprivation after the Asian economic bubble suddenly burst.

Although the cohesive force binding the groups together was fragile, they possessed unanimity in their weariness with skyrocketing inflation, discontent with a government that had stubbornly resisted economic reforms, and anger with their President, in part because of his see-no-evil attitude toward bureaucratic corruption and waste, and in part due to his refusal to dismantle the state monopoly of key national businesses, all of which were controlled by his seemingless endless multitude of brothers, half-brothers, sons, son-in-laws, and nephews.

Together the dissidents constituted a populist force to be reckoned with.

The government, however, had also prepared itself for a coordinated display of muscle.

Concerned that the unrest spreading through the nation's campuses, villages, and cities would eventually open the door to outright rebellion, many ruling party officials had concluded that strong action was needed to counter a perception of government weakness. All knew that quashing the protest in the manner of the Chinese in Tiananmen Square might provoke international condemnation, and potentially damage relations with their Western and Japanese allies. Yet after weighing that risk against the real or imagined likelihood of a full-scale people's uprising, certain influential aides to the President decided it was worth taking, and gained his approval of a scheme that would show their tolerance with dissidents had finally reached its limit.

According to reliable estimates, the throng of protesters was nearly five thousand strong at the height of the rally, and their complaints ranged from the dead serious to the frivolous. There were men with signs denouncing repressive social policies, demanding industrial privatization, and decrying the lack of variety offered by their cable television servers. There were women campaigning for better educational opportunities, new laws to prohibit workplace discrimination, and the scarcity of cosmetics due to import bans. There were journalists of both sexes crying out for freedom of the press, urbanites lamenting the absence of reliable public transportation, suburbanites complaining about their neglected roads and highways, and environmentalists calling out for the emplacement of stricter pollution controls. There was was even a small but vocal group of gourmands expressing outrage over the recent closings of several four-star restaurants.

While fewer in number than the demonstrators, the military troops deployed to manage and contain them were clothed in body armor, and equipped with a wide range of weapons and crowd-suppression gear that gave them a considerable defensive and aggressive edge.

They also had a dirty little secret up their collective sleeve: plainclothes security agents pretending to be demonstrators and dispersed throughout the crowd. The infiltrators' job was to incite a confrontation with the troops, who of course knew of the plan, and would respond with a swift and violent show of force against the real protestors. It would not matter whether their reaction was criticized as excessive by those with a human rights agenda; quite the opposite, its clear and desired message was that the government was finished with civil disobedience, and would begin to punish agitators in the severest manner regardless of anything its critics might say.

To make things look good, the first staged incidents were kept at the level of pushing and shoving matches, the ''protesters'' getting increasingly out of control, the soldiers showing restraint and discipline in driving them back. The clashes gained in frequency, following a realistic pattern of escalation, and soon the troops were being pelted with rocks and bottles. Tear-gas grenades, pepper spray, water cannons, and riot batons were used to subdue the rock-throwers, who were dragged from the scene in hand- and leg-cuffs.

Next, several of the government plants at the skirmish line began hurling gasoline bombs, covering the area with orange splashes of flame and dark clouds of acrid smoke. That no more than twenty people were engaged in this conduct went unnoticed in the milling confusion. That every one of the bombs were either intercepted by the soldiers' ballistic shields, or tossed intentionally wide of where they could do true harm to their supposed targets, also escaped detection. The image of the troops being physically assaulted, firebombs rupturing around them, was the excuse they needed to move into full offensive mode.

Shotguns and automatic rifles were brought out of mobile arsenals and chambered with lethal ammunition. Armored personnel carriers rolled into the mob, provoking exponentially greater anger and hysteria. A young man rushed in front of the lead APC, and was run over before its driver could halt or swerve, the vehicle's treads flattening him horribly, leaving him a mangled and bloody corpse. A young woman who had been near his side leaped upon a trooper in hysterical retaliation, cut open his cheek with a shard of broken glass, and was beaten to the ground with nightsticks and brass knuckles. A couple of men who tried coming to her aid were clubbed unconscious. Somebody triggered an automatic pistol, and by that point it hardly mattered whether the person was a uniformed trooper, an undercover provocateur, or an actual protestor who had been driven to a frenzy by the violence.

The troops smashed into the crowd from all directions, letting loose with their heaviest firepower. Live parabellum rounds poured from their guns. People trying to flee were trapped in the press of bodies and fell screaming and crying, swept with gunfire, slipping on their own blood, crawling through pools of blood.

The television crews already on the scene were speedily joined by satellite crews that could provide live coverage of the melee.

Watching the event closely on television, Nga Canbera couldn't decide how to feel about it. He had poured a fortune in *rupiahs* into financing the demonstrators, caring nothing about most of their issues, but liking to play political games with the administration, largely because he resented the competitive advantage held by the President's businessman relatives—and in particular by one of his sons, a former college classmate who owned a bank that was propped up by government loans and investments, and consistently outperformed his own as a result.

Still, Nga found the rabble crude and undeserving of sympathy. Would the crackdown play to the ruling party's advantage, or further inflame its domestic opposition? And what if the International Monetary Fund withheld the balance of its economic recovery package, or even aborted it entirely in a knee-jerk spasm of humanitarianism? What effect would such a turn have on the Canbera family's holdings . . . and most perplexingly, *why hadn't he asked himself that before?*

It was all very confusing and intimidating, especially when he stopped to consider that his involvement with the students would only be the beginning, the very tip of what would surface if someone started digging around in his affairs . . . and that his complicity, however indirect, in the killing of the American spy could be the very thing that led to where his secrets were hidden. Kinzo's thinly veiled warning was well taken—there was so much, so much that could bring catastrophe upon him. And what would Kinzo have said if he'd known about his role in what General Kersik and the others were plotting? Nga didn't understand how the game could have gotten so complicated and dangerous, how it could have gotten so *big*. He felt in over his head.

He stared at the television. At the armored cars, the troopers, the pathetically frightened demonstrators being cut down in their tracks as they tried to scramble to safety. The President and his advisors deserved credit, at least, for having the courage to strike decisively, to chance the repercussions of bold action rather than wait until the wolves were at their door . . . and perhaps, Nga thought, there was something invaluable to be learned from that, a clue to what *his* course ought to be.

Again, it all came back to the words of advice Kinzo had offered. If Max Blackburn's employers began tracing the circumstances of his death, it would inevitably lead to Nga's own door. How, then, to preempt such an investigation? Yes, Marcus Caine eventually would be feeding on UpLink, *devouring* UpLink—Nga was no less confident of that than before. But as he had tried pointing out at the Thai's dismal hiding place, the process of consumption would take time. Too much time.

Nga continued staring at the TV, but his eyes were no longer focused on the chaotic images flashing across its screen. He was wondering if the problem was not that the game itself had gotten beyond him, but rather that his strategy needed to be broadened. That he had reached the stage where studied and incremental moves would no longer work . . . and where one swift move could win it all.

Nodding to himself like a man who has suddenly

Tom Clancy's Power Plays

realized the solution to a complex puzzle, he picked up the telephone and called Marcus Caine.

"Hello?"

"Marcus, hello. I'm actually surprised I was able to catch you at home. According to what I've been reading, you're the toast of the town these days."

Caine raised an eyebrow at the sound of Nga's voice. He'd been in front of his television for over an hour watching raw CNN satellite feeds of the Jakarta bloodbath. By the time the footage made it to the regular broadcasts, it would be edited for mass consumption, sparing viewers the more grisly scenes of atrocity—but he preferred his glimpses of the world's ugliness straight up. Diluted reality afforded little in the way of insight.

"Libertine that I am, I occasionally give my follies a rest and try catching up with the news," he said, wondering if the timing of Nga's call was any coincidence. "Speaking of which, what's this madness going on in your country?"

"Our beloved head of state is clamping down on his opposition, it seems."

"Does that distress you?"

Caine heard Nga sigh. "I suppose it depends on how these events come to bear upon my own fortunes."

Caine's eyebrow arched a little higher. He'd expected an earful of Nga's phoney rhetoric . . . sympathy for the common man, and all that nonsense. The apparently honest answer Nga had given him instead was almost startling.

"As long as your bank continues doing well, I imagine you'd be in a good position regardless of who comes out on top," he said, uncertain whether that was true consid-

188

ering Nga's habit of fucking around in Indonesian politics, and hardly giving a damn in any case. He was just filling the silence, really.

"Marcus, listen to me," Nga said after a moment. "We have to talk about Roger Gordian. Something's arisen that could have damaging implications for us unless it is addressed right away."

Caine stroked his chin, thinking. He had no idea what to make of Nga's cryptic statement, other than that it presumably concerned the takeover.

"I'll be formally announcing my intention to acquire UpLink in today's *Wall Street Journal*," he said. "The company's lawyers are certain to stall things in court, but I think it will all be smoke. Give me a few weeks and—"

"I said *Roger Gordian*. Not UpLink."

Suddenly disquieted, Caine thought some more, wishing Nga would just spit it out. "Does this have any connection to the son of a bitch who was nosing around my Singapore branch? I thought you took care of him."

A pause.

"Marcus, are we secure?"

"I can only vouch for my end of the line."

"Then we should be able to speak freely," Nga said. "The one you speak of is dead. And that's where the complications begin."

Caine suddenly realized his heart was beating fast. "I— I don't understand. I mean, what went wrong? And what does it have to do with me?"

"How it happened is a long story, but be assured it wasn't intentional," Nga said. "Really, though, abducting him was a mistake, and I objected to it from the beginning. Had he been released, he would have been able to share information about his captors with the authorities and his employer. His death, meanwhile, is surely going to bring about an investigation. In the end, what is the difference? People are going to want answers, and all roads lead in our direction.''

''Wait a second,'' Caine said. ''You're speaking as though I had a hand in this. And I didn't. I didn't even want to know about it. Your friends came up with the brainstorm of taking him, when there had to be an easier way to find out what he was looking for. A *sane* way.''

''Calm down. We can't reverse what's past. The important thing now is that we have the courage to deal with the rest of it.''

''Don't give me that bullshit. You fucking deal with the rest, whatever it may be. I've repaid your loans ten times over. I've done everything you asked, like a fucking indentured servant. But this . . . I want no part of it.''

Another pause, this one of longer duration than the first.

''Marcus, I needn't remind you that you've already participated in activities that would be considered treasonous offenses by your government. If your actions come to light you'll be imprisoned for life, if not executed. Why do you think Blackburn had to be stopped? There was no choice—''

''Don't say his name. And don't you dare call me a *traitor*,'' Caine protested. His voice had become shrill. ''My God, I'm not used to this. Those sons of bitches you consort with, those thugs, it's their problem. What do you expect *me* to do about it, anyway?''

''Nothing directly. But there are men in the States who've performed certain kinds of tasks for us before. Who can get into and out of places without anyone witnessing anything. You know who they are, Marcus.''

Caine was incredulous.

"No," he said. "I won't hear any more—"

"Yes, you will," Nga said. "I will tell you what has to be done about Gordian because there is no other choice. And for that same reason you will listen."

"No, no, no—"

"I will tell you, Marcus," Nga repeated.

And before Caine could interrupt again, he did.

FIFTEEN

SITTING IN HIS PICKUP OUTSIDE THE BAYVIEW MOTOR Inn, Jack McRea resisted the impulse to check his watch for the third time in ten minutes. He was torn between contradictory desires, part of him eager to see the woman he was supposed to be meeting arrive in her car, part of him hoping she wouldn't show. He had been unfaithful to his wife only once in over a decade of marriage, and that had been when his drinking had gotten out of control and Alice had moved out for a while. Furthermore, he had never before breached his trust as a county sheriff's deputy or screwed up any of the jobs on which he'd moonlighted to pay the bills. Not even when his alcoholic binging was at its worst had he done that.

Yet here he was in a motel parking lot when he should have been on duty at the private airfield where he worked as a night watchman. Here he was waiting for a woman he had met in a bar where he still occasionally had a couple of beers between the end of his shift at the sheriff's office and the beginning of his shift at the airport. He knew nothing about her except that her name was Cindi with two *I*'s, and that she was blond and had pretty eyes and looked fantastic in short skirts and high-heeled shoes. Also, she wore this glossy stuff on her lips that made them look very moist, and had an incredible, sexy smile, the kind of sexy that made your stomach tight.

When they had met at the bar last night, she'd told him she was waiting for a friend who'd stood her up, and he had bought her a drink because she'd seemed kind of down, and somehow or other they'd gotten kind of flirty, and she'd edged a little close on her stool, and when he'd given her a look to show he'd noticed, she just smiled, and sat there a while with her skirt way up high and her thigh touching his leg.

Well, one thing had led to another, and they'd gotten very touchy, and because it was obvious where they were heading, and just so she knew where they stood, he'd decided to come clean and tell her he was married. She'd giggled a little at his confession, and when he'd asked what was so funny, had put her finger on his wedding band and said she'd sort of figured it was either that or he was trying to look hard to get, and he'd realized how lame he must have sounded and started laughing, too. And then she'd told him she had a regular boyfriend, which made them even, or *almost* even, and for some reason that had gotten both of them laughing harder, and they were still laughing as they leaned in close to each other and deep-kissed, then began necking at the bar, saying how much they wanted to be alone, forget the wife, forget the boyfried, alone, damn near getting it on right there at the bar.

Jack had known of the Bayview from passing it on the way to work every night—work being the airfield, which was owned by a group of local businessmen who had partnered up to keep their corporate jets there, and was just a hop-skip-and-jump from the bar—and also because a couple of his married buddies had been there with women they were seeing on the sly, and told him the owners went out of their way to keep things nice and discreet.

He'd mentioned it to Cindi while they were practically climbing aboard each other's laps, and said he had a couple of hours before work, and would she like to go there with him and finish what they'd started? And that was when she had explained about the guy she was kind of dating, saying he was a long-haul trucker who would see her whenever he was in town, and was stopping by that night midway through a long run, and that even though she didn't expect him until much later, she figured he'd want a little something from her like he always did, which made her feel funny about, you know, being with Jack that same night.

Jack hadn't known what to think of her story, except that it left him feeling like he needed a cold shower, and he'd asked her outright if she was having second thoughts about getting into something with him, and she'd said, no, no, you've got it all wrong, and had put her hand between his legs, and told him her boyfriend would be gone the next morning, and that it'd just be better if they could get together when she could be free to give everything she had to Jack ... that was exactly how she'd worded it, keeping her hand on him the whole time, rubbing him where it counted right in front of everybody in the place. And that smile of hers, that smile, it was—how did the song go?—sweet as cherry pie and wild as Friday night, something like that.

Everything I have.

Ah, God, how could he resist?

And so they'd wound up making their plans for tonight. His original idea had been to meet her at the bar around six o'clock, and then for them to drive over to the Bay-view, where they could be together for a couple of hours before he had to take over for the day guard at the airfield. But she'd said she had some important errands to run that evening, how about they made it a little later, maybe seven, seven-thirty, just to be on the safe side. And he'd told her that was no good for him because he really had to be at his night job by eight, which would leave them with, what, half an hour tops, and that he didn't think either of them wanted the first time they were alone to be a wham-bam-thank-you-ma'am kind of situation.

It had gone back and forth a while, the two of them trying to get at a way to make it happen, neither wanting to delay it again, but Cindi insisting she couldn't put off whatever she had to do, until at last she'd asked if he couldn't maybe be a little late for work, or find somebody to cover for him, or even sneak away from his post for an hour or so, which she thought would make it that much more exciting for them, kind of *dangerous* in a fun way, didn't *he*?

Crazy as it sounded when she brought it up, he'd im-mediately realized Cindi had hit on something. He *could* leave the gate unattended for a short time without any-body noticing; in fact, he'd done exactly that on occasions when he'd gone to buy a coffee or a pack of smokes for himself, and once or twice had even stopped for a brew before heading back to the airport. It wasn't as though he worked at Frisco International. There were rarely any comings and goings during his watch. He could clock in at his usual time, slip away for a couple of hours with Cindi, and be back without anybody being the wiser. And, yeah, she was right, it *did* somehow make things more interesting.

They had finally arranged to meet in the parking area of the Bayview—he'd given her directions, and she'd told him that she sort of knew where it was, anyway—at eight-thirty, which had given him long enough to punch the time clock at the guard booth, make sure the day man was gone, and head on over.

And here he was the very next night, looking at his watch yet again, waiting for her to arrive, wondering if she was going to let him down after all their planning . . . *negotiations,* you could even call them. Which, he thought again, might be for the best. Alice was a good woman and had gone through a lot with him, and he knew it would kill him to lose her. But it hadn't been happening in bed for them since Tricia was born, and he was a healthy guy who had his needs. What he was doing tonight was only sexual, and had nothing to do with how he felt about his wife. Still and all, though, once these things got rolling you could never be a hundred percent sure you wouldn't get caught with your pants down, and he guessed that was why there was a small part of him that would be glad if—

The sound of an approaching car suddenly interrupted the flow of Jack's thoughts. He glanced into his side-view, saw a red Civic enter the parking lot behind a splash of headlights, watched it pull into a slot in the row of cars behind him . . . and then felt his pulse start to race as her long legs slid out the driver's side and she came walking toward him, sweet as cherry pie, wild as Friday night, wearing clothes that might have come right out of his hottest fantasies, clothes that made it impossible for him to think about anything besides what she would look like once he peeled them *off.*

He hit the button on his armrest to roll down his window, and waited.

"Waiting for anyone special?" she said, smiling as she leaned into his car, her great big eyes and the scent of her perfume making his heart race.

"Not anymore," he said, and reached for his door handle, knowing very well that he would not be heading back to the airport anytime soon, that he couldn't have claimed to care if he *never* showed up at work, and that, like goddamned Samson in the old Bible story, he was wonderfully, deliciously doomed.

Its location chosen with privacy in mind, the airfield edged on a narrow inlet of the lower bay just northeast of the border between Almeda and Santa Clara Counties. Each of the four cinder-block maintenance hangars had a distinctive corporate logo painted large on its rooftop and at least one outer wall, making visual identification easy for approaching pilots. There were some small prefab outbuildings and two runways, one just over two thousand feet long, and a 3,400-foot high-speed stretch for the larger propeller and jet aircraft. Tonight only a handful of birds sat on the ramps beneath the calm and quiet sky: a single-prop Pilatus, a larger King Air C90B twin-turboprop, Cessna and Swearingen bizjets, and three or four kit-built sport planes. A fleet of passenger copters rested with their wheels on the numbers on a helipad at the north end of the airport.

A small oval of blacktop with space for perhaps two dozen motor vehicles, the airport's parking area was vacant as the unmarked commercial van swung in from the tree-lined access road at half past eight, and then nosed against the fence running behind the hangars and apron.

The pair of men inside had encountered no one at the guard booth, which had been their certain expectation. The guard had been lured to a motel by a woman whose expert distractions would make it impossible for him to remember his own name, let alone his responsibilities at the airport.

Moments after its headlights and engine cut out, its driver and passenger exited the van and passed swiftly through the entrance to the hangar areas. Both wore green utility coveralls. The driver carried a wallet with forged identification, two small adjustable wrenches in a patch pocket on his chest, and an empty pint jar in one hand. The passenger was also holding counterfeit ID, but had nothing else on him except a silenced Beretta in a concealed holster.

The service road ran in a loop around the airport, and had a concrete sidewalk leading past the hangars. Reaching the walk, they spotted the UpLink hangar about thirty yards to their right, and turned quickly and silently in that direction.

If they came across someone who questioned their presence, they would explain that they'd been hired to perform last-minute preflight maintenance on Roger Gordian's Learjet and arrived late because of difficulty finding the airfield. They had brought the Beretta as a fallback should that answer fail to quell any suspicions.

As it was, they reached the hangar without encountering anyone and found the hangar door open to the cool night air. They entered, located the overhead light switch, and turned on the fluorescents. The hangar's interior smelled of fuel, lubricant, and metal.

Stabalized by wheel chocks under the high, flat ceiling, Roger Gordian's Learjet 45 was a sleek eight-passenger plane with upturned wingtips and powerful turbofans. The driver stood admiring it for a moment. It was a beautiful work of engineering, but like all things had its Achilles heel.

Now the driver of the van turned to the other man, gestured toward the front of the hangar with his chin, and waited as he went to stand lookout. Once in the doorway, the man with the gun stretched his head outside, glanced left, right, and then over his shoulder at his partner, nodding to indicate there was still nobody in sight.

The driver returned his nod, and then went and slid down under the plane. Turning on his back, he produced the wrenches from his pockets and got to work. He unscrewed the lid of the pint jar and set the open jar on his stomach. Then he clamped one of the tools to the line running from the landing gear cylinder and, holding it steady by the handle, loosened the cylinder's hydraulic fitting with the other wrench. He held the jar underneath the fitting as the fluid bled out, and kept it there until it was full. Then he twisted the lid back onto the jar, put the tools back in his pocket, and wriggled out from beneath the aircraft.

Less than fifteen minutes after they had entered the hangar, the two men were back in the van. The driver placed the jar of drained-off hydraulic fluid in the glove compartment, and then turned on the ignition and pulled out onto the access road.

When they rode by the guard station it was dark and empty.

The watchman was still out enjoying himself, and would no doubt remember his hours of stolen pleasure with a smile, never realizing they had all but guaranteed Roger Gordian's fiery death.

SIXTEEN

"I'M TELLING YOU, IF THOSE PEOPLE IN THE PRESS
Office don't start doing their jobs, I'm going to give every
one of them the boot myself, and Terskoff is the first guy
whose ass gets to meet my foot," said President Richard
Ballard, referring in his momentary pique to White House
Press Secretary Brian Terskoff.

"Quite frankly, I don't think they're to blame," said
Stu Encardi, whose official job title was Special Aide to
the President, and who was now just waiting for the
breeze to stir. "You know how it is with reporters. They
cover what they want to cover."

Ballard pulled a disgusted face. "Oh, come on. We're
about to enter into a genuinely world-changing treaty with
Japan and other Far Eastern countries, we've got three
regional leaders *and* yours truly participating in a signing
ceremony aboard a nuclear sub, and you're trying to say
the crypto issue is *sexier*? That's absurd."

"You think so?" Encardi said. "Granted, the numbers
tell us people were hardly paying attention to crypto until
this week, and they still don't get what the whole damn
thing's about. But from my perspective, it's this escalat-
ing Gordian-Caine spat that's the hook for reporters. The

treaty represents cooperation and harmony, and, well, conflict being the essence of drama—''

"Spare me," Ballard said. "What the hell should we do as an attention grabber, get Diver Dan and Baron Barracuda down there underwater with us?"

"Excuse me, sir?"

"Never mind, you're twenty years too young," Ballard said, cocking an ear skyward. "By the way, doesn't the breeze sound pretty moving through those leaves?"

"Yes, sir, it does."

They were standing under a willow oak that a former First Lady had planted on the South Lawn as an everlasting reminder of her tenure at the White House, much as Encardi himself had been planted among the President's circle of confidants by *his* lovely missus, who had taken a shine to the thirty-year-old Yale man when he'd been one of the coordinators of Ballard's re-election campaign, sensing in him a kindred soul of similar outlook and attitude, and later finagling her husband into making him a member of his post-election advisory staff, feeling he would be the ideal surrogate to carry her approximate viewpoint to Ballard—be it on matters political or personal—whenever she wasn't physically present to do so herself.

Generally speaking, Ballard considered Encardi an insightful, practical, and dedicated pup, and liked having him around as the personification of his wife's *weltanshauung*. Still, he was occasionally bothered by the fact that the aide boasted a profusion of hair to rival a Hungarian puli, while only a miracle of artful combing concealed his own advancing, Rogaine-resistant baldness.

He also became annoyed when Encardi borrowed his wife's verbal tics, such as following every Presidential statement with a "You think so?" and beginning his replies with a pedagogic "Quite frankly," or "From my standpoint," both hearkening back to Mrs. Ballard's decades-long career as a college teacher. These were the sort of things that would make borderline days turn bad, and bad days a little worse, except when the gorgeous weather and the sound of the breeze rustling through Ballard's favorite tree made everything under God's blue sky appreciably better.

"Stu, let me give you some instant perspective," Ballard said. "Two days from now I'll be signing the crypto legislation while Roger Gordian makes a fuss down the Hill. Two months from now everyone will have forgotten all about it, and think Morrison-Fiore is the name of some Vegas animal-training act. But in the interim I'll have closed a deal that establishes the guidelines for America's security role in Asia over the next *twenty years,* and probably much longer. There's my posterity, or a decent chunk of it. We just have to make sure people notice."

Encardi regarded him in the light shade of the tree as the wind brushed through the drooping canopy overhead. There were gnats or something swirling around them. In fact, there were *always* bugs under this tree. For some reason he didn't quite get, they seemed particularly attracted to the vicinity of the goddamned willow.

He swished a squadron of tiny winged harriers away from his face, convinced he would be a much happier man if just once the POTUS would elect to stroll under a dogwood, elm, or alder while seeking to restore his inner calm.

"I'm thinking we need to make sure Nordstrum from the *New York Times* is given the red-carpet treatment," he said.

"And *I* thought we were already doing that," the President said.

"Well, we are, but we can always roll out more rug," Encardi said. "Nordstrum's the biggest proponent of our Asia-Pacific policy in the national media. Why not assist him in gaining interviews with the Japanese Prime Minister, as well as the Malaysian and Indonesian heads of state? Invite him to the dinner you'll be having aboard the Seawolf? Anything to give him a steady stream of material to write about."

Ballard stretched broadly and inhaled the fragrant air of the White House grounds, sunlight striping his face as it filtered through the long bushy willow leaves.

"*Ahhhhh,* I'm feeling almost relaxed," he said. "Isn't it a spectacular morning?"

"Spectacular," Encardi said listlessly, swatting away an insect.

Ballard looked at him.

"Your idea about Nordstrum sounds fine to me, but only for starters," he said, his brow creasing in thought. "You know, now that you mention him, it's kind of odd Roger Gordian hasn't convinced Nordstrum to write more about the encryption issue in his columns. He's a paid consultant for UpLink International, did you know?"

Encardi considered that a moment and shrugged.

"Could be he disagrees with Gordian on that one," he said.

"Or just finds the crypto stuff as dull and relatively inconsequential as anybody else," the President added.

Swathed in virgin wilderness, the atoll was one of hundreds speckling the Celebes Sea west of the Sabah coast and bordering on the Philippines' territorial waters. A circular reef formed a breakwater around its shoreline, where a dense band of mangroves buttressed it against tropical storms and enclosed the rain forest that lay further inland, itself a protective horseshoe surrounding the lagoon at the island's center on three sides.

The same terrain characteristics that sheltered the atoll from the ravages of sea and weather had made it an un-detected—and virtually undetectable—site for the pirate enclave. Few outside their brotherhood had ever located it, fewer still had penetrated its natural lines of defense, and none who did so without invitation had left it alive.

Zhiu Sheng had been there but once before, and then only for a quick pass around the island's rim at the request of General Kersik, who'd wanted him to have a firsthand acquaintance with the logistics of the planned Sandakan invasion. Today, however, he was headed for the interior. An hour ago, the Chinese fishing trawler that had brought him from the port city of Xiamen in Fujian province had steered slowly through the narrow inlet to the lagoon, and then dropped anchor near the sand belt. The timing of its arrival had been propitious; minutes af-terward, the stacked, charcoal-gray clouds of an anvil thunderhead had burst open with a flash of lightning that illuminated the sky for several seconds, ushering in a fierce tropical downpour. Had the boat still been in open waters, the rough surf and buffeting winds might have capsized it.

When the rain eased off, the vessel's crew, a dozen trusted, handpicked soldiers from commando units in the Guangzhou Military Region, had gotten to work off-loading its cargo of unmarked crates into the dinghies that bore them ashore. Per their orders, they had on civilian khakis. For their part, Xiang and the handful of pirates who'd met them on the beach wore army camouflage fatigues, something that had not slipped past Zhiu's keen sense of irony. Far too often in the world, he thought, the roles of men became confused and indefinable.

Now, the large crates balanced on their shoulders, their shirts soaked with perspiration, the soldiers were tramping through the knee-high water of a stream that bent and twisted between narrow lanes of cycads, their pirate guides leading them ever more deeply into the jungle. At first they had needed to hack their way through the epiphytic vines and creepers with machetes, but the undergrowth had thinned in the half-light below the treetops, allowing for better progress.

A lifelong city dweller, Zhiu nevertheless felt pressed, hemmed in, and that feeling was becoming more intense as he went along. It was as if he'd been bumped backward millions of years to some prehistoric epoch, a setting to which men like Xiang seemed as plainly suited as he himself was to the streets of modern Beijing. Trailing behind the giant as they crossed the stream, he recalled the moment he'd first seen him in the Thai's hiding place, guarding the door to where the prisoner was being held—his eyes staring with an impassive watchfulness that seemed to take in everything around them, yet let nothing escape their surface. Though that look had chilled him, Zhiu had not fully understood it, not then, not even after what Xiang had done to Max Blackburn. But here, in this old and alien forest, he did. Here, he had come to recognize it as a look with origins beyond human memory, a look of primordial jungle and swamp, a look which belonged entirely and exclusively to the cold-blooded, pitiless hunter.

Zhiu waded on. Though his shoulder pack contained

only rations, water, and a first-aid kit, the passage through moving water had tired him, and he could see his men approaching exhaustion under the heavier weight of their burdens.

He was glad when Xiang finally mounted the stream bank and led the party back onto the forest floor.

It took another twenty minutes before they reached the camp, a cleared area with a group of temporary thatch shelters in front of a spoon-shaped limestone outcropping. Zhiu peered through the foliage screening the perimeter, and saw Kersik and five or six others near one of the hooches, all except the general carrying ported combat rifles—battered Russian AKMs from the looks of them. Like Xiang's pirates, the men wore jungle camo fatigues, but that was the extent of the comparison. Their training and discipline were evident at a glance, making them far more similar to his own team.

These were experienced soldiers, no doubt chosen from the KOSTRAD Special Forces divisions Kersik had commanded before his retirement.

Zhiu raised his eyes to the arched ceiling of leaves without tilting back his head. He could not see the snipers guarding the perimeter, but knew they must be hidden somewhere up above him, ready to pick off unwanted intruders from their firing positions.

"Ah, Zhiu, you've arrived," Kersik said, spotting him. He came forward and parted the brush. "Our cause brings us to meet in unusual spots, don't you think?"

"Yes," Zhiu said, stepping past Xiang to take Kersik's offered hand. "This one, I confess, breathes down my neck with its heat and humidity."

Kersik smiled a little. "I suppose being a native of the islands makes me impervious to their effects." He gave

Zhiu's men an estimating glance, then nodded in apparent approval, as if impressed by what he saw. "Come, you all must be tired. I'll show you where to put the shipment."

Motioning for them to follow, he turned back toward the camp and strode to the rock formation behind the hooches. A matting of palm fronds, sun-dried and bound together with rope, covered a large section of the stone face. Kersick called over a pair of his soldiers, gave them a mild order in Bahasa, and waited as they lifted aside the matting to reveal a pocket cave, its mouth about five feet high and equally wide.

Curious, Zhiu approached the cave, bent over slightly, and leaned his head in for a closer look. The opening seemed to give into a space of some depth—in fact, he could not see to the back of the tunnel. Beetles and other insects crawled in the thick layer of guano covering the rocks beyond the cave mouth. He listened a moment, and heard the faint flutter of roosting bats.

Unusual spots indeed, he thought.

He straightened and faced his men.

"We'll bring the arms in there," he said, gesturing at the cave entrance. He paused, thought of the slippery bug-ridden coat of guano they would have to walk over. "And be careful where you step," he added.

Anna was sitting on the living room sofa, her legs tucked under her, when Kirsten came in from the guest room after having gotten off the phone.

"I've just spoken with the police in Singapore," she said. "I gave them my name, told them about the men that went after me and Max, told them where I'm staying.

They already seemed aware of what happened outside the hotel.''

Anna gave her a look that said she'd expected as much.

"In a country where chewing gum's contraband and spitting on the street is a crime, a scuffle of that sort wouldn't go unnoticed," she said. "What did they want you to do?"

"They tried persuading me to return to the island and meet with an investigator, but I said I wouldn't. That I felt it was too dangerous to go back unescorted. When they realized I wouldn't budge, they said they'd have to arrange something with the police in Johor and would get back to me."

Anna nodded sympathetically. "How do you feel?"

Kirsten wondered how to reply. She hadn't been to her own home for almost a week, was hiding from men who had been trying to abduct her or worse, and was still waiting to hear from Max after having left several unreturned messages on his answering machine. All of which left her very frightened and confused.

Furthermore, she felt vaguely as if she'd betrayed him by calling the authorities after he had specifically told her to wait for him to contact her, and had tried giving her the name of someone else to reach if he didn't. But he'd never finished getting it out of his mouth—either that or she hadn't heard him clearly from inside the cab—and though she was guessing the person might be someone at UpLink, her sister and brother-in-law had advised her not to call there, insisting it wouldn't do until she had a clearer idea of what Max had been into. For all she knew, they'd repeated endlessly, the Americans had dragged her into some kind of dishonest business. And without evidence to the contrary, it had been impossible for her to dismiss that possibility without seeming unreasonable.

Which left her with Anna's question. How, then, *would* she describe her psychic and emotional state? How to express the incommunicable?

She looked at her sister from the entryway, thinking.

"I feel," she said at last, groping for words, "as if the sky is upside down and world is in the wrong place. The *wrong place,* you understand?"

Overwhelmed, Anna started raising her hand to her lips in a gesture of mute distress, but caught herself at the last moment and let it drop back onto her lap.

"I'm trying, Kirst," she said in a dry, scared voice. "Please believe, I'm trying my very best."

"Truly, I consider the orchid to be the embodiment of our Asian heritage," Fat B was saying. "Lasting yet delicate, its success, its *flowering,* dependant upon an exacting set of conditions."

"Is that so?" Commander Sian Po of the Singapore Police Force said.

"Truly, truly," Fat B said. "Nurtured in the rich soil of their evolution, orchids thrive in abundance, generation upon generation draping our hills, blanketing our heaths and gardens. Change what is essential to their natural state . . . go too far trying to cross cultures . . . spoil the purity of their time-honored lineage . . . and they wane like homesick souls. And while you may call me eccentric, I have always held to the belief that their colorful blossoms are inhabited by the spirits of our ancestors."

"There is a widespread fancy that certain varieties may actually *steal* one's spirit, you know. That their sublime beauty, drawing its energy from the feminine principle, may entrance a man and capture his essence, drain his very *yin*."

"No, no, I think that is ridiculous."

"Well, I do, too. For that matter, I think this is all a pile of shit, so let's drop it. You arranged this meeting. If you have something to say, say it."

Fat B glanced at him and nodded.

They were looking out over the rail of a walking bridge that spanned a koi pond in the orchid gardens on Mandai Road in the north of Singapore Island, admiring the darting fish and the silver-tinged purple brightness of the bamboo orchids planted near the pond.

"Do the names Max Blackburn or Kirsten Chu mean anything to you?" Fat B asked.

The commander shook his head. "Should they?"

Fat B hesitated. "There was a disturbance on Scotts Road last Friday evening. Surely you're aware of it."

The commander did not shift his gaze from the orchids. A short, heavy man with rather mashed-looking features, he had arrived here for their clandestine appointment sans badge and uniform, not wishing to be identified as a police officer, let alone one of high rank. It would, he knew, be very bad indeed if he were seen consorting with a disreputable character like Fat B.

"Scotts is Central . . . 'A' Division," he said. "Not my jurisdiction."

Fat B found his brevity curious. He leaned forward with his elbows on the rail and gazed past the pond to where the flowers were quivering in a light breath of breeze, their glow in the copious sunshine surpassing even that of the hand-painted butterflies on his shirt.

"Your Geylang command encompasses thirteen neighborhood police posts and over three hundred officers," he said. "The incident to which I am referring involved a scuffle on the street in front of a large hotel. A very busy location. My information is that there were witnesses. Do you mean to tell me there were no reports? No departmental bulletins?"

The commander turned his head toward Fat B and gave him a phlegmatic look.

"Assuming there were," he said, "what connection do you have to the occurrence?"

"None, I assure you." Fat B shrugged. "Like yourself, I try not to stray beyond my own purview. But on occasion people ask me things, and I do my best to give them answers."

"And how generous are these people in their gratitude?"

"Very."

The commander inhaled, then let the air rush out his lips.

"Something odd *did* happen outside the Hyatt, and maybe inside as well," he said. "Exactly what, I'm not sure. But CID's involved."

"Criminal Investigation?"

"Yes. And more than one line element. Rumor has it that both the Special Investigation Section and Secret Societies Branch have their noses in this."

"Tell me everything that is known about the incident."

"There isn't much. Or if there is, the CID hotshots are keeping it to themselves." Sian Po shrugged. "I've heard a bystander gave us an anonymous call, and it was corroborated by another report. There was a confrontation at a taxi stand involving a *quai lo,* a woman, and some others. The woman rode off in a cab, and the white man stayed behind and is supposed to have been followed into the hotel lobby. We don't know what happened afterward, but it was all over by the time a patrol car arrived. Everyone involved seems to have vanished, and few bystanders admit to having seen anything. But that's the way it is.''

"Nobody wants trouble, *lah*.''

The commander nodded, and released another sigh.

"Even so,'' he said, "trouble comes.''

They were silent a while. Fat B's eye caught a compressed medley of color flitting under the surface of the pond—a large rainbow koi. It darted into the shade of a water lily and stopped abruptly, its long body hovering in perfect stillness.

"Should Missing Persons reports be filed on either the *quai lo* or the Chu woman, I would very much appreciate being apprised of their sources,'' he said. "Also, my inquisitive friends would find any clues I could pass along about the woman's present whereabouts to be of special value.''

Their eyes met.

"Your friends,'' the commander said. "What will they do if they locate her?''

"I don't ask.''

The commander looked at him for a full minute without saying anything, then slowly nodded.

"I'll see what I can do,'' he said.

Fat B grinned with satisfaction. "And I'll make it worth your while.''

The commander lingered on the rail another moment, then turned to leave. Fat B didn't move. He did not think Sian Po would be inclined to stroll from the garden in his presence.

The commander took two steps up the bridge and paused, motioning toward Fat B's shirt with his chin.

"Those butterflies are quite splendid," he said. "They are of the Graphium species, are they not?"

Fat B nodded.

"I've heard they survive by sucking the piss of higher animals from the ground," the commander said.

Fat B controlled his reaction.

"Thank you for sharing that with me," he said. "Outwardly we are very different types of men, you and I, but love and knowledge of nature is our bond."

The commander looked at him and grinned unpleasantly.

"The money helps," he said, and strode away.

SEVENTEEN

"THIS," NORIKO COUSINS SAID, "IS ONE *AMAZING* room."

Nimec reached for the little blue cube of chalk on the bridge of the pool table.

"So people tell me," he said, rubbing the chalk on the tip of his cue stick with a circular motion. "It's where I come to loosen up, get my thoughts right."

They were in the billiard parlor on the upper level of his San Jose triplex, a painstaking recreation of the smoky South Philadelphia halls where he'd spent his youth ducking truant officers, while pursuing an education of a sort that certainly wouldn't have moved them to reexamine his delinquent status. But in those days Nimec had only cared about one man's approbation, and in attempting to gain it had been a most attentive student . . . or, as he liked to put it, if SATs and grade-point averages could measure one's aptitude at bank shots, combinations, and draw English, he'd have been a shoe-in for a full college scholarship.

At any rate, he'd captured every detail of the old place—at least as filtered through the subjective lens of his recollection—from the cigarette burns on the green baize tabletops to the soda fountain, swimsuit calendars, milky plastic light fixtures, and Wurlitzer juke stacked with vintage forty-fives circa 1968, a machine he'd picked up for a song at an antique auction and which, after some minor repairs, could still shake and rattle the room to its ceiling beams with three selections for a quarter.

Right now it was belting out Cream's cover of the old blues standard "Crossroads." Clapton's improvised guitar lead slipped around Jack Bruce's bass line like hot mercury, taking Nimec back, conjuring up a memory of his old pal Mick Cunningham, a few years his senior and newly back from a hitch in Nam, bopping between rows of regulation tables, raving about Clapton being *fucking huge* in Saigon.

Mick, who'd had a problem with junk, which had also been fucking huge in Saigon, had been shivved to death in a prison exercise yard in '75 while doing a nickel for attempted robbery, his first offense, a heavy sentence by anyone's standards.

"One ball, over there," Nimec called, waggling his stick at the left corner pocket in the foot rail. He had won the opening break.

Noriko nodded.

He leaned over the side of the table and set the cue ball down within the head string, just shy of the center spot. Then he placed his right hand flat on the table's surface and slid the cue into the groove between his thumb and forefinger. Sighting down the length of the stick, he stroked twice in practice, then drove for the cushions on the opposite rail, giving the cue some left English and follow. The ball banked off the cushion at a slightly wider angle than he'd intended and hit the one thin, but still pocketed it neatly and scattered the triangular rack, leaving him with a couple of easy setups.

"You know what you're doing," Noriko said. When he'd shot, she thought, his eyes had shown the steely concentration of a marksman.

"I ought to," he said. "My father was the sharpest hustler in Philly. Shooting pool is what he did. His dream was that I'd carry on the family trade after he was gone, and I worked hard at learning it."

"Your mother have anything to say about that?"

"She wasn't around, maybe wasn't even alive. Blew the nest when I was three or four. Guess she wasn't impressed that I could count all my toes and fingers." He took his stance again. "Three ball, center pocket."

He aimed and shot, kissing his ball off the eleven. It pocketed with a solid chunk-chunk-chunk.

Noriko looked at him with mild wonder, waiting, twirling her stick vertically between her palms, its butt end on the floor. Nimec had always seemed the epitome of the straight-arrow cop—or ex-cop as the case happened to be. The side of her chief she was seeing was a revelation.

"If you don't mind my asking," she said, "how'd you wind up wearing a badge?"

Nimec faced her and shrugged.

"There was no dramatic turning point, if that's what you're curious about," he said. "Besides playing pool, our other favorite sport in the old neighborhood was hanging out on street corners and getting drunk and starting fights. Everybody wailed on everybody else, seven days a week . . . grown men pushing teenagers through windshields, teenagers pounding on little kids with trash cans, kids smashing bricks down on alley cats. It was hierarchical like that." He shrugged again. "I got tired of it after a while, and suppose the structure and the pay

and the benefits of being a police officer appealed to me.
One very typical day I took the exam and passed. A few
months later I got my appointment, figured I'd see how
it went at the Academy.''

''And it went well,'' Noriko said.

''Yes,'' he said. ''It did. And sort of killed my budding
career as a pool shark.''

He turned back to the table, called his next shot, and
put it down the chute. On the juke ''Crossroads'' ended
and Vanilla Fudge's rendition of ''Keep Me Hangin' On''
keyed up. Noriko waited.

''You know Max Blackburn?'' Nimec asked, his eyes
moving over the table.

''Only by reputation,'' she said. ''He's supposed to be
the best at what he does. Ever since Politika, everybody's
been talking about him like he's Superman.''

Nimec saw a possible combination rail shot at the
eleven ball, and lined up for it.

''Max is a good man, no question,'' he said. ''Enjoys
connecting the dots to solve a problem, which is why I
often use him as a troubleshooter. The past six months
he's been assigned to the Johor Bharu ground station,
taking care of a range of things, some of which were,
shall we say, not for the record. And dicey.'' He looked
over his shoulder at Noriko. ''Almost a week ago he
dropped out of sight in Singapore, and nobody's heard
anything from him since.''

She watched him without saying anything.

''Max would never stay out of contact this long unless
something were very wrong,'' Nimec went on. ''He's too
dependable a man.''

He took his shot, but his wrist tensed at the last instant
and he stroked the cue harder than he'd wanted. The ball

missed the hole and caromed off the cushion, too fast, its angle too narrow.

"The dicey stuff Blackburn was doing," Noriko said in a slow, considering voice. "Is it something we can talk about?"

"Later, certainly," he said. "First, though, I need to know if you'd be willing to head out to where he is. Or was. And help me track him down."

"I get a team?"

"Just me," Nimec said. "If we need support we can get it from the Johor crew."

She looked at him.

"I'd understand if you don't want to get involved," he said. "Your participation would be strictly voluntary."

"And off the record," she said.

"Right."

There was a pause.

"One question," she said. "Was I asked on this job because I won't stick out in a crowd of Asians, or because of my experience in the field?"

"You sensitive about your ethnicity?"

"Sensitivity has nothing to do with it. I'm half Japanese. It's a logical question. Was it my slanted eyes or my ability?"

Nimec gave her a small, tight smile.

"Both," he said. "Your background might open some doors a little quicker. It might make certain things easier for us in certain situations, and with certain people. It's a leg up. But I wouldn't want you without knowing absolutely that I could trust you with my life, no matter how thick it gets."

She looked closely at his face a while, then nodded.

"I'm in," she said. "What's our game plan?"

"Step one, we finish playing pool. Step two, I clear our trip with Gordian. Step three, we go get our suitcases."

"And if the boss doesn't give us the go signal?"

Nimec considered that a moment.

"Max is my friend," he said. Firmly. "Which means we'd have to skip right on ahead to step three."

Early on the day Roger Gordian was scheduled to depart for Washington, he was joined by Chuck Kirby and Vince Scull in the glass-enclosed veranda of his Palo Alto home. The three of them were seated at a large cane table talking seriously over their breakfast, drinks, papers, and open briefcases. The morning was bright and warm, and there was a flower-scented breeze wafting in through the louvered panels. On a freestanding easel near the table was a chart Gordian had prepared for their meeting. His daughter Julia had stopped by to wish him luck in D.C., and brought the greyhounds with her, and she and Ashley were running them outside on the grass.

Gordian had just finished summarizing his plan, and could already see the unhappiness on Chuck's face. He waited until the attorney wasn't looking and checked his watch, thinking he had a good half hour before his third visitor showed, time enough to deal with Kirby's inevitable objections. Not that it would be easy.

He glanced out at the yard, bracing himself. Whipping downhill in pursuit of a tossed plastic rabbit, the dogs were curves of graceful motion against the greenness of the sprawling lawn. As usual Jack, the brindle male, had outsprinted Jill, the teal-blue female. Though both had been bred for the dog track, and Jill was sleeker and younger, her skittish temperament had disqualified her from competition, while Jack had run a great many races before he'd been retired.

Julia had gotten the dogs from a greyhound adoption program out of Orange County about six months ago. Had they not been rescued and placed, they would have been euthanized, which was the common practice of racetrack owners when their dogs were no longer competitive, whether for reasons of age, disposition, or any physical deficit that hampered their coursing performance. Gordian had been originally amazed to learn from his daughter that, on average, unadopted track dogs were retired and put down when they were five years old, having barely reached a third of their natural life expectancy . . . and always when he watched their spirited and energetic play, the amazement returned in its fullness.

After all the acts of inhumanity he'd seen people carry out on other people, all the personal losses he'd accumulated as a result of war and terrorism, Gordian didn't know why such waste—lesser by far in the grand scheme of things—ought to surprise him anymore. But it did, and somehow he felt that was better than if it hadn't.

He took a sip of his coffee, and listened to Kirby begin arguing that he was about to commit the worst blunder of his life.

"Gord, I've heard every word you've spoken and tried my damnedest to keep an open mind," Chuck said. "But to do what you've proposed before considering a less extreme strategy—"

"Sometimes you have to lose a limb to preserve the health of the body," Gordian said. "Sometimes survival itself depends on it."

Kirby shook his head. "You're talking about wholesale dismemberment," he said. "Not the same."

Gordian's clear blue eyes were so calm it was almost unsettling. *Like Moses after receiving the Ten Commandments,* Kirby thought.

"Chuck, I haven't said this would be painless. And because you're my friend, I believe that pain is the thing you're trying to spare me," he said. "But I've already accepted it, you see. Mentally and emotionally, I've already let go."

"*Let go?* Of everything you built up over a decade? Everything you've worked your ass off to—"

"If you stop for a second you'll realize you're overreacting," Gordian said with unassailable forbearance.

Chuck turned to Scull. "Vince? Is that what you think? I know your analysis is that Gord's plan is doable, but my question is really whether it *ought* to be done. Whether you're endorsing it."

Scull nodded affirmatively.

"All we're asking is that you give us a chance here," he said. "Listen to what the coach has to say."

"And look at my graphic while you're at it," Gordian said. "Please."

Kirby pressed his lips together, breathed deeply through his nose, and looked. It was an organizational chart of UpLink broken down according to the market areas served by its corporate divisions and subsidiaries.

"As you pointed out yourself, Chuck, we've grown tremendously since the early nineties," Gordian said after letting him study the diagram. "When we secured the contract to provide our GAPSFREE missile-targeting system to the military, I knew the company's future was assured, and realized I was in the position I'd been hoping to reach all my life. I was successful and financially se-

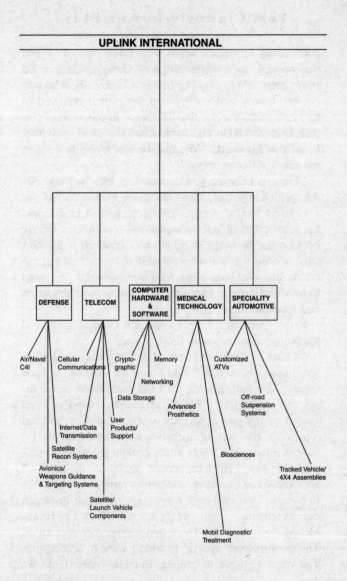

UPLINK INTERNATIONAL

DEFENSE

TELECOM

COMPUTER HARDWARE & SOFTWARE

MEDICAL TECHNOLOGY

SPECIALITY AUTOMOTIVE

Air/Naval C4I

Cellular Communications

Cryptographic

Memory

Customized ATVs

Networking

Data Storage

Off-road Suspension Systems

Internet/Data Transmission

User Products/ Support

Advanced Prosthetics

Satellite Recon Systems

Avionics/ Weapons Guidance & Targeting Systems

Biosciences

Tracked Vehicle/ 4X4 Assemblies

Satellite/ Launch Vehicle Components

Mobil Diagnostic/ Treatment

cure . . . my individual needs were taken care of . . . and that opened up a whole range of choices. Choices I'd never been able to consider before. Choices about how to put my money and energy into things that mattered to me, into making a positive difference in this world." He rose from the table and approached the easel, gesturing broadly at his chart. "My mistake was trying to do it in too many different ways."

"Heaven help us, you're sounding like Reynold Armitage," Kirby said. "And that gives me the chills."

Gordian smiled wanly. "We'd be foolish to discount his assessment of our strengths and weaknesses merely because the language in which he's couched it troubles us," he said. "It's always possible to learn from our enemies, and Armitage's essential point is valid. We need to look at the areas where we're bleeding away resources and liquidate them."

Kirby searched for a response, but Gordian continued speaking before he could think of one.

"Chuck, I'd be confident of our expertise in the defense business even if I didn't have the earnings to back me up," he said, placing his hand on the box at the diagram's upper left. "We're the best because I've been guided by my past experience as a combat pilot, and can remember the sort of technological improvements I'd have wanted when I was in the cockpit flying air strikes over Khe San." His hand moved one box to the right. "I also know our communications unit represents UpLink's tomorrow, irrespective of early-stage profits or losses on our investment . . . and that its potential has yet to be unlocked." He paused. "Those two are our core operations. The ones that are integral to what I want to accomplish. The ones we have to protect. But ask yourself, do we really belong in computers? Medical tech? Or how about specialty automotive? We only got into *that* because I wanted to make improvements to the factory-standard dune-hoppers we were using in our more rugged gateway locations.''

''Which you did.''

''And now that we've assembled a large fleet of vehicles, and our competition has incorporated our modifications into their own product—and in some cases outclassed us, if you want my frank opinion—why not release the company to management who can give it proper guidance? After all, its profitability as an UpLink company has been been marginal from the very beginning.''

Kirby rubbed the back of his neck.

''I don't know,'' he said. ''Putting aside the automotive unit for a minute, you've done well in the other supposedly nonessential areas. Just as a for-instance, the prosthetics subsidiary meets both of your fundamental criteria for an UpLink company. It helps people and makes money. The artificial limbs it produces are first-rate and have captured a respectable share of the global market—''

''And I'm very proud of that,'' Gordian said. ''But my passion and knowledge don't lay in medicine. I've short-changed the division in terms of personal attention, and have never quite gotten my market bearings. And the R&D budget for our biotech firm eats up something like forty million a year.''

''Which is not at all excessive,'' Kirby said. ''Your people are working on new drug therapies for everything from male impotence to cancer. Cutting-edge research costs money, but the financial and humanitarian payoff from a single major pharmaceutical advance certainly justifies the initial expenses.''

''I'd agree with you if this were a normal, as opposed to a predatory, business environment,'' Gordian said. ''The fact, however, is that we are under attack and need to focus. Because the medical division is in the red, it is lowering the valuation of UpLink's shares. As it stands, if I want the medical operation to continue, my choices are to either slash its budget or sustain it with the profits we earn from, say, our avionics branch. Money that could otherwise go toward higher-performance transmitters and receivers for our cellular network, or reducing the debts we incurred after the Russian debacle . . . and face it, Chuck, those are just two of many obvious examples I could offer.''

Kirby drank his Bloody Mary and was quiet a while. On the lawn one of the greyhounds had caught the plastic rabbit and flashed behind an alderberry bush, where it was throttling the toy between its jaws. The sound of its squeaker had apparently gotten the other dog envious, and it was jumping antic circles around the hedge. Standing nearby, Ashley Gordian and her daughter looked like they were having fun.

He wished he could have said the same for himself.

''Gord, listen to me,'' Kirby said at length. ''If I read you correctly, your strategy for averting a takeover is based on the assumption that the value of UpLink stock, and thus shareholder confidence, will be boosted once you've gotten back to basics and released capital to your most profitable ventures. Ordinarily I'd agree that it's a sound defensive approach, since a higher corporate valuation will curb sell-offs, force up a hostile acquirer's bid, and make him wonder if his move is worth the trouble and drain on his checkbook. Except this is *no* ordinary situation. Marcus Caine has already obtained a large chunk of UpLink stock. He's committed. Furthermore, UpLink's market decline has less to do with any real or perceived overdiversification than with investor fears that your stance on crypto will put you way behind rivals who are eager to sell overseas. And since you're obviously not going to sell off your cryptography firm—''

''Who says?'' Gordian interrupted, the patient, forbearing expression back on his face.

Kirby looked at him a moment, then turned briefly toward Vince Scull.

''Both of you *are* shitting me here, right?'' he said.

Scull shook his head.

Taken aback, Kirby waited a minute before saying anything more.

''Gord, I don't understand,'' he said disbelievingly. ''You've fought so hard to maintain control of your cryptographic technology . . . to turn it over to someone else . . . to chance that it will be distributed abroad . . .'' He spread his hands. ''You've never quit a fight before. I can't believe you'd do it under any circumstances.''

''Not *just* any,'' Gordian said. ''Chuck, I—''

Gordian broke off, his eyes going to the sliding doors that opened from the house to the veranda. Andrew, his domestic, had appeared with Richard Sobel, the third guest he'd been expecting for breakfast.

''Sir, I've shown Mr. Sobel in as you asked,'' Andrew said.

''Morning,'' Sobel said, tipping the other men a wave.

Gordian motioned him to an empty chair at the table. ''You're right on schedule, Rich,'' he said. ''Join the party.''

Kirby gave Gordian a level glance, saw his spreading grin, and suddenly understood everything.

"You can relax now, Chuck," Gordian said, his smile growing even larger. "Our White Knight has arrived to save the day."

EIGHTEEN

THE FAX WAS ON SIAN PO'S DESK WHEN HE CAME INTO work that morning—a dispatch out of Central HQ advising of a nationwide police search for an American named Max Blackburn, and accompanied by a passport photograph and some sketchy details about the circumstances of his disappearance. All personnel were to be on alert for information regarding his whereabouts, and immediately relay it to CID. The same notice, Sian Po knew, would have been forwarded to the divisional headquarters at Clementi, Tanglin, Ang Mo Kio, Bedock, and Jurong, as well as to hundreds of command center and vehicular computer stations over the Incident Based Information System.

Wishing to remain undisturbed, the commander immediately buzzed his receptionist, instructed her to hold his calls for the next half hour, and read the dispatch over a cup of green tea. It contained only a few brief paragraphs about last week's mysterious scene outside the Hyatt, and they conveyed little that was new to him. However, the material about the parties involved was most intriguing. There were fuller descriptions of the men who had accosted the American . . . and most importantly, there was the profile of Blackburn himself. Printed beside his photo, it included data about his age, general physical chacteristics, and employer, a satcom outfit called UpLink International operating in the Johor area.

Sian Po drank his tea and reflected back on his stroll in the park with Fat B. What in the world was the club owner into? His nose told him it was something big.

He set down his cup, thinking. The report was as interesting for what it didn't reveal as what it did, and had put several questions into his mind. There was nothing to indicate where the facts about Max Blackburn and the other men had come from. And no mention of the woman Sian Po had heard was involved. Why? Could it be that she was the source of the information? That she'd been located and was perhaps being kept under wraps? CID investigators were customarily tight-lipped, quick to mark their turf, and loath to accept assistance from other departments in the Force. It was conceivable those bastards knew where she was or had her in custody—or under police protection, whichever. If they did, they would not share that secret with anyone at ground level. Not as long as they could help it.

Still, Sian Po had his useful contacts, including a supervisor in intelligence who would be glad to talk to him for a cut of his own payoff from Fat B. And Fat B had strongly hinted the sum would be considerable. He had to be careful, though. Ask what he needed to ask without divulging too much in exchange. The main thing was to find out about the woman, find out where she was. For now that would be a sufficiently juicy morsel to pass along. He would see what else might develop afterward.

Placing the report on his desk beside his teacup, he reached for the phone and made his call.

• • •

Nimec managed to catch Gordian in his office at a quarter
past eleven in the morning. The boss was rushed, and
expectedly so; he'd arrived late after a business parley at
his home, and only planned to stay long enough to take
care of some odds and ends before leaving for the airport.
Vince Scull, Chuck Kirby, Richard Sobel, and Megan
Breen—the four of whom were flying to D.C. as passengers in Gordian's Learjet—had already driven on ahead
in a company car, and the hurried atmosphere had made
it all the more difficult for Nimec to tell him about Blackburn . . . and then persuade him to green-light a trip overseas so he could look into what was going on with Max.

Harder than either, however, was disclosing that he'd
let Max undertake a hidden probe into Monolith-
Singapore's books without first seeking Gordian's consent
. . . the unstated but clearly understood reason being that
had it been a sure thing the idea would have been
scotched out of hand.

Gordian's reaction to the news about Max—and Nimec's admission—was a predictable mix of anger, dismay, and concern.

"It's beyond me how you could have been part of
something this reckless, Pete," he said. He was leaning
forward with his right elbow on his desk blotter, his head
tilted slightly downward, rubbing the corner of his eye
with his index finger. "Completely beyond me."

Nimec looked at him from across the desk.

"I'm sorry," he said. "I won't try to justify it. But
consider the big picture. Marcus Caine had been using the
crypto bill to impale you in the press. And Blackburn
believed Monolith was engaged in a series of illegal business practices and hiding evidence of it in Singapore. It
was reasonable to suspect some of those activities might

have been aimed at causing damage to UpLink—''

''So instead of coming to me with those suspicions, the two of you launched a caper that could have easily sunk us in quicksand. And likely has, from what you're saying.''

Nimec was quiet for a minute, then nodded.

''Yes, we should've notified you, and we didn't,'' he said. ''It was a stupid mistake. And I'm afraid to think about how dearly Max may be paying for it.''

Silence.

Gordian was still leaning against the edge of his desk, massaging the corner of his eye with his fingertip.

''Let's back up a second,'' he said. ''You're convinced Blackburn's in some kind of trouble?''

Nimec gave him another nod.

''And you want to go extricate him from it.''

''If I can,'' Nimec said. ''With some help.''

Gordian shook his head. ''It's tough for me to believe Caine's people would go so far as to harm Max. Regardless of what he might have gotten wind of.''

Nimec moved his shoulders. ''We can't make assumptions about how much Caine might or might not know. Or who his people are. Or what sort of people *they're* involved with.''

Gordian placed both hands on his desk and studied them, his lips pressed together.

''It's a hell of a time for me to make this sort of decision,'' he said, looking up at Nimec. ''I'm flying to Washington in a little while. And I've got my mind on other matters beside that.''

''Caine's hostile bid,'' Nimec said.

''Yes.''

There was another period of silence. It fell over them with a weight that was almost palpable.

"All right," Gordian said finally. "See what you can do. But if something comes up, you'd damned well better consult with me. I lost too many good men and women in Russia to tolerate anyone in this organization taking unnecessary chances."

Nimec breathed.

"Thanks," he said, rising from his chair. "I only regret not being able to join you in D.C. You'll have a crack security detail, but it's going to be a madhouse."

Remaining seated, Gordian looked at him and shrugged dismissively.

"Just be careful to watch your own back," he said. "My guess is I won't be facing anything deadlier than potshots from reporters."

Nimec offered a thin smile.

"Probably right," he said. "But somebody's got to worry."

"Marcus, what's wrong?"

"Nothing."

"Obviously *something's* wrong."

"Give it time. I need to relax."

Lying in bed with Caine amid the restored deco furnishings of their room at the Hotel De Anza, her face beside his on the pillow, her naked body pressed against him, Arcadia Foxworth licked her fingertip and slid her hand under the sheets, tracing a slow line of moisture down his stomach.

He lay there, tense and unresponsive.

"Tell me," she said, raising her head off the pillow. "Is there somebody else?"

"Only you," he said distractedly.

"Well . . ."

"Well, what?"

"There's your wife," she said. "She's one I know of, anyway."

He broke off his thoughts and looked at her.

"What's that supposed to mean?" he said. "Must you be jealous of Odeille?"

"Hardly," she said. "It isn't important what you do with her when we're not together. But when we are, I want you here. Thinking about me."

"Arcadia," he said, "let's not argue."

"I'm not arguing."

"Then let's not continue with whatever sort of conversation we're having. I've been under a great deal of pressure lately. That's all there is to it."

She looked at him, easing closer over the mattress, the bare white flesh of her breasts against his shoulder.

"Okay," she said, taking him into her hand, tightening her fingers around him beneath the sheet. "Usually, though, it's pressure that gets you going."

He lay there on his back, very still, staring past her face at the ceiling. What was he supposed to say? That his dealings with Nga had taken him over a line he'd never expected to cross? That he'd been coerced into ordering the *murder* of Roger Gordian—and Lord knew who else would be on that plane—and would soon have blood on his hands? Would *that* help her understand why he wasn't feeling especially aroused?

"Stop," he said abruptly. "It isn't happening."

"I've come two thousand miles from New York to be with you," she said.

"Nobody twisted your arm."

Her eyes widened. She pushed away from him, her hand retreating from where she'd had it, grabbing the sheet, tugging it up over her chest.

"You son of a bitch," she said.

Caine threw his legs over the side of the bed and strode naked across the room to the chair on which he'd put his clothing. He kept his back to her as he silently got dressed.

"Aren't you going to say anything?" Arcadia said. She had sat up against the headboard.

He waited until he was fully clothed before turning to answer.

"Yes," he said. "I'm thinking that you're right. I should be honest about what's bothering me. You *deserve* honesty."

She looked at him.

He didn't know why he said what next came out of his mouth, other than that it made him feel better, released some of his pent-up anxiety and frustration.

"You're lovely, Arcadia. First-class. But you've walked a long road from the streets of Argentina, and I like my women younger," he said. "The simple fact is that you don't excite me anymore."

Her mouth actually dropped open. She looked as if she'd been slapped.

It occurred to Caine that he might have gone further than he'd intended, that there was little chance she would ever want to see him again after this ugly scene.

Once more over the line, he thought. Yet strangely, it didn't seem to matter . . . although *why* it didn't was a question he'd have to consider later on.

"Don't bother yourself about the hotel tab, I'll take care of it," he said.

And turned from her shocked face, opened the door, and left the room.

NINETEEN

"LOCAL TRAFFIC, LEARJET TWO ZERO NINE TANGO
Charlie, ready to go off Runway Two at the east end,"
Gordian was saying into his mike, informing any nearby
multicom users of his departure. The small private airfield
UpLink shared with a handful of other Silicon Valley
firms had no ground radio facilities, but the nationwide
advisory frequency of 122.9 was often monitored by pilots, and his practice was to broadcast his takeoff and
landing intentions as a courtesy to them and a hedge
against unwanted—and potentially disastrous—midair
encounters.

Not that it looked as if there would be anything but
smooth flying today. With a clear blue sky, high ceiling,
and gentle winds, Gordian was anticipating a takeoff into
ideal weather conditions. His only fillip of concern, and
very slight concern at that, had come when he'd lowered
his flaps while taxiing and noticed the hydraulic-pressure
gauge drop off a hair more readily than normal.

This was something a less cautious pilot probably
wouldn't have detected, nor found of much interest if he
had, and quite understandably so. Gordian himself
couldn't see any reason to worry. Though the aircraft's
flaps, speed brakes, and landing gear all operated on the

same hydraulic line, they would continue to respond properly, if perhaps a bit slowly, with the fluid level on the low side. Further increasing his confidence was the knowledge that his engine instrument-and-crew-alerting system—or EICAS—annunciators would flash a warning to indicate a problem with the circuit, serious or otherwise. And they had remained dark.

Still, he couldn't help but feel disappointed in Eddie, who'd inspected the plane the day before, and was usually an even bigger stickler for safety than he was . . . too thorough to let even a minor abnormality slip past his attention.

But later for that, he thought. As always in the moments before going airborne, Gordian could feel the sky exerting an almost physical pull. Moving the throttles forward, he concentrated on the EFIS panel in front of him, his eyes shifting between its flat-screen primary flight displays—arranged in the same ''standard T'' of old-fashioned analog instruments—and the bars of his ITT gauge, which measured the internal temperature of the turbofans. A hot start could lead to engine failure within seconds, making the ITT readout one to watch carefully.

Nothing to trouble him on that score; the turbos were operating well within standard limitations.

Its compressors whining and sucking in air, its wheels rumbling over the tarmac, the Learjet rolled up the centerline straight as an arrow. Gordian felt the shove of acceleration, and then the excitement that had accompanied each of the hundreds of takeoffs he'd flown over the past thirty years. He snapped his eyes to the window and quickly observed the distance markers along the runway—a feature as rare to civilian fields as it was common to military ones, and emplaced at Gordian's direction as a nod to his fighter-jock days.

Returning his attention to the EFIS, Gordian saw his virtual airspeed bug indicate that he had reached 104 knots, go-or-no-go speed. He conducted a last-minute check of the crucial displays. Everything was running smoothly, the bank of caution lights still out, his system readings A-okay. *Go.*

He released the stick, gripped the yoke with both hands, and rotated the jet to a seven-point-five-degree nose-up angle for liftoff. There was a slight jolt and another familiar tingle of excitement as his wheels left the pavement. His hands on the control column, Gordian increased his pitch to ten degrees and continued his ascent.

After several seconds he again looked outside to confirm what the altimeter and his own physical sensations had already told him. He had reached a positive rate of climb, the ground rapidly dwindling beneath him, the undivided blue of the sky pouring into his windshield.

His gear and flaps up, Gordian accelerated to two hundred KIAS, or over three hundred miles per hour. At a thousand feet he would very gradually trim airspeed until he attained cruising altitude.

Right now, though, it was time for an announcement to his passengers.

He switched on the cabin intercom.

"Vince, Megan, Rich, we're on our way," he said. "ETA in D.C. is nine o'clock. So make yourselves comfortable and try not to discuss business. There'll be plenty of time for that later." He reached for the "off" switch, thought about the chattery teeth Scull inevitably got when he flew, and added a few words for his benefit. "There's a bottle of Glenturret in the wet bar for anyone who wants it. Courtesy of your captain. Later, folks."

Smiling a little, feeling easier with himself than he had in weeks, Gordian cut the intercom and settled back into his pilot's chair for the trip.

In a drawing room at the Leominster country club in Southampton, Reynold Armitage was gazing out the window at the ocean. It was a drab, chill day in eastern Long Island, and the threat of rain had driven the gulls close to shore. They wheeled in erratic circles, their wings tearing ragged holes in the stationary film of mist that had settled over the beach and jetties. Distantly across the water, Armitage could see a lighted buoy twinkling bright and red.

Ensconced in the armchair opposite him, William Halpern released a long, heaving sigh. Wearing dark flannel pants and a herringbone blazer, he was a spare, white-haired man in his mid-fifties with an undershot chin and virtually neutral complexion.

"Awful outside, isn't it?" he said in a haughty Connecticut Yankee accent. "The forecast was for sunny and warm, you know."

Using his wheelchair's joystick control, Armitage swiveled around to face his host. He was feeling winded from the dampness, which exacerbated the respiratory problems associated with his condition. The mere act of breathing was a reminder of the limitations of his failing body. Yet from the way the president and chief executive of MetroBank seemed to take the bad weather as a personal affront, one would think *he* was the man in poor health.

"It's difficult to make predictions for the shore," Armitage said. "Don't bother yourself about it, William. I'm hardly up to a stroll on the beach, and found the ride in your corporate helicopter to be quite entertaining."

"I'm glad," Halpern said, although he still had the look of someone who had booked reservations at an exclusive restaurant and found his meal to be a cold disappointment. He glanced out the window again and then settled back, appearing resigned and vaguely disgusted, as if realizing there were no one in charge of the climate to whom he might complain. "I wanted a discreet and quiet spot for our meeting, you see."

Armitage said nothing. There were, he thought, any number of quiet places in Manhattan where they could have met with greater convenience. But even in their elevated circles a Leominster membership was a glowing symbol of status, and Halpern obviously liked to showcase it. He was also well aware of the attention being paid to Marcus Caine's grab for UpLink voting stock, and with MetroBank retaining a significant percentage of the company, wouldn't want to start rumors flying by being seen with Roger Gordian's most noted media critic.

No, there was nothing mysterious about Halpern's desire to meet where they were. The real question for Armitage was why he'd wanted to get together in the first place. And with their mannerly preliminaries out of the way, he wasn't about to kill time waiting for an answer.

"So," he said. "What gossip about the financial community can we exchange? Let's think of something blisteringly hot and in the news. Something that gets flashbulbs popping. Shall we?"

Halpern looked at him.

"There's Monolith and UpLink," Armitage said with an arid little smile. "Not to mention UpLink and Monolith."

Halpern seemed perplexed by his sarcasm. "I've sat down with some of the men on MetroBank's executive board to discuss liquidating our UpLink shares," he said. "Prior to a formal meeting, you understand."

"And?"

"The consensus to go ahead with the sell-off hasn't materialized as I'd expected."

"Interesting," Armitage said.

"It gets more interesting," Halpern said. "As you know, I have no allegiance to Roger Gordian, and think his mission to save the world by planting a wireless telephone booth in every garden is nothing but horse crap."

"You're mixing metaphors," Armitage said. "And being a tad reductionist about his goals, wouldn't you say?"

Halpern shrugged. "Call it what you will, I am concerned with MetroBank's stake in his corporation only insofar as its profitability, or lack of same. But there are directors on the board who feel a personal loyalty to the man, and have been reluctant to part ways with UpLink despite the diminishing returns on our investment. Before yesterday, though, I'd convinced most of them that hanging tight would be an abdication of their fiduciary responsibilties."

"And what's changed that?"

"Not 'what,' but 'who,'" Halpern said. "Gordian himself phoned three senior executives. He requested they hold off on considering any offer from Marcus Caine until he's had a chance to meet with them."

Armitage wondered if he was expected to be surprised.

"A sensible preemptive move," he said. "And one with nothing behind it. As long as UpLink's value continues to deteriorate, your board is obliged to take a serious look at Marcus's bid. Money, not loyalty or misplaced faith in Roger Gordian, is what will count in the final tally."

"And Gordian has promised to address shareholder doubts about UpLink's future at his press conference tomorrow," Halpern said. "He assured the directors he would be making a major, positive announcement. And that they would, at the very least, want to reassess their options after hearing what he has to say."

This time Armitage raised his eyebrows.

"I thought his reason for going to Washington was to protest the Morrison-Fiore legislation," he said.

"So did I," Halpern said. "And I'll tell you something else. His top securities attorney caught a red-eye out to San Jose last night. Canceled all his other appointments at the last minute."

"How do you know?"

Halpern stared at him.

"I have my contacts," he said, shrugging again. "You . . . and Marcus . . . can take my word for it. Something's in the air."

Armitage inhaled. His chest felt tight. If the feeling persisted, he would have to page his nurse into the room and be administeed a respiratory dilator. He felt a sudden bolt of hatred, and wasn't sure why. Nor was he even certain toward whom it was directed.

Outside the window a seabird emitted a shrill, ribboning cry as it plunged through the low veil of fog.

He looked at Halpern.

"I appreciate the tip, William," he said. "But the one thing you haven't told me is where you come down in this."

Halpern crossed his legs and was silent a moment.

"We've known each other for years, and you've always given me sound financial advice," he said finally. "But as you said yourself, this business is about money, not loyalty or faith . . . and like all bankers, I'm an agnostic.''

"Meaning you'll be listening to Roger Gordian's statement before deciding whether to stay behind the bid.''

Halpern nodded, brushing a speck of lint off his trousers.

"Yes,'' he said without hesitation. "And very closely.''

On a stubby finger of rock jutting off his island base's ocean side, Kersik stared out across the benighted water at the lights of Sandakan Harbor. Restless, he had left camp alone, thinking the freshness of the breeze would somehow dispel his somber mood, but instead it had made him feel worse. He supposed it was his knowledge of the violence that soon would be launched from his pristine shoreline, the deaths that were inevitably to come. There would be dozens, perhaps hundreds . . . if not many, many more. For a just cause, yes, or anyway a cause in which he squarely believed. But wasn't that the same ancient, self-righteous madness which drove every act of war?

Men fought. They had always fought, whether armed with stones, arrows, guns, or nuclear torpedoes. And they found their reasons. Indeed, Kersik sometimes felt that belief in a cause was nothing but a dark funnel into which both heroes and villains leaped with equal certitude, all tumbling together like clown players in a circus. Like the man who presently ruled Indonesia as if he were a Javanese king, parsing the nation's wealth out to his courtesans . . . like his predecessor, and Suharto, and those who had come before them, Kersik saw himself as being on the right side of history. Zhiu Sheng, Nga, Luan, they too were *right* from their individual perspectives—and yet the forces that had moved them into alignment were far too complex to be defined by absolutes.

Kersik's brow creased above his bushy eyebrows. Wasn't the judgment of right or wrong only a matter of who survived to render the verdict when the smoke cleared and the spilled blood of the dead was washed away? He had renounced his allegiance to his country's government and was about to place himself in defiance of ASEAN, Japan, and the United States. The entire world, really. Before all was said and done, he would be called a rogue, an international pariah. And what would he think of *himself* in the end? Might a division ultimately form in his own mind . . . half of him feeling validated, half condemned?

Kersik gazed out at the lights of a city that in the last 150 years had been governed once by the Germans, twice by the British, and exploited by traders, gunrunners, and timber lords from diverse corners of the globe. That during World War II was invaded by the Japanese and leveled by American bombs . . . and that now literally and ironically held the keys to the fate of both those nations.

Kersik stood and thought and looked out across the ocean swells . . . and after a while became dimly aware of a scurrying in the mangrove thicket behind him.

He turned, snapping on his flashlight, his right hand falling to the holstered Makarov at his waist. The sound had not really alarmed him; the only men on the island were the Thai's seawolves and his own commando units, and both groups had lookouts posted along the shore. Still, he was beyond all else a soldier . . . and good soldiers had cautious habits.

He trained the beam of his flash at eye level, saw nothing but smooth, gangling mangrove trunks and prop roots, and lifted it higher. Just below the leaf cover, a flying lemur clung to the bark and watched him with huge orb-like eyes.

For a moment Kersik experienced a queer, almost dizzying transference, imagining how he might appear to the strange little creature—clumsily threatening, out of place, himself the real alien. He withdrew his hand from his pistol grip as if it were red-hot, feeling an intense and incomprehensible guilt.

The creature studied him for another second or two with its perfectly round eyes, and then spread its flight membranes and kited off into the forest blackness.

Shaken and hardly knowing why, Kersik stepped into the brush and walked back toward camp.

As one of the test pilots of the original Learjet had told Gordian about its maiden run, the flight had gone better than expected and he'd expected it to go well.

That about said it for the trip to Washington.

Now, approaching Dulles International Airport at 8,500 feet and 350 knots downwind, autopilot off, the night sky clear and moonlit, Gordian cross-checked the Global Positioning System and VOR windows on his horizontal-situation indicator for a course fix, then radioed ahead to request airspace clearance.

"Washington, Learjet Two Zero Nine Tango Charlie, over Alexandria VOR at eight thousand, landing Dulles. Squawking one two zero zero," he said, finishing his initial communique with the standard numeric identification code for civilian aircraft.

A moment later the traffic controller responded, providing the computer code by which his radar-beacon system would differentiate Gordian's plane from other aircraft in the vicinity as it was guided down.

"Good evening Nine Tango, Washington Approach. Squawk five zero eight one and ident. Radar contact established, cleared into Washington Class B airspace. Descend and maintain four thousand."

"Roger. Learjet Nine Tango, squawking five zero eight one. Understand cleared into the TCA. Out of eight for four."

The buildings and illuminated landing strips of Dulles in sight below, Gordian trimmed power and entered a steady sink, carefully monitoring the instrument panel, making small heading corrections as he descended. Less than ten minutes later he again contacted the man on the ground floor.

"Approach, Learjet Nine Tango, level at four."

"Learjet Nine Tango, roger. Am familiar and would like Runway One Four Left."

"Cleared for approach One Four Left," the Approach controller began after a brief pause, then vectored and sequenced him into the lineup of arriving aircraft.

Not at all to Gordian's surprise, Approach concluded the transmission by informing him he would have to hold and circle at four thousand feet. In D.C. and other major cities, the terminal environment was often stacked with inbound traffic, in which instances one could look forward to a tedious wait.

He re-engaged the auto and informed his passengers they would have time for at least a couple of Scull's equally tedious jokes.

It was twenty-five minutes before the controller assigned a further descent altitude and then handed Gordian over to the tower—not as long as it might have taken, although he was still glad to be out of the pattern. The repetitive banking maneuver had been tiresome, and gobbled up more fuel than he would have preferred.

He switched to the tower frequency and identified himself.

"Learjet Two Zero Nine Tango Charlie cleared to land Runway One Four Left," the ATC acknowledged.

Gordian took the wind headings from him, rogered, and then read down the items on his computerized final checklist, mentally ticking them off to the line above Gear and Flaps. Although it sometimes seemed he had memorized the various checklist tasks when he was still in diapers, Gordian conscientiously ran through it before, during, and immediately after each flight. To do otherwise would be to deny his own fallibility, and that was not a mistake he ever intended to make—most especially not at the risk of people's lives.

Gordian returned his attention to the HSI, saw that he was coming in range of his final landing fix, and prepared to resume his checklist procedures. At just below six hundred feet and about a mile west of the runway, he was set to enter the base leg, and could see the brightly lit sprawl of the airfield in easy detail.

He pulled down the lever to deploy his wheels, expecting to feel the mild thump of the gear mechanisms lowering through the doors.

Instead the red master warning light suddenly illuminated.

The landing gear alerts on his EICAS began to flash.

An electronic alarm tone sounded from an overhead speaker.

Gordian's eyes widened. The breath catching in his throat, he pulled the landing gear handle up, then down again.

The red lights kept blinking.

The horn kept blatting into the silence of the cockpit with deadly insistence.

Gordian felt his heart clench as the ground rushed closer and closer up on him, the runway spooling toward his windshield.

The wheels, he thought.

With less than two minutes to go until he hit the ground, the landing gear hadn't lowered.

TWENTY

WHETHER JAMMED TIGHTLY INTO THE COACH SEC-
tion of some ready-for-the-scrapyard commercial jetliner,
or, as was presently the case, hugged gently by a leather
club seat in Gordian's state-of-the-art executive Learjet,
Vince Scull was a white-knuckle flier all the way, no
matter that he had logged hundreds of hours in the air
fulfilling his professional responsibilities at UpLink.

A lot of risk-assessment people, especially those whose
job it was to research international markets, relied on
second- or third-hand source material—news reports, so-
ciological studies, statistical reviews, and so on. Scull,
however, thought that was for slackers who might as well
have spent their time picking their underwear out of their
cracks as writing up analyses. In his opinion, if you
wanted to learn about a place, you went there, breathed
the air, ate the food, and if you were lucky, kissed a few
of the local *frauleins* or *signoras*. And, unfortunately, if
you wanted to get to the foreign country you wanted to
learn about, you had to fly.

So he flew. Which didn't mean he had to like it, or
pretend to anyone else that zipping around the world the
way he did merited flight wings, unless maybe they were
the ones that belonged to that Greek kid Zorro or Aesop

or whoever it was that went too close to the sun and got his tail feathers fried.

It was during the takeoffs and landings that Scull always had his worst anxiety attacks, mainly because somebody had once told him they were the times at which the airfoils were under the most stress from physical forces . . . not that he knew shit about physics or flying, except that it seemed there *were* more accidents at those critical stages than when the planes were under way, so maybe there was something to what he'd heard.

Be that as it may, the reason Scull was now gripping the armrest of his seat like a convict in the electric chair waiting for somebody to turn on the juice was that Gordian was making his final approach into Washington, one of those very stages of air travel that scared the living crap out of him, never mind the boss was an Air Force–certified Flying Ace. It was also why he was crooning a jumbled medley of Sinatra hits under his breath—*the summer wind came blowin' in across New York, New York, ring-a-ding and doobie-doo*—serenading himself with old standards being another tried-and-true Scullian method of coping with tension and blocking the unwanted from his mind.

He did not care if he would have to endure ribbing about his nervousness from Megan Breen, who was sitting just across the narrow aisle to his right. Nor did he care if he heard about it from Nat Sobel or Chuck Kirby, who were immediately behind him, bullshitting with Meg like a couple of makeout artists at a cocktail party instead of helpless prisoners of a tin can that just happened to be capable of shooting through the troposphere at close to Mach One, the fucking speed of sound.

All he really *did* care about was reaching *terra firma*

in one piece, and the rest of them could keep the Glen-turret, which had admittedly gone down nicely, although his personal favorite malt was this brand from far western Scotland called Bunahabhain, an unpronounceable name that always left his mouth sounding like something Ralph Kramden might have said when Alice caught him red-handed in a lie. . . .

Clutching his seat, singing quietly off-key with his eyes shut, Scull was trying his best to remain oblivious to the plane's descent when a sound from the cockpit—the slid-ing door to which was partially open because Gord had been talking to Chuck about something earlier in the fight—bored into his awareness like a drill bit.

He snapped open his eyes and peered into the cockpit. From the position at which he was sitting, he could see about half of Gordian's back, and about the same amount of the pilot's console. The boss didn't seem to be in any kind of panic, but that didn't mean anything. This was the guy with the cool head and bombardier eyes, the guy who had been released from a five-year getaway at the Hanoi Hilton, their special all-the-torture-you-can-take package, with his head high and his back straight and his lips sealed as tightly as the day of his involuntary check-in. This was definitely the guy you wanted beside you in the proverbial foxhole, and if something was wrong, you would never be able to tell from looking at him.

But the noise coming from the cockpit, the noise was like an electronic version of an automobile horn, a grat-ingly repetitive *blaat-blaat-blaat* that damned well sounded to Scull like a warning alarm.

He looked at Megan, glanced around at Richard and Chuck. All three of them were also trying to see into the cabin, and their faces said they were, if not quite as

253

worried as he was, then still pulling high Nielsen distress ratings.

Blaat-blaat-blaat-blaat . . .

"Anybody know what the hell's going on?" he asked in a loud voice. "Christ in a barrel, what's that *noise?*"

The others were silent.

Scull swallowed. His palms felt suddenly moist. And no goddamned wonder.

Coming from a plane full of talkers, that mute silence had frightened him more than just about anything he could have imagined.

Gordian breathed, filling his lungs with oxygen, his mind working rapidly. He was belting toward the runway at over a hundred feet a second without wheels, a situation that would have the gravest consequences unless he took action to change it. Which left no room for indecision.

Think logically, he told himself. *The problem's evident, now isolate its cause.*

He recalled the unusually quick drop in hydro pressure when he'd extended the flaps on takeoff. Yet if the pump motor had failed, the crew-alerting system would have detected it. Ditto if the sensors had gotten readings that indicated a low fluid level in the reservoir. Furthermore, the compressed nitrogen inside the fluid accumulator was supposed to provide supplemental pressure to system components in the event of leakage . . . within a certain threshold. When the fluid loss from a specific component became too great, or there was too much air in the line, it would be unable to keep up with demand and bring the pressure back to where it should be.

Meaning what? Gordian gnawed his bottom lip. Meaning he was looking at a drastically reduced fluid level—and therefore a sudden and unmanageable demand—in a particular area of the system, possibly the landing gear actuator cylinder. The gear had a mechanical uplock that wouldn't release without hydro power, even with the lever in the down position . . . and there was no manual override.

Okay, next. Options.

He could Mayday the ground facility, wait for them to foam the runway and bring fire and medical crews to the scene should he need to make a gear-up landing. But having to circle the field had depleted his fuel reserve, and foaming took time. While he had enough Jet A in his nacelles to safely abort and execute a go-round, he didn't believe he could stay in the air long enough for the process to be completed. In which case he would have to belly onto the pavement, something that would very likely spark an explosive engine fire and leave little but ashes for the ground crews to clean up.

Come on, come on. You want to avoid a messy outcome, get to the essence of all this.

He had compromised hydraulics. Gear assemblies stuck in the up position. And an urgent need to bring them down.

No, wait. Not down. Off.

He had to be precise in his thinking. What the hydraulic pressure really did was keep the gear assemblies in the retracted position by making them rest on the uplocks. If he could only get the assemblies *off* the uplock brackets, their own weight load would finish the task, causing them to drop through the well doors. In other words, they would bring *themselves* down.

Gravity.

Gravity was the problem, and it was also the solution. Gordian reached for a selector button under his multifunction display and punched up the G-meter screen. The bar was level at one-G—which meant the gravitational force on the aircraft was "normal," or equivalent to that of an object at rest on the ground.

Shooting a glance at the display, Gordian reduced flaps, gripped the control column with both fists, and pulled back on it abruptly, tilting up the nose of the plane, hauling it into a sharp climb. An instant later he shoved *forward* on the column, dropping the plane toward the runway again.

Gordian's stomach lurched. The airframe shimmied around him. The roller-coaster bump in altitude thrust him back and down into his seat, then up and out so violently he would have smashed into the windshield had he not been strapped in.

So far, so good.

He reached for the landing gear lever, not bothering to check the MFD. With his bottom floating off his seat as if he were being hauled up by an invisible hand, Gordian already knew he was at zero-G. And if he'd reckoned correctly, he would not be the only thing floating.

The gear would be too.

Right off the uplock.

Praying that God, Sir Isaac Newton, and his own common sense were at oneness, he pulled the lever down for the third and last time.

The wide band of his seat belt cutting into his flabby middle, his eyeglasses first clamping down on the bridge of his nose and then flying off his face, his thin fringe of hair flattening out and then sticking straight up, Scull felt like the ball in some maniacal game of ping-pong.

Buffeted by wildly shifting Gs, the cabin pitched and

shook. Magazines swept past him in a tumultuous flap. His eyes large with fear and confusion, he saw Megan's briefcase shoot up the carpeted aisle like a stone skipping over water, followed by a file folder Chuck Kirby had been perusing behind her, paper spewing from inside it. A banana somebody had been eating was next, then a pen that fired past like a small missile. He heard bottles of liquor, soda, and spring water clank and rattle in the wet bar, heard Richard Sobel uncharacteristically shouting out invective. Carry bags whumped against the interior of overhead storage bays.

"*Shit!*" he screamed, attaching his own contribution to Sobel's sting of epithets.

Suddenly he heard a thump under his feet.

Several thumps.

Pure, unalloyed terror leaped into his throat, jetted icily up his spine.

He stopped yelling.

Certain he was going to perish, Scull suddenly remembered that he wasn't alone, remembered there were four other people in the plane with him and—call him a dinosaur chauvinist, what was the fucking difference now anyway?—realized one of them was a woman who might need comforting.

Thinking he would do what he could, he turned toward Megan, reaching out to grip her hand—

And was stunned to see relief beaming from her face.

"It's okay, Vince, calm down," she said, leaning toward him, *her* hand falling gently over *his* wrist. "Listen, the cockpit alarm's stopped."

"Huh?"

"The alarm," she repeated slowly. "It's stopped. We're landing."

He perked his ears. It had indeed stopped. And so had the rocking. But what had those thumping noises been about?

Suddenly the intercom crackled to life.

"Everyone, I'm sorry for the jostling. There was a little problem releasing the landing gear, but our wheels are down now and we're fine," he heard Gordian say, as if in answer to his unvoiced question.

"Landing gear," he muttered.

"What?" Megan said. "Couldn't hear you."

He looked down at where she was still holding his arm, and smiled.

"Just saying I love you, too, babycakes," he said.

TWENTY-ONE

WASHINGTON, D.C./SOUTHEAST ASIA
SEPTEMBER 25/26, 2000

FROM AN ASSOCIATED PRESS WIRE REPORT:

Washington, D.C.—UpLink International Chairman Roger Gordian and a group of core supporters have arrived for a news conference at the Washington Press Club scheduled to coincide with tomorrow's White House enactment of the Morrison-Fiore cryptographic deregulatory bill. It is thought Gordian will restate his well-known opposition to the bill, a stance which has drawn criticism from many quarters of the government and high-tech industry.

The stakes are high for Mr. Gordian amid reports of mounting and widespread stockholder discontent, and Monolith Technologies' recent bid for a large voting share of his corporation. Questioned by reporters soon after his self-piloted Learjet touched down at Dulles International Airport, the besieged defense and communications titan gave no comment on rumors that his press conference will include a surprise announcement of his resignation as CEO of UpLink.

President Ballard and his media aides, meanwhile, have chosen to downplay the crypto bill's significance, wishing instead to emphasize the President's visit to Asia later this week for the signing of the SEAPAC maritime defense treaty, an event to be held aboard an advanced nuclear submarine in Singapore's coastal waters. . . .

FROM THE *STRAITS TIMES:*

Body Found by Coastal Villagers

Banda Aceh, Indonesia—Local police authorities have reported the discovery of human remains by fishermen operating off Lampu'uk, a remote village at the nation's northernmost point, near a frequently traveled sea lane where the Straits of Melaka open into the Indian Ocean.

There has been no official word about the body's condition, nor any indication whether its identity has been established. However, eyewitnesses present when the corpse was found describe it as belonging to a male who had apparently been afloat at sea for some days.

A forensic examination to determine the cause of death is said to be pending.

While little else about the case is known, the International Maritime Bu-

reau and other regional investigatory
agencies are said to have been contacted. It is routine procedure for the
IMB and ASEAN law-enforcement
groups, who maintain close cooperative links and shared databases of persons reported missing or lost at sea, to
consult when handling incidents of this
type.

Gordian remained at the field after the others had gone
ahead to their hotel rooms and, accompanied by a couple
of Pete Nimec's security aces, met with the airframe and
power-plant mechanic at UpLink's leased hangar.

Minutes after being told what had happened to the gear,
the shocked A&P man was under the Learjet's wing on
a wooden creeper.

"No sign of exterior leakage, and the fittings seem to
be intact," he said now. "Wait, hold it a second, I want
to take a closer peek at something."

The mechanic ran the tips of his index and middle fingers over a spot at the bottom of the fuselage, closely
holding a flashlight on it with his other hand. Then he
rubbed the fingers against his thumb and sniffed them.

"Got a whiff of Skydol, and there's some on my finger
from outside the actuating cylinder." He pulled his head
out from beneath the plane to look up at Gordian. "Can't
tell anything from that alone, though, since you're always
going to have some minor fluid loss. I'm going to need
to get in and check the whole circuit. From the sequence
valves to the main system line."

Gordian squatted down beside him.

"I want to know what went wrong, Mike," he said.
Then, thinking about Max Blackburn, he decided to fol-

low a hunch. "Do me a favor and check for any signs of tampering, will you? Four people almost lost their lives today because of me. Four of my dearest friends."

Mike turned off the flash, rolled out from beneath the plane, and stood, wiping the fluid residue from his hand with a rag.

"Maybe this is only a groundhog's way of seeing it," he said, "but from what you told me a couple minutes ago, I'd say it was you who *saved* their lives, sir."

Gordian shook his head.

"It isn't a matter of perspective," he said tersely. "Federal aviation regulations state the pilot in command has ultimate accountability for the aircraft. And for the safety of its passengers. Makes no difference whether they were jeopardized because of a sloppy preflight in San Jose, a mechanical failure in the air, my own judgment, or a combination of factors. I am responsible for everything that happens in the air."

Mike looked at him without speaking.

"I got lucky, Mike," Gordian said, his face tight. "You understand? I just got lucky."

Mike swallowed and gave him a slow nod. "I won't leave this hangar till I've combed over the bird from top to bottom," he said.

Gordian briefly patted his arm. "Thanks. It's appreciated."

He turned to the pair of Sword ops.

"I'd like you to stick around here with Mike. Give him any help he needs."

The two security men exchanged glances.

Gordian could see they were unhappy with his order, which was understandable. Lean and serious and zonedin, they were professionals whose effectiveness hinged on rigorous discipline. Their assignment was to protect him, and it went against everything in their training and mental conditioning to ease up.

"It's okay, I'll be fine," he assured them. "I'm heading straight to my hotel room and plan to stay there all evening."

"Sir, we received direct orders from Mr. Nimec to stay with you," one of them said.

Gordian nodded. "I know, Tom," he said. "But if you don't tell him you left my side for a few hours, I won't either."

The bodyguard looked pensive.

"It would be best, sir, if we could check in with you over the phone this evening," he said.

"Certainly, but please try not to reach any premature conclusions if I don't answer," he said. "It's been a rough day, and I need a long shower and some sleep."

The bodyguard hesitated a moment, and Gordian resisted a smile. He'd suddenly remembered his paternal angst when Julia was a teenager going out on dates, and found himself amused despite his tension and lowering fatigue.

"Gentlemen, my car's waiting, and the driver must be getting impatient," he said. "I'll see you later."

Tom was quiet another moment, and then nodded, his expression a mixture of chagrin, worry, and vague disapproval.

"Have a good rest, sir," he said.

"I'll try," Gordian said.

And still wrestling back a smile, turned, flapped his arm up over his shoulder in a loose, weary wave, and strode out of the hangar.

• • •

"So, Alex, what I'm saying is that it looks like I can get you to dine with the POTUS and the other heads of state in the officers' wardroom."

"Is that what you're saying?" Nordstrum said.

"That is exactly what I'm saying," Stu Encardi said. "Right there in the belly of the beast we call Seawolf."

They were talking over a lunch of quesadillas, cactus salad, and chili at the Red Sage on Northwest Fourteenth, roughly midway between the Kennedy Center and the White House.

"And who's setting this up?"

"Terskoff."

"The Press Secretary."

"The Press Secretary *himself,*" Encardi emphasized.

Nordstrum ate some of his quesadilla. "What's the catch?" he said.

"Excuse me?"

"The catch, the snare, the hook," Nordstrum said. "Whatever it is that's going to sink into my flesh if I take the bait."

Encardi combed back a wave of his lush black hair with his fingers.

"Oh," he said. "You mean President Ballard's request."

Nordstrum looked at him. "Stu, I think you're a decent fellow," he said. "But if you don't stop playing dumb, and get to the point, I'm going to leave this table, stroll into the kitchen, find one of the cactus plants they use for the salads *before* its spines have been removed, then come right back here and shove it up your ass."

Encardi frowned. "Ouch," he said.

"Yes," Nordstrum said, and speared another wedge of quesadilla with his fork. "Very definitely *ouch.*"

Encardi leaned forward confidentially. "Okay," he said. "All the President requests is that you absent yourself from Roger Gordian's press conference tomorrow. That is, assuming you've considered attending."

"Ah-hah," Nordstrum said, chewing.

"Now don't think the White House is trying to restrict your ability to express your opinions," Encardi went on. "Ballard merely feels SEAPAC is a far more vital part of his agenda—and his legacy—than approving the crypto legislation. And that it's slipped out of the spotlight because Gordian versus Caine makes snappier news copy."

"Ah-hah," Nordstrum said.

Encardi spread his hands.

"Think about it," he said. "You're the one heavy hitter in the press who's reported on SEAPAC from its earliest stages of negotiation to the present. Who's consistently stressed its importance to our regional interests in Southeast Asia. Don't you think it'll further sidetrack the public if they see you with Gordian at the podium? There are already enough things distracting their attention."

"Ah-hah," Nordstrum said, chewing placidly.

Encardi frowned with exasperation. "God damn it, Alec, *now* who's being incommunicative? You asked me to be right-on with you and I'm doing it. So, please, let's have some feedback."

"Sure," Nordstrum said.

He carefully set his knife and fork down on his plate and straightened.

"I had planned on standing beside Roger Gordian to-morrow and will do that come hell, high water, or sugar-coated coercion from the highest levels of government," he said.

Encardi brushed back his dense swirl of hair again.

"Alec, you could be interviewing Prime Minister Ya-mamoto over caviar and champagne instead of chowing down in the goat locker with the enlisted personnel. Don't pass up the opportunity of a lifetime."

Nordstrum crossed his arms. "You're annoying me," he said.

"Alec—"

"Don't whine, it makes you look like a schoolboy."

Encardi frowned, wiped his mouth furiously with his napkin, and tossed it down on the table.

"Okay, I quit," he said.

"Good," Nordstrum said. "Anything else you want to ask while I finish eating?"

Encardi looked at him and sighed.

"Yeah," he said after a brief interval. "You ever hear of Diver Dan and Baron Barracuda?"

Nordstrum shook his head disinterestedly.

"Some help you are," Encardi said.

The transcontinental haul from San Francisco to Johor Bahru had been a grueling and seemingly endless affair for Nimec and Noriko Cousins, with a late-night change-over from their 747 to a prop-driven rattletrap in Kuala Lumpur, and, following their jump to JB, a treacherous forty-minute drive over dark, winding, poorly mapped roads in the rental car Nimec had reserved at the airport.

Though Nimec had been at the Johor ground station on only one prior occasion, and though it had occurred to him before departing the States that it might be wise to have somebody from the local Sword contingent come out to the airfield and meet them, he had finally decided to drive to their end destination himself. He supposed that part of it was a natural predisposition toward seeking camouflage, a trait that made him lean toward maintaining a low profile until he was clearer about where Max's probe had been taking him . . . and what might have gone wrong. But there was also a part of him that simply liked cowboying it, and while he would have admitted it to no one—including, to some extent, himself—the truth was that being lifted from his ordinary milieu had aroused that long-dormant facet of his personality.

At any rate, it was just shy of five in the morning when Nimec found UpLink's corporate emblem on a sign marking a dirt service road and, looking off beyond the tree line to his right, glimpsed the concrete and aluminum buildings of the ground station in the near distance.

He swung up over the hard-pack toward the station's perimeter gate and braked about twenty feet before reaching the guard booth. There was an ATM-sized biometric reader on a concrete island to his left—one of the recent improvements Max had made to the security net. Whereas most UpLink facilities used either iris or fingerprint scanning at various levels of access, Blackburn had wanted to tighten the identification requirements at restricted entry points by using multiple biometric passkeys, and had the scanner platforms designed to his specifications.

Nimec lowered his window now and swept his thumb over the platform's thermal-imaging strip while simultaneously waiting for the iris scanner to digitally photograph his eyes—two cameras matching them to a computerized facial template, the third taking a high-res snapshot of his iris. All three images were then checked for a variety of characteristics and compared with information previously enrolled in the security mainframe's database.

Seconds after he'd pulled up to the multiscanner, the "toll light" above the motorized gate in front of him shifted from red to green and a computer-synthesized female voice issued from a speaker in the platform.

"Identification complete, Peter Nimec," it said in English. "Please proceed."

Nimec drove on through the gate toward the complex, nodding to the uniformed man in the guard booth as he passed him.

"This isn't quite the sort of place I expected," Nori said from the backseat, looking out the window in the dawnlight. "It's so . . . I don't know . . . colorless."

Nimec shrugged with his hands on the wheel.

"Utilitarian's the word I'd use," he said. "Didn't realize you hadn't been to any of our ground stations. They all come out of the same cookie cutter. After a while you get used to the no-frills decor."

"I suppose." She sat back and yawned.

Nimec glanced into the rearview.

"Tired from our journey to the East?" he asked.

"And wired," she said.

"Not a good mix if you plan to get any sleep." He lifted a folded newspaper from the passenger seat and held it out to her over his shoulder. "Here, take this copy of the *Straits Times* I grabbed at the KL airport. Maybe it'll help you relax."

"I don't remember seeing you read it."

"That's because I haven't yet," he said. "And I doubt I'll manage to keep my eyes open long enough to do so."

Nori took the paper from his hand, set it down beside her, and yawned again.

"Thanks," she said. "I'll be sure to fill you in on the local news over breakfast."

He nodded.

"Just don't forget my horoscope," he said in a tone that might or might not have been serious.

Sian Po had no sooner gotten to bed after returning home from his night shift at the precinct than he closed his eyes and dreamed he was in a gambling parlor managed by Fat B. There were women and flashing lights and he had somehow won an astronomical sum of money, hillocks of which surrounded him on every side.

The knock at his door awakened him just as, in his dream, he had begun to dance with a magnificent blonde who'd slid down off a pole and then told him she'd come all the way from Denmark to make his acquaintance.

Sian Po opened his eyes, jolted from the sparkle and glitz of his fantasy to the bland, curtained dimness of his studio apartment. Where had the sexy dancer gone?

He frowned with the realization that she didn't exist, and glanced at his alarm clock. It was five A.M. Had he thought he'd heard something?

There was another rap on the door.

Still a little disoriented, he got out of bed and went over to it in his pajamas.

"Who is it?" he grunted, rubbing his eyes.

"I've something for you from Gaffoor," a hushed male voice said from out in the corridor.

Sian Po's bleariness instantly dissipated at the mention of his insider with CID. He unbolted his lock and pulled open the door.

The man was about thirty and dressed in civilian clothes, a light cotton shirt and sport jacket. Another investigator, or so Sian Po believed.

"You in Gaffoor's unit?" Sian Po asked.

The man shrugged noncommittally, extracted a white legal envelope from his jacket's inner pocket, and held it out to Sian Po.

"Take it, *ke yi bu ke yi,*" he said.

Sian Po snatched it from his hand.

The man stood there giving him a blank look. "I'll tell Gaffoor you received his message," he said, and turned down the hall.

The door shut behind him, Sian Po eagerly tore open the envelope. Inside was a folded sheet of paper. He slipped it out and read the note that had been written across its face.

Excitement flooded his squashed features.

Unbelievable, he thought. Just unbelievable.

Heedless of the hour, Sian Po hurried over to his bedside stand, located Fat B's phone number in his datebook, and rang him up.

As though the dream had been a true and marvelous premonition, his jackpot had arrived.

TWENTY-TWO

IN THE CORRIDOR OUTSIDE THE EAST ROOM OF THE
White House, a room throbbing with reporters, prominent
members of Congress, and other official guests invited to
the Morrison-Fiore bill-signing ceremony, the President
was both aggravated and anxious to put pen to paper.

He was aggravated because he had wanted to sign the
bill while sitting behind the staunch and sturdy solidity
of the Resolute Desk in the sound and secure comfort of
the Executive Office, wanted to sign it at midnight when
the folks around him were home in bed, or elsewhere in
bed, or in some cases skulking between beds, zipping up,
unzipping, getting tangled up *inside* their zippers, whatever the hell they chose to do with themselves when the
sun went down and the lights were out here in the golden
city on the Hill.

He was anxious because now that he'd been induced to
make a huge ceremonial affair of the signing—C-SPAN
cameras dollying about, kliegs in his face, the whole nine
yards—he wanted it over and done with so that public
attention could be turned to something of real significance
to him, namely SEAPAC, a child he had guided from
infancy, watching it take on polish, refinement, and sophistication under his savvy political eye. A treaty that he

viewed as the most important policy effort of his tenure in the White House. That he believed was the blueprint for a new strategic and logistic collaboration in the Pacific Rim. That he was certain would reinforce America's ties with its Asian partners, and decide the future of its own security interests in the region. What was Morrison-Fiore in comparison, besides a piece of moot legislation, easing commercial restrictions that had already been bypassed with countless loopholes?

Impatient to get to his desk now—no Resolute by any means, no strong, lasting article of furniture made from the timbers of a bold expeditionary vessel, but rather a comparatively lightweight and characterless hunk of wood rolled out under the portrait of George Washington especially for this morning's swinging Big House hulla-baloo—the President glanced into the room, where the function's primary mastermind, Press Secretary Brian Terskoff, stood to the right of the entryway schmoozing with a young woman Ballard recognized as an executive from the news department of one of the major television networks. A place where Terskoff might very well be seeking employment once the sorry, obstinate bastard got the ass-kicking he'd long deserved.

And what better time than the present to do that? Ballard suddenly thought.

He caught Terskoff's eye and crooked a finger at him, then waited as he pushed his way through the sea of invitees and into the corridor.

"Yes, Mr. President?" he said, stepping close.

"What's the delay?"

"They're working a bug or two out of the satellite feeds, technical stuff," Terskoff said. "We'll be on in five."

The President looked at him.

"On in five," he echoed.

Terskoff nodded. "Maybe less."

The President kept looking at him.

"You sound like the stage manager of a talk show."

Terskoff seemed flattered.

"In a sense, that's my role here today," he said.

The President leaned in close. "Brian, if I'd had it my way, the signing would have been handled as a routine piece of business, something that passed quietly in the night," he said. "Instead, thanks to you, we've got ourselves a spectacle."

"Yes, sir, I believe we do," Terskoff said proudly, glancing into the room. "A *stately* spectacle. That is my preferred approach to these events."

"Your preferred approach."

"Very much so, Mr. President."

Ballard frowned, nibbling the inside of his cheek. "You know," he said, "it occurs to me this approach might have been utilized to promote another of my little endeavors. One I feel hasn't been quite the attention-grabber I'd anticipated it might be."

Terskoff scratched behind his ear, all at once unsure of himself.

"You're referring to SEAPAC," he said.

"Yes," the President said, snapping his index finger at Terskoff's chest. "You guessed it. And what I'm thinking, Brian, is that it's still not too late to change things. For example, we could have football cheerleaders accompany me to Air Force One as I leave for Singapore tomorrow. Or better yet, *Playboy* models *dressed* as cheerleaders. They could be spelling out the name of the treaty while they do their pom-pom waving on the field.

'Give me an S, give me an E,' and so forth. And they could have the word SEAPAC written out across their bikini tops in sequined letters, one letter to each model. How's *that* for a stately spectacle, as you phrased it?''

Terskoff grimaced. ''Mr. President, I know you feel the treaty has been neglected in favor of Morrison-Fiore. But please understand, the press feeds on the sensational. The best one can do is give them what they want, and I choose to do it in whopping portions—''

''I've heard that song a hundred times before, which is more than enough,'' he said. ''Let me tell you something, Brian. You fucked up. You and the pack of propeller-heads you call a staff. And as a result, an initiative to which I've dedicated tremendous effort has been side-lined.''

''Sir—''

Ballard raised his hand like a traffic cop.

''I'm not finished,'' he said. ''Crypto isn't my fight. It never has been. I've never wanted to go to blows with Roger Gordian over it, not publicly, and yet that's exactly what's happening today. At this very instant, he's across town putting on his big Everlast gloves. And that does not make me happy.''

A pause.

''Mr. President, if there's anything you feel I can do . . .''

''Actually, there is,'' Ballard said. ''For starters, you can notify those television people that I'm entering the room in thirty seconds, whether they're ready or not. And then you can take that pretty news executive you were chatting up out to lunch—the Fourth Estate might be an appropriate restaurant—and see whether she can find a place for you in her department. Because I'll be expecting your letter of resignation on my desk when I return from Asia next week. You got me?''

Terskoff had paled. ''Sir . . .''

The President pointed to his wristwatch.

''Twenty seconds,'' he said.

His lower lip quivering, Terskoff hesitated for another two of those seconds, then whipped around and plunged into the East Room.

Precisely eighteen seconds later, the President heard his name announced and made his entrance.

The Murrow Room at the NPC Building was packed with newsies. Like some huge, self-replicating organism, the Washington press corps had divided between two fronts of a battle that it hoped was about to reach a roaring public climax, with the President and Roger Gordian hurling verbal thunderbolts across Pennsylvania Avenue. They wanted banner headlines, they wanted dramatic sound and video bites, they wanted to keep the legion of attorneys and ex-politicos who had been reborn as television commentators regularly bickering through the next ratings sweeps period. They wanted bombs bursting in air, and Gordian was a little intimidated by their expectation— probably because he knew there wasn't much chance of reaching the level to which the bar had been elevated. A lifetime of conducting one's affairs with businesslike restraint scarcely prepared a man to generate oratorical hellfire.

In the end, though, it didn't matter to him whether they were disappointed. Nor would it have been devastating had none of them showed up, leaving his electronically amplified words to float unheard above a roomful of empty chairs. He had come to make his stand, and win or lose, that was ultimately the best anyone could do.

Mounting the podium, he waited for a long moment, Chuck Kirby, Megan Breen, Vince Scull, and Alex Nordstrum behind him on the right, Dan Parker, Richard Sobel, and FBI Director Robert Lang on his left.

"Ladies and gentleman of the press, thank you for coming today," he finally said. "Right now, only a few short blocks away from here, the Morrison-Fiore cryptographic deregulation bill is being signed into law. I don't know what personal feelings any of you may have about it, but for the past several months I have tried to make mine clear. My opposition to the decontrol of cryptographic hardware and software remains firm and uncompromising. Still, there seems to be some confusion about my views, and that is at least fifty percent of the reason I am addressing you today."

Gordian paused, adjusted his microphone.

"I know a little about technology and its importance as a binding and unifying global force," he continued. "I believe that knowledge is freedom, and information the core and cornerstone of knowledge. I have tried with my communications network to break down the barriers that keep people around the world in darkness and tyranny. And I am extremely proud of my successes.

"But the reality is that America has its enemies. We would be mistaken to confuse the globalization of advanced technology with the abdication of our rights and imperatives as a sovereign nation, and I believe Morrison-Fiore is a disturbing step along that road. My critics, on the other hand, argue that I am vainly trying to put the genie back in the bottle by advocating we control encryption technology as we might any other powerful tool.

They argue that because cryptographic software may be smuggled across the transparent borders of cyberspace with relative ease, we ought to pretend those borders do not exist, rather than better define and regulate them. That because we acknowledge the inadequacies and inconsistencies of current laws, and the real and great obstacles to applying them across *territorial* borders, we should abandon them altogether rather than work toward bringing them into greater harmony.

"This sort of thinking admittedly baffles me. Are we to cease attempting to check electronic piracy only because it may be difficult to do so? Refuse to engage a problem only because it may be daunting? If that's to be the case, where do we draw the line? Should we next allow arms and narcotics to flow unchecked between nations? This is no strained comparison. International criminals and practitioners of violence already know encryption technology can afford them a formidable advantage over law enforcement, a new and sophisticated layer of secrecy by which their activities can be concealed. They know it, and they are fast learning how to capitalize on that knowledge.

"I assure you, when we concede an advantage to crime and criminals, we do worse than allow the disintegration of legal boundaries. We risk the disintegration of our will as a civilization. And that, ladies and gentlemen, frightens me more than anything as an individual. . . ."

Nordstrum skimmed his eyes over the crowd of reporters. He thought Gord was doing superbly, and although his notoriously jaded colleagues were a tough bunch to read, and there were very few nodding heads, they at least seemed inclined to listen . . . which was really the critical thing today. Gordian needed their agreement much less than their interest. That translated into coverage, whereas boredom meant obscurity in the back pages.

Nordstrum was only disappointed that he'd forgotten to convey Craig Weston's message to Gordian. *It's not the locks, it's the keys,* he'd said, obviously alluding to the proprietary codes which were used to access, or rather, non-technically speaking, "descramble," data that had been encrypted. The problem of their safe storage was an aspect of the issue that certainly might have borne a touch more emphasis in Gordian's statement, and Nordstrum had fully intended to suggest that to him. But somewhere in the process of meeting Gord and the others at their hotel, and hearing about the near-calamity that had occurred when they'd been landing at Dulles, it had slipped his mind.

Well, perhaps he'd be able to prompt Gord to address the subject during the journalistic grilling—politely known as a Q and A session—that would follow his prepared comments. In fact, that might be the best time for him to do so, since Gordian would likely need a respite from the inevitable bombardment of questions about the Monolith bid, and the surprise announcement he was going to make on that track.

Reminding himself all over again of the hell he would catch at the gym if he failed to keep his promise to the admiral, Nordstrum turned his full attention back to the press conference.

Sitting aboard the monorail as it ran a smooth, circular course around the high-tech theme parks, man-made beaches, and other bustling tourist attractions of Sentosa Island, Omori peered through his binoculars and watched the boosted fleet of naval patrol boats maneuvering in the waters off Singapore's coastline. Their presence had become increasingly noticeable over the past few days, entire squadrons assembling in advance of the Seawolf's run. Security in the city itself was likewise tighter than Omori had ever seen it; walking from the train station to the ferry terminal, he often had been forced to detour around police barricades along the motorcade routes to be taken by arriving dignitaries. Indeed, the Malaysian Prime Minister was already in town, having come a day ahead of his counterparts from Indonesia and America to visit with the governor of Pulau Ubin, with whom he shared close personal ties.

The mission that had brought Omori from Tokyo also reflected long-standing ties . . . to the Inagawa-kai syndicate of which he was a high-placed *kuromaku,* or power broker; to Nga Canbera; to the politicians within the Diet whose opposition to SEAPAC had brought them into alliance with a broad group of foreign and domestic interests, all of which had pledged to make the treaty come undone, and bring about the humiliation and downfall of its internationalist sponsors.

Omori felt a jostling against his right arm now, lowered his glasses, and looked over at the little boy in the seat beside him. He was shifting restlessly about, repeatedly asking his mother when they would reach the Entertainment Mall. Omori frowned, and patted the child's shoulder to gain his attention.

"You should be patient and behave for your mommy," he said. "She is very good to bring you here and cannot make us go any faster."

The boy fell still, looked at him in the wide-eyed, anxious way children did when scolded by strangers, and then looked up at his mother.

Omori glanced at her and smiled in commiseration. The boy was a cute and precocious one, like his own son of about the same age. Omori prayed he would live to see his wife and family again. Children were his truest joy.

He turned back to the window, raised the goggles to his eyes, and continued looking out at the harbor. The number of vessels in the patrols had no meaning to him. Let them bring in the entire Navy if they wished. A small team of men, properly equipped and striking with accuracy, could penetrate any massive line of defense.

Tonight, after he'd finished reconaissance and freshened up a bit, he would meet with the members of the insertion party and review their final preparations. Then there would be nothing to do but await word to proceed, and check his E-mail for a critical file from Nga.

For the moment, however, Omori would relax and enjoy his ride. He hoped the world leaders aboard the Seawolf would enjoy theirs as well.

"In conclusion, I'd like to return for a moment to the example of the genie. Would I like it put back in the magic lamp, the lamp itself sealed away from the eyes, the very *awareness,* of man? My life's work is evidence to the contrary. As I interpret the story, it wasn't the genie's power to work wonders that heaped so much pain and trouble upon poor Aladdin. The cause, I think, was Aladdin's lack of judgment about how to use his gift, a failure to understand the exceeding degree of caution and restraint with which it needed to be managed. Power itself is never to be feared. Its uses are determined by the hands into which it falls. With passion and intelligence anything is truly possible.

"But as evolving technologies create new possibilities for us, as in a sense we use science to work magic, our eternal responsibility is to choose those uses which will build rather than destroy, liberate rather than imprison, bring gain rather than loss upon us as a species. It's a responsibility that hasn't changed in essence since the discovery of fire or the wheel, although as the tools become more complex, so do our choices. Mistakes are inevitable, but I hope and believe we will learn from them, and be wise enough to correct those we can. If so, then you can take my word for it . . . the genie belongs among us. And he's in the very best of hands."

Gordian pushed aside his written notes, and sipped from the glass of water on the lectern. *Not too shoddy,* he thought. It didn't bother him that the applause was merely polite. Rushed, even. The main thing was that he believed his delivery had been okay, and that his comments had a pretty good chance of penetrating the sieve of the media and getting out to the public.

He took a deep breath, drank some more water, and leaned toward the mike again.

"At this point, I'd be glad to take some questions," he said.

A clattering commotion as three quarters of the room sprang off their chairs.

Gordian pointed to the guy in the first row with the famous Website.

"Mr. Gordian, we were informed you would be making a significant announcement on the corporate front," he said. "And though you did not address the issue in your speech to us, I'm wondering if there's anything you can reveal about your future as chairman of UpLink International.''

Gordian looked at him with genuine surprise.

Damned if he hadn't nearly forgotten in all the excitement.

''Oh, yes,'' he said. ''Now that you remind me, there certainly is.''

The East Room erupted into noisy, enthusiastic applause the instant the President hastily and perfunctorily put his signature on the last page of Morrison-Fiore, no longer a bill now, but law of the land. Congratulations flew. The Senate whips clasped hands. The Speaker of the House and his rival from the minority party embraced in bipartison triumph. The Veep posed for photographs, basking in his Commander in Chief's reflected light, hoping it would enhance his own glimmer when his turn to seek his party's nod for the Presidency came about in two years or so.

Disgusted, President Ballard wanted to get to sleep.

He had a long flight to Singapore ahead of him in the morning, and then a historic ride on a submarine that it looked like nobody on the planet was going to notice.

''. . . and Mr. Sobel will acquire the firms comprising UpLink's entire computer products division, including Stronghold Security Systems, our cryptographic hardware and software subsidiary. As someone who has known and worked with Richard for over a decade, I have confidence my corporate children will attain impressive and unprecedented levels of success.''

Gordian pointed to one of the upraised hands in front of him.

"The young lady from the *Wall Street Journal,* " he said. "Ms. Sheffield, is it?"

She nodded and stood. "Sir, with all due respect, how will that growth be possible as long as Mr. Sobel preserves your restrictions on crypto export? Many industry analysts disagree with your contention that a cryptographic firm can focus primarily on the domestic market and remain profitable. Or will those policies be relaxed after the sale?"

Richard suddenly stepped up to share the podium.

"With our host's permission, I'm going to answer that myself," Sobel said. "I can unequivocally state that I support Roger Gordian on the encryption issue and will carry on his present policies to the letter. Success is all in how you approach the marketplace, and my electronics firm is existing proof that the analysts you mention are wrong. Our net profits have increased every year for the past five years. We have grown slowly by intention and built a solid reputation designing latchkey systems for corporate clients . . . using many of Roger Gordian's cryptographic products. As a service-and-support-oriented company, we believe Roger Gordian's superior data-encoding systems will both attract new clients, and present limitless advantages to our existing ones."

Sheffield asked Richard a brief follow-up about his specific last-quarter earnings, and then it was Gordian's turn again. Before taking the mike, though, he tapped Richard on the elbow, leaned close, and whispered for him to stay put, figuring they were certain to have the chance to drop their final bombshell before too long.

"What sort of reaction has the breakup proposal generated from your board?" a reporter asked.

"I've spoken over the telephone with everyone on it,

and can tell you my plan has been welcomed with almost complete unanimity," Gordian said. "I foresee no problem obtaining the board's endorsement when we convene sometime next week."

Another reporter. "Your computer division aside, there are a number of subsidiaries in UpLink's medical and automotive branches which you've said will also be up for sale . . . and which have yet to find buyers. How do you expect your shareholders react to these, ah, forced separations?"

"Very positively, I hope," Gordian said. "The spun-off entities remain under skilled and imaginative management, people who will be able to implement their ideas with greater freedom than ever outside the pressure of a large corporate bureaucracy. And while it would be unrealistic for me to expect full confidence from our shareholders at the onset, I think most will be initially reassured by the package of financial bonuses we're preparing, and eventually become true believers. We're dedicated to our investors and guarantee their concerns will be addressed."

A half-dozen more wearisome questions, most regarding the technical aspects of the breakup. What sort of financial bonuses? Will you be retaining any stock in the divested companies? If so, what percentage is to be floated to shareholders?

Question Number Seven was the charm, fired at him courtesy of someone from *Business Week*:

"Mr. Gordian, how will your plans be effected should the Spartus Consortium finalize the sale of their stake in UpLink, which amounts to fully one fifth of the company—an *enormous* minority holding—to Marcus Caine, who we all know hasn't been over to your home for dinner lately?''

It was a setup Richard couldn't resist.

"As part of our overall deal, UpLink will be placing an equal portion of its stock in my hands," he said, stepping in seamlessly. "If Marcus Caine wants to make himself an uninvited guest at the table, he'll have to sit across from Roger Gordian and myself from now on, look us both squarely in the eye, and learn it isn't an all-you-can-eat. And let me tell you, people, if Caine tries grabbing anything from *my* plate, he'd damned well better watch out for my fork."

A beat of surprised silence from the audience, and then laughter over Richard's quip.

A great, rising swell of laughter.

Gordian looked out at the room, and was embarrassed by the realization that he was grinning himself.

But not *too* embarrassed.

Boom, he thought. *Bombshell delivered.*

And dead-on in the crosshairs, no less.

In his office watching C-SPAN, Caine lowered the croissant he'd been eating to his desk, then glanced circumspectly over at his secretary. When Deborah had come in with his coffee and pastries, he'd asked her to stay and take notes regarding the press conference, and she was now sitting on the sofa with her laptop, typing, her gaze fixed on the screen. Perhaps too intently. She'd passed a hand across her mouth a moment ago, briefly shielding it from sight. Had she found Sobel's remarks amusing? he wondered. He would have liked to tear out her throat just on the suspicion. If his belief ever hardened into surety, she could look forward to her walking papers. He would see that she never set foot in an office again, not as an employee.

Caine felt his stomach burning savagely. It was as if he were on fire inside.

Those bastards, he thought incredulously. Those bastards. They should have been dead. Killed when Gordian tried to land that plane. The people he'd sent to work on it had *assured* him they would be. But somehow . . . somehow nothing had happened to them. And instead—

Instead . . .

He had to credit Gordian's resourcefulness. By segmenting off entire divisions of UpLink, he would almost certainly gain the capital to dispose of his outstanding debts. By parting with the cryptographic operation, he had eliminated the greatest cause of his shareholders' dissatisfaction, and no doubt raised the price of UpLink stock to its highest level in years. And by handing Sobel a chunk of the core outfit—making him White Knight and Squire all in one—he had forged an alliance that would decisively give him control of the company just when it had been within Caine's grasp. In order to overthrow that alliance, or even mitigate its control, Caine—or any buyer of voting stock—would now need to acquire an improbable and newly expensive number of shares.

A terrible, nauseous crashing sensation added itself to the pain tearing at Caine's gut, and he was suddenly afraid he might be sick. Even knowing what he'd set in motion at Gordian's data-storage facility tonight didn't help. Nga and his confederates would get what they wanted . . . but he . . .

Think it, an inner voice insisted. *At least have the courage to think it.*

No. No. No.

His hand shaking, he lifted the plate of croissants off his desk, slipped it into his wastebasket, and stared at the television screen in an agony of his own hatred.

No.

He would not, could not concede that he was beaten.

TWENTY-THREE

*"—ELLO, MAX? MAX, IT'S KIRSTEN. CALL ME ON MY
mobile soon as you can."*

*"Max, this is Kirsten again. Still waiting to hear from
you."*

"Hello, Max? Same message as before."

*"Max, where are you? It's been four days and I'm
getting really concerned. My sister and her husband are
telling me to call the police, and maybe they're right. This
is all so confusing for me. So please, if you hear this, get
in touch."*

*"Max, I've decided to do what Anna wants and contact
the authorities—"*

Nimec clicked off the answering machine and looked
at Nori in silence.

Though it was still not yet full morning in Johor, and
both were running on empty, they were in Blackburn's
spare, single-room living quarters at the ground station,
having decided to check it out for clues to his
whereabouts before heading off to bed. There had been
nothing to help them on that score, but Kirsten Chu's
frequent and increasingly worried messages—the most recent of which had been left two days earlier according to
the machine's time/date stamp—at least revealed that *she*

had not completely vanished from the face of the earth as well. And while the messages also seemed to confirm Nimec's feeling that Max had gotten into some kind of serious fix, they ultimately engendered more questions than they answered.

"Sounds like she's staying with her sister," Nori said after a while.

"Hiding out's more like it," Nimec said. "You catch the sister's name or do I have to run through the tape again?"

"Anna," Nori said. "No second name, though. And Kirsten mentioned there being a husband, so it'd be a different surname from her own. Makes it harder to track her down."

"A lot of married women keep their family names these days."

Nori shook her head.

"You're thinking like an American," she said. "Asian societies aren't quite so liberated."

Nimec sighed.

"Why the hell would she ask Max to call on her cell phone?" he said. "Wouldn't it have been simpler to just leave *Anna's* number for him?"

Nori thought about that a moment.

"Simpler for us, absolutely, but her situation's another matter," she said. "Put yourself in Kirsten's shoes. Whatever she's been into with Blackburn, it's something her family's probably better off not being enlightened about."

"For their own safety, you mean."

"Right," Nori said. "The less they know the better. Also, it sounds to me like Max would have been against Kirsten calling the authorities to report whatever happened—"

"Or at least *she* feels that way," Nimec said. "We can figure out why later, but go on, I didn't mean to interrupt."

"My point is that she seemed to be under pressure from her family to make the call, and would've been torn in two different directions about actually doing it. Could be the sister and her husband had misgivings about Blackburn . . . why wouldn't they, when you consider the whole situation? If you're Kirsten, you're going to feel uncomfortable about having him get in touch with you on their home phone, maybe kicking off a round of difficult questions from Sis. The other way's a lot more private."

"Except, as you've already indicated, it stinks as far as we're concerned," Nimec said. "Joyce has numbers for Kirsten's home and business phones, but not the cellular."

"No address?"

"Besides her office at Monolith, no."

"What about Max's notes on his investigation? The ones he gave to Joyce?"

"I didn't even know they existed until yesterday, when I called to tell her I'd be coming to Johor. They're encoded on his PIM, and it'll take some time to decrypt and go through them."

She nodded, thinking. "I assume we want to steer clear of the badges."

"For the time being, yes. Not that we even can be sure she's phoned them. Or, if she has, that she's told them where she's staying."

"It's even an open question *which* police force she'd call," Nori added. "Her sister could live on either side of the causeway. Or elsewhere. National borders are close in this neck of the woods."

"True enough, but we do we know *Kirsten* lives in Singapore. If we're lucky, she'll be listed in the public telephone directory. And that might give us the info we need."

"Maybe, maybe not," Nori said. "Most young, single women leave their addresses out of the listings. It's standard protection against sickos."

"Now *you're* the one thinking like an American . . . and a New Yorker at that," Nimec said with a wan smile. "Singapore isn't the kind of place where there's going to be a problem with obscene phone callers. If she's in the book, we'll likely find out where she lives. . . ."

"And the next step would be to get in there and look around for something with Sis's address written on it," Nori said, completing his thought.

Nimec nodded agreement.

"I hate to risk breaking and entering," he said. "But if we have no better alternative . . ."

Nori wobbled her hand in the air to interrupt him, then gestured to the key he was holding, a spare they had obtained from Station Security to gain access to Blackburn's room.

"Leave that part to me," she said.

It was a little past four in the afternoon when the two men in the Olds Cutlass drove up to the entry gate of the UpLink Cryptographics facility in Sacramento, slowing to a halt as they reached the guard station.

"Detective Steve Lombardi," the driver told the guard through his open window. He tilted his head toward the man in the passenger seat. "My partner here's Detective Craig Sanford."

The guard regarded them through his mirrored sunglasses.

"How can I help you?" he said.

"We need to speak to the supervisor in charge," Lombardi said. "We've got a subpoena for crypto keys, you know the deal."

The guard nodded. It was SOP for law enforcement to deliver court orders whenever there was an investigation or legal action involving the release of data-recovery keys used by UpLink software. With everybody from banks to supermarkets to Mafia hoods using crypto in their daily business operations nowadays, and thousands of keys stored in the data-recovery vaults, and all kinds of civil and criminal cases in which computerized files were requested as evidence, it wasn't unusual to get as many as four or five visits a week from police officers delivering subpoenas.

"Just need to see your ID and papers," he said.

The driver took the requested items out of his sport jacket and gave them to the guard. A moment later the passenger reached over and passed the leather case holding his own badge and identification through the window.

The guard angled his mirrored lenses down at what he'd been handed, glancing over the police tins, unfolding the court papers.

"Everything kosher?" the driver asked.

The guard studied the ID and paperwork another second, then nodded and returned them through the window of his booth.

"Go right on ahead, fellas," he said.

The doorman at the luxury condo near Holland Road, on the eastern part of Singapore Island, had scarcely arrived for his morning shift when he saw the pale blue taxi pull up near the entrance and discharge its passenger, a slight, nicely dressed young woman carrying a couple of over-stuffed travel bags. The luggage aside, she *looked* as though she'd been traveling, her hair slightly messed, a somewhat frayed expression on her face.

As she struggled toward the building with the bags, he set down his tea and rose from his desk to get the door.

"Can help?" he asked in typical Singlish fashion, blending English words with Chinese sentence structure.

She set the bags down on the carpeted floor of the vestibule and fussed her hair into place.

"Yes. Or I hope so, anyway," she said. "I'm here for Kirsten Chu."

The doorman regarded her a moment. Her American accent explained why he had not recognized her as an occupant of the high-rise. But he was familiar with the woman whose name she'd mentioned.

"Apartment Fifteen, I can call up, *lah*." He reached for the intercom's handpiece. "Your name, please?"

"No, you don't understand," she said. "Kirsten won't be home until tonight, and I was supposed to let myself in. But now I can't...."

She let the sentence trail off.

"Yes?" he said.

"Maybe I'd better start over." She looked upset. "I'm her sister Charlene, and I'm here visiting from the States. Did she mention my name to you, by any chance?"

He shook his head.

"Well, I suppose there wouldn't have been any need...." she muttered to herself, rubbing her forehead.

"Yes?" the doorman said again. He was becoming in-creasingly baffled.

When she looked up at him, her large brown eyes were moist.

"You see, I have a key to her door . . . well I *had* a key to her door . . . but I think I may have lost it at the airport. . . ."

"Yes?" he said for the third time, suddenly afraid she might burst into tears.

"Listen," she said agitatedly. "I don't quite know how to ask you this . . . it makes me feel so *foolish* . . . but could you let me into her apartment? I haven't any idea where else to wait for her . . . she went to pick up our other sister, Anna . . . and isn't supposed to be home until very *late,* you see . . . and I've got these *bags* . . ."

He gave her an uncomfortable look. "That against rules, miss. Okay if you want leave bags with me, but I not can—"

"Please, I'll show my passport if you need identification," she said at once, her voice trembling. She crouched over the bags she'd deposited on the vestibule's carpet, unzipped one of them, and began fumbling around inside it.

"Miss—"

The doorman cut himself short. Just as he'd feared, she had begun to sob. Tears spilling down her face, she bent there in front of him, pulling items out of the bag, dropping some of them in her distress, stuffing them hastily back into the bag and fishing out others. . . .

"Wait, wait, my papers are in here *somewhere* . . . I'm so sorry . . . I just have to find them. . . ."

The doorman looked at her, feeling sorry for her, thinking he couldn't just stand there and watch her cry.

"It okay, miss. It okay," he said finally, reaching for

the intercom button. "I call superintendent, tell him let you in, no problem."

Noriko stood and wiped a hand across her eyes.

"Thanks, that's so kind," she said, sniffling. "Really, I don't know what I'd've done without you."

The driveway leading up to the encryption facility terminated in a parking area outside the main entrance, the left side of which was reserved for staff, the right for visitors. The men in the Cutlass swung into the visitors' section, found an empty slot, strode across the lot toward the flat cinder-block building, and approached the armed guard posted at the door.

"Detectives Lombardi and Samford?" he said, smiling pleasantly.

They both nodded.

"I was informed you gentlemen were on your way from the gate," he said, and gestured toward the walk-through weapons-detector beside his station. "If you'd please leave your service weapons with me, and place any other metal articles you may have in the tray to your right, you can step through the scanners and come in."

"We're cops, and cops carry guns," the man who'd announced himself as Lombardi said. "It's in our regulations."

"Yes, and I apologize for the inconvenience. But a facility of this nature has to take added precautions, and most departments cooperate with them," the security man said. "If you'd prefer, I can call ahead to Mr. Turner . . . he's the supervisor you're going to see anyway . . . and request that he waive the requirement. I'm sure it wouldn't be much of a problem."

Lombardi shrugged.

"No need," he said. "Policy's policy."

The two men unholstered their firearms—both were carrying standard Glock nines—and turned them over to the guard, then deposited their coins and key chains in the tray and passed through the archway.

"Thanks for your cooperation," the guard said. He looked at his LCD display, gave the items in the tray a cursory glance, then held it out for the detectives to retrieve their property. "Follow the entry hall straight back, turn right, then cut another right at the end of that corridor. Supervisor's office will be the fourth door down. I'll have your weapons right here when you leave."

Lombardi stuffed his key chain into his pocket.

"Just hope we don't have to chase any armed robbers while we're here," he said, smiling a little.

The guard laughed. "Have no fear," he said. "This place is as safe as they come."

Nori slipped into the rear of the white company Land Rover parked in a shopping mall off Holland Road, three blocks up from Kirsten Chu's residence.

"Found what we wanted," she said. "And more."

"Any problems getting in and out?" Nimec asked from the front passenger seat.

"Nope. The doorman has a crush on me. He talked the super into giving me a key," she said. "Anyway, I've got a personal phone book with a number and address for a Lin and Anna Lung in Petaling Jaya."

"Where the hell's that?"

"Back over the causeway, *lah*. Outside KL." This from the driver, a Malay named Osmar Ali who was with the Sword detail at the ground station.

Nimec nodded.

"You sure you have the right party?" he asked Noriko.

"Pretty much," she said. "I also dug up an open mailing envelope with a return address that matches the one in the book. There were some photos of a couple and two kids inside it. And a letter starts with a 'Dear Sis.' "

"Okay." Nimec turned to look at Osmar. "Petaling Jaya . . . is it within driving distance?"

Osmar shrugged. "Can go, yes, but it a few hundred kilometers," he said in rough English. "Be faster we drive back to ground station, take helicopter."

Nimec thought in silence a moment. Then he reached for the cell phone resting in the molded-plastic cup-holder beside him.

"Better let me have that number, Nori," he said. "I want to see if anybody's home before we come knocking on their door."

The pair of men strode through the corridor after leaving their guns at the checkpoint, their eyes noting the button-sized lenses of surveillance cameras near the ceiling. Unlike commercially produced cameras, these miniature units were recessed behind the walls rather than mounted on visible brackets, and would have gone unnoticed by the average person.

They reached the T-juncture at the end of the hall, but instead of immediately turning right as instructed, paused to scan the doorways in both directions.

Midway down the corridor branching to their left was an office door marked SECURITY. The one who called himself Lombardi gave the other an almost imperceptible glance and they went over to it, walking side-by-side at an easy pace, nodding amiably to a woman who passed them going the opposite way.

Two plainclothes security men were sitting at a bank of closed-circuit monitors when the office door opened inward from the corridor. They were not surprised, having seen the approaching detectives on their screens, and assumed they wanted information.

"Can we help you gentlemen?" one of them said, swiveling to face the door.

The man called Lombardi entered, followed by his partner. They let the door close behind them.

"We're looking for the supervisor's office." He smiled, his hand casually tucked in his pants pocket. "Thought it was supposed to be right around here somewhere."

"Took a wrong turn," the security man said. "When you leave this office, hang a right and—"

Lombardi's hand came out of his pocket holding his key ring. Before the security guards could register what was happening, he brought up its rectangular fob and quickly tugged back the attached chain with his free hand. This cocked the firing mechanism of the weapon, which was only three inches long and contained two .32-caliber bullets. He pointed it at the man facing him and pushed a button on its side.

The slug that coughed from the tiny gun's bore would have been lethal at twenty yards, and the shooter was a mere fraction of that distance from his target. It struck the guard in the middle of the forehead and killed him instantly, slamming him back into the panel of monitors.

The shooter pivoted toward the other guard. His face white with shock, he was reaching for the holstered weapon under his jacket. The shooter pushed the button and fired his second shot, striking the guard in the center of his face. And then the face was gone. The body sprawled backward, blood, bone fragments, and tissue spraying the screens and walls behind him.

The shooter looked at his partner, gesturing toward the dead men.

"Close," he said. "I only expected there to be one of them."

The man near the door nodded.

"Let's take their guns and get on with it," the shooter said.

When she heard the phone ring at nine-thirty, she wondered if perhaps Anna had forgotten something in her rush to leave the house. The kids had acted up and been late getting ready for school, and Anna, who dropped them off every morning on her way to work, had made her exit amid quite a hustle and bustle.

"Hello?" she said, picking up.

A strange male voice. "Kirsten Chu, please."

She hesitated, her heart suddenly banging in her chest. She'd been expecting a call from the police, which was the reason she hadn't volunteered to help out her sister and deliver Miri and Brian to their classrooms herself. The police, this had to be the police. Anna and Lin . . . and Max, of course . . . were the only other people who'd know to find her here. And the person at the other end wasn't any of the latter.

"Who's calling?" she asked in a cautious tone. Purposely offering no acknowledgment of her identity.

"My name is Pete Nimec, and I'm—"

She didn't even hear him finish the sentence, so completely overwhelming was the recognition that swept over her. Her heart beat harder, faster. She inhaled, feeling as if the breath had been knocked out of her.

"Dear God, that's the *name,*" she said, the words springing from her mouth on their own. "You're Max's friend, aren't you? The one he wanted me to call?"

A beat of silence. "Yes, I am. I—"

"How is he?" she interrupted. Worry had swept chillingly through Kirsten's initial excitement. If Max were all right, why wouldn't *he* be calling?

"Kirsten, we need to meet. I have to speak with you in person, find out what's happened to him. To both of you."

"You mean you don't know. . . ."

"No, Kirsten. I don't. No one's heard from him."

She clutched the phone, her hand shaking around it. Her entire *arm* shaking.

"Then how . . . how did you get this number?"

"I'll explain all that later. I promise. Right now it's just urgent that we get together. I'll come to you there. It's probably best if you stay put."

Kirsten breathed.

What reason was there to trust this man? This name Max had mentioned once in a moment of urgency? This *voice?* The truth was that she hardly even knew whether *Max* was the person he'd seemed to be. . . .

Except that wasn't true. She *did* know. Maybe not everything about him. Maybe not as much as she should have known. But as she'd told Anna just days ago, she loved him. . . .

Had loved him long before he'd put his own life at risk to save her . . .

And what was love, always, always, but a leap of faith?

"All right," she said. "I'll be waiting."

•   •   •

The supervisor at the encryption facility—the name plaque on his office door read Charles Turner—was shaking his head as he pored over the court papers he'd been issued.

"I must tell you, this is rather atypical," he said, glancing up at the two detectives standing before his desk.

"How so, sir? I checked the subpoenas myself to make sure they crossed all the t's."

"No, please, don't misunderstand me," Turner said. "The papers are fine. But normally I get advance notification from the officers coming for the codes. They're stored on compact disc in our vaults, you understand, and there's a rather stringent checkout process. Going through it at the last minute, well, I'll have to drop everything, Detective Lombardi. . . ."

"We're really sorry for the inconvenience," the man standing in front of him said. "But this is our first time dealing with a matter of this type as officers."

Turner sighed and rose from his desk, looking annoyed and somewhat flustered.

"You may accompany me to the data-storage wing, though only authorized personnel are allowed in the vaults. You'll have to stay out in one of the waiting areas while I track the disk you want."

"Will it take very long?"

"It shouldn't," Turner said. "The corporation whose key-codes are being requested isn't one I recognize off-hand, but the disks are catalogued on our electronic database. I can rush everything through in half an hour, maybe a little faster."

"That'd be fine with us."

Turner *harrumphed,* and came around the desk toward the door.

"Lead the way, sir," the detective said, falling in behind him.

The men had left Penang State, southeast of the Malaysia-Thailand border, shortly after they'd received the call from Luan. That had been some hours ago, at dawn, and they'd been driving their van down the main coastal highways to Selangor ever since. The trip would have been lengthy under the best of traffic conditions, but there were herds of beachgoing tourists jamming the roads near the bridge and ferry terminals to Georgetown, and the delays had stretched miserably in the hot, beating sun. The men in the van had, furthermore, wanted to keep a moderate speed so as not to risk being pulled over by police. The kris tattoos on their hands would bring about an instant search, and once that happened their problems only would be starting. If the police found their weapons, they could look forward to many hours of painful interrogation, followed by many years of being locked away in prison holes. And that would be a far cry from the reward they were expecting for the successful completion of their task.

The Thai had promised them a fortune.

A fortune in greenbacks for capturing a woman and delivering her to him in Kalimantan.

They had joked crudely about her physical attributes when they received the call. And in spite of their grindingly slow progress, it would not be long before they saw the object of Luan's desire for themselves. They were already better than halfway down through Perak, and would be crossing into Selangor within a couple of hours.

Tom Clancy's Power Plays

With luck, Kirsten Chu would be at the address they had been given. And if not, they would gladly wait there for her to arrive.

She was, after all, one woman who was very much worth it.

TWENTY-FOUR

"**IS THERE SOME KIND OF PROBLEM, MR. TURNER?**" the man calling himself Lombardi asked from where he sat in the waiting area.

Holding the court papers, a puzzled expression on his face, Turner glanced at him as he returned through a doorway he'd entered just moments ago.

"The name of the corporation simply doesn't show on our database," he said, approaching his chair. "I don't know what to make of it."

Lombardi rose and sidled up to him, studying the papers over his shoulder.

"I'm no expert at this high-tech stuff, but could be it's just misspelled," he said.

Turner shook his head. "The computers will essentially correct for that sort of error by searching for approximate matches. In this case, nothing came up."

Lombardi grinned.

"Then I guess those papers are fake and the company doesn't exist," he said.

Turner looked at him. "I don't understand. . . ."

Lombardi reached under his jacket and drew the Beretta he'd taken from one of the murdered security guards.

"Oh, I think you do," he said, and rammed the handle

of the weapon upward into Turner's nose, shattering his septum and sending tiny slivers of bone into his brain. Turner dropped instantly to the floor, his eyes rolling up in their sockets, dark blood spouting from his nostrils. He spasmed twice, emitted a labored gurgling sound, and died.

Lombardi gestured to the other man as he got up off his seat. Then both went around the body and passed through the entry to the vault area.

A short while before the ringing of the doorbell startled her into alertness, Kirsten had slipped into a doze on the sofa, a kind of syrupy exhaustion having settled over her in the late morning, and stayed with her as she'd done some routine chores—washing the breakfast dishes, straightening up the living room, and gathering the kids' toys from around the apartment and garden and hauling them back into their bedroom closet.

Afterward, sitting down to listen to some light jazz on the stereo, hoping it would calm her mind, she had been surprised at how fast her eyelids had started getting heavy, and thought it quite incredible that she could be simultaneously clipping along full-steam on nervous energy and feeling so mentally fatigued that her brain almost seemed immersed in a pool of thick, lukewarm glue. It was a little like the way she'd felt as a university student studying for final exams, living for days and nights on coffee and chocolate . . . only many times more intense.

And now the sound of the buzzer had practically sent her bouncing off the couch, still half out of it, yet conscious of her nerves revving up to speed again.

She glanced at the clock on the wall opposite her. Could Nimec have arrived already? Under average circumstances it would have been highly unlikely he could have made it in so short a time . . . but he'd explained that he would be returning to the UpLink ground station in Johor, and would probably travel from there into KL by helicopter. Which had also told her a couple of things about him beyond the obvious fact that he was in a hurry. One, he was at least as concerned about Max as she was. And two, he had the sort of clout with Max's boss to pull some major strings, maybe even worked for UpLink himself—

Bzzzzzzzzz!

She crossed the room to the door, straightening her blouse, smoothing her skirt down with her hands. Whoever was out there was really leaning on the bell.

"Yes?" she said, reaching for the doorknob. "Who is it?"

"Johor police," a man said from outside. He was speaking Bahasa. "We want to see Kirsten Chu."

"Excuse me?" she replied in the same language. The blunt, gruff quality of his voice had surprised her as much as his response.

"It's about her call," he said. "We need to ask her some questions."

Kirsten didn't move, hardly even breathed. She was still holding the knob, her fingers suddenly sweating around it.

The Singapore cop with whom she'd spoken had said the Johor authorities would be in touch . . . but she hadn't expected them to just show up at the door. Wouldn't they want to phone and make an appointment, if for no other reason than to spare themselves a needless trip in case she wasn't home?

And does he really sound like a police officer? she thought.

Her pulse fluttering in her temples, she raised the spy-hole cover, peered outside. . . .

And felt her stomach turn to ice.

Never mind how he'd sounded, none of the men standing in the walk outside—she could see four or five of them through the little two-way mirror—looked anything *like* police investigators. Their hair was long, their clothes sloppy, and their eyes . . .

Even had they been wearing bright silver badges and starched blue uniforms, their eyes would have given them away.

"Come on," the one nearest the door said. "Open up."

She pulled away from the spyhole and inhaled shakily.

"Just a minute," she said. "I need to put something on."

The man slammed the door with his forearm.

"Forget the games," he said. "Open it."

Her fingers harrowing her cheeks, Kirsten took a step backward across the living room.

"Open up!" the man said, beating the door again, hitting it so hard she was afraid it might fly off its hinges.

Terrified, her breaths coming in sharp little bursts, Kirsten whirled and plunged through the apartment.

An instant later the door crashed open behind her.

The entryway through which the intruders had left the waiting room led to a short passage, which itself gave into another small, boxy room that was bare except for a computer workstation on the right, and a wall-mounted biometric scanner across from it beside a reinforced steel door.

"Lombardi" went straight over to the scanner. This was the part of the job that made him uptight. He'd been telling Turner the truth when he remarked that he was no technical wizard, and felt it would have been easy enough to steer the supervisor back into the room at gunpoint, force him to let the system take his readings, and in that way gain access to the vault. But the concern was that Turner might have triggered some discreet alarm had that been done. Caine's instructions had been explicit, and they'd been warned not to deviate from them under any circumstances.

Standing before the scanning unit, Lombardi raised his left hand to the level of the cameras designed to image his facial and iris characteristics, turning it so the artificial star-sapphire ring on his fourth finger would be visible to their lenses. Then, keeping that hand perfectly motionless, he placed his right hand flat on the machine's glass optoelectrical pad. Ordinarily this would both activate the unit and take readings of his fingerprint and palm geometry, which would then be converted to algorithms and matched to stored employee-identification data. But by an arcane process he did not quite understand, the specific star pattern on his ring would key a match with a simple data-string buried in the system mainframe's hard drive, which caused—or, according to Caine, was supposed to cause—the normal image-recognition sequence to be bypassed.

Lombardi held his breath and waited, one hand up, the other on the unit's clear glass interface, staring at its eye-level VDU. A red light had begun to glow beneath the glass, indicating the scanner had been activated by his touch . . . but if all was going as planned, the readings of its thermal sensors would be ignored by the computers.

Five seconds went by.

Ten.

He waited.

And then the words CLEARED TO ENTER appeared in the middle of the screen.

He exhaled, heard the faint click of the vault's lock mechanism retracting, and turned to his partner, who was already working open the heavy steel door.

They were in.

Kirsten ran toward the back of the apartment, hearing the door burst open behind her, hearing the men who'd been outside come pounding through the living room at her heels. She had only a vague notion of what to do, but it was *all* she had, and there was no choice except to go with it. If she could make it to the back door before they caught up, get into the building's central parking court, then maybe—

Suddenly a hand reached out from behind and snatched the sleeve of her blouse, pulling at her, yanking her backward. She stumbled, and almost lost her balance, but somehow managed to keep her legs underneath her, keep *moving,* carried by her own forward momentum. She twisted sharply as her pursuer tried to get his other hand around her, heard a loud ripping sound, and then was free of his grasp, racing across the room again, scrambling toward the door, a ragged streamer of cotton dangling from her arm.

"Hey!" he shouted. *"Stop, you bitch!"*

Kirsten was within several feet of the back door now, the kitchen on her immediate right, the hallway leading to the bedrooms on her left. She lunged ahead, shooting her hand out in front of her, reaching for the doorknob, thinking she might make it, thinking she really might, when the man whose grip she'd managed to escape a moment earlier sprang at her in a flying tackle, the full weight of his body whumping into her, his arms clamping around her waist.

He spun Kirsten around and swept her in toward his chest, trying to get a firmer hold on her. Frantic, she snatched a glance past his shoulder, saw his companions rushing up through the living room, and thrust her hands out at his face, clawing at him, digging her fingers into his eyes.

That bought her a momentary reprieve. Emitting an animal yelp of pain, her attacker shoved fiercely away from her and covered his face with his hands, spinning in a blind semicircle, bowling wildly into the men behind him. At the same time, Kirsten flung herself at the door, clutched the knob, and tore it open.

Gasping for breath, a gale wind of terror and desperation roaring through her brain, she dashed out into the automobile court.

When the white-smocked techie first opened the door to the security office, the coffee she brought the guys every day at the same time balanced on a cafeteria tray in one hand, she simply couldn't credit her eyes. She stood there in the doorway, looking at the bodies and the blood streaming from the unrecognizable remains of their heads, the blood spattered everywhere in the room, the blood and strings of gristle covering the monitors on which closed-circuit images of the halls were still flashing through their preset sequences as if nothing eventful had occurred to disrupt the daily routine, and then suddenly the world went into a crazy tilt and the two coffee cups spilled from the tray and hit the floor where there was all that blood and gore and she opened her mouth wide and screamed, screamed at the top of her lungs. . . .

Screamed until long after half the people in the building had come running toward the office to see what in the name of God and his blessed angels was the matter.

Kirsten squatted on her haunches between two parked cars, trembling with fright, trying not to move, afraid the slightest sound would give her position away to her pursuers. She could hear their feet crunching on the asphalt as they moved up and down the aisles, searching for her amid the rows of slotted vehicles. There weren't as many cars in the lot as there would have been at night, when many more residents of the apartment complex would be home from work, but she would take what small blessings she could . . . and for the first time in her life feel grateful for the large government-sponsored housing developments that had virtually wiped out the city's traditional architecture.

More footsteps. Closer. She hugged herself, trying to think clearly through her fear. If she could manage to hide until someone came along either to leave or fetch his car . . . or perhaps inch her way around toward the driveway leading to the street, then maybe she'd have a chance to get some help. . . .

Kirsten heard the crunch of another footfall, this one no more than two aisles down to the left of her, then an entirely different set a little further off to the right.

They were boxing her in on either side.

She stiffened, biting down on the fleshy part of her hand, stifling a mutinous scream. While part of her kept insisting that she give in to the urge, there was a more rational part that understood it would be the worst mistake she could possible make. If she screamed, they'd know exactly where she was, would be on her in an instant, well before anyone could come to her aid.

No, she dared not do it. Dared not make a sound. Dared not move a muscle.

The moment she did, Kirsten was sure she would be theirs.

The optical mini-CDs were stored in specially designed, alphanumerically-tabbed electronic "stacks" lining the walls of the vault. Once inside, the pair of intruders had been able to locate the object of their search within seconds. At the touch of a button, the disc was scanned, identified by a bar code imprinted on its surface, and then ejected from the repository in a gleaming stainless-steel tray.

Slipping the disk into a protective plastic sleeve he took from a wall dispenser, Lombardi dropped it into the breast pocket of his jacket and gave his partner the ready signal.

The two men strode from the vault less than three minutes after entering it, passed through the waiting area without a glance at the dead supervisor, and reentered the outer corridor as if they had nothing to hide.

They were swinging back into the main entry hall when the lab tech's screams pierced the air and all hell broke loose around them.

Kirsten knew she wouldn't be able to hide from her pursuers much longer.

The man she'd heard on her left had reached the end of the aisle he'd been searching, swung into the aisle immediately beside the one where she was crouched, and then turned back up in her direction, pausing every couple of steps to poke his head back and forth between the cars. He was now standing directly across from her, separated from her by a single row of vehicles. And the others were closing in from elsewhere around the court.

The man on the left took a step up the aisle, then another. Kirsten's breath came to a stop. She could see his boots and the bottoms of his jeans under the chassis of the car she was leaning against. Her heart was booming in her ears like a timpani, and in the panicky, half-crazed moment before she got a handle on herself, Kirsten was afraid he'd be able to hear it as well.

In a minute or so he would turn up her aisle, and it would be over.

She had never in her life felt so terribly helpless and alone.

God, God, what am I going to do?

No opening had presented itself. Nobody had driven in or out of the lot, and she had no reason to think anybody would before it was too late to make any difference.

She suddenly realized the only thing she could do was run for it, break for the driveway, and hope that by some miracle she could reach the street before they did. She knew even that wouldn't necessarily mean she was safe— the men who'd come after her and Max had been willing to strike on a thoroughfare as busy as Scotts Road, strike with hundreds of pedestrians around, for godsakes. If this group was just a fraction as bold, they might not have the slightest concern about who saw them.

But she hadn't any choice. It was either leave the pot or be cooked.

She waited another second, took a deep gulp of air, and then forced herself to spring to her feet.

The man on the left spotted her instantly. Their eyes made the briefest contact, hers full of hunted terror, his absent of any hint of sympathy or compassion.

Then he rasped an order to his companions and came hurtling across the aisle at her.

Kirsten turned and fled.

The first indication that something was wrong came the moment they pulled their rental car up to the curb, and was the only one they needed. If there were a way to think things were normal after arriving at a person's home and finding the door kicked in, Nimec didn't know it.

He glanced out the windshield at the street, at the outside stairs, at the walkways spanning the rows of doors on the building's upper stories. All were empty.

"Have your weapons ready," he said to Noriko and Osmar. He withdrew his own Beretta 8040 from its concealment holster, ejected its standard ten-round clip, and chocked in the twelve-round magazine/grip extension. "Don't seem to be any eyes around, but if somebody does call the local gendarmes, we'll get it straight with them later."

Following his lead, the others jogged out of the car and across the ground level unit's front yard to the partially open door.

Nimec instinctively moved to the right of the door frame, gesturing the others to the left, making sure there was some wall between them and whatever potential threat might be inside.

"Kirsten, this is Pete Nimec!" he called through the opening, leaning his head around the splintered jamb. "Are you okay in there?"

No reply.

He pulled back against the wall, cocked his pistol, and looked across the doorway at his teammates.

"Go!" he said.

They rushed into the apartment and fanned out in a practiced crossover maneuver, Nimec moving to the left of the entrance, gun held ready, Noriko and Osmar following him and buttonhooking to the right. The three of them rapidly pivoted to cover the center of the room with their weapons, legs apart, making broad sweeps of their sectors of fire.

They seemed to be alone in the place.

"Kirsten, you here?" Nimec called again.

Still no answer.

Noriko tapped his arm. "Look," she said, pointing straight across the living room.

The back door was wide open.

Nimec's eyes flicked between her and Osmar.

"Come on," he said, and rushed toward the door.

The two intruders paused in the hall and exchanged glances. Confused, frightened staffers poured from doorways on either side of them. Not a word was spoken. They could see that the greatest commotion was down the left bend of the corridor, and knew the bodies of the guards had been discovered. Their original intention had been to walk out the main entrance, and they would have to gamble on still being able to leave that way in the disturbance. It would be dangerous, but any attempt to leave the building through emergency exits would trip sensors that would likely pinpoint the specific door being opened. And they had no illusions about having eliminated the threat from security. The men at the surveillance monitors would not have been the sole members of the

plainclothes team on premises. And there was the uniformed guard at the door.

The intruders could only keep their fingers crossed that
he'd be sufficiently distracted for them to slip past. Otherwise, they'd have to kill him, too.

They moved forward through the scared, noisy people
in the corridor, and were nearly at the checkpoint where
they'd had to leave their guns when an alarm sounded, a
loud on-and-off noise that grated on the eardrums. The
guard at the door seemed to be tracking them with his
eyes as they approached.

"We're going out to radio for assistance," the one
who'd called himself Lombardi said. His hand was in his
jacket pocket.

The guard looked at him.

"I'm sorry," he said. "The building's been sealed."

"Don't insult me," Lomardi said. "We have a job to
do."

He started to move forward, Samford walking beside
him. The alarm grated on and on.

The guard clamped a hand around Lombardi's arm.

"You need to call somebody, we have phones in
here," he said. "But nobody's leaving."

Lombardi smiled. His hand was still in his jacket.

"Don't bet on it," he said, and squeezed the trigger of
the pistol he'd taken from the guards in the monitor room.

Hit at point-blank range, the security guard catapulted
backward off his feet, a cloud of blood exploding from
his chest. Lombardi pumped two more bullets into him
as he dropped to the ground, finishing him.

He turned to his companion and waved him along. He
was aware of screams, pale faces, racing feet behind them
on the concrete floor.

They hastened toward the door, and got as far as the archway of the weapons detector when someone behind them shouted out an order to halt. They kept walking.

"I said freeze!" the voice repeated. *"This is your final warning!"*

Without turning, they quickened their pace.

A gunshot fired out from behind them. Lombardi whirled and saw a plainclothes guard in the center of the corridor, both hands around a gun, his knees bent in a shooter's stance. Lombardi returned fire, missed, heard a *thud-thud-thud* from the suited guard's gun, and then was slapped across the middle by something he didn't see. He looked down at himself, his eyes wide with shock, and had just enough time to glimpse the bloody amalgam of flesh and shredded clothing that had replaced his stomach before he crumpled in a dying heap.

The other intruder reached for his own gun, but before he'd gotten it out of his pocket saw two more plainclothesmen emerge from the branching corridors at his rear. They all had their weapons drawn, and had triangulated their aim to put him in a perfect crossfire.

"Hold it!" he said. Dropping the gun to the floor, kicking it away from him, and slowly raising his hands above his head. "Don't shoot, okay? *Okay?*"

Their guns extended, the Sword ops moved in and took him.

Swinging around the grille of a car, Kirsten tore into the aisle and ran like hell, making for the driveway in a wild headlong dash.

She heard overlapping footsteps behind her, close, close, and pushed herself to move even faster, her legs pumping, arms working at her sides like pistons—

And then, suddenly, one of her pursuers sprang from behind a parked car several yards in front of her.

Between her and the driveway.

His right eye was bloodshot and swollen, and there was a thin line of blood trickling down his cheek from its lower lid.

It was the man she'd grappled with in the apartment. He had some kind of gun in his hand—a submachine gun, she thought, though she was hardly an expert—and was holding it out at her.

"No more shit from you," he said in Bahasa.

She halted, glanced over her shoulder.

Two more of the men who'd come for her were walking quickly up the aisle in her direction, their firearms held downward, flat against their legs. The fourth stalker had emerged near the spot where she'd been hiding.

"Just come on over here, I won't hurt you," said the one blocking her path to the driveway. He motioned with his gun. "Let's go."

Kirsten didn't budge, and was amazed to realize she was shaking her head in the negative.

He shrugged, holding his weapon steady. She could hear the other three coming close behind her.

"You want to wrestle some more, we wrestle," he said, and took a step forward.

"Hold it right there! *Bayaso reya!*"

The voice echoing through the court stopped all four of the men in their tracks. An expression of stunned surprise on his features, the one in front of Kirsten abruptly looked around for its source.

"*Drop the gun!*" the voice said in Bahasa.

Still looking from side to side, the man blocking the

driveway moved the gun off of Kirsten, but didn't lower it.

Kirsten heard a crack like the sound of a detonating firecracker. And then a blossom of crimson appeared in the middle of the man's rib cage and he pitched facedown to the asphalt, his submachine gun clattering from his grasp.

"I hope the rest of you are smarter," the voice said. "It's finished."

Kirsten turned her head, saw one of the gunmen behind her start to raise his weapon, instantly heard two more sharp cracks—only now coming from a different part of the court. The man screamed and fell over clutching his knees, blood spraying out from between his fingers.

The remaining pair of men tossed down their weapons and started to run, scrambling out of the aisle, and then bolting wildly toward the driveway exit. No one tried to stop them.

Her eyes wide and staring, Kirsten looked uncomprehendingly around the court, and all at once saw a brown-skinned Malay spring to his feet behind the tail of a car, several aisles down and directly across from where the first stalker had fallen dead. An instant later two more people appeared near the one who'd been shot in the knees—a white man with close-cropped hair and an Oriental woman.

The man with the short hair holstered his gun beneath his jacket and approached her.

"Kirsten, it's okay, you're safe," he said in a calm, level voice. "I'm Pete Nimec."

She started to say something in response, but her throat had closed up, and her teeth were chattering too violently.

Instead, she strode over to him, put her face against his shoulder, put her arms around him, and started crying.

Noriko had gone to wait in the apartment with Kirsten while Nimec and Osmar took care of business in the parking court.

"Mr. Nimec," Osmar said. "There is something I must show you."

"Right."

Nimec finished flex-cuffing the wounded man, folded a blanket he'd gotten from the apartment under his head, then went over to Osmar.

Kneeling over the body of the one he'd dropped, the Malay lifted his motionless hand off the asphalt.

"You see kris tattoo?" he said, glancing up at Nimec.

Nimec nodded. "Guy I cuffed has exactly the same marking on him. What the hell is it, some kind of cult sign?"

Osmar shook his head.

"Is more like what you Americans call . . ." He made a low sound of concentration in his throat, as if groping hard for words. Then he snapped his fingers. "Ah," he said. *"Colors."*

"Gang colors, you mean," Nimec said. "As in the Crips and Bloods."

Osmar nodded, and placed his finger on the tattooed skin. "The kris, many pirate gangs have such marks. But you see designs on blade?"

Nimec squatted beside him for a closer look. He did indeed see them—grotesque anthropomorphic figures that reminded him a little of the paintings on Egyptian tombs.

"They are *rakasa*," Osmar said. "Demons. Different for each brotherhood."

Sudden understanding spread across Nimec's features.

"These two punks . . . someone familiar with regional gang crime would be able tell their affiliation from the markings," he said

Osmar nodded again. "And this one, I know well from when I was with police," he said. "The men work for Khao Luan. He is Kuomintang."

The word rang a vague bell. Nimec searched his memory a few seconds.

"A heroin trader?" he said finally.

Another nod. "None are more powerful. The Thai army, they make him to flee during pacification program. Ten years ago, maybe more. Since then, he is in Indonesia."

Nimec gave him an imperative look. "Where? Does anybody know *where*?"

"Everyone knows, and everyone fears to touch him," Osmar said. "In parts of Banjarmasin, the Thai has longer arms than the government."

Nimec was quiet, letting it all sink in. What connection could a man like that have to Monolith? What on *earth* had Max stumbled onto?

After a moment he clapped a hand on Osmar's arm and nodded firmly.

"My friend, we're about to do some more island-hopping," he said. "And I promise you, if this guy's involved in Blackburn's disappearance, I'll cut his fucking arms off myself."

TWENTY-FIVE

THE SURVIVING MEMBER OF THE PAIR THAT GOT INTO the Sacramento vault hadn't talked—not to the Sword detail that apprehended him, not to the Feds after he'd been given into their custody. And it was anybody's guess whether he was *going* to talk.

Gordian, however, wasn't sure that was essential to determining who had been behind the act.

The main question for him, then, was of motive.

Back in San Jose now—he had booked reservations aboard a commuter flight while the A&P mechs continued their inspection of the Learjet in Washington—Gordian sat at his desk opposite Chuck Kirby, trying to put the pieces of a complex and profoundly troubling puzzle into place. They had already run through the whole thing a couple of times, but neither man felt it would hurt to bounce it around once more.

"Let's try it back to front," Gordian said. "Starting with the break-in at the Sacramento facility."

"Sure, why not," Kirby said. "Doing it the other way hasn't nailed it."

"I don't know whether it *can* be nailed, not with the fragmentary information we have," Gordian said. "But we can get closer, make some more important connections.''

Kirby nodded. "The disc they took off the dead man, then," he said.

"The disc," Gordian repeated, sighing. "The key-codes are used in communications systems UpLink has designed for a wide range of naval vessels. Obviously they would be of enormous value to any number of interests, both foreign and domestic."

"Allies and enemies, for that matter," Kirby said. "Everybody spies on everybody else. It's wide open until you look at how the thieves penetrated the vault."

"Exactly." Gordian's face was sober. "And if not for the surveillance videos capturing what happened after they killed poor Turner, the techies might've taken weeks, even months to find out. The wicked beauty of it is that the system defeated itself."

"And that's still the part I can't quite grasp," Kirby said.

"It probably isn't vital that you do . . . although the concept isn't really that difficult," Gordian said. "It involves basic computer file architecture, the way hard drives are set up. There's a minimum amount of space allocated for every file on a hard drive . . . the larger the drive, the larger the allocation. Regardless of how much data you have in a file, the computer reserves that minimum space." He thought a moment. "Imagine a department store that only has gift boxes of a single size for their merchandise, no matter whether you're buying a ten-gallon hat or a gold forget-me-not for your wife's necklace. Since the box needs to be pretty big to contain the hat, that tiny charm's not going to be too visible when it's placed inside. In fact, it may even get lost."

RUTHLESS.COM

Kirby nodded. "The data-strings that let the thieves through the system's backdoor . . . you're saying they were too small to be noticed. Like the charm. And they slipped past your whiz kids when the software employed by the biometric scanner system was examined for backdoors prior to installation."

"And the techs can't even be held at fault," Gordian said, nodding. "Do a careful diagnostic of *any* hard drive, and you'll find the percentage of file-space being utilized out of whack with the actual number of stored bytes. You store one word-processing file with a couple of words on it, another with several pages of text, and it's probable both are grabbing the same amount of space. When the technicians are looking for Trojan horses, they typically sniff around for long, complex algorithms such as the type needed to match fingerprint or voice characteristics. In this case, the backdoor key was short and sweet . . . a basic geometric pattern . . . a small item in a big box."

"The star on the sapphire," Kirby said. "Incredible."

"To me, what's more incredible is that our security system's primary biometric software was produced by— and acquired from—Monolith Technologies, of all goddamn outfits under the sun," Gordian said. He shook his head. "Talk about an incomprehensible oversight . . ."

"Don't beat yourself over the head with it, Gord," Kirby said. "Their stuff's the best being made. And the system was implemented a while before the problems between you and Caine started brewing. Viewed as an isolated incident, the break-in wouldn't even necessarily place Caine under suspicion. There could be rogue hackers within his company—"

Gordian's face tightened.

"It isn't hackers who tried to steal UpLink out from

under me. Nor was it hackers who used Reynold Armitage as a point man in advance of the raid, or had my plane's landing-gear system sabotaged, or made Max Blackburn vanish into thin air.''

Kirby released a breath. ''We can't prove Caine's direct involvement with any of that. . . .''

''It's just the two of us here, Chuck. This isn't about what I can prove, but what I know,'' Gordian said. ''Over the past seventy-two hours, the A&P team in D.C. has traced the plane's entire hydraulic circuit for leaks a half-dozen times. And found nothing. Also, the mechs here at home have paper checklists verifying they conducted the full preflight a day before we left, including eyeball inspections of the system's gauges and connections.'' He paused. ''Somebody tampered with that plane after it was prepped. And the guard at the airport, a man named Jack McRea, fessed up to having left his post for several hours a couple nights ago.''

''And has since been released from your employ, I hope,'' Kirby said.

Gordian nodded. ''Far as he's been willing to admit, he was lured off to a motel by long legs and a miniskirt. Suckered into leaving the hangars wide open.''

The room was silent a few moments.

''The logical jump still bothers me,'' Kirby said. ''Tying Caine to an attempted murder without evidence, for godsakes.''

''Mur*ders,* plural,'' Gordian said. ''You were on that plane too, Chuck. As was Megan and Scull.''

''Gord, my point is—''

''I know what it is. And again, I'm not talking about specific evidence, but getting a handle on the totality of events that have been wheeling around my head. Max is investigating Caine's business operations in Asia, Max drops out of sight. I take on the Morrison-Fiore Bill, Caine jumps into the ring as a challenger, then as a person who wants to devour my corporation. Somebody breaks into my encryption facility, they do it using a backdoor in Caine-designed software. And so on and so forth. There's too much coincidence. And now the whole thing seems to have taken on a sense of acceleration . . . almost desperation. . . .''

''Or urgency,'' Kirby said. ''If we're going to walk the road you're inclined to lead us down, the keys on that disc they tried to snatch are at the heart of this.''

Gordian nodded, his hands steepled under his chin.

The two men sat there quietly a while, thinking everything through.

Five minutes passed, then several more.

More thought, more silence.

Suddenly Gordian sat forward, his eyes widening.

Chuck looked at him. ''Something the matter?''

''That word you used,'' he said. ''*Urgency.* It's just that . . .''

He let the sentence trail off, moistened his lips.

Chuck kept looking at him.

''Oh, my God, how could I not have seen? That's why it's come to a head now. *My God,* the ceremony . . . the maiden run is today!''

''Gord, what the hell's *wrong*?''

Gordian shot his hand across the desk and gripped Kirby's wrist.

''The Seawolf,'' he said, speaking rapidly. ''Its command and control systems . . . the systems that run the sub . . . they use UpLink encryption software. And the spare keys, the keys are on that disc.''

Tom Clancy's Power Plays

Kirby was staring at him incredulously. "Gord, I'm not sure I'm reading you, or *want* to be reading you. But even if I am, the thing to remember is nobody got hold of them—"

Gordian sliced his right hand through the air to silence him, still digging the fingers of his left into Kirby's wrist.

"They aren't the only keys, Chuck," he said abruptly, his face white as a sheet. "You understand? We're talking about a nuclear submarine, a boat the President's going to be aboard. *And they aren't the only keys.*"

Watching his team ready themselves on the transportable dock, Omori was convinced he had done well, both in selecting his divers and finding a suitable launching area for the insertion. Notched into the coast of Pulau Ringitt— a small island less than five kilometers south of Sentosa— the saltwater inlet was protected by a zone of mud and marsh that made it the sort of place few people wanted to go sloshing around in.

Omori checked his watch. Not much longer now. Not much longer before his men climbed into the underwater delivery vehicle and the time for preparation was over at last.

He was eagerly looking forward to that moment.

Invisible beneath its camouflage netting, the delivery craft rested on a floating dock amid the thick rushes near the bank. Its bullet-shaped, fiberglass hull was windowless, and though this aided in reducing its detection signature, it also meant Omori's team would be navigating solely on their instruments once they lowered the canopy.

He regarded them from the stern of the speedboat which had towed the dock into position twenty-four hours earlier, and with which he would soon guide it back into

deeper water. The four divers had already slipped into
their wetsuits and Oxy-57 breathing apparatus. While
these had not been designed for the depths at which they
would be operating, Omori had been assured the closed-
circuit gear would provide breathable air for the limited
time their use would be required.

He glanced at his watch again, his frequent reading of
its face the only outward sign of the pressure he was
feeling. The act to which he had wholeheartedly committed himself would boost the *Inagawa-kai* to unchal-
lenged dominance over competing Yakuza syndicates,
and would guarantee him a personal status to surpass that
of Oyabuns and Emperors. But even that did not begin to
describe what it would mean. Nothing like it had ever
been done. Nothing. It would be remembered forever.

The prospect of future glories pushing any thought of
failure from his mind, Omori switched on his minicom-
puter and waited for Kersik's electronic message to appear.

The show was not turning out to be quite what Alec
Nordstrum had expected.

No, scratch that, he thought. As a writer, it was his job
to use language precisely. And as a member of the press,
he had an ethical obligation to be fair.

The show was fine. A tour of the Keppel Harbor area,
much fraternal camaraderie between President Ballard and
his fellow heads of state, a beautifully organized and executed military parade composed of American, ASEAN,
and JMSDF forces, and now the speechifying phase of the
ceremony, held on the dock against the sleek, dark shape of
the Seawolf. Soon Alex would be invited aboard the sub

with the small party of invited journalists, and off they would slip into the octopus's garden for the signing of SEAPAC . . . at which point he'd probably be forced to sit in with the bilgewater.

And that, he supposed, got to the crux of his complaint.

The show was fine, but his seats were lousy. Whereas he'd thought he'd be getting a backstage pass, and had planned to watch the action from the wings, thus far he'd gotten the equivalent of general admission at a rock concert.

He stood in the crowded press area on the waterfront, listening to the Japanese Prime Minister's remarks, getting bumped, jostled, and elbowed by scores of his rude and disorderly international colleagues, thinking this was surely just the first foul taste of Encardi's revenge, and that pretty soon he would be made to drink long and deep of its bitter waters. Already the President had snubbed him. The President's coterie of advisors had blown him off. Perhaps he was being oversensitive, but once or twice he'd even thought that some members of the President's Secret Service detail—men Nordstrum knew by name, and in some cases worked out with at the gym—were shooting dirty looks his way.

He had dared to go with his conscience, to stand with Roger Gordian, and for that had become a marked man, banished from grace, cast among the rabble.

Politics, he mused. *Always politics.*

Nordstrum sighed, trying his best to follow Yamamoto's speech . . . which was not easy with some reporter from an Italian news organization shouting and blowing kisses across his face to a female news anchor from a French television show. *Questa sera, mi bella.*

Dear God, the price one paid for holding to convictions in this world.

He glanced disconsolately at his watch. Another forty minutes or so before he'd be able to make his path to the ramp with the others getting into the nuclear-attack submarine. Even if he *was* restricted to the waste-processing facilities, he'd be grateful to be aboard. Damned grateful.

As far as he could see, his situation couldn't get any worse than it already was.

The Chinese hovercraft had arrived at the atoll under cover of darkness, transported in the well decks of two civilian tankers that had been refitted for military usage. Nearly ninety feet long and half as wide, each amphibious landing craft was powered by four sixteen-thousand-horsepower turbines—two of which fed the shrouded airscrews that would thrust it along at better than fifty knots, the others driving the centrifugal fans that provided vertical lift, allowing the craft to float above sea and strand on a smooth cushion of air. Their decks bristled with pintle-mounted 12.7mm Type 77 machine guns and 40mm grenade launchers.

Standing on the beach of the lagoon, General Kersik Imman watched his men board their vessels in preparation for the Sandakan raid, most of them filing up the ramps onto the four lozenge-shaped flotation craft assembled at the tide line, the rest climbing into a swarm of slender aluminum-hulled cigarette boats. All were suited as he was, in woodland fatigues, their faces veiled by cammo netting, their rucksacks and load-bearing harnesses laden with combat equipment. In strict adherence to Kersik's specifications, the light-assault rifles slung over their shoulders were factory-new, and would make effective personal weapons. Zhiu Sheng had delivered as promised, and for that—as for many other qualities—Kersik deeply respected him.

Perhaps one day they would meet again in some civilized place, a place far from this wretched island where the mosquitos were as fat as grapes from the blood on which they endlessly gorged, a place where they could sit at tables and chairs instead of hard straw mats that cramped their buttocks, a place where they could comfortably reminisce about all they had seen and done since they'd first met as younger men, one an Indonesian general full of pride and aspiration, the other a spirited Communist builder seeking to give shape to Utopia. Both holding dreams of Asian unity and greatness.

Yes, Kersik thought, perhaps they would indeed meet at some future time, and discuss how their greatest dreams had been attained at stages of their lives when most men were snugly wrapped in soft blankets of contentment. And together they would recollect the monumental day the Japanese and Americans who sought to dominate the region—and the ASEAN *wayang kulit* puppets with whom they worked their intricate shadow plays—were swallowed by an underwater behemoth of their own creation.

For now, though, there was only the certain prospect of the attack about to be launched, and the soul-heaviness of an old warrior who knew in his weary heart that the basic equation of war was always out of balance, the accretion of violence always beyond control, the smallest of gains always bought and paid for with the blood of far too many irreplaceable human beings.

Adjusting his pack on his shoulders, Kersik strode

across the sand and boarded the vessel that would carry him to battle.

Khao Luan strode along the boardwalk toward his dwelling on the canal, popping fried, sugared pieces of *tempe goreng* into his mouth, thinking he'd been foolish not to have the canoe vender fill an extra container for him. At the rate he was going, there would be nothing left of the soybean cakes by the time he sat down at his table.

Stress always made him hungry, and he had awakened famished today. With good reason, too. This business he'd gotten into . . . Sandakan . . . the hijack of a nuclear submarine . . . the *hostage taking* of the President of the United States. . . .

For him, it had all been about keeping the sea routes open for his trade. SEAPAC represented a threat to that trade, a solidifying of cooperation between regional governments in matters relating to the patrol of their waters, a substantial impediment to the flow of contraband from Thailand and elsewhere. Disrupting the treaty signing, perhaps even suspending its implementation indefinitely, had seemed a reasonable and pragmatic aim, a sound business strategy for one intent on staying at the top of his game.

Ah, though, how it had evolved.

He walked on, tossing another bit of food into his mouth. Until this morning, he'd been able to concentrate on the particulars rather than the broad contours of the plan, doing his part, taking it a step at a time. Which was how he generally approached things. But with its realization at hand—less than an hour away, unbelievably—the full weight of what he and his allies had undertaken had begun pressing down on him. And while he'd decided that the best way to deal with that pressure was to pretend this was any other day . . . well, it was difficult, that was all.

Luan reached the ladder that climbed to his door, paused at its foot, and looked into his box of *tempe*. Two pieces left. Really, really, he would have to send the men out for more.

He shook both remaining cakes into his mouth, absently tossed the container over his shoulder into the water to his right, and gripped the ladder frame to hoist himself upward.

Inches from where the cardboard box had joined the other refuse floating along the canal, a young female vendor in a loose-fitting sarong hunched forward in her canoe, her head lowering behind mounds of fruit, her hand slipping under a natty hank of cloth.

When that hand reappeared a moment later, it was holding a flat, palm-sized radio.

"Empire State to South Philly, do you read?" the vendor said in a quiet voice, transmitting over a trunked digital channel.

"Loud and clear, Empire State. The rooster back in the barn?"

"Just strutted in, big and nasty in life as in pictures," she said.

A brief pause.

She bent lower, waiting, holding the radio out of sight.

"Sit tight, Empire State," the voice replied after a second. "We're on our way to pluck his feathers."

Jointly sponsored by the ASEAN republics from its original blueprints to its funding and final construction, the Sandakan cryptographic key-storage bank was the largest in Asia, and the second largest in the world, ranking only

behind a subsequently built facility of its type in Europe.
In terms of proportion, it was to most of the world's other
key-recovery banks what Citibank was to a small-town
S&L. Sprawling across many acres of shoreline, the
concrete-and-steel structure gave a fortresslike impression, and was protected by a sophisticated array of alarm
systems and guard units of chiefly Malaysian and Indonesian composition. All this security was in place for a
simple reason: The spare key-codes stored within its
vaults were those of the region's largest governmental,
military, and financial institutions.

It had been regarded as a logical, convenient, and secure place for the Japanese and American governments to
store the spare keys to many of Seawolf's encrypted operational systems, including those which controlled its
Advanced SEAL Delivery System—or ASDS—docking
hatches. These would allow a fully pressurized mini-sub
containing from eight to twelve special-op divers to
launch and recover its personnel during insertions requiring long-distance, deep-submergence transport. As
planned, when the SEALS returned from a mission
aboard the sixty-five-foot ASDS vehicle, the computers
aboard their vessel would signal the Seawolf's control
systems to open the ASDS hatch so that the crew and
passengers—and their equipment—could reenter the submarine via its docking chamber, and move from there
onto its main decks.

Nga Canbera did not know, and would never know,
precisely which Japanese government official had passed
this information on to the Inagawa-kai, which had in turn
relayed it to him through Omori.

And what difference does it make? he thought, sitting
in his den now, watching the SEAPAC ribbon-cutting cer-

emony on television. He had remained home from the office to watch it undistracted, putting on his finest silk robe for the occasion. So far—given his knowledge of what would happen once the dignitaries were under way—it was proving to be quite a source of amusement.

For him the challenge of the game was the important thing, and though Nga had experienced his moments of apprehension lately, he felt the play would have been meaningless without an edge of danger. Today he would put aside his worries and *enjoy* himself. Could the Seawolf be tricked into swallowing a poison pill? After all, it was in theory only a matter of putting the right keys in the wrong hands—wrong from the American and Japanese standpoint, that is. And while Marcus Caine's failure to deliver the command-and-control keys had been a setback, it had in a sense only added to the excitement. Once Kersik got his hands on the Sandakan keys, Omori's divers would still be able to open the ASDS hatch. After that, they would simply have to put greater reliance on force than finesse, and use guns and bullets rather than keystrokes and passwords to take the submarine.

And maybe, if he were very fortunate, there even would be a little bloodshed to make things more interesting.

His eyes wide with disbelief, U.S. Secretary of Defense Conrad Holden looked at the telephone receiver in his hand as if it had been invaded by an evil poltergeist . . . albeit one that possessed the voice and speech mannerisms of Roger Gordian, someone he'd known for many long years.

"Roger, are you certain?"

"I'm telling you it's going to be Sandakan, Conrad.

And it will roughly coincide with the sub's embarkation. They won't want to give us time to disable the keycodes."

"But the sub's launching in a half an *hour*—"

"Then get off the phone with me and call somebody who can stop this from happening!"

Hotter and sweatier than he was accustomed to feeling, Luan was about to change his shirt when he heard it: the regular *thup-thup-thup* of rotors beating the air, rapidly getting louder and closer.

He looked across the room to where Xiang and his bodyguards had been throwing a pair of dice.

"What's that sound?" he said, already knowing the answer. The army helicopters had been ubiquitous when he was driven from the hills of northern Thailand.

The pirate tossed down the dice and turned abruptly to his fellows.

"Get your weapons," he grunted. "We're being attacked."

Leaning out the door of the Bell Jet Ranger chopper, Nimec extracted shells from his utility webbing, slapped them into his 12-gauge and pumped the forestock to chamber the first round. Like Osmar and the other three Sword ops in his team, he had on a pullover cowl, gas mask, and black Nomex Stealthsuit. The Zylon body armor underneath his shirt was both lighter and stronger than Kevlar.

Nimec gestured for the pilot to lower the chopper to a stabilized hover, and peered at the wooden structure below. There were a number of windows on all sides. He chose one of them as his target and pulled the trigger of his pump gun.

The finned CS bomblet disgorged from its muzzle in a train of propellent vapor, punched through the window, and burst open to release a cloud of tear gas.

Nimec chambered another round, fired, and loosed a third at the Thai's hideout. Billows of white smoke erupted from the windows.

He slung the weapon over his shoulder—he also had an MP5K against his side—donned his gloves, and signaled his companions to the door.

A moment later the rope line was dropped from its hoist bracket. One after another in quick succession, the men gripped the line and fast-roped to the boardwalk like firefighters sliding down a pole.

Submachine-gun volleys erupted on the ground almost the instant they alighted—stuttering from inside the house, from the dwellings around it, and from the wooden walkway that ran the length of the canal.

His head ducked low as his teammates laid down a lane of covering fire, Nimec raced around to the front of the hideout.

A man surged into his path from the gushing smoke of the building, bringing an FN P90 up in his direction. But he was half-blinded from the CS, and Nimec was quick to react. He jogged out of the way as the pirate released a stream of 9mm rounds. Nimec raked him across the middle with a burst from his MP5K, then kept dashing for the entrance without a backward glance.

He paused in front of the heavy plank door, sprayed the lock with bullets, and kicked it in with the flat of his foot. With his peripheral vision he could see Osmar running up on the left.

He looked over at him, signaled a crossover entry, and ticked off a three-count with his fingers.

Together they rushed forward into the house.

Minutes after the ribbon-cutting fanfare concluded, the delegation of world leaders was ushered across the gang, over the black anechoic tiles covering Seawolf's hull-like rubber flagstones, and then down into the sub by its executive officer. President Ballard dropped through the hatch first, followed by Prime Minister Yamamoto and the Malaysian and Indonesian heads-of-state.

The press contingent came next, Alex Norstrum at the back of the line, straining to see past a tall, broad-shouldered Canadian reporter who had been directed to board ahead of him.

As the group filed through a passageway toward the control room, Ballard felt as if he were about to step into the set of a Hollywood space opera, something about starships and wormholes in the space-time continuum. And in a sense he *was* entering a time machine, one which was capable of hurling him back through the accumulation of years and distance that had brought him to middle age, stripping the overlay of political cynicism and calculation from his face, and briefly revealing the excited countenance of a ten-year-old orphan from the Mississippi boondocks whose dreams had fueled a long, difficult journey from poverty to the Presidency. He goggled at the equipment and status boards filling up every corner of the brightly lit space with open wonder, his wide eyes no sooner landing on one piece of gadgetry than getting snagged by another of equal or greater fascination.

The sub's commanding officer, Commander Malcolm R. Frickes, USN, was saluting his guests from the control room entryway.

"It is my honor and privilege to welcome you all aboard," he said, stepping aside to let them enter.

Ballard enthusiastically returned the salute, swallowed, and gestured toward the periscopes on a raised platform in the center of the room.

"Do I get to look through one of *those*?" he asked.

Frickes smiled.

"Sir, you're the Commander-in-Chief," he said. "And that means you get to do anything you wish."

General Yussef Tabor, commanding officer of the Malaysian Army's 10th Parachute Brigade, could scarcely believe the orders that had just come down the line. He was to deploy his three airborne battalions—almost three thousand men—to Sandakan at once and assist the regular key-bank guard units in defending the beachhead.

Against *who* or *what* it was to be defended was unclear—but he at last saw an opportunity to be a true soldier. As the closest element of Malaysia's Rapid Deployment Force, stationed in Sabah less than thirty miles from the city, his would be the first of the support units to arrive. And that sat just fine with him.

After a decade of hunting illegal immigrants like a dogcatcher chasing down helpless puppies, it was high time for a mission he could be proud of.

Overcome with tear gas, his face tomato-red, Khao Luan was uncontrollably retching and coughing as Xiang tried to drag him into the barn. Gripping him under both arms from behind, the pirate opened the door and started to back his way through, but was still trying to maneuver his boss's weight when Nimec and Osmar burst into the house.

Osmar thrust his weapon out.

"Hold it!" he shouted in Bahasa. "Both of you!"

Breathing hard, Xiang stared at him a moment through thick braids of CS gas. Then, still partially supporting the Thai with one hand, he whipped the other behind his back and brought a donut-shaped P90 around on its strap.

The burst went wide, peppering a roof support, chewing out splinters of wood, Osmar got down into a crouch and fired back, intentionally aiming low. With Luan between him and the big man, he wanted to avoid shooting to kill, knowing the Thai might hold the answer to Blackburn's disappearance.

Luan sagged, clutching his meaty thigh, blood spraying from his femoral artery. Xiang tried to keep him erect, but was unable to manage it, and he went down with a crash. Retreating into the barn, the pirate triggered his weapon, sweeping it in an arc between Osmar and Nimec. Glass shattered somewhere in the house.

This time it was Nimec who fired back, squeezing off two crisp trigger pulls, *brrrat-brrrat*. He could hear sporadic exchanges of fire out on the walkway, and now and then a groan from one of the incapacitated pirates on the floor.

"Cuff Luan and the rest of these bastards!" he shouted to Osmar through his gas mask. *"I'm going after him!"*

Sea spray roiling up behind them, the four hovercraft scudded over the waves on pillows of air, flanked by dagger-shaped speedboats. They had covered nearly two thirds of the distance to the beach, and would be making landfall within a matter of minutes.

In the forward deckhouse of his vehicle, Kersik lifted his binoculars to his eyes to scan the LZ. He had mustered a force of close to three hundred men, outnumbering the key-bank guard by a third, and with the further advantage of surprise—

Kirsik blinked once, twice.

His eyes widened and widened against the lenses of the binoculars.

At first the dots he had seen against the fleecy backdrop of the cloud looked like insects. A sweeping, descending swarm of locusts.

But he knew all too well what they were.

Paratroopers.

Hundreds of them. *Thousands.* Alighting on the beach-head.

Had his ears not been filled with the deafening roar of the airscrews he might have heard the transports arriving sooner, heard them as he could now, *buzzing,* the buzz becoming a whine, the whine becoming a drone. . . .

He let the glasses drop from his trembling fingers and ran to the deckhouse radio, but by the time he'd trans-mitted his warning to the other vessels the incoming fire had begun, and the world was exploding all around him.

Omori had hardly seen the small email notice appear on his LCD before he realized the message was not from Kersik at all, but his contact in the Japanese Diet . . . a member of the Nationalist minority whose leaking of top-secret intelligence about the Seawolf had been at the core of the hijack plan since its initiation.

He opened the message and felt his stomach turn on itself.

Though there was only one word on his screen, it was sufficient to make him realize his plans had just come to an abrupt and crashing end:

YAMERU.

ABORT.

Omori dug his knuckles into his forehead and released a high mewl of anguish that instantly drew the attention of all four divers on the floating dock.

He did not look at them, or say anything to them. They would know what had happened just from looking at him.

Kersik, he thought, his fist pressing deeper into his brow.

Kersik had failed.

If he'd been holding a knife in his hand, Omori would have plunged it into his heart and brought the pain to an end then and there.

A blow to the rib cage almost dropped Nimec the instant he plunged through the door.

Stunned, scintillae whirling across his vision, he reeled against the wall of the barn, his MP5K sailing from his fingers.

He clamped his jaws around the pain in his chest. Whatever hit him had felt like an iron mallet, and if he'd been running straight rather than angling through the door, would have probably caught him below the diaphragm and made him lose consciousness. But the muscles of his chest had absorbed enough of its impact to keep him on his feet.

He gulped down a mouthful of air, struggling to get hold of himself—

And saw the giant's fist coming at him barely in the nick of time. He rolled sideways, twisting his head to avoid its pile-driver force, then slipped another blow as the pirate came charging in at him, his arms raised to get him in a squeeze hold, meaning to crush him against the wall with his bulk.

Nimec wasn't going to give him the chance. He could feel the strength flowing back into his legs and knew he had to move, stay out of the giant's reach, avoid going toe-to-toe with him at any cost. It had been his hand, his bare *hand,* that caught Nimec the first time. He'd have to make sure he didn't let it happen again.

Waiting until Xiang was almost on top of him, Nimec cocked his front leg and kicked it speedily up and out at his solar plexus. He heard the slam of his foot against the giant's flesh, saw him lurch backward, and followed through with a second snap kick to the same area.

Xiang staggered back another step and Nimec used the moment to scramble away from the wall, dancing on the balls of his feet like a boxer, getting a rhythm under him, working up some steam.

But the pirate was quicker on his feet than his size would have indicated. Rounding on Nimec, he lunged forward, rushing him head-on.

Nimec tried feinting sidweays, but was a hair too late. A sinewy forearm smashed across his lips and his head rocked back on his neck. He tasted blood, felt his knees weaken a little. Xiang hit him again, this time in the throat with his elbow. Nimec gagged, his eyes blurring.

And then, suddenly, Xiang's massive palms clapped down on either side of Nimec's head, his fingers forming a cage around his jaw and cheekbones. Nimec raised his own hands, wedged them up inside Xiang's forearms, gripped his wrists, and tried with all his strength to pry them apart. But the giant only held on and began steamrolling forward, carrying Nimec along with him, backing Nimec across the floor of the barn then ramming him up against the wall opposite the door with an impact that jarred him to the bone.

He brought his face in close to Nimec, his features a quivering mask of rage, his breath gusting into his nostrils.

"You want to fight, I'll break your fucking neck right here!" he bellowed, shaking Nimec, battering his head against the wall. "Right here like I did to that other American!"

Nimec's eyes widened. His heart pounded and swelled within him until its beating seemed to fill the universe.

Like I did to that other American.

Groaning from exertion, he pushed against the pirate's wrists, pushed, pushed—

Right here.

That other American.

Pushed—

For an instant he thought the pirate's grip would never relent . . . and then, miraculously, it did.

Shoving off the wall, Nimec brought his knee up fast, driving it into his crotch. Xiang's hands fell away from his head. Nimec hit him again, hard to the face with his fist, kept pressing. Threw another jab, another, another.

The giant started to sag, but Nimec didn't let up. He just kept thinking that Max was dead, and this was the man who'd killed him.

Two, three, four more powerful jabs, and then Xiang surprised him. He fell forward heavily, lumbering into Nimec and knocking him backward.

In that moment, as the two men separated, Xiang lifted his bloody face, his lips twisted into a sneer, and pulled his kris from its sheath.

Nimec froze, staring at that long, wavy blade, but Xiang didn't give him time to react. The giant lunged forward, the knife flickering toward Nimec's throat.

Nimec moved back a half step, pivoting on the ball of his left foot, and reached out. His right hand caught the back of Xiang's knife hand. His left hand slapped the inside of the giant's elbow, then turned and lifted the elbow up and out. Without pausing, Nimec stepped forward, pulling the giant toward him, and buried the knife deep into Xiang's chest, directly below the rib cage and angling up toward the heart.

Xiang remained on his feet another few seconds, looked down at the knife jutting from the center of his rib cage with an expression of utter astonishment, and dropped onto his face.

Nimec stepped back, breathing hard, the pain of his wounds rising up within him, and looked down at the fallen giant.

It was, at last, over.

EPILOGUE

"JUST DAYS AGO, I SAT HERE AND EXPLAINED TO someone how I knew about Marcus Caine's crimes without being able to prove them," Gordian was saying. He placed his hand on the wallet-sized digital recorder on his desk. "Now I've got proof, thanks to you."

"And Max," Kirsten said from the seat opposite him. "If not for him, I'd never have gotten it. And to be honest about it, might have kidded myself into thinking nothing strange was going on at Monolith."

Gordian looked at her, his frank blue eyes meeting her brown ones.

"For a while, maybe," he said. "But sooner or later you'd have stopped kidding yourself. And you'd have done exactly what you did."

She shrugged. They were silent a moment, just the two of them in the office. Outside the window behind Gordian, Mount Hamilton rose through the late afternoon smog, massive and somehow benign in its fixed solidity.

"Maybe you're right," she said at last. "But I'd noticed a lot of unexplained payments to American lobbyists crossing my desk. Sums that went far beyond what they should have been receiving for their services. And as I started paying closer attention to them, I realized they always followed visits to my department head from someone who was with the Canbera bank in Indonesia." She shrugged again. "Anyone with open eyes could have seen the money was graft to American politicians. The lobbying group to whom it was going was specifically hired to promote deregulation of cryptographic technology in Washington. But it wasn't until I mentioned it to Max that I allowed myself to see the truth."

"And it was Max who convinced you to snoop around in the computer databases for financial discrepancies."

"And plant the voice recorder in the Corporate Communications director's office." She shook her head. "It's hard for me to believe how indiscreet they were. I mean, I walked right in there every day before my boss arrived, tucked it behind the sofa, and picked it up every evening between the time he left work and when the maintenance woman came to do her cleanup. Then I'd walk back to my own office and upload everything onto a computer disk before heading home. It went on like that for two months."

"People get away with murder long enough, they get arrogant. They get arrogant, they start to think nothing can touch them. And as a result we've got half a dozen conversations about the payoffs between the director and Nga Canbera . . . and a couple with Marcus Caine's voice added to the mix. Coming over your former boss's speakerphone loud and clear."

"The CEO of Monolith himself imparting his wisdom about which government officials to target for bribes," Kirsten said. "Incredible, really."

They were quiet again for a while. Then Gordian

leaned forward, meshed his fingers on the desk, and looked steadily at her face.

"Kirsten, I didn't ask you here to the States because I needed to have the voice recorder and disks hand-delivered," he said. "I wanted to tell you in person how deeply I appreciate what you've done. And also let you know that I'd be honored to have you working for UpLink—wherever in our organization you'd prefer—should you want a job with us."

She smiled a little. "That's a very generous offer . . . but I hope you won't be offended if I decline to accept it, at least for now. I'd like some time to myself. Time to . . . re-group. You understand?"

His eyes were still holding steady on her.

"Yes, yes, I do," he said. "As long as you understand that the offer stands if you ever change your mind. And that I never forget my friends."

She nodded, her smile growing larger. It was very gen-uine and very beautiful, and Gordian thought he knew what Blackburn must have seen in it.

"Is it back to Singapore for you, then?" he said.

She was quiet a moment, then nodded again.

"For a time, anyway. But there's one more thing I have to do here in America before I go."

Armitage sat by the answering machine in his office, his eyes staring out of his wasted features with a cold vitality which seemed to demand and consume all that was left of his life force—like small, mean creatures arising from detritus, feeding on decay.

There had been a number of messages from Marcus Caine waiting for him this morning, each more panicked and desperate than the one preceding it.

No more of that, he thought.

Bound to a failing body and his wheelchair, he was determined to cast off unnecessary ballast. It was hard enough to manage without the dead weight.

"Erase messages," he said, activating the device with a voice chip produced in one of Monolith's San Jose factories. He paused a moment, then set it to screen and disconnect any calls originating from Caine's home or office, verbally inputting the numbers to be blocked.

He did not want to be dragged down with Marcus as his role in the SEAPAC affair, the campaign finance scandal, and numerous other damning episodes became known. Indeed, any association with him at all would be a severe liability.

How quickly things changed. He had believed Caine a likely candidate to win Uplink International and forge a media/technology monopoly that would extend around the globe as no single entity of its type had done before . . . and as a plum for being instrumental in bringing that about, Armitage was to have been handed Uplink's biosciences division on a silver platter. Who could say what new treatments for his condition might have emerged with the company's resources at his disposal? Who could truly say?

But Marcus had disappointed him, *failed* him, and none of that was to be.

He pulled air through his throat and released it in a watery sigh. Perhaps the ALS would get him in the end. Almost certainly it would. But he would live long enough to see Marcus go down first. . . .

And no doubt write many interesting and widely read columns about his fall.

●   ●   ●

"There it is. You can check everything out if you'd like."

Marcus Caine sat on the leather-cushioned sofa in his study, a square of mahogany wall paneling pulled back on his right to reveal an open wall safe.

The man he'd spoken to stepped across the room and peered into the safe. He reached a hand inside, extracted a banded pack of bills, rifled their edges, then put them back and looked into the safe another minute.

"It contains over a million dollars in cash. And some trinkets . . . diamonds, my dear wife has always loved her diamonds . . . worth a great deal more."

The man shifted his gaze toward Caine. He was smallish with a pencil mustache and gray eyes that matched the color of his sport jacket.

"You sure you want me to do this?" he said.

Caine spread his arms over the top of the backrest, tilted his chin up, and laughed—a sound that reminded the man a little of crows.

"What's the problem? Are you afraid you'll screw up, the way your friends did at the airport? Or how about Sacramento—shall we discuss that merry fucking romp?"

"There's no reason to talk to me that way," the man said. "Those were tough assignments."

Caine laughed his harsh, cawing laugh again.

"Then let's see you tackle an easy one," he said. "Earn your money this time. And spare me the humiliation of becoming the poster boy for Court TV for a year or so, to be followed by a lifetime of prison interviews."

Silence.

The man walked across the room, stopped in front of Caine, and reached under his jacket. The weapon he brought out from underneath it was a Heckler & Koch .45 P9S.

A moment passed. Still standing there, he took a sound suppressor from his inside pocket and screwed it onto the barrel.

"You worried about how your wife finds you?" he asked.

Caine straightened, and brought his arms down off the backrest. The pained humor was gone from his face and his eyes were watery.

His mouth suddenly tightened.

"Earn your money," he snapped. "Make a fucking mess for her."

The man nodded, cocked the gun, and angled its bore up at Caine's head. There was the sound of Caine sucking in air, and then the muted thud of bullets leaving the gun as he pulled the trigger ten times, emptying the magazine.

When his job was finished, the man holstered the gun, walked back around the couch to the safe, and quickly emptied it, transferring everything that had been inside to his briefcase.

He paused briefly at the door on his way out. Looked at the body and the blood on the sofa and walls. And nodded to himself with satisfaction.

Got what you paid for, he thought.

The inscription on the gravestone was elegant, a quote from Wordsworth:

> *O joy! That in our embers*
> *Is something that doth live,*
> *That Nature yet remembers,*
> *What was so fugitive.*

Reading it, Kirsten wiped a hand across her eyes.

"I remember, too, Max," she said. "I remember."

Behind her, Pete Nimec waited quietly, standing in the shade of the Japanese maples that grew where Blackburn had been laid to rest, his body flown back from Malaysia soon after his identity was confirmed.

Kirsten knelt over the soil that filled the grave, still loose under her fingers.

"Atman and Brahman," she said. "Sometimes, Max, we need illusion to show us the truth in ways we can manage . . . and though I can't be sure, I sometimes think you didn't understand that, and sold yourself short because you didn't. That you felt guilty about asking me to make difficult choices, and let that guilt get in the way of your opening up to me." She felt moisture on her cheeks. "The thing is, Max, I believe Roger Gordian is right. That you were really showing me the way to my own conscience. To my own heart."

She tasted salt, touched her fingers to her lips, touched the place where Max's name was carved on the gravestone.

"You . . . what we had . . . it was *Brahman,* my sweet love," she whispered. "It was truth."

Kirsten lingered there a moment, her eyes closed as if in prayer or repose.

Then she rose, turned from the grave, and strode slowly to where Pete Nimec was waiting.

"You okay?" he asked softly.

She looked at him, smiled a little.

"I will be," she said.